This book is affectionately dedicated to Michelle, my love. Without whose confidence in me, I would not have ever been able to write this.

Traveling in the company of those we love is home in motion

Leigh Hunt

Long Way Around

JP Beauchemin

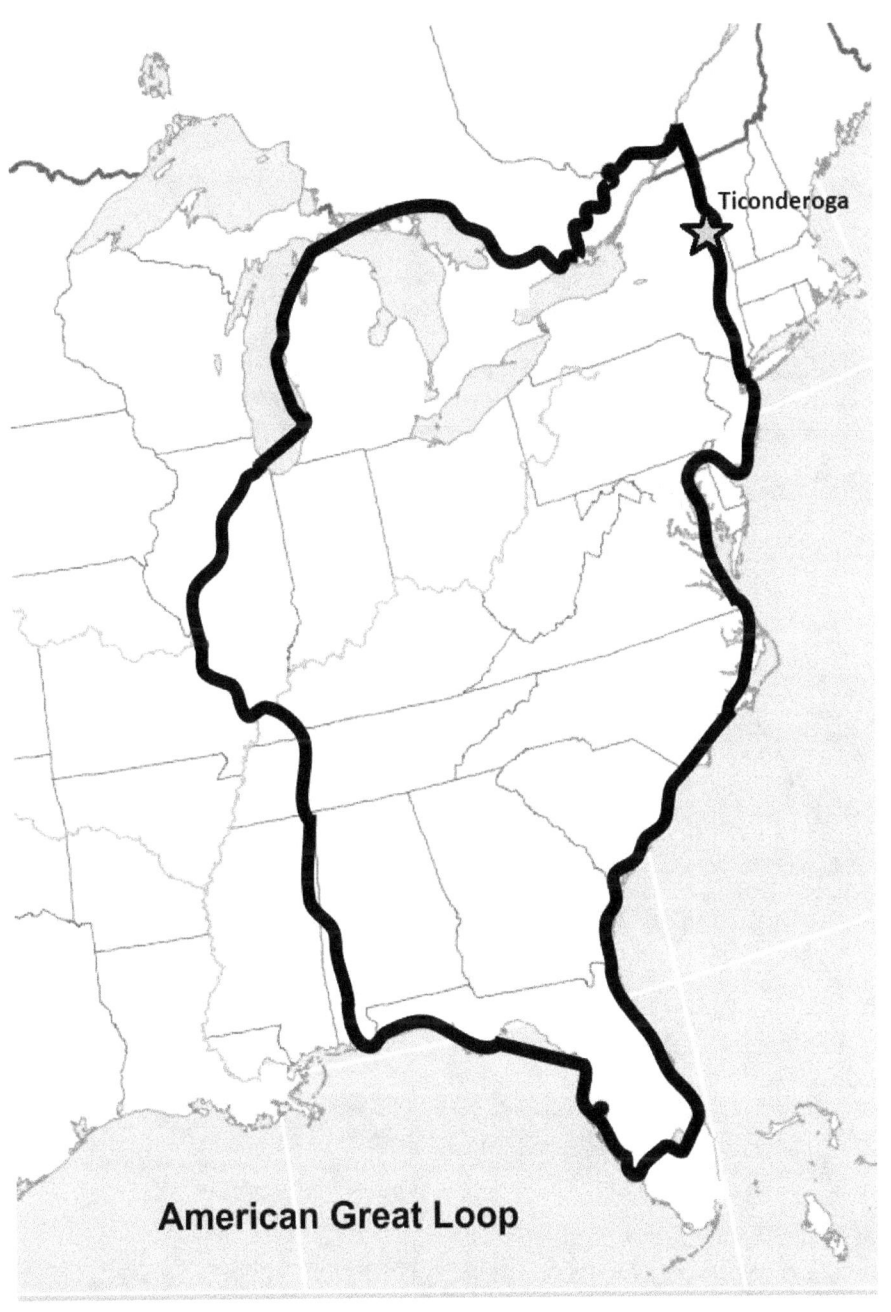

Ticonderoga

American Great Loop

Chapter 1

Seven Pounds, Six Ounces

Ticonderoga, is a charming small town nestled in the Adirondack region of upstate New York, situated between the scenic shores of Lake Champlain and the northern end of Lake George. Known for its rich history and stunning natural beauty, Ticonderoga is a favored summer getaway.

History enthusiasts can explore the renowned Fort Ticonderoga, while sci-fi fans can enjoy tours of the Star Trek Original Series Set. The town's breathtaking landscapes, including the Adirondack Mountains and Lake Champlain, also make it a hotspot for outdoor adventurers.

Emma, a lifelong resident of Ticonderoga, has always cherished meeting and talking with the many visitors who come to explore her charming town, especially enjoying the stories they share about their own backgrounds and where they come from.

At twenty-two, Emma works as a custodian at a local nursing home and dreams of changing her career by attending community college. Though she occasionally struggles with procrastination, she remains hopeful and determined about her future.

Her family is small, just her and her dad. A car accident claimed the lives of her mother and grandmother when she was a child, leaving her with only her father.

Her maternal grandparents live in Vancouver and visited only once since the accident, when they were already in the region anyway.

Their family was made even smaller by a falling out between her father and his own father around the same time. Emma and Ben had always enjoyed a close father-daughter relationship.

Every weekend, they made it a point to spend quality time together, exploring new places or indulging in their shared hobbies. Their favorite activity was hiking the scenic trails near their home, where they would talk about everything—from work to life dreams.

The town's small size and limited job prospects often prompt young adults to leave, though many eventually return to settle down or retire. Emma has found this trend challenging for her love life, as relationships often end when her partners move away. Although she dreams of eventually relocating, for now, she remains firmly anchored in Ticonderoga.

Standing at a modest height, Emma exudes a quiet elegance. Her long chestnut brown hair falls in gentle waves down to her lower back, often worn in a ponytail with a few strands softly framing her face. She tends to tuck her hair behind her ears when she's nervous, revealing delicate features and a complexion that's soft and fair.

Her eyes, a warm hazel, are often cast downward or to the side when she speaks, reflecting her shy nature. They are framed by subtle, natural brows and eyelashes that emphasize her contemplative gaze. When she does meet someone's eyes, her glance is quick and fleeting, almost as if she's surprised to be noticed.

She finds deep contentment in the simple, everyday moments and embraces a life of modesty and calm. Her demeanor is characterized by a thoughtful and unobtrusive nature, as she tends to listen more than she speaks, offering her insights only when prompted.

Emma's wardrobe reflects her preference for practicality and comfort over style, usually consisting of unadorned, comfortable clothing. In social settings, she is reserved yet approachable, radiating a subtle grace that attracts those around her. Her life is defined by simplicity, finding joy in routine and the understated beauty of her surroundings.

Ben, Emma's father, is in his mid-forties but has a youthful, baby-faced appearance that belies his age. His clean-shaven face reveals soft features, with smooth skin and bright, kind eyes that exude warmth and gentleness. He carries an air of approachability, often wearing a subtle smile that puts others at ease.

His demeanor is calm and inviting, making him seem like someone you can easily confide in. Ben's style is understated yet polished, reflecting a blend of maturity and an effortless charm. He is a dedicated professional who had spent twenty-five years climbing the corporate ladder at a major logistics company, ultimately becoming vice president.

He frequently worked long hours and commuted a considerable distance, but he felt it was worth it to live in Ticonderoga.

On his infrequent days off, he focused on caring for his modest bungalow on a spacious lot. Though simple, Ben took immense pride in his home, keeping the lawn impeccably mowed and the flower beds meticulously arranged.

In the evenings, he would unwind in his recliner with a beer, watching TV.

He had a particular fondness for travel shows, which Emma found amusing since he rarely ventured beyond work, the diner and beer runs. Occasionally, Ben would go out with colleagues and return home slightly tipsy after a night of socializing and after a quick snack he would go straight to bed, which was a good thing because she always found him to be grumpy after having too many drinks.

Even though Emma was in her twenties, she still lived at home, finding the arrangement convenient and practical for both her and her father. She handled the cooking, grocery shopping, and upkeep of the interior of the house, while her father managed most of the bills and took care of the exterior maintenance. The division of responsibilities suited them well and made their living situation harmonious.

Despite the monotony of her job, Emma found great joy in interacting with the seniors. She treasured their conversations and the warmth they brought, as they were always friendly and happy to see her. Sometimes, she struggled to complete her tasks because she was so engaged with them. Whenever a new resident moved in, she made a point of introducing herself.

One early June morning, while Emma was washing the windows between the administrative office and the lobby, she saw her father inside conversing with an administrator and a nurse. Nearby, an elderly man with gray hair and a bald spot was seated.

Curious, Emma entered the office to inquire about the situation but was promptly dismissed by the administrator. "Emma, would you please excuse us? I'm sure your father will explain everything when you get home."

Emma was left feeling bewildered and confused but quickly exited the office and returned to her work.

When Ben arrived home, Emma was waiting eagerly, hoping for an explanation. Ben sat down across from her and began to explain, "I received a call at work this morning about your grandfather. He had a stroke that has left him with limited mobility on his right side, and he can no longer care for himself. I had no choice but to place him in a nursing home. I simply don't have the time or the desire to look after him myself."

Emma was stunned. She barely remembered her grandfather. He lived just past Port Henry, a half-hour drive away But even though it was so close she still had never been there. The unresolved conflict between him and her father had kept her from knowing him. "Dad, how are we going to afford that?" Emma asked. "He has his own money, I'm just legally responsible for him now" replied Ben.

Emma started to think to herself, "Hmmm - he's at my nursing home now, is this my chance?" her father abruptly cut off her thoughts. "Stay away from him.

He's a selfish old man, and we're better off without him," he snapped. Emma begged with her father asking him what he did that made him hate him so much. But Ben just cracked open a beer, went into the living room and turned the TV on.

The next morning at work, Emma eagerly checked the room assignments and spotted her grandfather's name, "Jasper Nicholson," listed for room 411.

Since her schedule had her cleaning that area later in the afternoon, she had to wait before she could visit him.

It was her habit to introduce herself to new residents, and she felt it was only right to do the same with her grandfather. As she completed her morning duties,

she mulled over how best to approach him. She considered a range of introductions—from serious to humorous to ironic—but nothing seemed quite right.

When the time finally came, she made her way to room 411 with a mix of excitement and anxiety. She entered the room and saw him sitting in front of the TV, engrossed in a documentary about manatees.

He looks like an older version of Ben, radiating a distinguished charm. He has a slightly balding head that adds to his character, while his salt-and-pepper beard gives him a rugged yet refined appearance. Despite the signs of age, he still looks youthful, with a vibrant sparkle in his eyes and a warm smile that captivates those around him.

His features are strong but softened by the years, and he carries himself with an effortless confidence. Jasper's style is sophisticated and classic, enhancing his good looks and makes him appear both approachable and charismatic.

Clearing her throat to announce her presence, she watched as he turned to face her. He met her gaze and said, "I was wondering when you'd come to visit me." Emma was taken aback. "How did you recognize me? I must have been about eight the last time you saw me."

Jasper chuckled, holding up his phone. "It's called social media," he said with a grin.

Emma was surprised "You checked my profile?" He smiled and replied, "Kind of, You don't post often, so if it weren't for your profile picture, I might not have recognized you."

Emma shrugged. "I guess I don't lead the most exciting life." He nodded thoughtfully. "That's a shame, Life is meant to be lived." Just then, the nurse entered. "Emma, don't you have work to do?"

Emma replied, "Yes, I'm heading out. Jasper, it was nice meeting you." Jasper responded, "I hope we can talk more in the future." "Absolutely," Emma agreed as she left the room.

That night, while Emma was serving dinner, Ben walked in and gave her a sharp look and said, "You met him, didn't you? I bet you melted and rushed into his arms. I'm eating in my room." Without waiting for a reply, he grabbed his plate and retreated to his room, slamming the door behind him.

It was unusual for him to eat alone in his room, something he only did when he was upset. Emma anticipated his displeasure but was taken aback by its intensity. She thought to herself, "I didn't melt or rush. I kept it cool and even called him Jasper, not Grandpa. How could he assume that about me?" Emma, now irritated, felt a pang of frustration.

The next day was her day off, and Emma decided to indulge in one of her favorite activities, kayaking on the LaChute River in town. She sets out from a small boat ramp located between a stunning waterfall and the classic covered bridge known as the Kissing Bridge. She loves this little bridge. It's very cute but dreams of one day seeing some of the great bridges of the world.

Paddling downstream for about an hour before turning around, she enjoyed the scenery, which today included a juvenile great blue heron and several charming painted turtles.This tranquil time on the water offered Emma a chance to clear her mind and reflect.

Today, her thoughts were consumed by her grandfather. She was excited about the prospect of connecting with another family member but was conflicted about the potential impact on her father.

She wished she knew the cause of their estrangement, as understanding it would make things easier. It was hard for her to fathom what could have angered her father so deeply.

As she floated downstream, she started to convince herself that, despite her reservations, she had no choice but to get to know her grandfather. After all, she had to clean his room, which meant she'd inevitably have to interact with him. And that would be the way she would try to explain it to her father.

After running errands, Emma arrived home to find Ben already there, seated at the table while she unpacked the groceries. "I'm sorry," he said, his tone genuine. "I didn't mean to take out my frustration about him on you." Emma paused to absorb his apology and gave a nod. It was a small but meaningful gesture of reconciliation.

She then asked, "Would you mind telling me why you dislike him so much?" Ben sighed and replied, "Let's just say he was a selfish man who wasn't there when it mattered. That's all you need to know." Realizing that was all she'd get, Emma decided to drop the subject.

"You know Dad, I have to see him at work," she said. Ben acknowledged this with a nod. "That doesn't mean you have to become his best friend," he added.

Emma tried to reassure him by explaining that when she met her grandfather, she referred to him as Jasper, not Grandpa. However, Ben didn't seem to be comforted by that.

"Since you'll be seeing him, could you take him those boxes over there?" Ben gestured to a small stack of boxes, about the size of shoeboxes.

"Sure Dad," Emma responded, accepting the task. The next day, Emma arrived at work earlier than usual to drop off the boxes for her grandfather. She placed the boxes in the hallway outside his room and knocked lightly on the side of the open door. "Are you awake?" she called out.

Her grandfather rolled over with a warm smile and greeted her with a cheerful, "Good morning." She responded with her own friendly, "Good morning. I brought you something."

"Oh, what's that?" he asked, his curiosity piqued. Emma picked up the boxes and showed them to him. "Oh, that's wonderful!" he exclaimed. "I was waiting for those."

Curiously she asked, "What's inside them?" "Mostly photos and mementos," he replied. "Nothing of great value, except to me. Since it seems I'll be spending the rest of my life here, I want to keep my memories close."

Emma responded, "You make it sound like your life is over." He shook his head. "No, I still have two things I want to do before I die."

Emma decided it wasn't the right moment to ask about those two things. Instead, she said, "You're still young, you have a lot of life ahead of you."

He grinned and said, "Well, I'm seventy-one, and I have some heart issues—nothing fatal. I've had a stroke that's left my right arm and leg severely limited. I can barely walk, even with my cane. I can't take care of myself, and I'll never be able to use Arabella."

Emma's heart sank at his mention of Arabella. Arabella was her grandmother's name, but she had died in a car crash over fourteen years ago. The comment left her sad and puzzled. Could he be suffering from Alzheimer's or dementia?

She hoped not, she was just starting to get to know him and feared he might soon forget her.

Emma glanced at her phone and said, "I'm sorry, but I have to start work. I'll see you again soon."

"Any chance you're free on your lunch break?" Jasper asked. She pondered it for a minute and replied "Yes, I'll see you then," she replied.

As Emma continued her work throughout the morning, she couldn't shake her thoughts about what she had told her father regarding her relationship with Jasper, the two things Jasper wanted to accomplish before he died and whether his mind was still sharp.

She considered asking a friend on the nursing staff if she could get a glimpse of Jasper's medical file. However, she wasn't sure if her friend would agree, and if her friend was caught, she'd face significant trouble.

Typically, Emma spent her lunch breaks alone, reading a book on a bench beneath a large maple tree. It was her time for solitude in the middle of the workday, and she cherished her reading. But today, she would spend her lunch break with her grandfather. Just the thought of saying that in her head felt both strange and exciting.

The morning seemed to drag on forever, and when lunch finally arrived, Emma hurried to Jasper's room, eager to spend time with him. She was taken aback when she walked in—the room was filled with a vast collection of framed photos, both on shelves and hanging on the walls.

"Wow, Jasper, you really transformed this room. Do you mind if I take a look around?" she asked.

"Not at all," he replied with a smile.

As she wandered through the room, each photograph seemed to narrate a chapter of a richly lived life. There were snapshots from his youth, brimming with the vitality and dreams of early ambitions, and vibrant framed portraits commemorating significant achievements and milestones. Vintage photos, some slightly faded, depicted him with family and friends, illustrating a web of relationships and shared experiences.

However, the majority of the photos showcased exotic locales from his travels around the world, capturing adventures and explorations. Many pictures featured his wife and Emma's father from their younger years.

Each frame, thoughtfully arranged, offered a window into his passions, triumphs, and the people who shaped his journey. The room wasn't merely a display of images but a meticulously curated narrative of a life well-lived, rich with accomplishments and cherished moments.

One photo on the desk caught Emma's attention; it showed her father maneuvering a long skinny funny looking houseboat through some large doors.

Jasper noticed her interest in the photo "That was your dad, he was taking a narrow-boat through a lock on the Llangollen Canal in England. Emma replied "I didn't realize Dad knew anything about boats. And, um, what exactly is a lock?"

Jasper chuckled softly. "When your father was younger, we spent a lot of time on boats; he loved the water. We even sailed a schooner across the Atlantic once, from the Caribbean to the Azores. As for a lock, it was an engineering marvel two hundred years ago. It allows boats to move between different water levels on a river or canal, like a giant boat elevator.

The lock in that picture was used to bypass a waterfall. Have you spent much time on the water?"

Emma nodded and said, "Some, I have a kayak that I use on the LaChute River downtown and an ex of mine wanted me to try sailing, so I went with him to his place on the water, about a half-hour bike ride south of town.

I was okay puttering along with the auxiliary engine, but when we started sailing and the wind picked up, the boat tilted and we were moving fast. It felt overwhelming, so I asked him to take me back. Sailing just wasn't for me."

Jasper felt disappointed. Sailing and boats had always been a central part of his life, so hearing that Emma didn't share that interest was disheartening. However, he decided not to press the matter further. Instead, he asked, "You've mentioned your bicycle a few times. Do you not drive?"

Emma shook her head. "No, I prefer my bike. It suits me better. It's a small town, so getting around without a car is easy."

Jasper continued, "But what about when you leave town? How do you manage then?"

Emma shrugged and looked for a change of subject. Next to a picture of her father was a newer photo of Jasper standing beside an old-looking sailboat with his arms crossed looking proud. She pointed to it and asked, "What about this picture?"

A broad smile spread across Jasper's face. "That's my baby, her name is Arabella."

It took a moment for Emma to process, but once she did, she let out an audible laugh. Jasper looked puzzled.

"Why is that funny? Arabella was my wife's name," he said, sounding slightly offended.

Emma quickly apologized. "No, no, that wasn't what I was laughing at, I promise!" She tried to explain, "This morning, you said you wouldn't be able to use Arabella, and I didn't know you named the boat after your wife."

Jasper chuckled, cutting her off. "So you thought I was off my rocker, didn't you?" He laughed heartily. "For the record I didn't name the boat after my wife, it already had the name. It was what drew me to buy her in the first place".

Emma looked interested so he started to tell the story "I found her in South Carolina. She was damaged in a hurricane and left sitting for over a decade. I had it brought up here and spent the last seven years restoring it to its original condition. It's a thirty-four foot center cockpit 1939 sloop built with meticulous craftsmanship that you just can't find anymore.

She was built during the golden age of yacht design. She has elegant lines and graceful curves … " Jasper kept talking but Emma's mind drifted away. She could tell this was a real passion for him and that he put his heart and soul into it. She also knew that it was sad he won't be able to use it anymore. But she didn't like sailing and didn't have any interest in any boats bigger than her kayak.

Suddenly she heard him ask her "would you like to see her one day?" She quickly replied "I'd love to," knowing that she never would.

She could tell he was starting to get sad so she attempted to cheer him up by saying "at least you have your memories of sailing her right?" That seemed to have made it worse.

He explained, "you misunderstood me. I've never sailed her, she has never been in the water since I owned her."

"On the first of this month I had given up my place and moved most of my stuff aboard her. I was having her launched next weekend and I was going to sail away. It's how I was planning to spend the rest of my life. Not being stuck in here".

Tears welled in his eyes. But then he turned to her and said "But now I have two new things I need to do and that will keep me going." Emma quickly replied, "What two things?" He said "I'll tell you someday, just not today ok" He seemed to have cheered up a bit. "That's ok you tell me when you're ready."

"I'm sorry but I really should be getting to work. We will talk again soon if that's ok?" "Please," Jasper responded, his expression brightening. Emma thought to herself for a little while and asked "Any chance you want to go to a restaurant in town tonight" he looked at her strangely "Um how are we going to get there. I can't walk any distance and you don't drive."

Emma thought to herself for a moment then said "Oh right. Well what if we grabbed one of the wheel chairs downstairs and I pushed you". He absolutely hates being pushed in a wheelchair but loves the idea of spending more time with her and getting out of the building. The dining area is a little bland in appearance and in the food they serve.

"That sounds great, I'd love that". Emma knew that meant lying to her father he would be very upset if he knew about it. She hated the very thought of lying to her dad but felt in this case it was worth it. If she only knew what caused the rift between the two of them to start with.

Maybe she can get it out of Jasper since her dad won't tell her and tonight would be her chance to ask him.

She decided to call her dad at work so he could pick up something on his way home for supper.

He always goes to the same place to eat when she doesn't cook. It's a small diner on the far side of town. So she knew she would not run into him while she was out with Jasper. She told him she was going out for supper with a colleague, she knew he would like that as he is always trying to get her to go out and socialize more.

That evening, Emma arrived at the nursing home, retrieved a wheelchair, and headed up to Jasper's room. She knocked on his door, and he opened it eagerly. "I'm already ready," he exclaimed.

"All right, take a seat and we will be on our way. Jasper sat in the chair and exclaimed "And away we go." Emma was having fun pushing him quickly down the hallways, but once they got outside it didn't take them long to realize that the wheelchairs from the nursing home were not really designed to go outside. The thin solid hard rubber wheels made for an extremely rough ride.

Emma suggested they might need to turn back, but Jasper was determined to continue.. Finally they got to the restaurant where outside was a sign that read "Sunny Meadow Café." As they went to go through the front door they realized there was a small four inch step. It's something she never even noticed before. In the past she had stepped over it many times.

Jasper just said don't worry I can walk from here". Emma couldn't help thinking about all of the people who are full time in a wheelchair it would be so simple to fix. She thought to herself "I won't mention it now so I don't embarrass him but next time I come back I'm going to have a word with the manager about it".

Jasper grabbed his cane and went inside, found a table quickly and sat down. Emma folded the wheelchair, took it inside and leaned it up against the wall. Then she went and joined Jasper at the table. The restaurant had a warm, rustic charm. The interior features wooden tables and chairs with cheerful checkered tablecloths. The walls are adorned with colorful murals of rolling meadows and playful farm animals, creating a bright, welcoming atmosphere.

Jasper smiled warmly at Emma and started "So, Emma, why don't you tell me every little detail about your life? I want to hear all about you." Emma burst into laughter, amused by his playful tone. "Well let's see," she began, trying to play along "I was born seven pounds six ounces..." Jasper chuckled and interrupted her with a grin, "Haha, very funny. I didn't mean for you to start with your birth weight! You know what I mean."

Emma chuckled again, shaking her head. "Alright, alright, I get it. You want to hear more about my life, but without all the tiny details. Well, to be honest, my life might seem a bit mundane. I still live with my dad, I haven't done much traveling, and while I've had a few boyfriends, nothing really serious has come out of those relationships. I work at the nursing home, and that pretty much sums it up."

Jasper's eyes twinkled with interest as he responded, "Oh, come on, you can do better than that. I'm guessing you don't want to spend your whole life just cleaning, right? What are your goals and dreams?"

Emma looked down slightly, a touch of shyness in her expression. "Well, to be honest, I've always wanted to take a writing course at the local community college. I've dreamed of becoming a novelist someday.

I love writing, and I think it would be amazing to create stories that people might enjoy reading."

Jasper's eyes widened with genuine surprise and admiration. "Wow, that's incredible! Why haven't you pursued it yet?"

Emma sighed, a mix of frustration and resignation in her voice. "There are a few reasons. Life has just sort of gotten in the way—work, responsibilities, and all that. Plus, it feels like a big step to take on top of everything else. But it's something I really want to do, if I ever find the time and resources."

Jasper nodded thoughtfully. "It sounds like you have a real passion for it. Sometimes, taking that first step can be the hardest part, but it's often worth it. You should definitely consider going for it. If you need any support or advice, I'd be happy to help in any way I can."

Emma's face lit up with a grateful smile. "Thank you, Jasper. That really means a lot to me. I'll definitely consider it. It's comforting to have someone believe in my dreams. Most people, including my dad, keep saying that I need to live more of my life before I can write about it."

Jasper looked thoughtful and shook his head. "That's a bit silly, don't you think? You're twenty-two. I'm sure you've experienced quite a lot. You mentioned not having had any serious relationships, but what about traveling? Have you been anywhere?"

Emma looked a bit embarrassed as she confessed, "The truth is, I haven't really left Ticonderoga since I was a kid. I've stayed pretty close to home."

Jasper's eyebrows shot up in surprise. "Really? What about New York City? Ever visited?"

Emma shook her head. "Nope, never been."

Jasper's astonishment grew. "How about Albany, the state capital? Have you been there?"

Emma shook her head again. "Nope, never been."

Jasper, clearly bewildered, continued, "What about Lake George? It's just at the far end of the lake from here."

Emma, still sheepish, replied, "Nope, never been there either."

Jasper was in utter disbelief. For him, travel wasn't just a hobby; it was a vital part of life, a passion deeply shared with his wife. Even her parents had been avid travelers when they were younger. Travel had woven itself into the fabric of his existence, shaping countless experiences and cherished memories.

"I find it hard to believe," he said, still grappling with the realization. "Travel was such an integral part of my life and my wife's. It's almost like second nature to me. To think that my own grandchild hasn't ventured out much—well, it's just surprising."

The silence that followed felt heavy and awkward, stretching out interminably. Emma shifted uncomfortably, clearly wrestling with her thoughts. Finally, she broke the silence with a hesitant voice, "If I tell you something, do you promise not to laugh, judge me, or tell anyone?"

Jasper's expression shifted to one of genuine concern, mixed with a touch of curiosity. "I promise not to laugh or judge. And honestly, who would I tell? I'm just here to listen."

At that moment the waitress showed up, a young girl barely old enough to be out of school "Can I take your order?" Emma and Jasper were slightly annoyed by her timing but knew she was doing her job. "Could you give us a few more minutes" Jasper replied and the waitress said "no problem just let me know when you're ready" as she left on her rounds.

Jasper then looked back at Emma telling her to continue with what she was saying.

Emma took a deep breath, her shoulders relaxing slightly as she prepared to share something personal. "It's not that I haven't wanted to explore more of the world," she began, her voice steady but reflective. "It's just that I have a mild form of tachophobia—a fear of speed. Whenever I'm moving faster than about ten miles per hour, I start to feel overwhelmed and experience panic attacks. It's a really intense reaction for me."

She glanced at Jasper, hoping he would understand. "That's why I prefer activities like kayaking and biking. They're slower and give me a sense of control. With my bike, I always make a point of checking the brakes thoroughly before I head out, especially if there's a chance I might encounter a downhill stretch. Safety is key for me to manage my fear."

Emma paused, taking a moment to gather her thoughts. "On the rare occasion when I do have to ride in a car with my dad, he drives exceptionally slowly. He even puts on the hazard lights to warn other drivers that we're moving at a crawl. It's his way of helping me manage my anxiety about speed, but it can be quite isolating too. It affects my life in more ways than one—especially my relationships. Most of them end because I can't bring myself to get into a car, and that's a major barrier for anyone who wants to be with me."

Jasper sat in stunned silence, struggling to find the right words. After a long pause, he finally said, "If that's what a mild form of tachophobia looks like, I can't even imagine what an extreme case must be like. It does make sense now why you haven't ventured far from Ticonderoga."

Emma nodded, her expression thoughtful. "Yeah, it's a real challenge. Some people with tachophobia can't even stand to see things moving quickly, not just being in them.

I consider myself lucky in that regard because I can still manage to handle slow-moving things like my kayak and bike. It's just one of those things I've had to adapt to in order to live a somewhat normal life." She looked at Jasper, hoping he understood.

Chapter 2

Nope Still Crazy

Ben found himself at the diner that night; it's the same place he always goes when Emma doesn't cook. The diner is called "Tico's Diner," a nostalgic spot that captures the essence of classic American diners with a modern twist.

As you step inside Tico's Diner, you're immediately transported back to the 1950s. The décor is a vibrant mix of turquoise and chrome, with shiny vinyl booths, black-and-white checkered floors, and walls adorned with vintage memorabilia like old movie posters and retro signs. Classic diner jukeboxes are set on tables, allowing patrons to select their favorite tunes from a curated list of oldies.

Ben loved the style even if he wasn't around for the 50's. Over time, Ben had become a familiar face at the diner and developed a friendly rapport with the staff, who knew him by name and were well-acquainted with his preferences.

The moment he walked through the door, they could almost predict his order. He had settled into a routine, often opting for the same beloved dishes that had become his personal favorites. His usual meal was a perfectly cooked cheeseburger with a side of crispy fries and a classic chocolate milkshake.

Ben had always enjoyed sitting at the counter. It wasn't just about the food; it was the opportunity to chat with the friendly staff while he ate. The counter offered him a front-row seat to the bustling kitchen and allowed him to engage in lively conversations with the cooks and servers.

Tonight, however, was unusually quiet. The usual hum of activity was replaced by an almost serene stillness. The occasional clink of dishes and the soft murmur of conversation seemed to echo in the calm atmosphere. It was on such nights that Ben would often find himself having more personal interactions with the staff, and tonight was no exception.

Douglas, one of the diner's cooks, took the opportunity to step out from behind the kitchen counter and strike up a conversation with Ben. Douglas was a familiar face for Ben, having lived just a few doors down for many years. He was a few years older than Ben, likely around fifty, and they had shared many casual chats over the years. Douglas had a friendly demeanor and a knack for storytelling, making their conversations enjoyable and engaging.

As Douglas leaned casually against the counter, engaging in conversation with Ben, the two men easily transitioned from playful banter to more meaningful topics. The atmosphere was relaxed, and the quiet of the diner allowed their discussion to flow naturally.

However, Douglas noticed a subtle shift in Ben's demeanor. There was a concern etched on Ben's face that seemed out of place amidst their usual light-hearted exchanges. Sensing that something deeper was troubling his friend, Douglas leaned in a bit closer, his tone shifting to one of genuine concern.

"It's Emma," Ben said. Douglas listened attentively, his expression one of empathy. "Ben, whatever it is, I'm sure she'll be fine. I've never seen a father worry for his child as much as you do. She is twenty-two and you still don't stop worrying about her. If you want to talk about it, I'm here to listen. I've got plenty of time tonight, and I don't mind at all."

Ben appreciated the offer of a listening ear. Douglas's genuine concern and willingness to help provided a small but meaningful comfort. As they continued their conversation, Ben began to open up about his worries and fears concerning Emma, finding solace in the supportive presence of a long-time friend.

Ben began, "You know that my relationship with my father has always been strained. Well he had a stroke a few days ago."

Douglas immediately interrupted with a sympathetic, "I'm so sorry to hear that." Ben's response was terse, "Don't be."

Ben continued, "The stroke left him unable to care for himself. Since I'm his only family, I had no choice but to move him into a nursing home." "That must be expensive," Douglas replied.

Ben shook his head slightly, "Nah, he still has plenty of money from his royalties. He just needed me to be legally responsible for him." Douglas, piecing things together, remarked, "ah it's because its the same nursing home where Emma works. I get it."

Ben nodded. "Yes. Emma's a kind-hearted person, and no matter how much I caution her, she's determined to befriend him." Douglas was puzzled. "Why is that a problem?" Ben's face tightened with concern as he explained,

"He's a charming and likable man on the surface, but he's fundamentally self-centered. I know he'll eventually hurt her."

Douglas looked Ben directly in the eyes. "Ben, you know Emma isn't a child anymore.

She's a grown woman who can look after herself." Ben sighed, his worry evident. "I understand, but she's still quite naïve in many ways. Even with her maturity, she doesn't always see people's true nature."

Douglas nodded thoughtfully. "I know you're worried about her getting hurt. But she's stronger than you might give her credit for." "Perhaps you're right," Ben said, his voice heavy with concern as he took a bite of his food. "But I still want her to be careful with him."

He chewed slowly, his thoughts clearly elsewhere as he considered the situation. His expression softened with the weight of his concern, though the food seemed to offer little distraction from his troubled mind.

Later that night, Ben was at home relaxing with a cold beer and watching one of his favorite travel shows on TV. The atmosphere was peaceful until Emma walked in. "Emma, come in here," Ben called out, reaching for the remote to pause the show.

As she entered the room, Ben looked serious. "I need to talk to you." Before Ben could say anything further, Emma cut him off, her face etched with deep regret. The weight of her guilt over not being completely honest with her father was overwhelming, and she felt an urgent need to come clean.

"Dad, I'm sorry. I need to tell you something," she began, taking a deep breath to steady herself. "I wasn't at the restaurant with a colleague; I was there with your dad."

Ben's anger surged with an intensity he couldn't recall ever experiencing before. He leaped out of his seat, his gaze fixed on Emma as he desperately tried to find the right words.

His mind was a whirlwind of confusion and fury, leaving him speechless. He was completely at a loss, grappling with the overwhelming shock and sense of betrayal that engulfed him.

Ben was scared he was going to say or do something he would later regret. "Emma I can't do this right now, I'm going to bed we will talk about it later." Emma knew she had betrayed him and she really felt sorry. Maybe she had been a bit selfish trying to get to know someone who clearly upset her father.

Deciding to go to bed early, she fell asleep with a heavy heart, her mind racing with thoughts and worries about the right course of action. She had a chance to reconnect with her grandfather, which was important to her, but she didn't want to cause any more trouble with her father. So, she resolved not to visit him today. Her relationship with her father had to come first.

The next morning, Emma woke up to her alarm as usual, feeling groggy. She trudged to the shower, reflecting on her restless night. Despite her resolution, she couldn't shake the feeling that she was torn between reconnecting with her grandfather and honoring her father's wishes.

She completed her morning routine and headed off to work. Typically, she would ride her bike, but with the rain pouring down, she opted for a walk with her big pink umbrella adorned with little white hearts. At work, she checked her schedule and felt a wave of relief when she saw that she wasn't assigned anywhere near her grandfather's room. She let out an audible "phew."

However, fate had other plans. While cleaning the dining room, she felt a tap on her shoulder and heard Jasper's voice, "Are you free for lunch again?" Emma spun around and replied, "Yes, I'm free; that would be great."

She chuckled to herself, thinking, "So much for avoiding him and respecting Dad's wishes." Emma reasoned with herself, "I'm an adult now; I have every right to talk to whoever I want. If Dad would just explain what the argument was about, it might make things clearer."

She suggested to Jasper, "How about instead of the bland dining hall food, we order something and eat it in your room?" Jasper's eyes lit up. "Sure, that sounds really nice. Is there anywhere in town that delivers Chinese food? I've been craving it."

"Absolutely," Emma responded. "There's a great little place on Main Street that delivers. We can check out the menu on my phone and order now so it arrives by lunchtime." They placed their order, and Emma returned to work, feeling a mix of emotions—happy about reconnecting with her grandfather, yet conflicted about the impact on her father.

When Emma arrived at Jasper's room with a bag featuring Chinese symbols, Jasper greeted her with a warm smile. "Come on in," he said. "I brought the food," Emma announced.

Next to the bed was a small table with two chairs. However, Jasper's table was cluttered with papers, old maps, and books. "Is it okay if I clear some of this onto the bed so we can eat?" Emma asked. "Sure," Jasper replied.

As Emma began to move the items, she noticed a paper with a list of names. "What's this?" she asked. Jasper's face fell. "Oh, that's just a list of places I wanted to visit by boat. Before my stroke, that is." Emma glanced at the list, noting names like Nova Scotia, Costa Rica, and Aruba. But halfway down, she saw "The Loop."

"Jasper, what's 'The Loop'?" she asked, chuckling, since it didn't sound like a real place. "That's the Great American Loop," Jasper explained, grabbing a map from the pile. "It's a six thousand mile, year-long boating trip around the U.S. and parts of Canada, along a series of rivers, canals, lakes, and bays. Despite being in the middle of the list, it was the first thing I had planned after launching."

He traced the route on the map, starting at Lake Champlain, heading north through Canada, then going through various waterways till you get to the Great Lakes, Down the Midwest Rivers to the Gulf, around Florida before returning to New York state via the Intracoastal Waterway. "Wow that would have been amazing," Emma said, her excitement palpable. "But what's the Intracoastal Waterway?"

"It's a route along the east coast that lets you avoid the open ocean as much as possible," Jasper explained. Emma started spreading the Chinese food on the table and her heart sank a little. "I'm so sorry you never got to do that. It sounds like it would have been an incredible trip."

As they ate, Jasper was unusually quiet, seemingly lost in thought. After Emma finished her meal and started cleaning up, Jasper suddenly stopped her and looked her straight in the eye, and said in a somber tone, "You know Emma, I could still do that trip."

Emma gave him a puzzled look, prompting Jasper to continue. "I can still pilot my boat; it's just the docking and errands like groceries that I struggle with. Even if I never made it to shore, the changing scenery would be worth it. I've easily got enough money to make it happen. I could pay you something and even help with your writing.

Your dad said you need to live more before you can be a writer. Besides, you don't seem to like this job anyway." Emma cut him off, her tone firm. "Stop. I've told you before, I don't like sailing, and even if I did, I wouldn't know how. Plus, my dad would be furious, and who would look after him? This whole idea is just crazy! And no offense, but how would you even help me with my writing?"

Jasper reached over and grabbed a paperback book from the bed, tossing it to Emma with a casual flick. The book's cover depicted a rugged cowboy holding a revolver aloft, with a horse standing majestically in the background. Emma's confusion was evident as she stared at the book, her brow furrowing. "Um, okay," she said, shaking her head slightly. "I don't really like westerns."

Jasper's smile widened, and he said, "Turn it over." Emma, still puzzled, flipped the book over. On the back cover was a photograph of a much younger Jasper. It was unmistakably him, though significantly younger. "You're a writer!" Emma exclaimed, her eyes lighting up with genuine excitement. "Well, I was," Jasper replied, a hint of wistfulness in his voice. "I haven't written anything in a few years. All the books you see scattered on the bed? I wrote those."

Emma's eyes darted to the pile of books, and she eagerly began flipping through them. She picked one up, holding it out. "I've seen this movie!" Her enthusiasm was palpable. "I thought you didn't like westerns," Jasper observed, a teasing note in his voice. "I don't! My ex-boyfriend made me watch it... but it was actually pretty good," Emma laughed, her excitement unabated.

"Thank you so much for offering to help me with my writing, but I still don't want to go on this trip with you. I really don't like sailing," Emma said, her voice tinged with regret.

Jasper's eyes twinkled with a new idea. "It wouldn't be sailing, really. The trip is mostly through rivers and canals, so we'd just be using the engine. You mentioned before that you're fine with puttering around—it's sailing you don't like.

There might be a few stretches where we could technically sail, but we could just use the motor the entire time. I wouldn't even raise the mast. In fact, it might be easier if I just leave the mast at home until we return. This trip is slow and steady. It's perfect for you."

Emma paused, considering his words. "Nope, it's still crazy. I have to think about my dad." Jasper's expression softened with understanding. "I'm sure your father can take care of himself, Emma."

"Yeah, but what about the fact that he would be furious? He's already not talking to you, and I don't want to jeopardize our relationship. I'm sorry, but I need to get back to work and I can't go with you," Emma said, a hint of finality in her tone. She gave a small, half-hearted smile before turning and walking out of his room.

As the afternoon wore on and the evening settled in, Emma found herself unable to shake the conversation with Jasper from her mind. Over the next few days, she noticed Jasper's absence and learned that he had scarcely left his room. Concerned, she made inquiries but discovered little information—just that he seemed to be in seclusion. Emma felt a growing sense of guilt and helplessness.

That night, during dinner with her father, Emma decided to address the situation. "Dad," she began, trying to keep her tone calm, "I'm sorry, but I need to talk to you about Jasper."

Ben's response was immediate and brusque. "I don't want to hear it." Emma pressed on, her voice pleading. "Please, Dad. Just hear me out." Ben finally relented with a resigned sigh. "Fine, go ahead."

Emma recounted everything she had discussed with Jasper, her voice steady but laden with concern. When she got to Jasper's idea about the trip, Ben's reaction shifted dramatically.

Emma had never seen her father like this; it seemed he was mad, sad and terrified all at the same time. Ben started yelling "He took my wife, he took my mother, even our ability to travel but I'll be damned if he is taking my daughter as well" tears rolling down his cheeks. "No way are you going with that son of a bitch".

Emma cut him off screaming and virtually crying "Dad I'm not going anywhere. I'm staying right here" Emma rushed over to her father and wrapped him in a warm, tight embrace. Her arms clung to him as if she could somehow erase all the worries that had plagued him.

"I'm so sorry, Dad. I love you so much," she said, her voice choked with emotion." After what felt like a long, comforting silence, they slowly pulled away and returned to their seats. Emma wiped her tears and looked at her father with a renewed sense of determination. "Dad, I didn't realize how much this was affecting you," she said, her voice still trembling. "I promise you, I'll never leave. I'll always stay here with you. No matter what happens, this is where I belong."

Later that night, Ben lay wide awake in bed, his mind a chaos of conflicting emotions. He grappled with the intense resentment he felt toward his father, a bitter feeling that had lingered for years.

But more pressing was the unsettling memory of Emma's words: "I'll stay here forever." The notion of her spending her entire life in Ticonderoga, bound by the limits of their small town, had always been a source of deep anxiety for him.

Now, faced with the possibility that she might finally have a chance to leave and embark on an adventure, the irony was almost too much to bear. The journey she might take was with the one person in the world he despised most—his father.

The thought of Emma being exposed to Jasper's potential for harm tormented Ben. He imagined every conceivable scenario in which Jasper might hurt her, fueling a sleepless night filled with restless tossing and turning. The hours dragged by, and as dawn approached, Ben had not managed to close his eyes even once.

The weight of his thoughts and fears kept him trapped in a wakeful state, dreading the possibility of Emma's departure.

The next morning, which was Emma's day off, she managed to sleep in a bit longer than usual. Still dressed in her soft lavender cotton pajamas—adorned with delicate white floral patterns—she emerged from her bedroom and headed to the kitchen.

It was then she noticed something unusual, her father had not left for work. Ben was always up and out before she even stirred. Concerned, she padded over to his bedroom door and gave it a gentle knock.

"Come in," Ben's voice called out, slightly muffled through the door.

Emma opened the door slowly, peering inside. The room was dimly lit, and Ben was lying in bed, covered by a faded duvet decorated with a nostalgic floral pattern.

The sight of the duvet tugged at Emma's heart. She knew it had been a gift from her mother, and it was clear why Ben had never replaced it.

His habit of sleeping on the left side of the bed, while the right side remained untouched, was a poignant reminder of her mother's absence. "Dad, are you okay?" Emma asked softly, her concern evident.

Ben shifted slightly and replied, "I'm fine. I just didn't sleep well last night. I called in sick today; I didn't feel up to going into work."

Emma was taken aback by her father's unusual decision to stay home from work. She struggled to recall if she had ever known him to call in sick before; it was certainly out of character for him. While she couldn't pinpoint a specific instance of him taking a sick day, she realized it must have happened at some point. Nonetheless, his unexpected absence and evident distress sparked a fresh wave of concern.

Emma remained by the door, her mind racing with a barrage of questions and worries. Despite her growing anxiety, she decided to give him space "ok dad I'll let you sleep" she responded and gently closed the door, understanding that he had likely had a rough night.

As the hours passed, her concern only deepened. By late afternoon, around four o'clock, she could no longer ignore the unease gnawing at her. She knocked softly on his door and asked quietly, "Dad, are you okay?"

"Come on in, Emma. We need to talk," Ben's voice came through the door, tinged with an urgency that made Emma's heart sink. "That's never a good sign," she thought as she slowly turned the knob and entered his room.

Ben was lying on the bed, his gaze serious as he motioned for her to sit. "Come on in, sweetie. Have a seat next to me," he said, patting the space beside him. Emma sat on the edge of the bed, her mind brimming with unease.

"Emma, you know more than anything that I want what's best for you, regardless of what it means for me personally," Ben began, his voice earnest and heavy with emotion.

Emma nodded, her eyes searching his face for reassurance. "I'm sorry," Ben continued, "but I don't want you to take this trip." Emma's eyes widened, and she quickly interjected, "Dad, I already said I'm not going." "Let me finish," Ben urged. "I don't want you to go, but I honestly feel you need to go."

"What? You can't be serious!" Emma stuttered, her shock palpable. "You hate him. What if something happens? And who will take care of you?"

"Emma, calm down," Ben said, trying to soothe her. "Let's take this one step at a time. Yes, I hate him, and the thought of you going with him is tearing me apart. But this might be your only chance for an adventure like this.

If something goes wrong, remember that I'm less than a twenty-four-hour drive away from the farthest point you'll be. I can even fly if necessary. Plus, I'm going to buy you a new waterproof phone. If you get into trouble or just want to come home, In fact I want you to call regularly and keep me updated."

Emma listened, still reeling from the emotional rollercoaster. "But what about the fact that I don't have a passport? One of the first things he plans on doing is going into Canada." Ben's face softened with a reassuring smile. "That's easy. We can fill out the passport application online and expedite it.

If it doesn't arrive before you leave, I can drive it to you at the border. Do you know when he plans on leaving?"

"I'm not sure," Emma replied, her voice tinged with anxiety. "I think he mentioned that he's planning to launch the boat this weekend, which is only four days away. But Dad, I would miss you too much. We've never really been apart for more than a few nights."

Ben's gaze softened as he took in her worried expression. "Emma, you need this experience," he said gently, trying to ease her fears. "Besides, we can stay in touch.

We can talk on the phone, and we can even video chat. I'll always be just a call away."

Emma nodded slowly, still feeling the weight of the decision pressing down on her. Her father's reassurances were comforting, but the thought of being away from him for an extended period remained daunting. She took a deep breath, trying to reconcile her longing to stay close with the opportunity to explore something new.

Emma's mind raced as she absorbed her father's words. Despite her initial reluctance, she realized that with his backing, the practicalities of the trip seemed more manageable. She took a deep breath, preparing to discuss the details with him, feeling a new sense of resolve forming within her.

Ben continued, his tone pragmatic yet supportive. "Before we do anything else, you need to let Jasper know you're going and find out more details about the trip." Emma nodded, contemplating the best way to approach the conversation. "I'd prefer to tell him in person, so I'll have to wait until tomorrow morning. But what kind of details should I ask him about, Dad?"

Ben leaned back, thoughtful. "You should ask about the boat itself. Find out what kind it is and how much space you'll have for yourself and your belongings. Remember Emma, living on a boat is quite different from living in a house."

Emma furrowed her brow, recalling what little she remembered about the boat. "Well, he did mention something about the boat, but to be honest, I wasn't really paying attention."Ben chuckled, shaking his head. "What's so funny?"

Emma asked, puzzled. "You never listen to me, so why should Jasper be any different?" Ben laughed, his amusement clear.

Emma couldn't help but smile despite herself. "Haha, very funny, Dad. I do remember him saying it was thirty-four feet, old and had a center pit or something like that."

Ben's laughter intensified. "Ah, so it's a classic with a center cockpit. That fits him perfectly. The boat likely has a split cabin design. Think of it as a really small one-bedroom apartment. At least you'll have some privacy, though I'm not sure if he will give you the stateroom or keep it for himself." Emma's eyes widened. "Wait, you mean one of us will have to sleep on the sofa?"

Ben, still chuckling, nodded. "Yep, and consider yourself lucky. Most sailboats in that size range are more like mini studio apartments with no separate bedrooms. And just so you know, a sofa on a boat is called a settee, and a bed is called a berth."

Emma's initial excitement was tempered by a flurry of questions and concerns. As she pondered the details, she began to wonder why she was even considering doing this. But as she reflected more, she realized that she didn't have much stuff and was generally a pretty simple person.

This opportunity was a once-in-a-lifetime chance, and despite the uncertainties, it was something she felt she couldn't pass up.

For the next few hours, Emma peppered Ben with a barrage of questions. His responses were filled with insights and practical advice, covering everything from the boat's layout to the exact route they would take. He described the incredible sights they would encounter—palm trees swaying in the breeze, towering skyscrapers, intricate bridges, and even the gentle manatees that might appear along the way.

As the evening grew late, Emma's initial apprehensions were replaced by a growing excitement. She felt a renewed sense of anticipation for the adventure ahead and couldn't wait to share her decision with Jasper in the morning. The prospect of exploring new places and experiencing life on the water began to overshadow her initial doubts, filling her with a sense of eager anticipation for the journey to come.

Chapter 3

Being an "Old Salt"

Jasper awoke to the soft, soothing sound of a nurse's voice at his door. "Good morning Jasper," she greeted him with a warmth that was hard to ignore. Her voice had a gentle, calming quality, and her presence seemed to fill the room with a comforting sense of care.

The nurse stepped into the room, her smile radiating genuine kindness. "Jasper, a group of us are taking the bus to the Fort today. I know you've probably been there a thousand times, but I think it would do you some good. Please, say yes."

Her eyes were full of empathy as she offered him a sympathetic smile, making her plea seem both heartfelt and earnest. "Please, please, please come," she added, her tone almost playful as she begged in a friendly, coaxing manner.

Jasper sat up and met her gaze, the corners of his mouth twitching into a faint smile. "I'm sorry, I'm just not in the mood today," he replied, his voice betraying a hint of reluctance. The nurse's expression shifted to one of mock seriousness.

"Jasper, if you don't get up out of that bed, I'm going to have to get a couple of orderlies in here to drag you out," she said, her voice firm but not unkind.

Jasper chuckled softly at her playful threat. "That was a great performance, but I'm not buying it. The truth is, I've been there a thousand times, and I'm just tired today, okay?" he explained, his tone earnest yet light-hearted.

The nurse's smile remained, and she seemed to accept his response with grace. "Alright, if you're sure you don't want to come," she said, her tone warm and understanding.

"Yes, I'm sure," Jasper affirmed with a firm nod, his expression resolute. "Alright then, I'll talk to you later," she said, her voice softening as she began to leave. As she walked out the door, Jasper could faintly hear her speaking to someone in the hallway.

"Oh, Emma, what are you doing here so early?" the nurse asked, her tone warm and surprised. She paused for a moment before adding, "Oh, he'll like that. Have a great day!"

A moment later, Emma appeared at the door, her face brightening with an eager, friendly smile. "Hi, Jasper!" She greeted him with a warmth that seemed to fill the room."Hello, Emma," Jasper responded softly, his tone carrying a hint of sadness that seemed to linger beneath his otherwise polite words.

Emma stepped into the room, her excitement barely contained. "I have some good news for you," she said, her eyes sparkling with anticipation. She paused for a moment, clearly savoring the moment before delivering her news.

Her enthusiasm was palpable, and she looked at Jasper as if she couldn't wait to share something special. "I know it's something that will make you feel a lot better."

"I don't know, Emma. Do you still think I'm crazy?" Jasper replied, his voice carrying a somber tone that revealed a lingering hurt. The question seemed to echo with a touch of vulnerability, hinting that he was still affected by last night's conversation.

Emma's heart ached at Jasper's words, realizing that her earlier reaction might have stung more than she intended.

Determined to mend things, she approached him with a gentle, reassuring smile. "Jasper, I need to clear something up," she began, her voice soft but sincere. "I never meant to imply that you're crazy. I just thought your idea seemed a bit out of the ordinary. But I've had a change of heart."

Jasper raised an eyebrow, his curiosity piqued. "What do you mean? You don't think it's crazy anymore?

Emma's eyes lit up with enthusiasm as she continued. "No, not at all. In fact, I'm excited to go. I want to experience life beyond this town. Do you know, in all my memory, the tallest building I've ever seen is only three stories high. I've never seen a large bridge. The largest I've seen is the little ones that cross the LaChute River, which I can practically touch from my kayak.

I want to see the world. I want to see the ocean, palm trees, and dolphins." Her voice grew animated as she spoke, her excitement evident. "I've been dreaming of seeing these things for so long. This is a chance I can't pass up. I'm really looking forward to it now."

Jasper's smile was thin and unconvincing as he replied, "I'm sorry Emma. I know this was my idea, but after thinking it over, I don't think I can go through with it." Emma's eyes widened in shock.

She stared at him, her expression blank as she struggled to process his sudden change of heart. After a moment of awkward silence, she managed to ask, "Wh-why? Why can't we go?"

Jasper's voice was heavy with regret. "I refuse to make things worse with your father. I'm sorry, but I just can't do it."

Emma's confusion quickly melted into a wide, beaming smile. "Jasper, it was actually Dad who convinced me to go. He wants me to go, he really does. He told me this is a chance I might never get again. He even went online, ordered me a passport, and had it expedited, and offered to drive it to the border if it didn't arrive in time."

Jasper's eyes widened as he absorbed this new information, his earlier resolve wavering in the face of Emma's excitement and determination.

Jasper's eyes widened in disbelief. "I can't believe it," he said, his voice tinged with astonishment. "Are you sure? You're not just telling me what I want to hear, are you?" Emma chuckled softly, her own excitement bubbling over. "No, it's the truth. We're definitely going."

Jasper, still in shock, felt a surge of emotions all at once. He could barely contain his joy, overwhelmed by the thought of escaping his current situation for at least another year, the prospect of traveling again, and the chance to spend time with Emma.

But above all, he was elated that it was his own son who had convinced her to go.

With a huge, almost childlike smile spreading across his face, Jasper managed to stand up on his bad leg.

He hobbled over to Emma with a look of pure elation. Wrapping his left arm around her, he managed to get his right arm around her lower back, pulling her into a heartfelt embrace.

His voice trembled with emotion as he said, "Emma, this is the happiest I've been in fourteen years. Thank you so much."

Emma's heart sank slightly as she quickly calculated that fourteen years ago was the year of the accident. She felt a pang of empathy mixed with joy for him, As they slowly released their embrace, Emma looked at Jasper with a mix of excitement and concern. "I have a lot of questions," she began. "I learned quite a bit about the route from Dad last night, but there are still some things I'm unsure about. My dad also has questions about the departure details, the specifics of your boat, and what my responsibilities will be."

Jasper's face brightened with a warm smile. "Of course, I'm happy to fill in the details. Let's start with the boat. Do you remember what I mentioned about it before?" Emma offered a sheepish grin and shook her head slightly. "Sorry, not really."

"That's alright," Jasper said with a nod. "She's a classic thirty-four-foot sloop, which is a type of sailboat. I'll call the marina today to arrange for them to remove the mast from its crutches and store it for the year. The boat has a center cockpit, which means the cabin is divided into two main sections: the fore cabin and the aft cabin."

"Starting at the front of the boat and working our way to the back first you have the fore cabin, which is the front part of the boat—'fore' meaning 'forward,' there's a U-shaped sofa, called" Jasper began. "A settee," Emma interrupted with a grin. "I learned that one last night."

Emma's laughter brought a smile to Jasper's face. "Good, you're picking up the lingo already," he said. "Yep, got my first two words down," Emma replied with a laugh. Jasper chuckled and added, "Oh, there are just a few more terms to learn."

"Really?" Emma asked, intrigued.

"No Not really," Jasper said with a twinkle in his eye. "I used to have an entire dictionary of sailing terms. But since we're not actually sailing, you won't need to know that much."

"Okay, so back to the boat," Emma said, her face beaming with an unwavering smile. "Right," Jasper continued, "so I mentioned the U-shaped settee right at the front. It has a table in the middle that can be adjusted up and down to form a double berth, but since I'll be sleeping there alone, we can just keep it set up as a table."

Emma's eyes lit up as she interjected eagerly, "So I'll be sleeping in the other cabin?" "Yes, exactly," Jasper confirmed with a nod. "And I'll get to that in just a minute."

"So working backwards from the front to the back, behind the U-shaped settee on the port side, there's a small desk," Jasper explained. "Traditionally, this would be where you'd lay out your charts, but with modern technology, I use electronics for navigation. The desk still serves as a navigation station, but it can also be used for other tasks, like your writing."

Jasper's smile was warm and encouraging. Emma's face brightened as she remembered his promise to help her with her writing. "Thank you so much for this, Jasper," she said, her gratitude clear.

Jasper felt a fleeting pang of longing for a more affectionate term like "Grandpa," but he chose to let it go for now. Instead, he smiled and said, "It's my pleasure, Emma. Now, back to the boat. Behind the desk, there's the enclosed head."

Emma immediately interjected, "Which side is the port side, and what exactly is the head?"

Jasper chuckled, enjoying the moment. "Port is the left side of the boat when you're facing the front, and starboard is the right side. Unlike right and left, which change depending on your orientation, port and starboard are fixed relative to the boat. So, no matter which direction you're facing, Port is always on the left side of the boat."

Emma's brow furrowed slightly in confusion, so Jasper elaborated. "Imagine you're standing in the cockpit and facing the front of the boat. Port is to your left. If you turn around and face the back of the boat, Port will be on your right. It's all about the boat's orientation, not yours."

"Oh, I get it now!" Emma exclaimed. "The easiest way to remember is that 'port' and 'left' both have the same number of letters." Emma's curiosity remained piqued. "So, what was the other thing you mentioned?" she asked.

Jasper smiled, happy to explain further. "Ah, yes, the head. That's the nautical term for the toilet. On this boat, it's referred to as a 'wet head' because the entire room can double as a shower. When we're at anchor, I often prefer to shower in the cockpit to keep the cabin dry.

Alternatively, I might just use a bar of soap and take a dip in the water—though that's best done in freshwater. In the ocean, you'd still need to rinse off the salt water to stay clean."

Jasper continued with the boat details, his tone upbeat. "Alright, back to the layout. On the starboard side, which is the right side, behind the U-shaped settee, there's a small dresser.

On top of that dresser is a tiny wood-burning stove called a cubic. And behind the dresser is the galley which is the nautical word for kitchen. That wraps up the fore cabin.

Now, moving to the middle of the boat, we have the cockpit. It's quite straightforward, just a couple of settees facing each other with a tiller in the center that can flip out of the way. The settees are long enough to lie down on, and there's a tent-like enclosure that can turn the cockpit into an additional room if needed.

Behind the cockpit is the aft cabin, which will be yours. It's not very big, so I hope you're not claustrophobic. This cabin has two quarter berths. Emma interrupted with curiosity, "I know what a berth is—it's the nautical term for a bed, right?"

Jasper smiled and nodded, "Exactly. But it's also the term used for a slip at a marina where you dock your boat. A quarter berth, in this case, is a small bed that your feet are tucked under the cockpit. My boat has two of these in the aft cabin, one on each side, with a small end table between them.

There's also another head in the aft cabin hidden under that table—this one's just a toilet, but since you'll have the cabin to yourself, it's all yours. There isn't much standing room in the aft cabin, but the hatch, which is the nautical term for the door, lifts up to give you headroom. You'll be able to look outside while standing.

For storage, there's space under each quarter berth, and since you're alone in the cabin, you can use the space on top of the other berth for all your things. Is there anything else you want to know?"

Emma's eyes brightened with curiosity. "Your boat sounds amazing, but my dad had a few more questions.

He wanted to know about the electricity and electronics on board. He mentioned something about you being an old salt and probably navigating by the stars."

Jasper chuckled, shaking his head. "Oh, your dad's just looking out for you. Rest assured, I'm not stuck in the past. I've got all the latest electronics on board. We'll have GPS to keep us on track, and he can even track our progress online via our AIS signal, so he'll know exactly where we are at any given time."

"And yes, in the worst case scenario I could navigate without Electronics." Emma looked relieved. "That's good to know. What about electricity? I assume you need power for all those gadgets."

"Absolutely," Jasper confirmed with a smile. "I've got a big solar panel array on the back of the boat to provide most of our power, and the engine generates some electricity too. So, you'll have plenty of juice for your laptop and phone.

You can stay connected and charged up without any problems." Emma nodded, her smile widening. "That sounds perfect. Thanks for explaining all of that!"

Jasper smiled "Oh and by the way I also have satellite internet onboard which has no data cap so you can sit and talk to your dad or your friends all you want."

Emma's face lit up with a broad smile. "Well I don't have a lot of friends but I'll call my Dad each night so he doesn't worry. I guess the last big question is, when?" she asked eagerly.

Jasper replied promptly, "I'd like to get going as soon as possible.

I'm scheduled to launch the boat this weekend, but we still need to sort out how to get you to the boat or bring the boat to you. Plus, I'll need to make some shore visits, so I'd like to get a proper wheelchair before we set off."

Emma's eyes widened as she suddenly checked the time. "Oh no, I'm really late for work!" She quickly added, "I'll have to explain things to them, but I'm sure they'll understand. We're actually really overstaffed at the moment, so it shouldn't be a huge problem. I'll come back and talk to you right after work when I have more time. See you later, and thanks again!"

She barely gave Jasper a chance to respond before rushing out of the room. That day felt like a dream come true for Emma—everything seemed to fall perfectly into place.

She stopped by the administration office and shared her exciting news with the administrator, who greeted her with enthusiasm. "We'll make Friday your last day," the administrator said warmly. "You still have some vacation pay coming, so we'll add that to your final paycheck. It'll be ready for you then."

Emma's heart soared with relief and joy. All the pieces were falling into place, and she couldn't have been more thrilled. As she moved through her tasks, she felt as though she were floating on air. Her steps were lighter, her smile wider—she practically skipped around the office, radiating happiness as she worked.

After work, Emma hurried back to Jasper's room, her excitement barely contained. It looked like Jasper had already started packing things up. Emma chuckled to herself thinking, hard to believe, but he seems as excited as I am. "Hello!" she called through the open door.

Jasper turned his head and smiled. "Hi Emma!"

"I did it! Friday is my last day here," Emma announced, her face beaming. "That's fantastic news!" Jasper replied. "And I have some good news too. I ordered a wheelchair online—it'll arrive tomorrow and even comes with a travel bag.

I also contacted the marina. They're going to remove the mast and deliver the boat to the boat ramp near the ferry crossing. You can ride your bike there, and I'll take a taxi. Then we can load the boat, attach your bike and my wheelchair to the pulpits, and we're on our way."

Emma's curiosity was piqued. "Wait, what's a pulpit?" Jasper explained, "It's the area at the front of the boat where there's a railing around it. We can attach your bike and my wheelchair there."

Emma's eyes lit up. "That's fantastic! I didn't even think about bringing my bike. We're all set. So, when will they bring the boat to the ramp?" "Is Monday okay, or is that too soon?" replied Jasper. "No, that will be perfect," Emma replied with excitement. "I can't wait!"

Chapter 4

Tending the Flower Gardens

Ben stumbled toward the front door, the cool night air barely piercing through the fog of drunkenness that enveloped him. His gait was unsteady, and his normally confident stride was replaced by a series of erratic steps. His dress shirt, once neatly pressed, was now disheveled and stained, and his tie hung loosely around his neck. The glint of streetlights caught on the half-empty bottle of bourbon he clutched in one hand, the source of his current state.

He fumbled with the keychain, the keys jangling loudly as he tried to fit them into the lock. His fingers were clumsy, unable to grasp the right key, and he muttered incoherently to himself, his speech slurred. After several frustrated attempts, he finally managed to unlock the door with a triumphant, if unsteady, push.

Ben pushed the door open but lost his balance as he stepped inside. His body with the doorframe, staggering sideways. He tried to correct his balance but misjudged the distance, and his foot caught on the threshold. With a yelp of surprise, he pitched forward, his arms flailing wildly.

He crashed into a small table just inside the door, sending a vase toppling and flowers scattering. The impact knocked him off his feet, and he crumpled to the floor with a thud.

The bourbon bottle slipped from his hand, rolling away with a dull clink. As he lay there, sprawled on the floor, Ben let out a groan, his head resting on a scatter of flowers and broken vase pieces. He blinked up at the ceiling, trying to piece together what had just happened, while the muffled sound of his own clumsy entrance echoed in the quiet house.

Emma dashed out of the kitchen, her heart racing after the loud crash. Her eyes widened in shock as she saw her father sprawled on the floor, surrounded by broken vase shards and scattered flowers. She gasped, her voice trembling, "Dad, are you okay?"

Ben's head lolled slightly as he looked up at her, his words coming out in a thick, slurred drawl. "I'm fine," he mumbled, his voice barely coherent. "Just had a tiny, tiny itsy bitsy accident."

Emma's fear quickly turned to frustration as she knelt beside him. "Dad, how did you get home?" she demanded, her voice edged with worry. "Az—azzer—Adirondack," he managed to say, struggling to focus.

Emma sighed in relief, though she was still frowning. "Oh good, you took a taxi," she said, noting the name of the local taxi company he had garbled. "But still, you shouldn't have been out like this."

Ben, still lying on the floor, suddenly raised his head with a weak, pleading look. "Where's my drink?" he asked, his voice tinged with desperation.

Emma's expression hardened, and she shook her head firmly. "Nope, you're going to bed now," she said, her tone brooking no argument. She helped him to his feet, steadying him as he swayed unsteadily.

With a determined but gentle grip, she guided him towards the bedroom, knowing that getting him to bed was the first step in dealing with the mess of the night.

Emma carefully removed his shoes and guided him into his room. After helping him into bed and tucking him in, he looked up at her with blurry eyes.

"You are the love of my life," he mumbled with a slurred voice. "I'd do anything for you." With that, he drifted into a deep, alcohol-induced sleep. Emma sighed, smoothing the blankets over him, and quietly left the room, her heart heavy with a mix of concern and frustration.

The next morning, Emma's alarm jolted her awake. As she dressed quickly and made her way to her father's room, a wave of disbelief washed over her. She couldn't believe that he had left so early after such a chaotic night and had gone to work. Emma couldn't imagine herself being able to work after a night like that.

As she continued her morning routine, Emma couldn't shake the nagging question of what had driven her father to drink so heavily the night before. Was it a celebratory indulgence or an attempt to drown his sorrows? She hoped it might be unrelated to her, but deep down, she suspected it was most likely connected.

As she headed into work she felt very conflicted. On one hand she was leaving in a few days on this amazing trip and on the other hand leaving her father in this state felt awful and she was going to miss him so much.

She had to keep reminding herself that not only was this a once in a lifetime opportunity but it was what her father wanted for her.

She decided to tell Jasper today that she was going to spend as much time with her dad as possible before they leave but she will still spend lunch with him.

After all she had a ton of questions and loved hearing of all the places she was going to go and things she was going to see.

That night, Emma prepared her dad's favorite meal and made sure it was ready for him when he walked through the door. Thankfully, his favorite meal was simple to prepare; he was a man of straightforward tastes. She cooked a perfectly barbecued steak, medium rare, paired with a baked potato topped with sour cream, and fresh green beans on the side.

When Ben walked through the door, he saw the meal Emma had prepared for him. It was all ready—he just needed to sit down and eat. Normally, she would offer him a cold beer, but tonight she decided to skip that.

Ben's initial reaction was not one of joy but of deep shame. The sight of the perfectly cooked meal only served as a stark reminder of his behavior the previous night. He was painfully aware of how disgraceful his actions had been and felt even worse knowing that Emma had witnessed his drunken state.

Ben began to speak softly, his voice filled with regret. "Look Emma, thank you for this, but I owe you a huge apology for last night. I know if you go with him, you'll most likely have a wonderful time. You'll get to expand your horizons and see all the things I wanted to show you.

But my anger toward him for the past is something I just can't get over. You need to take this trip. I wish it could be me taking you, or anyone but him. At least I trust his skills, as I mentioned before, he is an old salt."

"Dad, I love you and I do understand. I wish you would explain to me why you're so mad at him, but I get why you're feeling this way today. If you wished it was you taking me, then why didn't you?" Emma asked gently.

Ben looked at Emma, his expression sheepish. "I doubt you remember, but after your mom and grandma passed away, I was completely distraught for a long time. It was my work and my responsibilities that eventually helped me cope.

Do you recall all the therapy you had for your phobia? That cost a lot of money. As I moved up in the company, my responsibilities grew, and it began to consume all of my time. It still does. I guess, amidst all that, I just never thought of it."

It was now Emma's turn to feel a pang of embarrassment. "Dad, was it the cost of raising me and dealing with my phobia that kept you from traveling and made you stay in Ticonderoga?" she asked softly.

Ben lowered his head and nodded. "It's not your fault, Emma. You had a very real phobia, and it's not something you could control. Remember what your therapist used to say: 'It's not your fault; it's out of your control, so you should have no guilt over it.' I truly believe that."

Emma, tears welling in her eyes, still felt a deep-seated guilt. Despite what anyone said, it always felt like it was her fault. No amount of reassurances could fully erase that lingering feeling.

"Dad, if I'm going to be gone for about a year, why don't you take some time off and go on a holiday or something?" Emma suggested, her smile mingling with the tears on her cheeks.

Ben met her gaze with a forced smile, "I still have responsibilities at work, and besides, if I left,

who would tend to the flower gardens and mow the lawn?" He tried to chuckle, but it was clear it didn't come naturally. Emma didn't think it was a very convincing excuse but chose not to press the issue. Instead, she and her father spent the next few hours talking about everything imaginable, before finally heading to bed.

The next morning, Emma woke up earlier than usual. She glanced at the clock and saw that her alarm was still set to go off in another half hour, but she decided it wasn't worth going back to sleep. Today was Friday, her last day at work, and she planned to say goodbye to everyone.

She took a little extra time with her morning routine, making herself look as good as possible within the confines of her work uniform. Deciding to forgo her bicycle, she chose to walk to work instead, as the helmet always seemed to ruin her hair.

Emma enjoyed the crisp morning air and the tranquility of her walk, feeling a mixture of excitement and nostalgia as she prepared for her final day.

Emma spent her morning at work much like any other day, though with more frequent stops to chat and say her goodbyes. While she was in the hallway, deep in conversation with a co-worker, the Administrator tapped her on the shoulder.

"Emma, could you please clean Break-out Room 'B'? Someone spilled something," the Administrator said. "You're being paid until the end of today, so please make sure you get some work done." Emma quickly responded with a smile,

"Absolutely, I'll get right on it." She headed toward the break-out room.

When Emma arrived at the Break-out Room 'B', she was surprised to find a group of her closest co-workers gathered inside. A handmade banner hung across the back wall,

reading "Good-Bye Emma," and a table was set with a cake and three wrapped presents.

The Administrator followed her in and explained, "They wanted to throw you a going-away party. You have half an hour."

Emma's face lit up with gratitude. "Thank you everyone, this means the world to me."

A young woman, about Emma's age, stepped forward with a warm smile. "We went together and got you some presents and a cake. I hope you like chocolate."

Emma's smile grew even wider. "Of course I do! You'd have to be insane not to like chocolate." She glanced at the cake, which was decorated with the words 'Bon Voyage Emma'. With a beaming smile, Emma added, "Awww, thank you guys. This means so much to me."

"Great! Come and cut the cake, we don't have that much time," one of her co-workers said. Emma picked up the knife and began slicing into the cake, her joy evident as she cut generous pieces and handed them out to her colleagues.

Each smile and appreciative thank you from her friends added to her happiness. As they enjoyed their cake, her colleagues either wished her well or eagerly asked about her upcoming trip. The room buzzed with lively conversation and heartfelt farewells, making Emma's last day at work a truly special occasion.

After the last crumbs of cake had been enjoyed, one of Emma's co-workers spoke up, "It's time for presents. Honestly, there's not much, but we wanted to get you something."

She handed Emma a small gift box, tastefully wrapped and adorned with a delicate bow that instantly caught the eye.

Emma accepted the box with a smile and slowly unwrapped it, her curiosity piqued. Inside, she found a ceramic cup with a wider base than the top, designed with a non-skid rubber bottom to prevent tipping. The cup was a soft beige color, and printed on the outside was the inspirational saying, "Always Move Forward."

Emma's co-worker explained, "It's supposed to be tip-proof. We figured it would be good on a rocking boat." Emma's eyes softened with appreciation as she admired the thoughtful gift, its practical design perfectly suited for her upcoming trip.

Next, her co-worker announced, handing Emma a medium-sized gift bag adorned with a pattern of tiny red hearts against a white background. The bag had a playful, Valentine's Day feel to it, but Emma found it endearing nonetheless.

With a smile, Emma reached into the bag and pulled out a canvas Tilley-style hat, its practical design featuring a wide brim and a drawstring that could be secured under her chin. What made the hat truly special was the array of signatures scrawled across it in various colored pens, each one from a different colleague. The heartfelt messages and names were a testament to the camaraderie and warm wishes of her coworkers.

"Okay, last gift," the same co-worker announced with a smile, handing Emma another gift bag. This one was decorated with a whimsical design featuring a mouse on a sailboat, a motif that looked more suited for a child but was undeniably charming and fitting for the occasion. Emma admired the bag's playful design, appreciating its light-hearted touch.

As she carefully opened the bag, Emma couldn't help but smile at its cheerful pattern. The anticipation built as she reached inside, eager to see what awaited her.

Emma's eyes widened as she pulled out a small pink and white striped bikini from the gift bag. "Oh my god," she blurted out, completely taken aback. "It's so tiny," she said, her face flushing with embarrassment. Her co-workers erupted into laughter, clearly enjoying the moment.

The same co-worker who had been presenting the gifts wrapped her arm around Emma's shoulder and said, "We've seen your swimsuit, and while it was probably fabulous in the nineteen thirties, we figured you might meet someone on your travels. The selection has to be better than what we have here, and we thought this might help."

Emma blushed even deeper and stammered, "But it's so small." Her co-worker chuckled and reassured her, "There's actually twice as much fabric on this one than there is on mine."

Emma couldn't help but laugh along with everyone. She decided to embrace the playful gesture and smiled as she thanked them. "I appreciate it," she said, still a bit red but genuinely touched by the effort and humor.

"Alright everyone, time to get back to work," called out the Administrator, her voice cutting through the lively chatter in the room. "Emma, could you stay behind for a minute?"

Emma gave her co-workers one last round of goodbyes and heartfelt thanks before they filed out of the room. Once they were gone, the Administrator turned to Emma with a warm, serious expression.

She handed Emma an envelope and continued, "First Emma, this is your last check. It includes all your hours, up to the end of your shift today, plus your remaining vacation pay."

Emma took the envelope, appreciating the Administrator's thoughtfulness. "Thank you," she said, her voice sincere.

The Administrator smiled, her tone softening as she added, "Second, I know you've just reconnected with your grandfather and you two are about to embark on this grand adventure together. But heaven forbid anything goes wrong, I want you to know that you will always have a job here."

Emma's eyes widened slightly, touched by the offer. "Thank you so much. That really means a lot to me."The Administrator continued, her smile widening slightly, "And third - go home. You can leave now; you're already being paid until the end of the day."

Emma's face brightened with relief and gratitude. "Oh, really? That's so kind of you. Thank you!"

"Absolutely," the Administrator replied with a nod. "Enjoy the rest of your day, you've earned it." The Administrator nodded, a reassuring smile on her face "Safe travels Emma, and don't hesitate to reach out if you need anything."

Emma left the office feeling a mix of gratitude and excitement. As she walked out, she glanced at the envelope in her hand, her heart full of appreciation for the support she had received.

The rest of the day and the weekend flew by in a whirlwind of packing, goodbyes, and last-minute preparations. Emma was surprised at how quickly the departure day arrived. Her excitement mingled with a tinge of anxiety, keeping her awake through the night before. She lay in bed, tossing and turning, her mind racing with anticipation and what-ifs about the journey ahead.

Chapter 5

It's Your Turn

After Ben packed all of Emma's belongings into his car, he drove down to the ramp by the ferry, where Jasper's boat was securely moored alongside. As he arrived, he saw that Emma was still en route; she had left quite a bit before him, but her bicycle ride took longer than his drive.

He knew she enjoyed cruising down Main Street, while he had taken the quicker route across the north of town.

Ben knew Jasper had already taken a taxi earlier that morning and was likely already on board. Determined to avoid any awkward encounters with Jasper, Ben decided to unload Emma's belongings in the parking lot. The bags were manageable in size, so he figured Emma could easily transport them up to the boat herself once she arrived.

Just then, Ben heard from a distance, "Dad... Dad..." Emma was approaching, her voice carrying through the crisp morning air.

Emma stopped her bike, flicked out the kickstand, and dismounted with a cheerful grin. "Hi Dad. Thanks for bringing my stuff down." She looked at the collection of bags in the parking lot. Ben gave a small, forced smile, I'm sorry Emma but you're going to have to bring your stuff up to the boat from here.

Ben looked at Emma, his expression a mix of pride and sadness. "Alright Emma. I guess this is really it then. Just be careful out there and make sure to keep in touch. We'll definitely have to keep up with the video chats."

Emma smiled, trying to reassure him. "Of course Dad, we'll talk and video chat all the time. I promise, and don't worry about me too much. I'll be fine."

Emma gave her father a quick hug, which turned into a tight embrace as they both felt tears well up in their eyes. The emotion of the moment was palpable, with the reality of their parting settling in.

As they finally let go, Emma turned toward the boat, the mixed feelings of anticipation and nervousness washing over her. She took a deep breath and started carrying her belongings aboard, each step on the dock resonating with both excitement and the weight of leaving home.

Ben stood beside his car, watching her with a bittersweet expression. He knew this was an important step for Emma, and while he felt sad, he was also proud of her courage and eager for her new experiences.

He waved as Emma glanced back one last time before stepping onto the boat, her future stretching out before her. Ben got in the car and looked over at Emma getting onto the boat.

All of this was way too much for him. He drove to the parking lot at the train station. It was only two minutes away but he wanted to be out of sight of the boat.

After he parked he slumped over the wheel, his tears spilling out as he let the emotions he had been holding back come to the surface. It was a mixture of sadness and pride, a heartache for the goodbye and a deep sense of admiration for Emma's bravery.

After Emma had greeted Jasper, he led her to her cabin. She peered inside the aft cabin and thought to herself, "Wow, it's really tiny, but it will do." Despite its compact size, she appreciated the cozy charm it offered.

With a smile, she looked up at Jasper and said, "Thanks, this is great," as she began to organize her bags and settle in. The small space felt surprisingly comforting and she was ready to embrace the journey ahead.

After a few minutes Jasper called to her to take a tour of the rest of the boat. She really liked seeing the boat but was anxious to get going.

"OK ok" Said Jasper "We will get going, But normally when you leave for a trip like this you would have a rope cutting ceremony".

Emma looked at Jasper with curiosity. "A rope cutting ceremony? What's that about?"

Jasper chuckled and nodded. "It's a tradition. Normally, you'd have two people you trust most cut the lines when you leave. They'd then take the knot home with them. It's a symbolic way of marking the start of your journey, and those people would be trusted with things like forwarding your mail and handling any important tasks while you're away."

Emma raised an eyebrow. "Sounds interesting. But why aren't we doing it today?"

Jasper shrugged. "Given the circumstances of our departure, the cost of rope, and the fact that your dad is handling your mail while I'm using a mail forwarding service, I figured it would be simpler to skip the ceremony."

He glanced around to make sure everything was in order. "So, with that in mind, could you untie the lines for us? Since there's very little wind or current here, it doesn't matter which line you do first."

Emma nodded and began untying the lines, feeling a bit of excitement as she worked. Jasper's mention of the tradition made her appreciate the moment even more, and she was eager to start their journey.

"Should I push the boat off of the dock?" Emma asked." Jasper quickly said "No! It's silly things like pushing boats off of the dock or trying to use your body when we pull up to a dock is where accidents happen. So unless I ask you to, we can just power away from the dock."

With that Emma untied the boat and stepped back on board. She could feel the excitement building inside her as the boat slowly started to drift away from the dock. Jasper was right—he'd emphasized the importance of safety, and she could see why.

Jasper, noticing her eagerness, gave her a reassuring smile. "We're all set," he said. "Just let me know if you have any questions or if there's anything you want to see as we head out."

Emma watched as the dock receded into the distance, feeling a mix of thrill and relief. The adventure was finally beginning. Jasper guided the boat out of the dock with practiced ease, and Emma could see the shoreline stretching out before them. The freedom of the open water was exhilarating, and she figured she was ready for whatever lay ahead.

It truly was a beautiful day. The temperature was around 80 degrees, the sky was clear with not a cloud in sight and a gentle breeze barely stirred the water's surface. Emma couldn't believe how much she was enjoying herself, with a seemingly permanent smile on her face. The boat moved slowly, almost gliding, adding to the tranquil atmosphere.

Emma glanced at the control panel, searching for a speedometer, but found none. "Jasper, how do we know how fast we're going?" she asked. Jasper chuckled, looking around casually. "Oh, we're doing about eight knots." Emma laughed, enjoying the banter.

"Okay, I get it—no speedometer. But how fast is a knot, anyway?" Jasper smiled. "About nine miles per hour." Jasper continued, "That's about the speed we'll average for the length of the trip." Emma's face lit up with relief. She really enjoyed traveling at that pace.

"Do you know where we're stopping next?" she asked. Jasper laughed again. "We just left, and you're already thinking about stopping?"

Emma shrugged with a playful grin. "Well, we didn't bring much food with us, and I was thinking about what our first supper aboard should be." Jasper nodded. "I had planned for us to stop in the town of Westport later this afternoon. We can pick up supplies there."

"Do you know Jasper, this is the first town I remember visiting outside of Ticonderoga" said Emma. Jasper kind of knew this in the back of his mind but hearing it out loud for the first time really hit home for him.

"Wow Emma, that's right, Well, Westport is a charming little town, though to be honest, it's not that different from home. Just wait until you see a big city—now that's a whole different experience."

Emma couldn't wait "What is the first big city we will see and what's the biggest city?" Well the first big city we will see is just a few days from now and that's Montreal. It's actually the third largest city we will come across on the loop and they mostly speak French there."

Emma knew very little about Montreal, as it rarely featured in American movies. To her, it felt like an exotic destination. Jasper continued, "As for the biggest city on our route, that's New York City. We'll also pass through other major cities like Chicago and Miami. But we'll be visiting plenty of smaller cities along the way as well."

Emma's excitement grew. She had seen these places in movies and was eager to experience them in real life.

Emma didn't have to wait long, only about an hour and half before something incredible caught her eye in the distance. A massive bridge came into view, and as it grew closer, her amazement only intensified.

The bridge was silver, with enormous arches stretching upward and a lattice of wires connecting the road to the arches. It was the largest structure Emma had ever seen. She couldn't take her eyes off it as they approached. She was captivated by its grandeur.

Then, off to the side on a small hill, Emma spotted a lighthouse adorned with Greek-inspired columns. It was even more stunning than any picture she had ever seen.

Emma was speechless, her eyes wide with wonder. Jasper watched her with a smile, seeing her awe as if she were a child on Christmas morning. Emma finally spoke, "What a beautiful spot! This is amazing."

Jasper replied, "It's called Crown Point. just beyond the bridge, across from the lighthouse, are the remains of an old fort similar to Fort Ticonderoga." "Really?" Emma asked, her excitement evident. "Yeah, there are actually a few more as we head north, and many more along the loop," Jasper replied. Emma simply smiled, thrilled by the prospect.

A short distance later, Emma spotted a small town nestled along the side of a hill. "That's Port Henry, where I lived," Jasper said. Emma responded quickly, "You were so close. I can't believe it took fourteen years to reconnect." Jasper lowered his head and replied solemnly, "Yeah, sorry about that. It's partly my fault."

Emma decided to change the subject. "Are we going to be spending the night in Westport?" Jasper, recognizing the shift but smiling, replied, "Nope, just stopping for provisions. We need to pick up groceries and top off the diesel."

Emma looked at him curiously. "Which part of that am I responsible for?" Jasper grinned. "Well, it's time for you to start earning your keep. I'll need help tying off at the marina. Don't worry they will pump the fuel and I need you to go into town and buy groceries for a few days.

"The grocery store is close to the marina—just a short walk," Jasper said. Emma smiled. "No problem. But I need to know what you like and don't like to eat."

As they discussed food, a massive motor yacht sped by, passing dangerously close and creating a huge wake that rocked the small sailboat violently. Jasper struggled to steady himself and in a moment of frustration, gave the motor yacht the finger.

When he turned back to Emma, he saw her in absolute terror, pushed back into her seat, clinging on for dear life. Jasper quickly moved to her side, sitting down to comfort her. "It's okay," he said reassuringly. "The Arabella can handle anything this lake or reckless boaters like that can throw at her. It doesn't happen that often, but it does occur from time to time," Jasper said, trying to reassure her.

"Just think of it like being on a roller coaster." Emma, starting to regain her composure, looked at Jasper and whispered, "I've never been on a roller coaster." Jasper looked a bit puzzled. Emma explained, "The rides go really fast, and I feel out of control." Jasper hadn't considered how her phobia might affect her experiences.

He realized there were many things she might have missed out on, not just places. "Okay, Emma, I'm sorry—I didn't think of that. You seem alright now. Were you okay with the wake?" Emma replied, "No!! Not while it was happening, but at least it was over quickly."

Jasper began to think about how he could help Emma, especially since as much as he hated it, encountering large wakes was part of being on the water. He decided to shift her focus.

"When we get to Westport, the marina usually has staff who grab the lines and tie the boat off for us. But sometimes they're busy, and we'll have to do it ourselves. So, I'm going to teach you how to tie a mooring knot.

"Can you go to the back of the boat and uncoil the mooring line? It's long enough to reach up here,"

Jasper instructed. Emma went to the back, uncoiled the line, and brought the end forward to the cockpit. "Now, see these cleats here?"

Jasper said, pointing to a small piece of hardware on the side deck with two horn-like projections at either end. "Yes," Emma replied.

"These cleats are usually used for tying spring lines in tidal waters, but today we're going to practice on them," Jasper explained. "I'll demonstrate once, and then it will be your turn."

He began to loop the line around the cleats, guiding it over and finally under. "Alright, your turn," Jasper said. Emma proceeded slowly, with Jasper offering instructions as she worked.

After she completed the knot for the first time, Jasper said, "Great job. Now keep practicing until you can do it in your sleep." "Okay," Emma replied, and continued tying and untying the line.

While she did this she asked "so if we are not spending the night in Westport where are we spending it." "I told you I preferred to anchor at night, it's usually a lot quieter and to be honest much cheaper". Emma remembered him saying this but had forgotten. The thought actually scared her a little.

As the town of Westport came into view, Jasper expertly maneuvered the Arabella alongside the dock. Two marina attendants were there to assist with tying off the boat, and Jasper was engaged in conversation with one of them.

He then turned to Emma. "Okay, we're all set here. Could you go and get the groceries please?" "Okay," Emma said, her voice tinged with nervousness.

She started walking toward the gate at the end of the dock but then stopped, turned around, and headed back to the boat.

As soon as she reached Jasper, she said, "Jasper, can I talk to you for a minute?" Jasper looked at her with concern and replied, "Sure, come here." Emma approached him and said, "I'm sorry, but I don't know where the grocery store is."

Jasper smiled and said, "I told you it's just a couple of blocks away. You can use the maps on your phone." Emma dropped her head, looking embarrassed. Having never left her small hometown of Ticonderoga before, she hadn't had much use for maps and wasn't really sure how to read one. "I'm sorry, I don't know how," she admitted. Jasper understood immediately what she meant.

Feeling guilty for not noticing the issue earlier, Jasper quickly offered a solution. "I'm really sorry Emma. I should have realized you might need more help. How about this; let's bring my wheelchair ashore, and we'll go together. That way, I can help carry the groceries too."

Emma let out a sigh of relief. "Thank you so much," she said gratefully. Jasper smiled and nodded as Emma untied his wheelchair from the front of the boat. She carefully maneuvered it onto the dock, ready to head to the store with Jasper's assistance.

Jasper chatted with the marina attendants a bit longer, and they assured him they would fuel the boat while they were away, with payment to be settled upon their return. As they walked, Jasper took the opportunity to show Emma how to use the map on her phone. He demonstrated how to search for locations like the grocery store and how to navigate her way back to the boat.

When they returned with the groceries, Emma noticed that the boat was no longer in the same spot. She looked at Jasper, a question forming on her lips. Before she could ask, Jasper explained,

"They moved the boat away from the fuel dock so other boats could use it. It's fine, let's get our stuff on board and get going."

They hadn't been on their way for long when Jasper pointed out, "See that little bay over there? That's where we're going to spend the night." Emma squinted in the direction he indicated, but all she could see was a dense row of trees.

"I'm sorry, I can't see it," she admitted. Jasper pulled out his tablet and brought up a detailed map. He showed Emma the area they were approaching and pointed out a small bay hidden among the trees, labeled Partridge Harbour.

As they got closer, Emma's eyes adjusted, and she began to make out the bay, which had been perfectly camouflaged by the surrounding foliage. It gradually revealed itself as they approached, unfolding into a beautiful spot.

As they slowly glided into the bay, Jasper's voice took on a playful tone. "Okay, now it's your turn again Emma. Time to drop anchor.

"What?" she exclaimed. "Okay, what do I do?" "It's not hard," Jasper replied, pulling out a pair of gloves and handing them to her. "Go up to the front. You'll see the anchor hanging there." Emma made her way to the front of the boat, spotted the anchor, and noticed it was held in place by a pin.

"Do I just pull this pin out?" she called back to Jasper. "No," he shouted back. "First, we need to calculate how much chain to let out."

"The more chain you let out, the less angle the anchor pulls at, which makes it hold stronger. But if we let out too much chain here, we could end up onshore.

Each ten feet of chain is marked with a blue-painted link, so just count them as the chain pays out—ten, twenty, thirty, forty, and so on.

So you pull the pin out letting the anchor drop and when you've reached the correct length, secure it with the large hook around the links. We're only going to let out about sixty feet of chain. Ready?" "No but let's do it anyway," replied Emma "Okay Emma, grab the chain and give it a little pull to relieve the pressure," Jasper instructed.

Emma took hold of the chain with her gloves and pulled, causing the pressure on the pin to ease and allowing it to come free.

She then began to let the chain slide slowly through her hands. It passed through a hole in the deck, over a roller on a machine looking thing across the pulpit, through a small roller, and into the water.

When she reached the sixth marker, she firmly gripped the chain, took the hook, and attached it. Finally, she let the chain rest gently on the deck.

After turning to Jasper, Emma asked, "Is that it?"Jasper chuckled and replied, "For you, yes." He then put the engine into reverse. "I'm just backing down on it to set it into the bottom and check its hold.

Since we couldn't let out a lot of anchor chain, I want to be sure it's set properly." After a brief moment, he shut off the engine and said, "That's it; we're all set for the night." "Well, that was easy," Emma remarked.

"Yep, now let's get supper started," Jasper said, rubbing his hands together with enthusiasm.

When it came to cooking, he and Emma had struck a fun balance; they decided to alternate meals. Emma leaned toward comfort food—hearty dishes that reminded her of home—while Jasper preferred to whip up the exotic meals he had picked up during his travels.

As they gathered ingredients from the galley, Jasper rummaged through the shelves. "How about I make a spicy shrimp stir-fry tonight? It'll be quick and packed with flavor." Emma nodded, her eyes lighting up. "That sounds amazing! I'll prepare some garlic bread to go with it."

They worked side by side, the warm aroma of spices filling the air as they chopped vegetables and seasoned the shrimp. Over the next few hours, their conversation flowed easily, a mix of laughter and shared stories about their lives.

They talked about their favorite meals, the places they had visited, and their dreams for the future.

Emma found herself opening up about her childhood and the challenges she faced, while Jasper shared tales of his adventures—mishaps, successes, and the people he had met along the way.

As they finished cooking, they set the table, enjoying the meal they had prepared together. After dinner, Emma felt a sense of contentment wash over her. She glanced at the clock and realized it was time to call her father. "I think I'm going to head to my cabin for a bit," she said, gathering her things. "It's time for my nightly call to Dad."

Jasper smiled, sensing the importance of the ritual. "Sounds good. I'll clean up here. Enjoy your call!" With a warm feeling in her heart, Emma made her way to her cabin, the soft sound of the waves lapping against the boat accompanying her.

As she settled in, she took a deep breath, ready to catch up with her dad and share all the exciting moments from today's journey.

Chapter 6

Sit Straight and Not Wobble

The next morning, Jasper awoke with the quiet realization that Emma would still be sleeping for a little while longer. He carefully brewed himself a fresh cup of coffee, savoring the rich aroma as it filled the small galley. Once the coffee was ready, he made his way outside, finding his usual spot in the cockpit.

The early light of dawn painted the sky in hues of gold and pink, and the water beneath them shimmered like a field of diamonds. Jasper took a deep breath of the crisp morning air, relishing the tranquil solitude before the day began in earnest.

He settled into his favorite spot, and sipped his coffee slowly, allowing the serenity of the moment to wash over him. This time of day was his favorite—peaceful and still, with only the gentle lapping of the waves to break the silence. He glanced occasionally toward the cabin, knowing it would be a while before Emma stirred.

It was a couple of hours before he finally heard some noise coming from her cabin. "Good morning Emma! Do you want a coffee?" Jasper called out, his voice carrying through the thin walls. "Oh, yes please! In my mug!" came Emma's cheerful reply, though still tinged with sleepiness.

A few minutes later, Emma's head emerged from the cabin, her hair tousled and eyes still half-closed. "Good morning Emma. How did you sleep?" Jasper asked, his tone warm and friendly.

Emma rubbed her eyes and offered a small, embarrassed smile. "To be honest, not so well. There were a lot of noises I'm just not used to. I guess it's part of the charm of being on a boat though. I'm sure I'll get used to it." Jasper nodded sympathetically. "It's true, it takes a little while to adjust to sleeping on a boat. But you're doing great."

Emma brightened up a bit as she pulled a cozy sweater over her head. "Oh, I did get a text from my dad this morning. He said my passport is ready, and he was wondering where he could meet us to give it to me."

Jasper's eyes lit up with a thought. "Well, we're heading to Burlington today. How about we arrange to meet him there?"

Emma's face lit up with excitement. "Burlington, Vermont? That sounds fantastic!" Jasper grinned, pleased to see her enthusiasm. "Yes, Burlington isn't a big city but it has a lot to offer. I think you're really going to enjoy it."

Emma looked at Jasper with a mix of excitement and wonder. "This will be my second state and my first real city. I've heard so many good things about Burlington. I can't wait to explore!"

Jasper chuckled, enjoying her enthusiasm. "It'll be a great day. You can get your passport, and tour Burlington. How about we finish up our coffees and get ready for the day?" Emma nodded eagerly. "Sounds perfect. I'll be right back after I get dressed."

As Emma disappeared into her cabin, Jasper took one last look at the sparkling water, feeling a deep sense of contentment.

A short while later, Emma emerged from the cabin, now dressed and ready for the day. She had changed into a pair of white shorts, paired with a light, airy shirt. The shirt, a soft pastel blue with a subtle floral pattern. Her hair was pulled back into a loose ponytail, and she had added a touch of sunscreen to her face, indicating she was ready to embrace the day's adventures.

Jasper turned to Emma with a grin. "Ready to weigh anchor so we can get underway?"

Emma raised an eyebrow, her curiosity piqued. "I'm guessing 'weigh anchor' means pulling it up. That sounds like it could be tough."

Jasper chuckled. "Exactly, that's what it means. But don't worry, it's not as hard as it sounds. Arabella has a manual windlass, which makes it a lot easier. Just let me start the engine first."

Jasper turned the key and pushed a button and the engine came to life. He then reached into a storage locker and pulled out a bar, handing it to Emma. "Here, take this handle and fit it into one of the holes on the windlass. It's pretty straightforward—there's only one set of holes it will fit into. Then, you just need to place the chain onto the gypsy—that's the wheel on the side that looks a bit unusual."

Emma carefully positioned the chain and inserted it into the gypsy. She gave it a slight tug to make sure it was aligned properly. "Like this?"

Jasper nodded as he watched her work. "That's right. Just ensure the chain is seated evenly and aligned correctly; it should sit straight and not wobble.

Once you've got it in place, move the handle back and forth to pull the chain up. When the anchor is fully raised, insert the locking pin to secure it. After that, we'll be ready to get going" As soon as Emma finished she went back and sat in the cockpit across from Jasper. Jasper throttled up and they left the anchorage.

Early that afternoon, they finally arrived in Burlington, the vibrant city beginning to bustle with its midday activities. The city's charming skyline and the bustling waterfront came into full view. The sun cast a warm glow over the picturesque scene, adding a golden hue to the city's already lively atmosphere. Jasper navigated the boat into the Marina and up to a dock and Emma tied it off.

Turning to Emma, Jasper smiled and said, "We're here! I've been thinking it would probably be great for you to spend the day with your dad, catch up, and enjoy the city. I've been here many times. I don't mind waiting on the boat. There are some maintenance things I wanted to get done anyway."

Emma's face lit up with excitement. "Yes, I've arranged to meet him for ice cream on Church Street. Apparently It's a really popular spot."

Jasper nodded approvingly. "That sounds like a perfect plan. Church Street is a great place to explore - full of shops, street performers, and charming cafes. It'll be a nice way for you to connect with your dad and enjoy the local scene."

Emma grabbed her bag and made her way to the dock, her excitement barely contained. "Thank you for this," she said, her eyes sparkling. "I'm really looking forward to spending the day with him and exploring everything Burlington has to offer!"

Jasper gave her a warm smile and a friendly wave. "You're welcome, Emma. Enjoy your time with your dad. I'll take care of the boat and see you later this afternoon."

As Emma strolled down the dock, Jasper watched her with a sense of contentment. Her enthusiasm was infectious, and he was pleased to see her so eager to embrace the day. With Emma on her way to a day filled with new experiences and cherished moments, Jasper turned his focus back to the boat, readying himself for a bit of maintenance and relaxation.

Emma pulled out her phone and opened her Maps app. Within moments, she determined it was a short walk of less than fifteen minutes and plotted her route.

As she approached the ice cream shop, she spotted her dad, already waiting for her. "Dad!" she called out, her voice filled with excitement. She hurried over and enveloped him in a warm hug. "I hope you haven't been waiting long." "Not long at all," Ben replied with a grin. "I've got your passport right here."

Emma looked up at him with a bright smile. "Thank you! And I have some good news too." Ben raised an eyebrow, curious. "Oh? What's that?" Emma's eyes sparkled. "I'm all yours for the day! You're going to be my tour guide." Ben's face lit up with delight as he pulled her into another hug. "I love that! Thank you."

"But first let's take a moment to enjoy some ice cream. It's the perfect way to start our day on a sweet note".

After enjoying some ice cream, Emma and Ben set off to explore Burlington together. They spent the day strolling through the city, chatting about everything and nothing, browsing through local shops, and soaking in the vibrant atmosphere.

The time they spent together was filled with laughter and discovery, making for a memorable day in this beautiful little city.

It was late when Emma finally made her way back to the boat. Jasper was seated in the cockpit, engrossed in a book. As she approached, he looked up and greeted her with a broad smile. "Did you have a good day?" he asked. Emma's face lit up. "I had a fantastic day!" she replied enthusiastically.

Jasper nodded, clearly pleased. "I've taken care of the slip for the night, so we're all set to stay here. We can relax and enjoy the evening." Emma smiled and nodded, feeling content as she settled back into the cozy atmosphere of the boat.

"Well, I'm heading to bed," Jasper said, stretching slightly. "Tomorrow will be a straightforward day. We'll head to an anchorage near the Canadian border and spend the night there. That way, we can get an early start with Canadian Customs the next morning."

The following day unfolded at a leisurely pace. Emma spent most of it basking in the tranquility of the boat, lounging on the foredeck with a good book in hand. As she turned the pages, she occasionally glanced up to take in the beautiful scenery, watching as the landscape slowly drifted by, bathed in the soft light of the afternoon.

The calm and peaceful atmosphere made the day seem to stretch out in a pleasant, unhurried manner.

Emma relished the opportunity to unwind completely as she soaked up the sun and fresh air.

By evening, the soothing effects of the day caught up with her. Emma retired to her cabin, where she quickly succumbed to a deep, restful sleep.

The day's relaxation had left her thoroughly refreshed, and she slept soundly through the night, undisturbed and at ease.

The next morning, Emma was the first to wake, she was so excited as she anticipated crossing into Canada for the first time. This milestone marked her first venture outside the country, and she could hardly contain her enthusiasm for the new experiences awaiting them.

The day greeted her with a brilliant sunrise, painting the sky in warm hues of orange and pink, and the gentle sounds of the water lapping against the boat added to the sense of adventure that filled the air.

Despite her eagerness, Emma faced a minor dilemma; she cherished her morning coffee, a comforting ritual she looked forward to each day. The only issue was that the coffee was stowed in the fore cabin, where Jasper was still peacefully asleep. Emma stood quietly on deck for a moment, soaking in the tranquility and the stunning morning light.

Even without her coffee, the beauty of the day was enough to lift her spirits. She decided to sit and wait for him and watch the morning unfold.

When Jasper finally roused he was surprised to see Emma already awake "Good morning Emma" Jasper said with a friendly smile. Emma quickly replied back "Coffee, Now!" and started to laugh. Jasper laughed along "ok coffee is on the way" as he disappeared back into the cabin.

Once Emma finally had her coffee, she set about weighing anchor, ready to continue their journey. They navigated to the customs dock, where they tied up and completed the necessary paperwork.

The customs process was efficient and straightforward, and it wasn't long before they were on their way again.

Jasper looked at Emma "Emma why don't you take the tiller for the first part of your first new country?" "Really" Emma exclaimed. Jasper gave her a big smile "Sure you're going to have to learn sometime. I can't do it all the time. Besides it's wide here and there aren't many boats around so I highly doubt anything can go wrong."

Emma took the tiller out of Jasper's hands. Jasper continued "Now remember with a tiller you move it opposite than the direction you want the boat to go. So if you want to go left you push the tiller to the right.

In fact, while we have a wide open area why don't you practice maneuvering her around a bit so you can get the feel". "This is easy" Emma said excitedly. "Well it gets a bit more complicated when it comes to docking and things of that nature. But don't worry, by the time we are done with the loop you will be an expert."

Emma was overjoyed, marveling at the fact that she was steering Arabella in a new country. She couldn't wait for her nightly call to her Dad and tell him about today. Although Emma couldn't help thinking to herself, "so far Canada looked strikingly similar to the United States."

Nevertheless, the thrill of exploring a new place kept her spirits high as they set out to discover what lay ahead.

As they traveled north along the Richelieu River, Emma and Jasper passed through several quaint, picturesque towns. Along the way, they came upon a historic fort that bore a striking resemblance to Fort Ticonderoga back home. However, this fort had a different historical purpose; it was constructed to defend against potential American invasions.

Being an American herself, Emma found this to be fascinating. It gave her a new perspective on history as they journeyed through the Canadian landscape.

In the distance, a larger town began to emerge on the horizon. Jasper glanced over and said, "That's St. Jean Sur Richelieu. I believe the name translates to St. Jean on the Richelieu River, much like Castleton on the Hudson back in New York. This will be our stop for the night." Emma quickly interjected, "So, we'll be anchoring here?"

Jasper shook his head with a smile. "Actually, no. We're entering the canal system now. Our first canal will be tomorrow, after we stock up on groceries. From here to the Great Lakes, we'll navigate through numerous canals and waterways.

Tomorrow, we'll also go through our first lock of over a hundred that we'll encounter on this journey." Emma's eyes widened in surprise. "Over a hundred?"

"Yep," Jasper confirmed with a nod. "But don't worry—it might sound a bit daunting, but it's actually not that difficult. The locks here are among the easiest we'll deal with on our journey, making them perfect for getting the hang of things. It'll be a new experience, but definitely manageable."

He paused, then added, "In fact, how about you help me get my wheelchair onshore tonight? We can watch some boats go through the locks so you can get a better feel for how they work. Afterward, we can grab a bite to eat at a restaurant." "That sounds great!" Emma replied, her excitement evident.

It wasn't long before Jasper was maneuvering the boat up against a cement wall. Emma stepped ashore with the mooring lines and tied the boat off. "Secured"

She said aloud with a slightly raised voice. "Thanks Emma, could you get my wheelchair ashore while I get ready" said Jasper.

A few minutes later, Emma and Jasper were making their way up a path leading to the lock station. Emma was so excited; she practically skipped along the path. Just over a week ago, she hadn't even known what a boat lock was. The concept had only become real to her when she saw a picture of her dad maneuvering a narrowboat through one. Now, here she was, about to experience it firsthand.

As they walked Jasper explained that this was a historic canal built in the early nineteenth century. And it is still operated in much the same way it was when it was built. When they arrived Emma looked down into the chamber; it was rectangular in shape, with high stone walls rising above the water level, giving the lock a picturesque, almost timeless appearance. The chamber's huge gates are made of wood and are adorned with antique looking mechanisms for operation.

Jasper and Emma sat at a nearby picnic table, enjoying the crisp evening air as they waited. Their attention soon shifted to another boat approaching the lock. This boat, a small motorboat with distinctive green stripes, pulled up to the wall just a short distance from where their own boat was moored.

It was positioned closer to the lock, on a blue line painted on the edge of the wall.

The boat had barely begun to secure itself when the lock gates began to open. With a smooth maneuver, the boat drifted away from the wall and glided into the lock chamber. Inside, there was a floating dock attached to one side of the lock. The motorboat approached the dock and tied up, preparing for the lock's operation.

As the boat settled, the lock staff closed the gates behind them, and the process began. The water in the lock started to lower slowly, gradually bringing the floating dock and the boat down with it. The transition was smooth and methodical, showcasing the lock's efficiency in managing water levels.

Once the water level inside the lock matched that of the level on the other side, the staff opened the gates at the far end. The motorboat, now floating at the new water level, untied itself from the dock and smoothly exited the lock chamber.

Emma watched the entire process with fascination, taking in the practical mechanics and the seamless operation of the lock system. She found it captivating to watch. And excited and nervous about the fact she will be doing it tomorrow. Jasper then explained that the following day would involve navigating through nine lock chambers and covering about ten miles of the canal.

Emma's eyes widened in surprise. "Nine! We're doing nine of these tomorrow?" Jasper laughed, trying to ease her anxiety. "Don't worry, Emma. You'll be just fine." With her nerves somewhat calmed, they decided to head to a nearby fish and chips restaurant with a charming patio.

The relaxed setting offered the perfect place to unwind and enjoy a delicious meal while taking in the views of the canal.

Chapter 7

Nothing Short of Spectacular

As anticipated, the following day unfolded smoothly. The locks proved to be straightforward. Jasper skillfully guided the boat through each one with practiced ease, while Emma handled the tying and untying of the boat without a hitch.

The canal itself was exceptionally picturesque as it meandered through the city. For much of the journey, there was only a narrow strip of land separating the canal from the main river. This slender strip was bustling with a bike path that stretched alongside it, offering a continuous view of the lively activity. The river, with its cascading rapids, showcased the natural beauty and the reasons behind the canal's construction.

The canal twisted beneath several lift bridges, each adding to the charm and character of the route. Upon reaching the town of Chambly, they encountered three lock chambers that formed a stunning entrance to the Chambly Basin. The view from the basin was particularly striking, offering a perfect blend of architecture and natural beauty.

After leaving the canal behind, they rejoined the Richelieu River. The next few hours were spent cruising past scenic farmlands and quaint small towns. The journey was peaceful, marked by the serene landscapes that defined the region.

They eventually tied up for the night at the St. Ours Lock, concluding a day filled with picturesque views and smooth cruising.

That night, Emma jolted awake to a deafening thunderclap that shook the entire boat. Her heart raced as she quickly sprang from her bed and peered out of her cabin. The outside world was shrouded in darkness, illuminated only by intermittent flashes of lightning. She saw Jasper outside, busy securing the cockpit.

With a quiver in her voice, Emma called out, "Are we going to be okay?"

Jasper glanced over with a reassuring smile, "We'll be fine Emma it's just a storm. I suspect it's going to start pouring any moment now. I checked the forecast earlier, and it looks like we won't be going anywhere today."

Emma took a deep breath, finding solace in Jasper's calm demeanor. The storm might have been fierce, but she felt more at ease knowing they were well-prepared and safe aboard the boat.

They spent the rest of the day balancing their time between enjoying each other's company and seeking solace in their respective cabins.

In the morning, as the rain continued to fall steadily outside, they took advantage of the cozy interior of the boat. They shared meals and chatted, catching up on their experiences and plans while the storm raged on outside.

The sound of the rain tapping against the boat's windows provided a soothing background to their conversation. They also figured this was the perfect time to get another writing lesson in.

Later, as the storm showed no signs of letting up, they retreated to their own spaces for some quiet time. Emma curled up with a book in her cabin, finding comfort in the simple pleasure of reading while the rain created a rhythmic patter against the deck.

Jasper, meanwhile, enjoyed some solitude in the cockpit, sipping coffee and listening to music as he contemplated their journey ahead.

By evening, they reconvened for a quiet dinner, sharing a meal prepared in the boat's galley. The storm outside continued its relentless assault, but inside they felt snug and content, their bond strengthened by the day spent together in close quarters.

The next day dawned cloudy but dry, so they decided to resume their journey. They navigated through the single lock at St. Ours and continued north along the Richelieu River until they reached the St. Lawrence Seaway at the town of Sorel.

The St. Lawrence River was expansive, and a brisk wind created choppy waters, though nothing they couldn't handle. Emma glanced around, noticing the slower pace. "Are we going slower now?" she asked. Jasper nodded, "Yes, we are. We were previously moving with the current, but now we're going against it. Plus, since it's still early in the season, the high water levels are forcing us to proceed even more slowly."

Emma didn't mind, she wasn't in a rush and she wasn't paying the gas but she was curious about one thing.

"Jasper, wouldn't it have made more sense to do the loop the other way so we'd be traveling with the current?" Emma asked.

Jasper smiled and replied, "Actually, going this way, we're with the current for most of the trip. It's only in a few spots where we'll be heading against it, mainly on the rivers. We could have started by heading south, crossing the Erie Canal first, but I wanted to see Montreal and Ottawa. This way, we complete a full loop and avoid retracing our steps."

Emma looked puzzled. "What do you mean by that?" Jasper explained, "If we had gone south through the Champlain Canal and then tackled the Erie Canal, we'd have to come back through the Champlain Canal when we returned to New York.

By doing it this way, we only travel through the Champlain Canal once." "Ah, I see now," Emma said, nodding in understanding. "The only thing that concerns me," Jasper said, raising an eyebrow, "is that I've heard there's a strong current right in the heart of Montreal. I'm hoping our engine will be powerful enough to handle it." Emma's face showed genuine worry. "What if we can't get through?"

Jasper sighed, "If we can't manage it, we might need to hire someone with a more powerful boat to tow us. Alternatively, we'd have to turn back, head down to the Erie Canal, and complete the trip that way, bypassing this part of Canada." His expression grew somber as he spoke. "But I'm confident we'll be fine," he added with a more hopeful tone, trying to reassure Emma.

Just then, Emma heard the unmistakable sound of rushing water. She looked over the back of the boat, following the noise, and saw a massive ship approaching, coming up alongside them. It was only about a hundred feet off their starboard side. "Holy crap, that scared me!" Emma admitted, her eyes wide.

Jasper chuckled and said, "Yeah, you'll see plenty of ships like that here and on the Great Lakes, and even more once we reach the coast. Here and on the Great Lakes, some of these ships can be up to a thousand feet long.

On the Midwest rivers, you'll encounter very large barges being pushed up and down the waterways. As long as we give them plenty of space, there's nothing to worry about." He said this reassuringly, confident that their cautious approach would keep them safe. Emma watched as the ship went past them. She couldn't help notice how much faster it was going compared to them.

"Soon, we'll be stopping at a marina in the town of Verchères," Jasper said, "which is essentially a suburb of Montreal. I need to refuel there and make sure all our tanks are full before we tackle the current in Montreal. After that, there's an anchorage not far from there where we can spend the night."

A short while later, Jasper indeed maneuvered the boat into the marina at Verchères. He went about the task of filling up the fuel tanks, ensuring they were brimming with diesel.

Emma was seated on the foredeck, engrossed in her book, when she heard a voice say, "Bonjour. Comment vas-tu ?" She looked up to find a young man approaching. He was obviously a marina employee, dressed in cargo shorts and a polo shirt emblazoned with the marina's name.

He appeared to be in his mid-twenties, standing about six feet tall. His chiseled jawline and high cheekbones gave him a distinctive and attractive profile. His dark, slightly wavy hair was neatly styled, complementing his striking green eyes that held a gaze both intense and approachable.

His well-defined physique suggested he took good care of himself. With a warm and confident smile, he exuded a charm that made him both engaging and memorable.

Emma felt a bit self-conscious, realizing she wasn't wearing any makeup. She stammered, "I'm sorry, I don't speak French." The man smiled warmly, his green eyes twinkling.

"That's okay, I speak enough English." Emma grinned back at him. "Where are you headed today?" he asked.

Emma, still smiling brightly, replied "Tonight, we're just anchoring near here. But tomorrow my grandfather and I are planning to head to Montreal."

"Oh, will you be in Montreal for long?" the man asked. Emma turned and called back to her grandfather, "How long are we staying in Montreal?"

Jasper came forward to join the conversation, much to Emma's chagrin. "Probably a few days," Jasper replied. "We're not on a set schedule, so we have plenty of time." The man looked at Jasper and asked, "Would it be alright if one of those days I took your granddaughter to La Ronde? That is, if she wants to."

Jasper enjoyed this man's manners and glanced at Emma, who was beaming with a wide smile. He noticed her enthusiasm but realized she might not fully understand what La Ronde was. "It's up to her if she wants to go with you to an amusement park," he said, emphasizing "amusement park."

Emma's heart sank as she heard the mention of an amusement park. Her phobia made the idea of going to La Ronde the last thing she wanted to do, despite her attraction to the man. Just then Jasper spoke up. "You know what would be a better idea? Emma has been to plenty of Amusement parks 'a little lie' but this is her first time in Montreal why don't you show her around?"

Emma gave a smile of gratitude to Jasper. Emma then turned to the man "oh I would love that" The man then pointed to the bike tied to the front of the boat and asked, "Is that your bike?" "Yes, it is. Do you ride?" Emma inquired.

With a smile, he replied, "I do love biking. How about I grab my bike, meet you at the marina, and we'll explore Montreal together?" "That sounds great! By the way my name is Emma and my grandfather's name is Jasper" Emma responded enthusiastically, her excitement evident.

"I'm Antoine, Nice to meet you. So which marina are you planning to stay at?" he asked Jasper.

Jasper replied, "I had planned on staying at the La Ronde marina the first night so I'd have a full day to figure out how to power through the current between there and the Lachine Canal."

The man smiled and said, "Oh, I have some advice on how to handle that. I can even help if you'd like. My father has a small engine, and we've navigated that stretch in spring a few times before. You know in about a month from now when the spring run off has ended there is much less current."

Jasper sighed with relief and said, "Yes I know that but I don't want to stay here a month and yes that would be incredibly helpful. Thank you so much, but we really should

get going, it's getting late, we will see you tomorrow."
"Absolutely I will see you then" replied Antoine as he started helping with the mooring lines.

During the ride to the anchorage, Emma turned to Jasper and said, "Thanks for that. You're quite the wingman. But so far on this trip, you haven't had much chance to see anything. When do you think we'll get a chance to tour around?"

Jasper smiled and replied, "We haven't even left Montreal yet. There will be plenty of time for sightseeing. You're young and should enjoy yourself. Go have fun tomorrow."

They pulled into the anchorage, a quaint spot nestled between two islands. Though there were quite a few boats buzzing around earlier, they gradually disappeared after dark. Emma went to bed feeling excited and eager for the next day.

The next morning, after they weighed anchor, they set off towards Montreal. It wasn't a long cruise, but the approach into the city was nothing short of spectacular.

As they neared, Emma marveled at the sight of the towering cranes loading cargo onto ships, their long arms reaching out over the water. In the distance, the tall buildings of Montreal began to rise, growing larger and more impressive with each passing moment. Emma was in awe of the sheer scale of everything, unable to believe how grand and expansive the cityscape appeared.

Soon, they approached an island with an entrance to a bay on one side. Emma could make out the structures of amusement park rides silhouetted against the skyline. The distinctive shapes of roller coasters came into view as they drew closer.

A few minutes later, they were securely tied up at the marina. Emma looked around and thought to herself, This is where we're staying? The area was bustling with activity and noise. Directly adjacent to the bay was a huge wooden roller coaster that roared with every pass of its cars, sending echoes across the water.

In addition to the amusement park, a massive green steel bridge loomed overhead. Its towering presence was imposing, and Emma could hear the rumble of vehicles crossing it even from the marina below.

The combination of the amusement park's clamor and the constant hum of traffic from the bridge made for an exhilarating yet overwhelming environment.

Emma was mesmerized by the vibrant, energetic surroundings but wondered how she would manage to get any sleep tonight.

Once they were settled in, Emma began preparing for the day ahead. Deciding to embrace a more polished look, she let her hair flow freely instead of tying it back in a ponytail. She applied her makeup carefully, enhancing her features with a touch of mascara and a hint of lip gloss.

For her outfit, she chose a pair of casual black shorts, paired with her favorite blouse. The blouse was a light, airy white adorned with a vibrant pattern of pink and purple butterflies cascading from one shoulder. With her look complete, for Emma noon couldn't come soon enough.

Emma kept her eyes on the gate, eagerly waiting for Antoine to arrive. Then, right on the dot, he appeared. Emma grabbed her bike and walked up the dock toward the gate to meet him. "Hi, Emma!" Antoine called out, his voice warm and enthusiastic. Emma beamed and replied, "Hello, Antoine! How are you?"

"I'm great," he said with a grin. "I thought we'd ride over to the Biodome today. It's not too far, but we do need to cross that bridge," he added, pointing to the towering steel structure in the distance. "It's quite a hill up. Are you afraid of heights?"

Emma glanced at the bridge, its immense height and structure imposing against the sky. "Nope, I'll be fine," she said, though the truth was she'd never been up that high before. Back home, there was nothing comparable to this.

Despite her apprehension, Emma resolved to face her fear. If Antoine could handle it, she reasoned, so could she. With a deep breath and a determined smile, she followed Antoine, ready for the adventure ahead.

As they pedaled up the incline toward the bridge, Emma's anxiety began to rise. The hill seemed endless, stretching far ahead as they climbed the on-ramp. She steeled herself for the daunting ascent, deciding to focus straight ahead and push thoughts of the height out of her mind.

A few minutes later, Antoine halted his bike and pointed. "Look, Emma," he said, gesturing towards the marina. "That's where your boat is!"

Emma had no choice but to look down, and as she did, her fear began to dissipate. "Wow, what a view!" she exclaimed. The sight before her was breathtaking. From her vantage point, she could see the marina and the boats below, dwarfed by the enormity of the bridge.

The vastness of the view was awe-inspiring, and the once-intimidating height now seemed exhilarating. Emma's initial trepidation gave way to wonder as she gazed at the panorama. She eagerly asked Antoine questions about everything she saw, Antoine was delighted by her enthusiasm, curiosity and awe.

"Okay, Emma, let's keep moving. We've still got a lot to see," Antoine said as they resumed their ride. They completed the crossing of the bridge and continued along a path that meandered past the bustling port with its towering cranes. The route then followed a bike path alongside a road.

As they rounded the final corner, Emma's eyes widened at the sight of a distinctive angled tower topped by a domed building below it. "That's the Olympic Stadium," Antoine called back, pointing. "We're heading to the uniquely shaped building behind it."

When they reached the entrance, they found a set of black loop-style bike racks and secured their bikes. After Antoine purchased the tickets, they entered the building. Emma's jaw dropped in awe as she stepped inside.

She was greeted by a lush indoor rainforest with a warm, humid atmosphere. Towering trees and vibrant plants formed a dense canopy overhead, while exotic flowers and giant ferns added bursts of color and texture to the scene. The air was filled with the melodious sounds of chirping birds and the gentle rustle of leaves, creating a tranquil yet lively ambiance.

Emma felt like she was in paradise. This was a world she had only ever seen in books and online, and now it was all around her.

The biodome was divided into distinct sections; the Laurentiens, the St. Lawrence region and finally Antarctica. Emma was particularly captivated by Antarctica. The section featured real ice walls and icy caves to walk through.

At the end, there was a viewing area where visitors could sit and observe penguins in their chilly habitat.

Emma and Antoine settled into the seats, and Emma's gaze was fixed on the playful penguins. She had always dreamed of seeing these charming creatures, and witnessing them in person brought a surge of emotion. Her eyes welled up with tears as she watched the penguins waddle and slide around.

Antoine noticed her distress and asked gently, "Is everything okay?" Emma, not wanting to reveal her true feelings, replied with a smile, "I think it's just the cold making my eyes water." Antoine nodded understandingly and stayed by her side, letting Emma soak in the moment.

After leaving the biodome, they decided to take an alternate route home. The first part of the journey was a bike path running parallel to a busy road, which then led into a park with a large hill. Emma had to pause halfway up to catch her breath.

When they finally reached the summit, they followed a narrow path that opened up to a breathtaking view of downtown Montreal. Antoine explained that this was Mount Royal, designed by the same person who created Central Park in New York City.

As the afternoon was winding down, Antoine asked Emma if she would like to go out for dinner. Emma glanced at him and asked, "Is this a date?" Antoine grinned widely and replied, "I hope so."

Emma felt her heart flutter with excitement."Let me text Jasper to update him and let him know I'll be late," Emma said, pulling out her phone and starting to type. After a moment, a notification dinged.

Emma read the message and smiled widely. "He said he'll probably be asleep by the time I get home, so I should try not to wake him. So I'm all yours." "Really" Antoine laughed "You know what I mean" replied Emma.

"I know the perfect place to go," Antoine said, pointing to a building visible from the viewpoint. "And it's all downhill from here." "That sounds great, but can we take it slow? I'm not completely confident in my brakes," Emma replied.

"Of course, no problem," Antoine agreed. They began their descent, with Emma carefully braking the entire way. After reaching the bottom and continuing through some downtown streets, they arrived at the building Antoine had pointed out.

Antoine started locking up his bike, but Emma was puzzled. All she could see was an office building. "Don't worry, trust me," Antoine said with a playful smirk. Emma locked up her bike and followed him into the building.

As they approached a bank of elevators, Emma stopped and stared, confused. "Are you okay?" Antoine asked.

"Yes, just a bit confused," Emma replied, trying to hide her apprehension. Antoine chuckled, unaware of her nervousness.

Emma was secretly anxious - she had never ridden in an elevator before. What if it was really fast and she panicked? What would Antoine think of her? She couldn't admit her fear, so she resolved to give it a try.

Slowly, she walked toward the elevator and paused in front of the doors. Her heart began to race with each passing moment. Suddenly, the doors dinged open, and Antoine encouraged, "Come on, Emma." She stepped inside and shut her eyes tightly.

For a moment, there was nothing, and then she felt the elevator start to move. After a brief moment, another ding signaled their arrival. "This is us. Are you coming?" Antoine asked.

Emma opened her eyes, relieved to find the experience was much easier than she had anticipated. She stepped off the elevator, feeling a sense of accomplishment.

They walked down a short hallway and through another door. Antoine turned to Emma with a grin, saying, "It's a rooftop terrace restaurant."

As Emma stepped outside, she was immediately struck by the stunning atmosphere. The terrace was elegantly decorated, with each table covered in crisp, white cloth tablecloths. The air was filled with the sweet scent of blooming flowers from the hanging planters that adorned every corner. Triangular shade sails were stretched overhead, providing both shade and a touch of whimsy.

The wall where they had emerged was transformed into a lush, green living wall, draped with vibrant vines that created a natural and inviting backdrop.

Emma took in the scene and thought to herself that this was the most beautiful restaurant she had ever been to. The combination of the meticulous design, the vibrant greenery, and the enchanting ambiance made it a truly unforgettable setting.

The maître d' guided them to a cozy table positioned next to the glass railing, offering a breathtaking view of the city below. They spent hours savoring their meal and engrossed in conversation.

Eventually, a waitress approached and apologetically said, "I'm really sorry, but we officially closed half an hour ago." Emma glanced at her phone and exclaimed, "Oh wow, it's nearly midnight! I should head back to the boat."

Antoine said "yes after I ride with you back to the marina I still have to ride home and it's quite a ways" "You're not planning to ride all the way to Verchères tonight, are you?" she asked."Yes, it's a pleasant ride," Antoine answered.

"But it takes two hours to get back, and you also said you'd return here tomorrow to help Jasper with the current.

So you're going to bike home in the middle of the night and then drive back here first thing in the morning?" Emma replied, incredulously.

Antoine, looking a bit embarrassed, admitted, "Actually, to be honest, I don't drive and I don't even own a car. I'll either ride back or take the bus, but I don't mind at all. I hope that doesn't change how you feel about me."

Emma thought to herself, Could he be any more perfect? I just wish he lived in Ticonderoga. She looked at Antoine with a big smile and said, "No, it definitely doesn't make me think less of you. I don't drive either."

She continued, "Why don't you just sleep on the boat tonight? You could use the enclosed cockpit; the settees in there are long enough to lie down on." Antoine hesitated and replied, "Are you sure Jasper won't mind? I don't want to cause any problems."

Emma chuckled and reassured him, "It's not like you're staying in my cabin. I'll explain to him, and I'm sure he'll understand."

Jasper was awake in his cabin, reading a book as he waited for Emma to return. Although she was twenty-two, the fact that she was out with a stranger in an unfamiliar city made him uneasy. It was well past midnight when he finally heard them come aboard. Relieved that she was home safely, he decided to stay quiet and let them be.

As he settled in to go to bed, he could hear their muffled conversation and, more distinctly, the sound of kissing. Jasper wasn't entirely sure how he felt about this.

While he was glad Emma was having a good time and she was old enough to make her own choices, he was concerned about her getting hurt with their departure from Montreal just a few days away.

Eventually, Jasper fell asleep to the background noise of their conversation, unable to make out their words but finding some comfort in the fact that Emma was safe.

The next morning, Jasper was the first to wake up. He peeked out of the hatch and wasn't surprised to see Antoine sleeping there. Knowing Emma would be asleep for a while longer, Jasper went below deck to make two cups of coffee. He then poked his head back into the cockpit and saw that Antoine was awake, likely stirred by the noise of the hatch.

"Good morning Antoine. I made you a cup of coffee," Jasper said warmly. "Thank you. I hope you don't mind me staying here. Emma said it was okay, and after talking late into the night, I didn't want to make the two-hour bike ride home just to come back this morning," Antoine explained.

"It's fine," Jasper replied. "It might even be the responsible thing to do. But let me ask you something." His tone grew serious. "I heard you two last night, and it's clear you have romantic intentions. Since we're leaving in a couple of days, what exactly are you looking for - a one-night stand, a long-distance relationship, or something else?"

Antoine looked at Jasper for a moment before responding, "I'm sorry if you think I'm the type who would pursue a one-night stand with your granddaughter..." Jasper interrupted, "I don't know you, so I don't know what type you are. Sorry if you're offended, but that's the truth."

Antoine met Jasper's gaze. "Honestly, when I first saw Emma, I thought she was very attractive, and I was excited about spending the day with her and showing her around.

"But as I got to know her, I was genuinely impressed. She has an infectious smile that brightens any room she walks into.

Her eyes are always sparkling with curiosity and joy, reflecting a profound sense of wonder and appreciation for life. Her laughter, warm and spontaneous, has a way of transforming even the most ordinary moments into something remarkable." I'm sorry but I think I will be the one who is heart broken when you leave."

Jasper having a little loss of words "well... you do understand my worries right?" At that moment, a voice came from the aft cabin. "Are you guys talking about me?" It was

Emma, just waking up. "Of course we are," Jasper replied with a grin.

Emma poked her head out of the hatch and quipped, "Well, stop talking about me and make me some coffee instead!" She laughed, clearly enjoying the lighthearted exchange. Jasper disappeared into the cabin "I'm on it."

After enjoying their coffees and preparing for the day, they decided it was time to get underway. Their goal was to reach the Lachine Canal by nightfall, which was only about a mile away as the crow flies.

However, they were facing a strong current that moved at nearly the same speed as Arabella, if not slightly faster. Despite the challenge, they were determined to give it a try.

They maneuvered out of the marina's bay and rounded the tip of the island. "Stay as close to the island as possible; the current is weaker along the edge," Antoine advised.

Jasper followed the instructions, pushing the boat to full throttle as they traced the island's edge for about a mile and a half, past the canal entrance on the far side of the river. The journey took around two hours, and progress was slow.

"Now, keep your bow mostly facing into the current and slowly work your way across the river," Antoine continued. "The current will push you back a bit, but you'll make it across." Jasper adjusted the tiller slightly, angling the boat just enough to face the current. As they left the island's protection, the current began to push them backward, but they steadily made their way across the river.

After another two hours, they finally reached the far side of the river, almost directly across from their starting point.

Jasper laughed, "Four hours and all we've done is cross the river!"

"Yep," Antoine replied with a grin. "Now we just need to follow this side until we reach the canal entrance."

After six hours, they finally arrived at the canal. Jasper had radioed ahead, and the lock doors were open, so they pulled right in. They went through the single lock and tied up for the night behind a large tugboat that now serves as a museum.

"I think tonight we'll explore the Old Port and Old Montreal, and then continue our journey tomorrow morning," Jasper suggested.

Antoine and Emma exchanged glances, their expressions tinged with disappointment. Neither wanted to argue with Jasper. "Well, we still have today, right?" Emma said, trying to find a silver lining. "Do you mind if I join you today?" Antoine asked.

Jasper glanced at Emma, who had a beaming smile on her face, and then turned back to Antoine. "Absolutely, we'd love for you to join us. You can be our tour guide," he replied enthusiastically.

After carefully taking Jasper's wheelchair ashore, they made their way toward the path leading to the Old Port. It was clearly a bustling tourist area, full of vibrant sights and attractions.

The waterfront featured charming little waterfalls, colorful paddle boats bobbing gently on the water, and a towering Ferris wheel that offered panoramic views of the city.

Once they had explored the Old Port, they ventured into Old Montreal. This area was equally captivating, with its enchanting European architecture and picturesque cobblestone streets. The historic buildings, with their intricate facades and timeless charm, created a sense of stepping back in time.

As they meandered through the narrow alleys and lively squares, the blend of ambiance and modern vibrancy made the exploration truly memorable. After just the first two blocks, Jasper requested to turn back. Emma and Antoine quickly realized that the cobblestone streets were proving to be far too rough for Jasper's wheelchair.

Antoine suggested that, since it was already dinner time, they should stop and eat somewhere. There was a small restaurant directly across from where they were standing, so they decided to go there. While it wasn't anything particularly special, it was convenient.

Jasper had been worried about feeling like a third wheel, but Antoine made sure he was included in the conversation throughout the evening. Dinner was no exception; Antoine was genuinely intrigued by Jasper's stories of travel and adventure, keeping the conversation engaging and inclusive.

After dinner, Antoine asked Emma and Jasper if they wanted to go out for drinks. Emma eagerly responded with a "Love to," but Jasper, sensing they might want some time alone, graciously declined.

Once Jasper was safely back at the boat, it was already dark. Antoine took Emma to a lively street nearby, where throngs of young people were spilling out of bars and lounges lining both sides. "Do you like to dance?" Antoine asked Emma. "I've never really been before," Emma admitted shyly.

Antoine flashed a reassuring smile. "Well, tonight we're going to change that. I know just the place."

The next morning, as usual, Jasper was the first to wake. He peeked out of the hatch and glanced into the cockpit, where he saw Antoine sprawled half on, half off the settee. Jasper chuckled to himself, thinking, "That boy's going to be in a lot of pain when he wakes up."

Determined to let Antoine sleep a little longer, Jasper moved quietly back into his cabin, made himself a coffee, and began reading his book.

A few hours later, he heard the rear hatch open and Emma's voice calling out, "Antoine, Antoine, wake up!" Moments later, Antoine's groggy voice moaned, "I'm awake, but I think it would have been better if I had died." Emma laughed quietly and replied, "I know what you mean. I'm so hung over."

Feeling it was time to make his presence known, Jasper stuck his head out and observed them. Unable to resist a comment, he said, "Wow! You two look like a couple of corpses. Guessing it was quite a night? Would you both like a cup of coffee before we head out?"

"Please," they answered in perfect unison.

After they had their coffee and started to wake up a bit more, Jasper announced that it was time to say goodbye. "I want to get going," he said, preparing to continue their journey.

Emma looked at Antoine, Antoine's face was a mixture of sadness and resolve, his gaze steady as he tried to be strong for her.

"I don't want to go," Emma whispered, her voice trembling. Antoine gently lifted her chin, compelling her to meet his gaze.

"You have to," he said softly, his voice choked with emotion. "But we will talk every day. We'll find a way to see each other again, I promise." They shared one last, lingering kiss before Antoine turned to Jasper.

"It was nice getting to know you, Jasper. I'll help you with your lines." Moments later, Jasper and Emma set off again, leaving Antoine behind with a heavy heart.

Chapter 8

Quite Daunting And Complex

The Lachine Canal offered a different experience from the ones Emma had explored so far. While still historic, this canal ran directly through the heart of downtown.

As they neared the far end of the canal, they stopped at a bustling farmers' market to pick up some food. Adjacent to the market was a large grocery store, providing a convenient option for any items they couldn't find in the market.

After completing their passage through the canal, crossing a lake, and navigating another single-lock canal, they finally left the St. Lawrence River and entered the Ottawa River.

They discovered a modest anchorage, a small bay tucked away on the river's edge. The location was unremarkable—just a quiet spot surrounded by a few houses and a handful of boats moored nearby.

Emma expertly lowered the anchor, and they settled into their nightly routine. Emma couldn't wait to retire to her cabin. Instead of just her usual call to her dad now she has added calling Antoine into her nightly routine.

The days that followed were largely uneventful, marked by calm waters and steady progress. However, they encountered one particularly daunting lock along their route.

This lock was enormous and intimidating, with its doors moving up and down rather than swinging open. The mechanism's sheer size and the way it operated made Emma shudder, prompting her to joke that it looked like a French guillotine, adding a touch of humor to the otherwise nerve-wracking experience.

The Ottawa River stretched out before them, a broad and relatively straight waterway with farmlands lining one side and gently rolling hills on the other. As they approached their final day on the river, the City of Ottawa came into view.

To prepare for their entry into the Rideau Canal the next morning, they chose to anchor near the entrance. They found a perfect spot across from a charming little island, with a lush, forested park behind them and the Ottawa skyline prominently displayed in front, with two large curtain style waterfalls off to the side.

The view was stunning. Jasper pointed out that they were now in Canada's capital, highlighting the impressive neo-gothic Parliament buildings perched on a hill overlooking the river. He also noted the very large castle-like structure nearby, which was actually a grand hotel built by the railroads in the early 1900s.

The skyline was dotted with other unique and significant buildings.

As the sun began to set, the buildings across the river bathed in a magnificent copper glow. Emma watched in awe as the entire cityscape transformed into a warm, golden spectacle, making their anchorage spot even more magical.

From their anchorage, Emma could see the start of the Rideau Canal. Eight lock chambers, aligned in a row, ascended a hill into the city, nestled between the Parliament buildings and the castle-like hotel.

The sight was a bit intimidating; the locks appeared quite daunting and complex. Despite her apprehension, Emma decided to set aside her worries for the moment. "That's tomorrow's challenge," she told herself. For now, she resolved to fully enjoy the beauty of their anchorage.

Early the next morning, after completing their usual routine, they weighed anchor and made their way to the Blue Line. This blue-painted line along the wall before the locks signals to the lock staff that they wish to pass through.

The lock staff came down to inform them that there would be about a 90-minute wait, as a boat was already en route to the lower end of the locks. Though disappointed by the delay, they decided to make the best of the situation. Emma took the opportunity to do some cleaning, while Jasper used the time to inspect the engine.

At last, the gates swung open and a small red runabout emerged from the lock. Emma, feeling a bit anxious, untied the lines and took her place at the edge of the boat, prepared for the maneuver.

As they slowly eased into the first lock, she wrapped her lines with a firm grip. While the gate closed behind them and the water began to rise, Emma couldn't help but notice the large crowd of spectators lining the edges of the lock flight.

Tourists were gathered, eager to witness the operation of the locks. Emma felt a pang of nervousness, acutely aware that their every move was being watched.

The thought of potentially making a mistake with so many eyes on them made her even more anxious.

Jasper explained that one reason for the large number of tourists was that the Rideau Waterway is the oldest continuously operated waterway in North America. It has been in use for over 190 years and operates today much like it did when it first opened.

As they progressed through the locks, moving slowly from the bottom to the top, it felt like an eternity to complete the series. One lock after another, they made their way upward. Finally, they emerged beneath a broad bridge and continued through to the other side.

Jasper maneuvered the boat alongside a narrow dock, and Emma secured it with the lines. Next to the canal was a path, with a road running alongside it, and behind that stood a large, round glass building.

Jasper pointed out that the design of the building was intended to resemble a tulip lying on its side. Emma looked at it closely, trying to see the resemblance, but struggled to make out the tulip shape.

Emma was bubbling with excitement about exploring the city. Before Jasper could react, she had already wheeled his chair ashore and was enthusiastically urging him on. "Come on, Jasper, let's go!"

"Alright, I'm coming," Jasper responded with a smile. "We've got two nights here, so we have tonight and tomorrow to be tourists," Emma said eagerly. They spent their time in Ottawa soaking up the city's rich architecture, taking a tour of Parliament, and visiting several large, unique museums.

Before they realized it, it was time to leave. Emma untied the boat, and they set off once more. The Rideau Canal, much like the Lachine Canal, wound its way through downtown, passing several more lock stations.

They cruised by a massive stadium and a bustling beach before finally leaving the city behind. They reached Blacks Rapids Lockstation, only to find the locks closed for the night. They moored along the lock wall and settled in for the night, planning to go through the lock first thing in the morning.

Over the next few days, they navigated the entire 125 miles of the waterway. The journey was divided into three distinct sections: the first third featured expansive farmland with sprawling estates along the shore, the second third encompassed large lakes dotted with cabins and a plethora of boats and the final stretch was characterized by rolling hills and dense forests.

All of it was interspersed with charming small towns and historic cities. They ended the Rideau at Kingston, situated on the shores of Lake Ontario.

They had originally planned to spend just one night in Kingston, but Jasper deemed the wind conditions too severe for their planned crossing of a small stretch of Lake Ontario the next day. Despite his confidence in Arabella's capabilities, he knew it would be an uncomfortable journey.

After a three-day delay, Jasper finally announced that they were ready to leave Kingston. Emma was both thrilled and eager. While she had enjoyed her time in Kingston, she was eager to move on.

This was the largest body of water she had ever encountered, even if only briefly.

She untied the boat, and they set out, passing under a lift bridge that separated the Rideau Canal from Lake Ontario.

As they emerged from under the bridge, the conditions were a bit rough, but nothing too alarming. Initially, an island blocked their view of the lake, but as they navigated past it, Emma was taken aback to discover that she couldn't see the far side of the lake.

It stretched out before her like the vast oceans she had only seen in pictures. The sight was a bit intimidating, but she reassured herself that it wouldn't be long before they were back in the more sheltered waters of the Bay of Quinte.

It wasn't long before they reached the entrance to the bay. Emma noted that it resembles more of a river than a traditional bay. Despite its charm, she was surprised by the sheer number of fishing boats everywhere.

They had arrived during a weekend fishing tournament. Jasper looked for a peaceful spot to anchor for the night but had no luck finding one. He eventually chose Hay Bay, which provided good shelter from the wind. Despite this, the bay was teeming with activity, and the constant movement of boats kept the area lively throughout the night.

Emma was eager to set off the next morning after a restless night. She weighed anchor and they set course for the city of Trenton.

As they approached, the number of fishing boats decreased, but they were met with a new sound - the roar of jet engines. It turned out that Trenton was home to a Canadian Air Force base, and there was an air show in progress.

Despite their interest in exploring Trenton, the noise drove them to distance themselves as quickly as possible. They were now on the Trent-Severn Waterway, which they would navigate for the next week or so.

Though the Trent-Severn was historic, it was not as old as the Rideau. That evening, they reached Lock 3 in Glen Miller, just outside of Trenton, and settled in for the night.

After several days of tranquil travel along the picturesque Trent-Severn Waterway, Emma and Jasper approached the charming city of Peterborough.

As they navigated through the waterway, a striking and unusual structure appeared on the horizon, piquing Emma's curiosity. It was unlike anything she had ever seen before—a towering, futuristic edifice rising above the landscape.

Emma turned to Jasper with wide eyes and asked, "What is that thing?"

Jasper's face lit up with excitement as he explained, "That's the Peterborough Lift Lock. In fact, it's the highest hydraulic lift lock in the world." Emma's interest was piqued, but she was still a bit confused. "So, what exactly is a lift lock?" she asked, her tone a mix of curiosity and skepticism.

With a knowing smile, Jasper explained, "A lift lock is different from the traditional locks we have already done. Instead of just having a chamber with gates on the ends that fill or empty with water to raise or lower boats, a lift lock works like a giant moving bathtub. It has two large chambers that move up and down."

He continued, "Here's how it works; one chamber fills with water and lowers, while the other empties and rises. They balance each other out, letting boats move smoothly between different heights. The whole process is really efficient. Plus the view from the top is supposed to be spectacular".

"There are actually two of these along the Trent-Severn," Jasper said. Emma was both thrilled and a bit nervous about the upcoming experience. "Do I need to do anything differently from the other locks?"

she asked. "Not at all. We'll do everything the same. Just follow the usual routine," Jasper reassured her.

True to Jasper's word, they approached the blue line, and the gate opened. They eased into the chamber, tied off their lines, and waited as the lift lock began its ascent. As they rose, their view expanded from the surrounding trees to the distant buildings. Emma marveled at the sight and said, "Wow Jasper, you were right. This is spectacular! Antoine would have loved this."

Jasper's heart ached as he saw Emma's awe and excitement. He knew how much she missed Antoine, and he felt sad for her.

The next few days passed quickly, filled with stunning scenery and a series of locks that kept them busy. Emma even joked about becoming a lock expert, proudly declaring that there wasn't a lock she couldn't handle. Laughing, Jasper teased her, "Alright 'expert' time to tackle the next one!"

After a few more locks, Jasper chuckled and said, "Well, here comes something interesting, 'expert'", Jasper said with a grin. Emma looked ahead and saw the familiar Trent-Severn sign for a lock, but there was no lock in sight.

"Jasper, what's going on?" she asked, clearly puzzled. Jasper, still chuckling, replied, "Welcome to the Big Chute Marine Railway. The only one of its kind in North America." "The what?" Emma responded, still confused. Jasper repeated, "The Big Chute Marine Railway." Emma gave a small chuckle and said, "Alright, explain it to me."

Jasper began explaining, "Here's how it works; you pull your boat into a huge cradle that has straps hanging underneath to support it. Once you're securely in place, the cradle moves along tracks, much like a railway. The cradle lifts out of the water with your boat inside and travels over the top of a large hill. And down a long slope on the other side, then it gently lowers back into the water, and you're good to go."

Emma looked in shock "are you kidding me right now?" "Nope," Jasper replied. "In fact, the marine railway was originally constructed in response to shortages during World War I.

In the 1960s, there were plans to replace it with a single lock. However, the emergence of an invasive species known as the Sea Lamprey, which was wreaking havoc on the Great Lakes, led to the decision to maintain the railway to prevent the spread of these pests.

Today, the marine railway not only remains a favorite among boaters but has also become a popular attraction for tourists who enjoy watching its fascinating operation."

Jasper radioed ahead and had received confirmation that everything was prepared for their arrival. Emma, visibly anxious, tried to steady her nerves as they maneuvered their boat into position. They were carefully secured alongside the staff, who began their final checks to ensure everything was in order.

The cradle, while cradling their boat, began to move with a deliberate, gradual pace. It first took them up a short incline, lifting the boat gently out of the water. Water dripped from the hull, creating a shimmering trail as the cradle traversed across a road.

This marked the beginning of a new perspective—one that promised a view of the surroundings they hadn't yet experienced. The anticipation built as they moved forward, the incredible view unfolding before them.

The boat then started its descent, gliding slowly down the long hill, the cradle, meticulously controlled. As they reached the bottom, the cradle gently lowered the boat, allowing it to settle smoothly back into its natural element. The transition from land to water was seamless, with the boat finally floating once more. Jasper restarted the engine and they continued their journey.

That night, nestled in a tranquil and picturesque anchorage, they enjoyed a meal as the sun dipped below the horizon.

Jasper turned to Emma, his eyes reflecting the fiery hues of the sunset. "So far Emma, we've navigated over a hundred locks. But after the one we tackle tomorrow, we'll be entering the Great Lakes at Port Severn. There won't be any more locks until we reach Chicago on Lake Michigan."

Emma, captivated by the view, responded with a touch of wonder in her voice, "Yeah, it's been quite the trip, one I never imagined I'd experience. Thank you for this, Grandpa."

Jasper's heart fluttered at the familiar term; it had been years since she'd called him Grandpa.

"You're very welcome, Emma," Jasper said, his voice betraying a hint of emotion as he tried to mask the lump in his throat.

As the last light of day faded away, Jasper suggested it was time to turn in. They both retreated to their respective routines, eventually drifting off to sleep under the starry sky.

The next morning, Jasper awoke with a noticeable bounce in his step, eager to start the day. He grabbed his coffee and headed outside, but his enthusiasm was quickly tempered by the stifling heat and muggy air.

Despite the early hour, there was no sign of a breeze to offer relief. Jasper muttered to himself, hoping Emma would wake up soon. "Once we get moving, we might be able to create a bit of breeze," he thought, looking forward to the day's adventure.

Emma jolted awake to the sound of a large splash. Panicking, she rushed out of the cabin and quickly scanned the surroundings. There, just a few feet from the boat, was Jasper, swimming contentedly in the water.

"Good morning!" Emma called out to him. "Get your suit on and join me—it's really refreshing!" Jasper replied with a cheerful splash.

Emma raised a finger to signal she'd be right back and hurried below deck. When she emerged moments later, she was wearing a modest black one-piece swimsuit that was low cut at the legs. Jasper couldn't help but think how much it resembled a suit he remembered seeing on her grandmother.

Splash! Emma dove headfirst into the water and surfaced, laughing with delight. "The water is fantastic!" she exclaimed. "I can't believe it took us so long to finally get in!"

After a while, Jasper climbed back onto the boarding ladder. "Grandpa, could you do me a favor?" Emma called out. "What's that?" Jasper asked, curious. "Could you take a picture of me out here? I want to send it to my dad and Antoine," Emma requested.

"Sure thing," Jasper replied, grabbing his camera. He snapped a photo of Emma and asked, "Do you want me to take a few so you can pick the best one?" "Yes, please!" Emma said. Jasper laughed as he continued taking shots while Emma floated and struck various poses.

After a bit, Jasper called out, "I think we've got enough. I'm sure you'll find a great one to send them." As he reviewed the photos, Jasper thought to himself that these pictures are certainly a lot nicer than the selfies Emma usually takes.

"Alright Emma, we should get going," Jasper said, signaling that it was time to move on. Emma, still enjoying the water, hesitated but understood the need to leave. She reluctantly climbed out, dried off, and changed into dry clothes. Meanwhile, Jasper prepared a couple of coffees for them, readying them for the next part of their journey.

They weighed anchor and set off for the day, passing through the final lock before emerging into the bay. At this stage, the bay was relatively narrow, dotted with numerous small bays and harbors branching off from it.

For the night, they chose to dock at a spot called Honey Harbour. There, they could refuel and enjoy a nice dinner out.

Over the next week or so, they navigated what is known as the Small Craft Route. This shallow passage, winding behind islands and other natural barriers, offered shelter from the wind and waves.

The scenery was nothing short of breathtaking. Jasper explained that the region's geology is known as the Canadian Shield. The landscape was characterized by an abundance of islands and large, rugged rocks.

Both Jasper and Emma agreed that it was one of the most stunning places they had ever seen, with its dramatic, rugged beauty leaving a lasting impression.

Chapter 9

From Seattle to Singapore

One night, while anchored in a picturesque spot, at the entrance of the French River another boat arrived and anchored close to them. It was named the "Singing Swallow" and stood out as quite different from their own vessel. This boat was a sizable powerboat, though not a speedboat.

They had seen the boat a few times before as they were also doing the loop and had gone through a few locks with them. At that moment, the VHF radio crackled to life with a call, "Arabella, Arabella, Arabella, this is the Singing Swallow, over."

Jasper promptly responded, "This is the Arabella, over." After a few minutes of conversation, they agreed to gather for a campfire and barbecue that evening. They planned to meet on a barren rock peninsula extending into the water at the edge of the anchorage.

Jasper and Emma quickly loaded their gear into the dinghy and rowed to shore. Shortly after, the couple from the "Singing Swallow" arrived in their own dinghy. The woman disembarked first - she was about thirty, tall and slender, with blonde hair and wearing a white sheer cover-up that highlighted a vibrant red bikini.

Her hair was streaked with pink and blue and decorated with small beads at the ends. Emma immediately sensed that this woman enjoyed being noticed and had a distinct bohemian flair.

The man followed, appearing to be in his early forties. He had dirty blonde hair that fell past his shoulders and wore a pair of old cut-offs with a patterned shirt draped over his shoulders. He, too, exuded a bohemian vibe.   Once everyone was ashore, Jasper introduced himself and Emma. "Hi, I'm Jasper, and this is my granddaughter, Emma."

"Hello, we're Scott and Samantha Sheridan," they replied. Jasper chuckled and said, "Scott and Samantha Sheridan from the Singing Swallow—so many S's!"

"Yeah, it's kind of our thing," Samantha responded with a grin. "So, what do you guys do?" Jasper asked.

Samantha answered, "We're singers. We've performed everywhere from Seattle to Singapore. We just had a gig last night in Port Severn." True to form, every time they said the letter 'S,' they emphasized it.

"It's how we're funding this trip. That and our YouTube channel," Samantha continued. Emma chimed in, "A YouTube channel? Is it just a travel blog?"

"Sort of. We do travel blogs, but I also create instructional yoga videos. Though, since ninety percent of my audience is male, I'm guessing they're not tuning in to learn yoga," Samantha giggled.

Emma understood and decided to steer the conversation in a different direction. "Let's get this fire going and maybe grab some drinks." Jasper took the hint. "How about Emma and I go gather some firewood while you two start on the BBQ?"

Scott looked puzzled. "Um, wouldn't it make more sense for Jasper and me to get the firewood and let the ladies handle the food?"

"What? I'm just as capable of gathering firewood as any man!" Emma exclaimed. Scott immediately apologized, "Sorry, I didn't mean anything by it. I just thought it might give you both a chance to get to know each other. I wasn't trying to be sexist, I promise."

Jasper glanced at Emma and gave a shrug of apology. "Alright then, Scott, let's go gather the firewood," he said, taking the lead. The two men headed into the woods together, leaving the women to get things started.

"So Emma, tell me what made you do the loop with your Grandfather. Wait let me guess both your parents are dead, you got hooked on crack and your grandfather kidnapped you to straighten you out" laughed Samantha.

Emma looked at her "I don't do drugs and I'm very close with my dad" " I'm sorry I've been told many times that I lack tact. So on that note where is your Mom?" replied Samantha.

Emma gave a little chuckle "Well my Mom and Grandma died in a car accident when I was a kid but it was a long time ago and like I said my Dad is amazing" "Not to mention, you had your Grandfather as well" Samantha chimed in.

Emma looked at Samantha a little sheepishly. " Actually before this trip I didn't know him". Emma went on to explain to Samantha how they ended up on the adventure together."Wow, that's quite a story," Samantha said with genuine interest. "I take it you didn't have a boyfriend when you left?"

"Not when I left, but..." Emma began, trailing off and hesitating slightly. "Wow you really have been having an adventure" Samantha laughed. "So give me all the dirty details" Emma starts telling Samantha all about Antoine.

How they met, the time they spent together and the fact they have talked every single day since. " So you will get together when this Adventure is over right?" asked Samantha. "I don't see how, we don't live in the same country, never mind the same town", replied Emma. Just then, the men returned with the firewood.

"Hey girls, we've got the wood!" Scott called out as he and Jasper approached. Samantha turned to Emma with a playful grin. "We'll have to continue our chat later," she said, her eyes twinkling. "It seems the men have wood and are eager."

It wasn't long before the four of them were gathered around the fire. Scott had brought a few blankets, which they draped around their shoulders for warmth. As they ate, drank, and laughed together, the night unfolded in a cozy atmosphere. Above them, the stars sparkled brightly, while the gentle lapping of the water against the shore provided a relaxing evening.

The next few days passed smoothly for both boats. The Singing Swallow decided to remain in Little Current for about a week to reconnect with friends from Sudbury, while Jasper and Emma continued their journey into the North Channel. They had planned to meet up again at Mackinac Island, where they would team up to cross Lake Michigan together.

As Jasper and Emma ventured further into the North Channel, they were greeted with stunning vistas. The landscape revealed its rugged charm, with dramatic cliffs rising sharply from the water's edge. Each turn brought a new, awe-inspiring view, making the journey even more enchanting.

For Emma, the North Channel was unlike anything she had ever seen - its breathtaking beauty left her in constant wonder and admiration.

They traveled at a leisurely pace through the Channel, savoring every sight along the way. They spent their days swimming and having campfires, allowing the journey to slow down a bit.

They were slightly ahead of schedule, preferring to avoid arriving in the south until after hurricane season had ended. Additionally, they hoped to reach Mackinac Island just a few days before Singing Swallow.

Despite their differences, Jasper and Emma got along well with Scott and Samantha. Crossing a large body of water like Lake Michigan was much safer with a buddy boat, providing reassurance in case of any unforeseen problems.

At the end of the North Channel lies Drummond Island, a key landmark in their journey. This island represents not only the end of the Canadian segment of their adventure but also the conclusion of their westward travels.

From this point onward, they would be turning south, marking the beginning of a new chapter in their exploration.

After reaching Drummond Island, they spent the night anchored in U.S. waters. The anchorage was conveniently located close to the customs office, allowing them to clear the necessary paperwork the next morning.

With this transition, they officially left Canadian waters behind, ready to continue their voyage with renewed excitement and anticipation for the next leg of their journey.

The next morning, customs was bustling with activity due to the start of the Labor Day weekend, and many boaters were crossing through. Despite the crowd, they managed to complete their clearance before noon.

After navigating a somewhat choppy crossing at the top of Lake Huron, they arrived at Mackinac Island just

before dark. Although the marina was crowded, Jasper had secured a reservation in advance, ensuring they had a spot to dock for the weekend.

As they pulled into the marina and tied up the boat, Jasper turned to Emma with a wide grin. "I have a big surprise for you," he said, his eyes twinkling with excitement. Emma looked puzzled. "Oh? What's that?" she asked.

Jasper gently placed his hands on the top of her head and guided her gaze toward the marina gate. There, illuminated by a nearby light, stood Antoine.

"You're not sleeping on the boat this weekend," Jasper announced. "Antoine took a twelve-hour bus ride and ferry to be here. I've booked you both a room for two nights at the Grand Hotel."

Emma's eyes filled with tears of joy. She threw her arms around Jasper in a heartfelt hug, repeating, "Thank you, thank you, thank you!" "Alright, alright, go see him and let him in," Jasper said with a chuckle as he watched her sprint up the dock, calling out after her to watch her step.

Emma opened the gate, and Antoine stepped onto the dock. They embraced each other with the intensity of a classic romance scene, holding on as if they never wanted to let go.

Jasper laughed to himself, amused by their emotional reunion, and playfully shouted, "Get a room! Oh wait, you already have a room - go to your room!"

Reluctantly, they separated and made their way back to the boat. As Emma packed, Antoine expressed his deep gratitude to Jasper for making this surprise possible.

With their luggage in tow, they took a moment to admire the quaint harbor, where boats bobbed gently and even in the dark the island's charm was already apparent. They took the traditional carriage ride. Traveling along the streets, Emma and Antoine felt the gentle breeze on their faces.

Eventually, the path began to rise gently. The historic charm of the island was evident in every turn, with Victorian-style homes and fragrant gardens adding to the beauty of the ride.

The silhouette of the Grand Hotel gradually came into view, its elegant white facade and expansive porch standing majestically. Emma and Antoine's anticipation grew with each clop of the horses hooves. They could hardly wait to experience the allure of the famed hotel.

Finally, they arrived at the Grand Hotel. Stepping off the carriage with their luggage, the hotel's grandeur was even more breathtaking up close, with its sprawling lawn and iconic porch stretching invitingly before them.

They entered the grand lobby, awed by the opulence and warmth of the hotel's interior. As they entered, they shared a smile, knowing that their Mackinac Island adventure was just beginning, with the promise of unforgettable experiences ahead.

The lobby was a marvel of classic elegance, adorned with rich wood paneling, plush carpets, and sparkling chandeliers that cast a warm glow over the space.

A stately desk, polished to a high shine, welcomed them. Behind it stood a friendly receptionist in formal attire, ready to assist. Emma and Antoine approached, their eyes drawn to the intricate floral patterns on the carpet and the luxurious furnishings.

"Welcome to the Grand Hotel," the receptionist greeted with a smile. "How may I assist you today?"

Emma handed over their reservation details, and Antoine glanced around, taking in the grandeur of the lobby. The receptionist quickly processed their check-in, explaining the various amenities and activities available during their stay.

After a few moments, Emma and Antoine received their room keys - ornate cards encased in elegant folders. The receptionist pointed out their room's location on the map of the hotel, explaining how to reach the elevator and offering directions to nearby attractions.

With keys in hand, they made their way to the elevator, their excitement growing with each step. As the doors opened to their floor, they were greeted by the soft, rich hues of the corridor, leading them to their room.

Their room, spacious and elegantly furnished, featured large windows with views of the lush gardens and the sparkling lake beyond.

They took a moment to appreciate the touches; the antique furniture, the grand bed with its crisp linens and the tastefully decorated bathroom. With their bags unpacked and the hotel's charm fully embraced, Emma and Antoine knew they were in for an unforgettable stay.

Antoine began expressing his disbelief at Jasper's gesture, marveling at how memorable it will be. However, before he could finish speaking, Emma slipped into the bathroom.

When she emerged, she wore a white shirt unbuttoned at the front, revealing her cleavage, and a small pair of delicate white underwear. Emma looked at Antoine, who was staring in shock, and said with a glint in her eye, "You're right, this weekend will be very memorable."

The next morning, Emma and Antoine were eager to show Jasper around the island, and with some advice from the reception desk, they had a plan in place. They first headed to a bicycle rental shop, then made their way down to the marina.

When they arrived at the boat, they found Jasper sitting in the cockpit, enjoying a coffee and reading a book. "Jasper!" Antoine called out enthusiastically. "Get ready—we're taking you out!" Jasper looked up and responded, " I won't argue. ok, I'll get ready. You guys grab my wheelchair," before disappearing below into his cabin.

While Jasper prepared himself, Antoine busied himself with getting things organized and Emma took her place in the cockpit. A short while later, Jasper emerged, only to be met with a puzzling sight.

Instead of seeing his wheelchair being brought out, they were unloading Emma's bicycle. Jasper gave a bewildered look, and Emma, chuckling, gently placed her hands on the top of his head, Just as he had done to her the night before guiding his gaze toward the marina gate.

There, by the gate, stood a custom tricycle. "It's called a chariot bicycle," Emma explained. "It's designed for people with disabilities. One person pedals up front, and the other person sits in a comfortable seat at the back with their feet on the floor."

Emma, Antoine, and Jasper left the marina, their eyes wide with anticipation. The soft clinking of the bells and the gentle hum of the tires against the cobblestone streets setting the rhythm for their day.

The vibrant colors of Mackinac Island unfolded before them; the lush greenery, the charming Victorian houses, and the inviting blue of Lake Huron.

As they pedaled out of the bustling harbor area, the tranquility of the loop road soon enveloped them. Emma led the way, her laughter echoing through the morning air. Antoine and Jasper followed closely, Jasper ever the enthusiast had his camera ready to capture the island's beauty. soaking in the landscape.

The road wound through dense forests. Occasionally, they would pass a picturesque farmhouse or a cluster of historic buildings, their intricate architecture a testament to the island's storied past. Emma pointing out the quaint shops and horse-drawn carriages, each one adding to the island's timeless charm.

As they approached Arch Rock, one of the highlights of their journey, they dismounted and first Emma pushed her bike up the steep incline then went back and helped Antoine push his with Jasper still seated.

Jasper wouldn't stop apologizing but Emma and Antoine understood this was not his fault and he shouldn't feel guilty besides they didn't mind doing it. In the end the effort was well worth it.

At the top, they were greeted by an awe-inspiring panoramic view of the sparkling lake below, the vast horizon stretching endlessly. Jasper snapped a few photos while Emma and Antoine simply stood in awe, taking in the breathtaking scenery.

Refreshed, they continued their ride, passing by the island's famous fudge shops. The sweet aroma of chocolate and caramel filled the air, and Emma suggested a stop for a treat. They enjoyed the indulgence, savoring each bite as they sat on a nearby bench, their bikes resting beside them.

Their journey continued past beautiful beaches and tranquil gardens, each turn of the road revealing new delights. The afternoon sun dipped lower in the sky, casting a soft, golden hue over the island. Emma joked about the possibility of staying on Mackinac Island forever, and Jasper and Antoine laughed, agreeing that it would be a delightful place to linger.

As the day drew to a close, they circled back to the harbor, their hearts full and their spirits high. The bike ride around Mackinac Island had been everything they had hoped for—a perfect blend of natural beauty, historical charm, and joyful companionship. After dropping off Jasper at the boat and returning the rental tricycle. Emma and Antoine went back to the hotel for the night.

Late the next morning, Emma and Antoine made their way down to the marina, a sense of dread growing with each step as they neared the moment of their impending farewell. When they arrived at the boat, they found Jasper in his usual spot—sitting in the cockpit, sipping coffee and reading a book.

"Good morning Grandpa!" Emma called out as they approached the dock. Jasper looked up with a warm smile. "Morning! How did you sleep?" Emma sighed and replied, "Not too well, considering it's our last night and all." Jasper nodded empathetically.

Jasper then proposed that, since they still had to wait for Scott and Samantha aboard the "Singing Swallow," they should spend one more night on the boat. However, Antoine declined, explaining that he needed to get back to work. His seasonal job at the marina was crucial for his summer income, and winter was always a lean period for him.

"Well, at least let us give you a ride over to St. Ignace so you can skip the ferry," Jasper offered. Antoine's face lit up. "Okay, that sounds great," he agreed. "Let me just give Scott and Samantha a call, in case they arrive while we're away," Jasper said. He pulled out his cell phone and made the call. A few minutes later, he finished the conversation and turned to Emma.

"Well, there's been a slight change of plans," he explained. "Scott and Samantha are going to skip Mackinac since they've been here before. Instead, they'll meet us in St. Ignace for dinner. We'll stay at a marina there; it's much cheaper than at

Mackinac." "That works out perfectly," Emma replied with a smile.

Emma and Antoine quickly stowed their bags on the boat, and Jasper started up the engine. Emma untied the lines, and they were underway. As they emerged from behind the breakwater, they encountered some waves. They weren't particularly large, but they were enough to make the boat rock.

Jasper turned to Emma with a concerned look. "You okay?" "Yep, I'm good," Emma replied, her tone steady.

Jasper then glanced at Antoine, who was gripping the side of the boat tightly. "Are you alright?" Jasper asked. Antoine looked up with a hint of unease. "I'll be fine. I've only ever been on ferries before, and I'm a bit nervous about the water. But I'll manage," he said, trying to sound more confident than he felt.

Emma moved to sit beside Antoine, gently cuddling with him to offer comfort. "But you did sleep in the cockpit in Montreal," she pointed out. Antoine nodded. "Yes, but the boat didn't move there," he explained. Emma smiled reassuringly. "Well, don't worry. Everyone has something they're scared of. I guess this just means we might have to skip kayaking together," she joked.

Antoine managed a smile as he began to regain his composure. "Well, who knows? We all have to face our fears sometimes, right?" Emma nodded. "I suppose so," she agreed. Jasper chimed in, "Luckily for you, Antoine, this is only a half-hour ride."

It wasn't long before St. Ignace began to come into view. The first landmark they spotted was a slender, cylindrical tower rising gracefully from the water. "That's the Wawatam Lighthouse," Jasper said, pointing it out to Emma.

As they approached, the lighthouse's details became more distinct. Its intricate stonework and weathered brick base were crowned by a red lantern room that housed the beacon, standing as a proud sentinel.

As the rest of the waterfront came into focus, they soon found themselves navigating towards the new marina, preparing to dock. Emma swiftly tied off the boat while Antoine looked on in amazement. "Wow Emma, you're really quick at that!" Antoine remarked. Emma laughed, "Yep, I've had a bit of practice. You know, we've been on the water for well over two months now."

Antoine replied, "I know. We've talked every day throughout most of it, even though we've only been physically together for a few of those days. I feel like nobody understands me as well as you do." Jasper then asked, "Antoine, when is your bus?" Antoine checked his phone and said, "In about an hour and a half."

Realizing he was an intruder in their farewell moment, Jasper decided to give them some space. "Alright, I'm going to head below and take a nap. So, I'll say goodbye to you now."

"Okay Jasper," Antoine said, "It was an extreme pleasure getting to know you. I really can't thank you enough for the hotel room - it was amazing and something I'll remember for the rest of my life."

"Antoine, it was my pleasure," Jasper replied. "You make Emma happy, and as long as you keep doing that, I'll always think of it as money well spent. I'm sure I'll see you again in the future, so until then..." Jasper extended his hand. Antoine took it with a firm handshake.

"Goodbye, and thanks again," he said. Jasper smiled and nodded. "I'm off to my nap. Bye for now," he responded, then headed into his cabin.

Jasper never really slept, he just went below, cleaned a bit and laid down with his book. Emma and Antoine spent the little time they had left holding each other and making small talk till it was time to go to the bus.

Emma decided to accompany Antoine to the bus stop to say goodbye. It was just a few minutes away so they waited until it was about fifteen minutes till the bus left but when they got there the bus was already loading. "I have to go," Antoine turned to Emma. They embraced, gave a quick kiss and said their goodbyes. Antoine grabbed his bag and ran towards the bus.

By the time Emma came back Jasper was sitting in the cockpit. He could see she had been crying. "Emma, are you ok?" asked Jasper. "I'm fine, I just want to be alone for a little while," replied Emma.

Emma went into her cabin and closed the hatch. Jasper was worried and saddened for her but figured there wasn't much he could do and maybe being alone isn't so bad right now.

After a few hours Emma was still lying in bed when Jasper called out, "Scott and Samantha are here. It's time to head out for dinner." "Tell them I'm not feeling well," Emma shouted back.

After a brief pause, Jasper called out again, "Um, when I said they were here, I meant they're right here." Samantha's voice came through clearly, "Hi, sweetie. Are you okay?" Emma heard some mumbling and then, moments later her hatch slid open. Samantha appeared and climbed into the aft cabin, moving some clothes off the other quarter berth before sitting down.

"Hi, sweetie. Coming in," Samantha said cheerfully. Emma managed a smile as Samantha settled beside her. "Wow, it's really, um, compact back here," Samantha commented. Emma chuckled softly, her eyes still red from crying. "I prefer the word cozy myself,"

Samantha smiled at Emma "You guys go ahead. Emma and I are going to talk" Samantha yelled out of the cabin. "Ok so Emma `sing`! Tell me everything. "Emma overlooked Samantha's use of the word 'sing' and took a deep breath and decided to be completely open.

She began by sharing her fears and anxieties, including her phobia and how it has limited her experiences and interactions. She spoke about how much she missed her father. She spoke candidly about her feelings for Antoine, expressing her concerns about their future and worried whether Antoine would still want to be with her once he learned more about her fears.

Samantha listened intently, offering a comforting presence as Emma poured out her emotions and uncertainties.

Samantha nodded understandingly as Emma opened up. "I get it, Emma. It's hard, especially when you're dealing with something as personal as a phobia," Samantha said gently. "And missing your father, that's a lot to carry on top of everything else."

Emma's eyes glistened with unshed tears as she continued. "I just don't know how to handle it all. Antoine means so much to me, but I'm scared that once he knows the full extent of my fears, he might not want to be with me anymore."

Samantha reached out and took Emma's hand. "Listen, it's natural to worry about how your fears might affect your relationships. But if Antoine truly cares for you, he'll want to understand and support you, not push you away. Trust that he's with you for who you are, not just for what you can or can't do."

Emma took a shaky breath. "I hope you're right. It's just so hard to imagine what the future will look like when I feel like I'm holding so much back."

Samantha gave Emma a reassuring squeeze. "The future is always uncertain, but what matters is the present. Focus on the here and now. You're already taking a brave step by doing this adventure right?. That's something to be proud of."

Emma nodded, feeling a bit lighter. "Thank you, Samantha. It means a lot to have someone to talk to about this." "Anytime," Samantha said with a comforting smile.

Emma felt a wave of relief wash over her. "I needed to hear that. Thanks for being here." Samantha smiled warmly.

"Of course. Now, let's not keep the others waiting. We'll head out in a bit, but just remember—you've got this."

Chapter 10

Make a Break For It.

Waking up early, the two boats prepared for a significant day ahead. Both Jasper and Emma, as well as Scott and Samantha from the "Singing Swallow," were eager to make the most of the calm morning. Today, they faced a large crossing, a major leg of their journey across Lake Michigan.

As the first light of dawn crept across the water, Jasper and Emma moved quietly on their boat, their movements precise and purposeful. Jasper checked the weather reports one last time, ensuring that conditions were favorable for the crossing. The forecast promised clear skies and light winds, ideal for the journey ahead.

Scott and Samantha, who had spent the night aboard their boat docked nearby, were also busy with their preparations. The Singing Swallow gleamed in the early morning light, its crew working efficiently to ready their vessel for the long haul. By the time the sun had fully risen, both boats were ready.

The gentle hum of engines began to fill the air as they cast off from their moorings. Emma and Samantha exchanged waves, their faces reflecting a mix of excitement and anticipation.

Jasper gave a final nod to Scott before they set out. "Ready for the crossing?" he called out, his voice carrying over the water.

"Ready as we'll ever be!" Scott replied, a grin spreading across his face. "Let's get underway!"

The sun was high in the sky as Emma and Jasper navigated their boat toward the Mackinac Bridge. The bridge, an iconic symbol of the Great Lakes region, loomed in the distance like a steel sentinel.

Jasper stood at the helm, his eyes squinting into the horizon where the bridge's outline grew more defined. Emma, standing beside him, watched in awe as the structure gradually came into full view.

"Look at that," Emma said, her voice filled with wonder. "That's the largest bridge I've ever seen." Jasper nodded, a proud grin on his face. "I'm sure it is. The Mackinac Bridge connects Michigan's Upper and Lower Peninsulas, and it's one of the longest suspension bridges in the world. Quite the engineering marvel."

As they drew nearer, the scale of the bridge became even more astonishing. The massive steel cables, crisscrossed like giant spider webs, spanned gracefully from one tower to the other. Emma could see the intricate patterns in the bridge's design, the way the sunlight gleamed off its metallic surface.

"Can you imagine the work that went into building this?" Emma mused. "It must have been incredible."

The boat glided smoothly through the water as they approached the bridge. The closer they got, the more the bridge seemed to dominate the landscape.

The towering pillars, clad in their distinctive green paint, stood tall and proud, piercing the blue sky. Their sheer size made her feel small and awestruck.

As they neared the bridge, Emma could see the cars and trucks moving across it, tiny specks in the distance. She imagined the countless journeys that had been made across this bridge, connecting people, places and stories.

Jasper guided the boat carefully, maneuvering it into position. "We'll be passing under the bridge soon. It's quite a sight from underneath too."

Emma's excitement grew as the boat approached the base of the bridge. "Wow," Emma said softly, "The bridge has a way of making everything else seem insignificant in comparison."

As the boat glided beneath the arch of the bridge, Emma looked up, her neck craned back to take in the full height of the structure. The sunlight filtered through the cables, casting intricate shadows on the water below. The sound of the wind rustling through the cables and the distant hum of traffic above added to the grandeur of the moment.

When they emerged from beneath the bridge, Emma glanced back at the colossal structure, feeling a mix of awe and appreciation. "That was incredible," she said, her voice tinged with reverence.

After seven hours of open water, the boats finally approached the small town of Charlevoix. The long day on the lake had been punctuated by a mix of excitement and weariness, and the sight of land brought a welcome relief. As they neared the entrance a charming, small square red lighthouse stood as a beacon, guiding them into a narrow canal.

Jasper maneuvered the boat carefully toward the entrance, the lighthouse's vivid color providing a striking contrast against the lake. The canal itself was a quaint waterway, flanked by lush greenery and lined with cozy shops and homes that hinted at the town's charm.

As they navigated through the canal, the basin in the center of town came into view. The water here was calm, reflecting the afternoon sun and the colorful facades of the surrounding buildings.

The small basin was surrounded by bustling streets and picturesque buildings, giving the area a lively and inviting atmosphere.

Jasper expertly guided the boat toward the south end of the basin, where there was a designated anchorage area. The small space was snug but perfect for a brief stopover. Emma, ready for her task, moved efficiently to lower the anchor. With a series of practiced movements, she ensured that the boat was securely anchored, the chain clinking softly as it settled into place.

Singing Swallow followed into the basin, setting anchor near Arabella. Jasper and Emma, already on deck, waved to their friends, welcoming them with smiles.

"Glad you made it!" Jasper called out, his voice carrying across the water. Samantha responded with a hearty laugh, "It wouldn't be the same without you guys!" "Looks like a lovely place to spend the night," she remarked, her eyes lighting up as she observed the inviting scenery.

Later that evening, as twilight deepened into night, Jasper and Emma hopped into the dinghy, their faces illuminated by the soft glow of deck lights. The gentle splash of the oars against the water was a soothing rhythm as they made their way over to the Singing Swallow.

Upon reaching the boat, Emma and Samantha greeted each other with warm hugs and excited chatter. Samantha invited Emma into the cozy galley, where the scent of spices and herbs lingered from earlier meals.

The galley, though compact, was welcoming with its neatly arranged countertops and the soft hum of the refrigerator.

Samantha busied herself with preparing a selection of drinks, reaching for glasses and mixers while Emma assisted, her laughter mingling with Samantha's as they worked together to create the perfect concoctions.

Meanwhile, outside on the deck of the Singing Swallow, Scott and Jasper were engrossed in a discussion, looking at a laptop screen with weather reports. Jasper scanned the latest weather updates and frowned slightly. "The forecast doesn't look promising for the next few days," he said, pointing at the screen.

Scott nodded in agreement, his expression thoughtful. "Yeah, it seems like we might be stuck here for a while," he replied, his voice tinged with resignation. "It looks like the lake will be too rough to continue."

As the two men discussed their options and the potential delays, Emma and Samantha emerged from the galley with a tray of colorful drinks and snacks. They joined the conversation, bringing a burst of energy and optimism to the discussion.

With the drinks now in hand, the group moved to the deck, where they gathered around a small table. The mood was a blend of camaraderie and contemplation. The uncertainty of the weather was a minor setback, but it was also an opportunity to enjoy each other's company.

The following days were marked by a persistent gray sky and drizzling rain, but the small group made the most of their time in Charlevoix. The dreary weather couldn't dampen their spirits as they embraced the chance to explore the town and enjoy each other's company.

During the day, Emma, Jasper, Scott and Samantha ventured into the charming downtown. They wandered through quaint shops and local boutiques, enjoying the unique finds and cozy atmosphere of the town.

The streets were lined with colorful buildings and the occasional burst of flowers, offering a charming contrast to the overcast sky.

They stopped by a local market to stock up on provisions. The market was bustling with locals and the aroma of fresh produce and baked goods filled the air. They picked out a variety of fresh fruits, vegetables and artisanal breads, chatting with the friendly vendors and getting tips on the best local delicacies. Meals became an experience of their own.

They explored several local restaurants, each offering a taste of the local culinary scene. They savored hearty stews and freshly caught fish, and indulged in delicious desserts. The meals were accompanied by lively conversation and laughter, turning each dining experience into a memorable event.

Some evenings were spent gathered together, sharing stories and other evenings they each stayed on their own boat. For Jasper and Emma this meant writing lessons. The camaraderie grew stronger as they navigated the rainy days together, finding warmth and companionship in each other's presence.

After a few days of dreary weather and relentless rain, the skies finally cleared, and a break in the wind offered a perfect opportunity for the boats to make their move. With the weather improving, the group decided it was time to continue on their long-awaited crossing of Lake Michigan.

The crossing would span five days, with each day dedicated to making steady progress across the vast lake.

They set out early the next morning, eager to seize the favorable conditions. The boats, Arabella and Singing Swallow, departed the safety of the harbor and ventured into the open waters.

Each day of the crossing was marked by a rhythm of cruising and anchoring. They navigated through the

lake's expanse, enjoying the calm waters and the warm sun that replaced the earlier gloom. As evening approached, they would search for a suitable anchorage.

The evenings provided a sense of relief after a day at sea, and they took pleasure in finding quiet spots to anchor, away from the open waters.

Finally, after five days of steady traveling and anchoring, the skyline of Chicago began to take shape on the horizon, its towering structures gradually revealing themselves.

From the deck of Singing Swallow, Scott and Samantha waved enthusiastically. Samantha, her camera in hand, captured the moment as the two boats approached. "Look at that! We're finally here!" she called out, her excitement evident.

The massive skyscrapers of Chicago became more distinct as they drew closer. The tall, sleek forms of the Willis Tower and John Hancock Center loomed prominently, their glass facades shimmering in the morning sun.

The sight was awe-inspiring, a stark contrast to the tranquil waters and small towns they had encountered on their journey.

Jasper's voice came over the radio, "Arabella to Singing Swallow, we're approaching the entrance to Chicago Harbor. Let's keep our eyes peeled for the entrance buoys."

Emma nodded, adjusting the binoculars to get a closer view of the harbor entrance. She spotted the familiar green and red buoys marking the channel, their colors bright against the dark water.

As the boats navigated the entrance, the bustling activity of the harbor came into view. Large yachts, sailboats and the occasional commercial vessel moved with purpose, a testament to the city's vibrant maritime life. The Chicago skyline, now fully revealed, stood as an example to the journey's culmination, a beacon of urban energy against the lake.

With skilled hands, Jasper maneuvered Arabella to her assigned mooring buoy. Samantha and Scott on Singing Swallow followed suit, their boat finding its place in the adjacent buoy. "Well, we made it," Emma said, her voice a mix of relief and exhilaration. "Chicago, here we come."

As the sun began its descent, casting a warm golden glow across Monroe Harbor, Jasper, Emma, Scott and Samantha prepared for an evening of adventure into Chicago. The sleek Monroe Harbor tender service was their ticket to the city's vibrant nightlife and iconic sights. The tender, a sleek and efficient boat designed for short trips across the harbor, bobbed gently. Stopping first at Arabella then at Singing Swallows.

As they climbed aboard, the tender's crew greeted them with friendly nods. Jasper and Emma took a seat at the stern, while Scott and Samantha chose a spot closer to the bow to get the best vantage point for their photos.

Emma gazed out at the tranquil water, her eyes reflecting the shimmering lights. "It's so peaceful out here," she remarked, enjoying the calm before the buzz of the city. As the tender navigated its way across the harbor and approached the yacht club, the cityscape began to reveal itself in all its illuminated splendor.

The iconic buildings, now bathed in colorful lights, created a dazzling display against the night sky. The tall, shining towers of Chicago seemed to pierce the darkness, their lights twinkling like stars.

Samantha couldn't resist snapping photos of the changing scenery. "This is going to be some of the best night photography I've ever done," she said, adjusting her camera settings to capture the city's vibrant lights and reflections.

As the tender glided into the yacht club, the architecture became even more striking. The buildings seemed to close in, their grand facades illuminated by street lamps and lights from within.

The tender's slow pace allowed the group to fully appreciate the stunning contrast between the dark water and the brightly lit structures.

The tender eventually approached the dock. As the boat came to a stop, the group disembarked. Chicago's evening energy was infectious, and they were eager to explore.

The first stop was a nearby rooftop bar. From their vantage point, they enjoyed panoramic views of Chicago's skyline, the tall skyscrapers silhouetted against the darkening sky.

The cityscape sparkled with thousands of lights, creating a breathtaking scene.

Emma leaned on the railing, taking in the scene. "This view is incredible," she said, her eyes wide with wonder. She snapped a few photos, capturing the city's illuminated beauty. Scott, always with his camera ready, took the opportunity to get some shots of his own. "I've never seen Chicago like this. The city is just alive at night."

As the evening progressed, the group descended from the rooftop bar and wandered down Michigan Avenue, also known as the Magnificent Mile. The street was bustling with activity, storefronts and restaurants adorned with festive lights and holiday decorations. The sound of laughter and conversation filled the air, creating an atmosphere of excitement and possibility.

They strolled past the famous Chicago Water Tower, its gothic architecture standing out among the modern buildings.

Emma marveled at the contrast between the historic structure and the contemporary skyscrapers surrounding it.

"Chicago really has a mix of old and new," Emma remarked, looking up at the Water Tower.

Jasper agreed. "It's one of the things I love about this city. There's so much history alongside the modern hustle."

As the night continued, they decided to take a leisurely walk along the Chicago Riverwalk. The path was illuminated by streetlights, and the reflections of the city's lights danced on the water's surface. The serenity of the river contrasted beautifully with the bustling cityscape, providing a peaceful end to their evening.

Finally, as they made their way back to the marina, the city's energy began to wind down. The streets were quieter now, but the memories of the evening lingered brightly in their minds.

Standing at the edge of Monroe Harbor, looking out over the gently rocking boats, Emma turned to her friends. "Tonight was amazing. I'm so glad we got to experience Chicago like this."

Jasper nodded, a satisfied smile on his face. With that, they made their way back to their boats, their hearts full of the sights, sounds, and experiences of a truly memorable evening in Chicago.

Early the next morning, Emma was deep in sleep when a persistent knocking began at her cabin hatch. "Emma, Emma, I need to come in!" Jasper's voice called out, muffled through the cabin door. Emma groaned softly, reluctantly stirring from her slumber. She rubbed her eyes and stretched before responding, "Come in, Grandpa. What's going on?"

The hatch slid open quickly, and Jasper stepped inside, his expression serious. "I'm sorry to wake you, Emma, but we've got a problem. We're taking on water. I need to check the bilge to find out where it's coming from."

Emma's eyes widened as she followed Jasper to the bilge. When he lifted the sole, she saw about an inch of water sloshing around. Panic gripped her. "Oh my God, we're going to sink, she thought."

Jasper knelt down and examined the situation. "Yep, it looks like the water's coming in around the propeller shaft," he said, his voice steady. He turned to face Emma, noticing the terror in her eyes.

Jasper realizing how much he scared her, changed his tone to sound more reassuring "Emma, relax. We have dual bilge pumps and plenty of power. We're not going to sink. Do you hear that low hum and the water splashing outside? That's the pumps doing their job."

Emma's heart began to slow as she absorbed his words. "Are you sure?" she asked, her voice trembling slightly. "Yes, we'll be fine," Jasper assured her. "But we can't stay like this forever. I need to find a place nearby where we can haul out the boat and get this repaired."

Emma took a deep breath, nodding in understanding. Jasper's calm demeanor helped to ease her anxiety, and she resolved to focus on finding a solution together. Later that morning, Jasper was in the fore cabin when Emma walked in, looking concerned.

"I've found a place a little ways up the Chicago River, just across from downtown, that can haul us out," Jasper said, his tone practical but worried. "Depending on what needs fixing, we might be stuck in Chicago for a while."

"Ok I get it," Emma replied. "Well I'll call Scott and Samantha to let them know what's going on."

A short while later, Emma finished her call and turned to Jasper. "They're going to stay in the harbor for one more night. They'll stop by the marina to say goodbye on their way out but are planning to keep moving. They said they'll meet up with us somewhere along the loop."

"Alright Emma, let's weigh anchor and get moving. The sooner we get there, the better," Jasper said, sounding determined.

Emma nodded and began the process of weighing anchor. As they navigated out of the harbor and around the breakwall, they entered the Chicago River.

"One nice thing about leaving the mast at home," Jasper continued, "is that we have a really low air draft, which is our height above the water. This means we can slip under most bridges without needing them to lift."

Emma glanced up at the towering bridges spanning the river, grateful for the added convenience.

About an hour later, they arrived at the marina and pulled into a specially designated slip. Emma quickly retrieved Jasper's wheelchair, and they made their way up to the office.

After completing some paperwork and making the necessary payment, the marina staff drove out a large lift mounted on four wheels. It went over the boat on sturdy tracks.

With careful precision, huge straps were lowered over the boat's bow and stern. The staff double-checked everything to ensure it was securely in place before they began hoisting the boat out of the water. As the boat rose, Emma watched in awe.

This was her first time seeing the underside of the vessel. The hull, covered in copper cladding, was a striking contrast to the V-shaped hulls of the other boats in the marina. The long, sleek keel ran almost the entire length of the boat, from bow to stern, giving it a distinctive look.

Emma found the sight unique and fascinating. The marina staff, equally intrigued, bombarded Jasper with questions about the antique sailboat.

Jasper was more than happy to oblige, explaining the boat's features in detail. He described how it was Mahogany planked and had been fitted with thin copper cladding instead of traditional antifouling paint.

He talked about the restoration work he had done and how the interior, though appearing antique, had been updated in the 1980s.

Jasper also discussed the advantages of a long keel over a deep keel, such as better tracking and being capable of going into more shallow water, although it made the boat less suitable for racing.

The questions seemed endless, and Jasper, like a proud parent, reveled in sharing the boat's history and unique characteristics.

Meanwhile, the other staff worked diligently, moving the boat onto stands. After a while, the marina manager emerged from the office to deliver some disappointing news.

Due to their current schedule, it would be about a week before they could even begin inspecting the boat. Jasper and Emma exchanged glances, both disheartened by the unexpected delay.

Jasper turned to Emma, his face reflecting a mix of resolve and disappointment. "Well, let's go find a place to eat and figure out our next steps," he suggested. Emma nodded in agreement, and as they were about to leave, the marina manager chimed in, "There's a really nice place just a block over the bridge. Highly recommended."

"That sounds perfect," Jasper replied, grateful for the recommendation. With that, they made their way over the bridge, taking in the sights of the bustling city around them.

The short walk brought them to the restaurant, which lived up to its promise.

The restaurant had a striking large glass facade that allowed plenty of natural light to flood the interior.

The design was elegant yet welcoming, featuring a beautiful light wood trim that complemented the modern, airy atmosphere.

Emma and Jasper found themselves settling into a table with easy access for his wheelchair, the stress of the morning giving way to the comfort of a well-deserved meal.

As they browsed the menu and ordered, Jasper and Emma reflected on the day's events. The delay with the boat was frustrating, but they decided to make the most of their time in Chicago.

Their conversation turned to their immediate needs. It was clear they needed to secure a hotel room for their stay. They quickly agreed on their criteria: it had to be close enough to downtown to explore on foot, must accept bicycles, and ideally have a really nice bathtub - a luxury Emma had missed.

Additionally, having an on-site restaurant would be a huge convenience for Jasper.

While savoring their meals, they pulled out their phones and began searching for suitable hotels. They browsed through various options, weighing their pros and cons.

After considerable discussion, Jasper found a hotel that met all their requirements. Emma hesitated, noting that it seemed a bit pricey, but Jasper reassured her with a smile, "Don't worry about it."

Jasper placed a call to the hotel to make a reservation, confirming that Emma's bicycle could be accommodated in the elevator. Once everything was set, they felt a wave of relief wash over them. With their plan in place, they finished their meal, content and ready to tackle their next adventure.

They decided on their plan of action, they would head back to the marina to gather their belongings and Jasper would travel to the hotel by taxi, while she cycled over with her bike. The distance wasn't far, so Jasper shouldn't have to wait too long.

As Emma arrived at the hotel, she was awestruck by its grandeur. It was a stark contrast to the elegance of the Grand

Hotel on Mackinac Island. This hotel was sleek and modern, yet undeniably luxurious.

The lobby was adorned with chic decor. Jasper was waiting in the lobby, comfortably settled in his wheelchair. When Emma approached, he greeted her with a smile. "The bellhop has already taken our things up," Jasper said, handing Emma a keycard. "Here's your keycard. We're all set."

Emma thanked him and took the keycard, "Let's go up," Jasper said, gesturing toward the elevators. They entered the lift, which was lined with mirrored panels and wood trim, and featured a plush upholstered sofa at the back.

As they ascended, Emma admired the opulent design of the elevator. When they reached their floor, Emma glanced at her keycard, which read "Room 2204." She walked down the hallway, her eyes scanning the ornate brass room numbers until she found the right door. "Room 2204 this is it!" Emma said with excitement.

Jasper, who was following closely behind, pointed out, "And I'm in 2206, right next door."

Emma looked at Jasper with surprise. "We're not sharing a room?" "Nope," Jasper replied with a grin. "I thought you might appreciate a little space."

Emma's eyes filled with gratitude. "Grandpa, you are the best. I'm never going to forget everything you've done for me, Not ever." Jasper's heart warmed at her words, and he gave her a reassuring smile. "How about dinner tonight up on the terrace?" he suggested.

"Absolutely," Emma replied, her face lighting up with a smile. With that, they settled into their rooms, each one a luxurious retreat, before looking forward to a relaxing evening together.

Chapter 11

Human Ingenuity and Environmental Stewardship

The following week passed in a whirlwind of exploration and relaxation as Emma and Jasper made the most of their time in Chicago.

They immersed themselves in the city's vibrant atmosphere, with Emma often taking her bike to venture beyond the downtown core. She discovered charming neighborhoods, scenic parks, and hidden gems that the city's bustling center couldn't offer.

Jasper, meanwhile, enjoyed the luxury of the hotel and the ease of navigating the city with Emma. Together, they visited iconic landmarks, dined at excellent restaurants and soaked in the local culture.

Jasper figured this was also a great time for Emma to learn more writing skills. So each evening in the hotel they sat down and worked on Emma's writing skills.

Despite their enjoyable stay, the time spent waiting for Arabella to be ready felt like an eternity. It took nine full days for the repairs and maintenance to be completed, but finally, the day came when Arabella was back in the water, gleaming and ready for the journey ahead.

For Jasper and Emma, the return of the beloved boat couldn't have come at a better time.

They were eager to start traveling once more, relieved to move on from their extended stay and resume their adventure.

Jasper and Emma settled into Arabella with a sense of eager anticipation. The boat had been meticulously prepared for the journey, and as they cast off from the marina, a wave of excitement swept over them. They navigated their way south down the Chicago Ship Canal, embarking on what promised to be a uniquely urban waterway experience.

The Chicago Ship Canal stretched from the Chicago River to the Des Plaines River, and its surroundings were a fascinating contrast to the natural beauty they had grown accustomed to. Lined with a mix of old warehouses and factories juxtaposed against modern infrastructure, the canal was a bustling corridor of industry.

The waterway was wide and straight, marked by numerous man-made structures, including bridges and locks. Jasper and Emma observed a variety of traffic, from massive commercial barges to smaller recreational boats, each contributing to the dynamic flow of the canal.

While the scenery lacked the picturesque charm of more natural waterways, it offered an intriguing view into the industrial heart of Chicago and the canal's crucial role in the city's economic landscape. The hum of machinery and the occasional sight of freight moving along the canal highlighted its importance as a commercial artery.

As Arabella was making its way south down the Chicago Ship Canal, Jasper and Emma approached a critical and somewhat daunting part of their journey - the electric fish barrier.

This barrier, a formidable structure designed to protect the Great Lakes from invasive species, was a sight to behold. Its presence was marked by warning signs and high-tension wires, a clear indication of its importance and the serious nature of its function.

The barrier, spanning the width of the canal, was a series of submerged electrified cables. These cables emitted a low-level electric field intended to deter fish from crossing into the canal and migrating toward the Great Lakes. The technology was crucial for environmental protection.

Jasper glanced at Emma, who was observing the scene with a mix of curiosity and apprehension. "This is one of the more interesting parts of the trip," Jasper said with a reassuring smile.

Emma nodded, her gaze fixed on the barrier as it loomed closer. The water around the barrier was marked with cautionary buoys, and the signs indicated the presence of the electrical field below the surface.

The sound of the water against Arabella's hull was accompanied by the occasional hum from the barrier's electronic systems, a reminder of the advanced technology at play.

The electric fish barrier was an impressive example of human ingenuity and environmental stewardship. As Arabella passed through the designated channel, Emma exhaled a breath she hadn't realized she was holding. The barrier's impact was felt more in its symbolism than in its physical presence.

Once past the barrier, the canal resumed its usual character. Jasper and Emma shared a look of relief and accomplishment, knowing that they had successfully navigated one of the more interesting aspects of their trip. "Well, that was something,"

Emma said with a smile, her earlier apprehension giving way to satisfaction. "Yep," Jasper agreed, "Just one more experience ticked off the list. Now, let's enjoy the rest of the river."

As they approached the final lock in Lockport, Jasper maneuvered Arabella through with practiced ease. Once they cleared the lock and connected to the Des Plaines River, the atmosphere began to shift. The river offered a new perspective, transitioning from the industrial to a more quiet setting.

By evening, Jasper and Emma decided to tie up for the night at the town dock in Joliet. The dock, though modest, provided a welcome respite. They tied up Arabella and settled in for a peaceful night, enjoying the calm after the day's urban adventure. The change in scenery and the tranquility of the Des Plaines River offered a soothing contrast to the bustling canal they had just navigated, marking a fitting end to their day's journey.

The next morning Emma and Jasper embarked on the next leg of their journey, spending the following four days meandering down the Des Plaines River and onto the Illinois River. Their route took them through a series of locks, each one an essential part of their passage.

Their nights were spent at various town docks, each stop offering its own unique charm. The first night, they docked in a quaint riverside town where they were greeted by friendly locals and enjoyed a simple, home-cooked meal at a nearby diner. The town's warm hospitality provided a comforting end to their day of travel.

The following nights were similar, with each town offering its own character and amenities. In one town, they discovered a small farmers' market where they stocked up on fresh produce for their meals. In another, they explored historic buildings and learned about the local history, adding an educational touch to their journey.

By the end of the fourth day, Emma and Jasper had made significant progress on their journey, finally docking for the night at a picturesque marina in the charming town of Grafton.

Nestled at the confluence of the Illinois River and the mighty Mississippi, this quaint town served as an essential pitstop for their vessel, Arabella.

As they maneuvered into their slip, a young dockhand rushed out to assist them, eager to lend a hand with their lines. His friendly demeanor lightened the mood after a long day on the water. While securing the boat, he glanced at Emma and asked, "Are you a traveler or a tourist?" Curious, Emma raised an eyebrow and replied, "What's the difference?"

The dockhand smiled, ready to share his thoughts. "Well, a tourist tends to stick to the main attractions, following the usual routes and schedules. They often check things off a list—sights to see, restaurants to visit. But a traveler, on the other hand, immerses themselves in the local culture. They seek out hidden gems, engage with the community, and embrace spontaneity."

Emma considered his words, feeling inspired. "I see what you mean. I hope I'm more of a traveler," she said, glancing at Jasper, who nodded in agreement. The dockhand chuckled, "You're in the right place for that. Grafton has its share of secrets waiting to be discovered." Emma thought to herself how refreshing it was to see someone take pride in their town.

Emma felt a renewed sense of adventure as they prepared to explore the town, eager to experience all it had to offer.

The marina was bustling with activity; the docks buzzed with the sounds of engines and the clatter of boat gear. Jasper seized the moment to perform some essential engine maintenance, methodically checking over the systems and making necessary adjustments. He was meticulous in his work, understanding that the challenges of the Mississippi River demanded their boat be in top condition.

As he worked, Emma wandered along the docks, taking in the sights and sounds of Grafton. She marveled at the old buildings lining the waterfront, and the laughter of families enjoying the evening.

Emma took a more leisurely approach to preparing for the next leg of their journey. She explored the small town, picking up local delicacies and chatting with friendly townsfolk. Grafton had a welcoming atmosphere, with picturesque views of the rivers. Emma enjoyed a moment of relaxation.

As evening fell, Jasper and Emma had a quiet dinner at a local restaurant, reflecting on their journey so far and discussing their plans for the days ahead. They were both excited and a bit apprehensive about entering the Mississippi River.

The next morning, with the sun rising over the horizon, they prepared to leave Grafton behind.

The air was cool, and the river waters glistened in the early light. Emma and Jasper completed their final checks, ensuring that everything was in order before setting out.

Jasper started the engine, and Arabella gently pulled away from the dock. The feeling of moving onto the Mississippi River was a significant shift in their journey. The Illinois River had been a quiet and winding passage, but the Mississippi loomed large and powerful, with its wide expanses and strong currents.

As they ventured into the Mississippi, the scenery transformed dramatically. The water was darker and swifter, and the river's character was unmistakably more dynamic. Emma and Jasper marveled at the new

landscape, their excitement growing with each mile they covered.

They adjusted to the rhythm of the Mississippi, navigating its currents and taking in the diverse scenery. The riverbanks were dotted with a mix of industrial sites, wildlife habitats, and sprawling river towns. Each bend in the river brought a new perspective and a fresh appreciation for the scale of their adventure.

As Arabella glided southward, Emma and Jasper approached the city of Alton. The highlight of this segment was passing under the striking new cable-stayed bridge that arched gracefully over the river. Its modern design contrasted sharply with the old and industrial landscape of the Mississippi, and Emma admired the bridge's elegant lines and soaring cables.

With the bridge in their wake, the excitement of reaching St. Louis grew. Emma had heard so much about the city and was particularly looking forward to seeing the iconic Gateway Arch.

However, as they neared the city, her enthusiasm waned when she learned that St. Louis did not have docking facilities for pleasure boats. The realization was a bit of a letdown; it meant they would miss out on exploring the city.

Despite the disappointment, Emma was determined to make the most of their visit. As they approached the city, the majestic Gateway Arch loomed on the horizon, its stainless steel curves glinting in the afternoon sun. The Arch was even more impressive up close, standing as a powerful symbol of westward expansion and a striking landmark against the St. Louis skyline.

Emma and Jasper maneuvered Arabella into a position where they could get a good view of the Arch from the river. The sheer scale and beauty of the structure were awe-inspiring, and Emma took a moment to appreciate and photograph its grandeur from their unique vantage point.

As they continued south on the Mississippi, Emma reflected on the day's events. While their visit to St. Louis hadn't gone as she hoped, the river's ever-changing scenery and the chance to see the Gateway Arch from the water had made it worthwhile.

As they continued south the strong current and large barges made navigating the river a bit nerve-wracking for Emma.

Jasper, meanwhile, continued to communicate with the barge operators over the radio, ensuring they maintained a safe distance and avoided any potential collisions. Despite the heightened risk, Emma found some reassurance in Jasper's calm and competent handling of the situation.

As the day drew to a close, Jasper decided to spend the night at Hoppies Marina. The strong current had pushed them to unprecedented speeds, making navigation increasingly challenging.

With the day winding down and safe anchorage options scarce on the stretch ahead, staying at the marina provided a much-needed respite. It allowed them to refuel and rest before tackling the more difficult part of their journey.

Known for being the last refueling stop for over 250 miles, the marina offered not just fuel but also a chance to prepare for the stretch of the river ahead. Emma and Jasper took full advantage of the opportunity to relax.

The next few days drifted by with a steady rhythm, the clouds hanging like a soft blanket over the Mississippi. The muted light cast a serene, almost monochromatic view of the river, turning every scene into a study of grays and silvers. Though the weather remained overcast, it didn't detract from the tranquility of their journey.

Each night, they anchored in familiar routines, the gentle sway of the boat and the distant murmur of the river becoming a comforting lullaby. The constant, unchanging scenery of the riverbanks, dotted with occasional clusters of trees or small settlements, became a setting to their reflective moments.

Finally they arrived in Cairo and even though they didn't plan on stopping. Cairo was still a major landmark. Cairo, often referred to as the "Confluence City," marked the transition from one mighty river to another. Leaving the Mississippi and continuing onto the Ohio River.

They eventually arrived in Paducah, Kentucky, where they had planned to spend the night. Emma was so excited as she said, "Do you know, as of now we've been in six states and two provinces?"

"Really?" Jasper replied, counting the states on his fingers. "Yep! It wasn't that long ago I'd never really been out of Ticonderoga. This is amazing. Thank you." said Emma

Jasper smiled. "It's me who should be thanking you. If it weren't for you, I'd still be staring at the walls and eating that bland food back at the nursing home." Emma gave Jasper a heartfelt hug.

"Okay, Emma, we should get ready; we're almost at the town dock," Jasper said as he steered the boat towards Paducah's waterfront. Emma quickly prepared the fenders and lines while Jasper navigated the final approach.

As the boat eased into place, Emma nimbly jumped off and expertly tied off Arabella. "Emma, grab my wheelchair. Let's go see what this town has to offer. We need a break from the boat." said Jasper

Emma was already on it. She swiftly retrieved Jasper's wheelchair and helped him into it. The town had a charming, inviting vibe, with colorful buildings lining the waterfront. Jasper pointed out a massive wall that stretched along the shoreline. "That's the flood wall," he explained. "The town painted large murals on it to beautify it."

Emma's eyes widened as she admired the vibrant artwork. "It's so cool how the town turned a functional flood wall into a piece of art. It really gives the place character!" After a leisurely stroll, they found a cozy local restaurant with outdoor seating.

The atmosphere was warm and inviting, and the scent of fresh food wafted through the air. They enjoyed a delightful dinner, sharing stories and laughter, savoring every bite of the local cuisine.

As they made their way back to the boat, the sun dipped below the horizon. Emma smiled at Jasper. "Today was perfect. I'm so glad we decided to explore." "Me too," he replied, a content look on his face. "Sometimes a little time off the boat is just what we need."

As Arabella came into view, Emma's heart raced. Two figures loomed in the cockpit, their silhouettes sharp against the twinking water. "Grandpa, wait - " she started, but he was already yelling. "Hey! You get off of there!" Jasper's voice echoed across the water. "Shhhh, they might be dangerous!" exclaimed Emma.

Emma tried to pull him back, but he was undeterred. "Get off my boat!" he shouted again, his determination unwavering. Suddenly, the two figures bolted, darting through a nearby passage in the flood wall.

"See, Emma? Most thieves are also cowards!" Jasper exclaimed, a mix of triumph and adrenaline in his voice. Emma couldn't help but smile, imagining how he would have chased them down if he weren't in his chair.

"Come on, let's check the boat and see what they did," he urged, and they made their way down to Arabella. As they reached the deck, Emma's stomach dropped. The lock on the forward cabin was seriously damaged, metal twisted and broken, but the door remained closed.

"I guess we interrupted them just in time," Jasper said, examining the damage. "Yeah," Emma replied, relieved but shaken. "It could have been worse."

Jasper nodded, his expression serious. "We need to make sure this doesn't happen again. Let's reinforce the locks tomorrow." Emma agreed, but a lingering unease settled over her. "I don't feel comfortable sleeping here tonight," she said quietly, almost under her breath.

Jasper looked at her, his understanding evident. "Yeah, I get that. There's a bit of a bay straight across the river. Let's untie and anchor over there."

With a plan in mind, they quickly got to work, getting Arabella ready for the move. Emma helped Jasper navigate the boat, her anxiety easing as they set off. The water was calm, and the bay promised a more peaceful night.

Once they anchored, Emma took a deep breath. "This feels better already," she said, glancing around at the tranquil surroundings. "Definitely," Jasper agreed, his voice more relaxed.

As night fell, Emma settled into her nightly routine, preparing for the video chat with her dad and Antoine. She couldn't wait to recount their day's journey and share the excitement of the evening.

Over the next few days, they left the Ohio River and navigated across Kentucky Lake, making their way onto the Tennessee River. As they traveled downstream, Jasper began to slow the boat, intently studying his charts and GPS.

Eventually, he brought the boat to a stop in the middle of a wide stretch of the river.

"Why did you stop?" Emma asked, curious. Jasper smiled. "Right here, at this spot, you're currently in three states at once - Alabama, Tennessee, and Mississippi."

"Wow!" Emma exclaimed. "That's awesome!" Jasper continued, "It's also where we leave the Tennessee River and start the Tenn-Tom Waterway." "What's that?" Emma asked. "The Tennessee-Tombigbee Waterway. It connects the Tennessee River to the Tombigbee River. It's the newest navigation canal in North America and features some massive locks we'll have to navigate."

Emma's eyes lit up with excitement. "Well, it sounds amazing. What are we waiting for?" Jasper laughed, throttling up as they began heading towards the Waterway. The first section of the Tenn-Tom Waterway was a man-made channel, similar to others they had seen along their journey, but it marked the beginning of a new and intriguing part of their trip.

For the next four days, Emma and Jasper delighted in their voyage through the Tenn-Tom Waterway. Each day brought new experiences and sights as they navigated this impressive man-made channel.

The waterway's course meandered through a variety of landscapes, from dense forests to open fields.. Emma reveled in the beauty and took countless photos to capture the moments.

The locks along the Tenn-Tom Waterway were a highlight of their trip. Although they had been through many locks before, the grand scale of each of these locks presented a thrill, with the massive gates and chambers. Jasper's expertise in handling Arabella through these large, industrial marvels made the process smooth and efficient.

The Tenn-Tom Waterway, with its combination of natural beauty and engineering marvels, proved to be a memorable and enjoyable stretch of their journey. Emma and Jasper relished every moment.

Upon reaching Demopolis, Emma and Jasper recognized that they had reached the end of the Tenn-Tom Waterway, marking a significant event in their journey. As they approached the town dock, the sky darkened ominously, signaling an approaching storm. The strong current added an extra layer of difficulty, requiring extra care and precision to secure Arabella properly.

Jasper, focused and skilled, navigated the boat with steady hands, managing the powerful flow of the river with expertise.

Emma, ever vigilant and prepared, worked in tandem with Jasper, ensuring they were aligned with the dock amidst the swirling waters. The combination of their efforts allowed them to position the boat accurately despite the current's challenges.

Securing Arabella involved additional adjustments to their lines and fenders, but their meticulous approach paid off. Their teamwork, honed through their journey, was evident in how seamlessly they worked together to manage the situation.

Just as they completed the task, the rain began to fall. The first drops turned into a steady downpour, a timely reminder of nature's unpredictable role in their adventure.

Emma and Jasper, satisfied with their accomplishment, took shelter in the cabin. It wasn't long after they had taken cover that the wind started to pick up. Amid the heavy downpour, and the wind howled around them. The sky, already dark, was now punctuated by a dramatic crack of thunder that reverberated through the air.

The thunder rolled on, its echoes seeming to amplify the storm's ferocity. Each flash of lightning illuminated the turbulent water and the surrounding landscape, offering brief, dramatic glimpses of the storm's impact.

Even though Arabella was securely tied to the dock, the storm's force caused the boat to roll slightly, resulting in a gentle but persistent bumping against the fenders. The rhythmic thuds created a bit of an uncomfortable night for Emma and Jasper, as the constant motion and noise made it difficult to fully relax.

The sound of rain pelting the deck, combined with the occasional groan of the boat against the fenders, kept them both on edge. The storm's howling wind and the intermittent flashes of lightning through the cabin windows added to the uneasy ambiance. Despite their best efforts to make the best of the situation, sleep was elusive.

Very early the next morning, Jasper awoke from a restless night. The storm had kept him on edge, and the occasional thud against the hull had punctuated his uneasy sleep. He reasoned that it was probably just a large floating branch bouncing off the boat.

As he climbed out into the cockpit, he was greeted by the beauty of an incredible sunrise. The early light painted the sky in brilliant hues, a stark contrast to the stormy darkness of the previous night. Jasper always found sunrises particularly striking after a storm, a reminder of nature's ability to renew and refresh.

However, as his gaze shifted downward, he noticed that the water level had risen significantly onshore. The river, swollen from the storm, was choked with debris, a testament to the storm's intensity. The shoreline was littered with broken branches and the remnants of the storm's fury, and he could see visible damage to trees and roofs along the riverbank.

Jasper made his way around the front of the boat to investigate the source of the thud that had disturbed his sleep. To his dismay, he discovered that an entire tree had come floating down the river during the storm. It had become lodged between Arabella and the dock, a sizable obstacle that had caused the banging noises he heard earlier.

He assessed the situation with a mix of concern and determination. The tree was large and heavy, and it was clear that removing it would require some effort. Jasper knew that addressing this issue would be their top priority before they could continue with their journey.

Jasper decided that dealing with the tree could wait until he had a chance to enjoy a cup of coffee and give Emma some time to wake up.

The tree, while inconvenient, wasn't causing any immediate harm; it was simply lodged between Arabella and the dock, held in place by the water's current and the boat's position.

He headed to the galley to make himself a strong, comforting cup of coffee. The warmth of the beverage was a welcome start to the day, and the rich aroma filled the cabin as he waited for Emma to stir.

It was nearly eleven when Jasper heard some noises coming from Emma's cabin. He went below and made a fresh cup of coffee, anticipating that she might need a pick-me-up once she emerged.

A few minutes later, Emma poked her head out of the hatch. Jasper greeted her with a warm smile, holding out the steaming mug. "Good morning Sunshine," he said cheerfully. "I take it you had trouble falling asleep?" Emma groaned as she rubbed her eyes. "Ugh, yes. I could hardly get any rest with all the noise and movement."

Jasper handed her the coffee. "Here, this might help. I was just about to have some myself. There's a bit of a mess to deal with, but we've got time." Emma took the cup gratefully, savoring the warmth as she took a sip. "What happened?"

Jasper pointed out towards the river. "We've got a tree wedged between the boat and the dock. It floated down during the storm and got caught. It's not causing any immediate harm, but we'll need to sort it out." Emma went to the bow and saw the large tree lodged against the boat. "Oh wow, well I'm glad we're okay. Let's finish our coffee and then figure out how to get this thing out of the way.

"But I have to tell you, with the river like this, I don't believe it's wise for us to leave just yet," Jasper said, a note of concern in his voice. "You see, all this debris isn't just from the recent storm. The higher water levels have picked up debris from past storms and other sources along the shoreline."

Emma looked around, taking in the tangled mess of branches and trash floating by. The river was visibly swollen, and the increased flow had indeed brought a lot of debris into their path. "So you think it's too dangerous to continue right now?"

Jasper nodded. "Exactly. With all this floating debris, navigation could be hazardous. There's a risk of running into something we can't see or the propeller getting caught up. It might be best for us to stay put until the water levels drop and the river clears up a bit."

Emma considered this for a moment and then agreed. "That makes sense. Safety has to come first. We can use the time to rest and prepare for when conditions improve." With the storm's remnants slowly fading into memory, they enjoyed their coffee and prepared for the task ahead.

After finishing their coffee, Emma and Jasper formulated a plan to address the tree wedged between the boat and the dock. They decided that both of them would need to go ashore to effectively manage the situation. The plan was straightforward but required careful execution. Emma would handle the bow of the boat, while Jasper would manage the stern.

By allowing Emma to give out significantly more line than Jasper, they hoped the current would pull the boat away from the dock, creating enough space for the tree to slide out.

Emma prepared to untie the bow line, her movements precise as she made sure the boat's forward line was ready to be released. Jasper, positioned at the stern, checked his line and prepared to let it out slowly.

Once they were both in position, Emma began to feed out the bow line, letting it slip through her hands as the current began to act on the boat. Jasper, meanwhile, carefully managed the stern line, making sure not to release too much too quickly.

As the boat gradually moved away from the dock, the current did its job, creating a gap between the boat and the tree. The large piece of debris slowly began to shift, and with a bit of maneuvering, it eventually slipped free from its wedged position. Both Emma and Jasper breathed a sigh of relief as they watched the tree drift away, clearing the path. With the obstruction resolved, they worked together to re-secure the boat and ensure everything was in order. The plan had worked well.

With the decision made to stay in Demopolis for a few days, Emma decided to venture into town to get some food. She had hoped to find a few essentials and perhaps some comfort food to make their unexpected delay a bit more pleasant.

Before leaving, Jasper joked around with Emma "Hey Emma remember you are at the northern end of where alligators roam". With a bit of panick in her voice "What, maybe I should stay on the boat."

Jasper started laughing "Relax, I'm kidding, yes there has been the odd sighting this far north but they're extremely rare. Besides, the chances of being attacked by an alligator is like one in three million. Especially on land. Remember it's not hard to outrun one. Just don't take a nap right next to a swamp and you will be fine" That set Emma's mind at ease. It was one less thing she had to worry about.

As she walked through town, it quickly became evident that the storm had left significant damage in its wake. The further she went, the more the extent of the devastation became clear. Fallen trees, scattered debris, and damaged buildings were common sights.

Driven by concern and curiosity, Emma continued toward the areas where the damage seemed most severe. Her walk led her to a neighborhood that had been particularly hard-hit.

Houses had been partially or fully destroyed, with roofs ripped off and siding torn away. Trees had been uprooted and scattered across yards and streets, and some homes were still partially submerged from the swollen river.

The scene was sobering. Emma saw residents working tirelessly to clean up and salvage what they could. Volunteers and local officials were coordinating efforts to clear debris and provide assistance to those affected. Emma's heart ached as she witnessed the scale of the destruction and the resilience of the community in the face of such adversity.

Emma was deeply moved by what she had seen. She called Jasper and shared the experience with him, and told him that she resolved to help where could, even if only by contributing to local relief efforts. The community's strength and determination were inspiring, and Emma felt grateful for their own safety and the opportunity to be part of a supportive response to the storm's aftermath.

Emma asked around for information on where she could assist. She found a local community center that had been turned into a hub for relief efforts. Volunteers and local organizers were busy coordinating cleanup operations and distributing supplies to those affected by the storm.

Emma approached one of the organizers and offered her help. "I've seen the damage firsthand and really want to pitch in. Where can I be most useful?" The organizer, a middle-aged woman with a weary but grateful smile, pointed her toward a nearby area where cleanup was in progress. "We're focusing on debris removal and helping residents clear their properties.

There's a lot to do, and any help we can get is appreciated."

Emma thanked her and headed to the neighborhood. When she arrived, she saw a mix of volunteers and local residents working diligently. She joined a group clearing debris from a street, where she picked up fallen branches, broken fence pieces, and scattered trash.

Her efforts did not go unnoticed. Emma worked alongside others, exchanging stories and camaraderie as they labored. The community's resilience was evident in their collective spirit, and Emma felt a deep sense of fulfillment as she contributed to the recovery process.

Throughout the day, Emma's hands grew tired, but her resolve remained strong. She worked until dusk, making sure to leave no task unfinished.

The impact of her efforts, though small in the grand scheme, was meaningful to those she worked with and to the people whose lives were shaken. When she finally returned to Arabella, Emma was exhausted but satisfied. She shared her experiences with Jasper, who was moved by her dedication.

Chapter 12

Shadow of Doubt

Days later, with the cleanup efforts well underway and the community beginning to recover, Jasper decided it was time to continue their journey. Emma had contributed significantly to the recovery efforts, and the town had made noticeable progress. Construction crews, equipped with loaders and dump trucks, were now actively hauling away the debris and repairing the damage.

Emma felt a deep sense of accomplishment for having done what she could to help the community. She had seen firsthand the impact of their support and was heartened by the resilience and progress she had witnessed. As the town moved into the next phase of recovery, she knew it was time for them to move on.

On their final morning in Demopolis, Jasper and Emma prepared Arabella for departure. They checked their equipment, and made sure everything was in order. The boat, now clear of the tree and any remaining storm debris, was ready to resume its journey.

Emma took one last look at the town, reflecting on the experience and the kindness of the people she had met. She was grateful for the opportunity to help and for the warm reception they had received from the local community.

Jasper, seeing Emma's thoughtful expression, put a reassuring hand on her shoulder. "Ready to hit the water again?" Emma nodded "Absolutely. Let's get going."

With the boat secured and their course set, Jasper and Emma cast off from the dock. As Arabella pulled away, Emma felt a mix of satisfaction and anticipation for what laid ahead. The journey had been delayed, but it had also been enriched by her unexpected detour and the meaningful contributions she had made along the way.

As they navigated the Tombigbee, Alabama, and Mobile Rivers over the next few days, Emma and Jasper delighted in the ever-changing scenery and the challenge of passing through various locks. A particularly significant event came when they reached Claiborne Lock—the final lock on the Midwest rivers.

This marked a special moment for Emma, who had never experienced tidal waters before. The transition from fresh to saline water heralded their approach to the coast, infusing their journey with a fresh sense of excitement.

Not long after passing through the locks, Emma spotted her first palm tree. The sight of it brought an emotional wave of joy, symbolizing their progression into new and unfamiliar territory.

Over the next few days, they completed the final 118 miles of their journey through the Midwest rivers, eventually reaching the northern end of Mobile.

The stretch along the waterfront was strikingly industrial, with towering cranes and sprawling warehouses dominating the landscape. The constant hum of machinery and the sight of massive cargo ships painted a vivid picture of the city's bustling maritime activity.

Given the industrial nature of the surrounding area, Emma and Jasper decided to make a brief stop at the courtesy dock located downtown. They wanted to take advantage of the opportunity to explore the area a bit before heading to their marina for the night.

Upon docking at the courtesy dock, they took a quick tour of the nearby downtown district. They strolled through the streets, admiring the blend of classic and modern architecture and stopping by a few local shops and cafes. The downtown area, though not particularly picturesque, had a unique charm of its own and offered a glimpse into the area's character and history.

After their short but enjoyable excursion, they returned to Arabella and prepared for the final leg of their journey. With the sun beginning to dip lower in the sky, they cruised the last ten miles to their marina.

The calm water and the prospect of reaching their destination provided a satisfying end to their day's travel. As they approached the Marina, the anticipation of a well-deserved rest and a peaceful evening grew, marking the end of another successful leg.

The next morning, Jasper and Emma departed from the marina, ready to tackle the width of Mobile Bay.

The sun was just beginning to rise, casting a golden hue over the tranquil waters. As they left the protection of the marina and ventured out into the bay, they felt a renewed sense of adventure.

The bay's vast waters stretched out before them, a shimmering body of water that promised both beauty and challenge. The early morning light danced across the surface, setting the tone for an invigorating day on the water.

Jasper carefully navigated Arabella through the bay, his experienced hands steady on the wheel. Emma stood by his side, taking in the panoramic views of the open water and the distant coastline. The transition from the confined waterways they had been navigating to the wide-open bay was exhilarating.

Emma couldn't wait for the bay to end, the combination of it being a busy commercial corridor and being wide open made her uneasy.

A few hours later as they completed their crossing of Mobile Bay, Jasper navigated Arabella into the Gulf Intracoastal Waterway. The transition from the expansive bay to the more sheltered waterway was both smooth and relieving.

The Gulf Intracoastal Waterway stretched out before them, a carefully maintained channel that offered a more protected route through the coastal regions. As they entered, the scenery changed dramatically. It was narrower, flanked by lush marshlands and scenic waterfronts.

Jasper adjusted the navigation settings, ensuring they stayed on course within the well-marked channel. Emma took over the tiller as she enjoyed the new surroundings, marveling at the changing landscape. The waterway offered a different kind of beauty—serene and tranquil, with occasional glimpses of wildlife including Emma's first pelicans.

The Gulf Intracoastal Waterway provided a unique perspective on the region, with its intricate network of canals and inlets weaving through picturesque environments. As they cruised along, Emma and Jasper enjoyed the slower pace and the chance to appreciate the subtler details of the coastline. The journey through the waterway was a refreshing change, offering both relaxation and a deeper connection to the natural beauty of the Gulf Coast.

It wasn't long before Emma and Jasper entered the Florida Panhandle, greeted by a stunning transformation in their surroundings. The Gulf Intracoastal Waterway began to open up to reveal the region's renowned beauty.

As they cruised along, the landscape shifted to reveal the picturesque coastline. The sandy shores were lined with pristine, white-sand beaches that seemed to stretch endlessly. The turquoise waters of the Gulf of Mexico sparkled under the bright sun, offering a breathtaking contrast to the more muted hues they had encountered earlier.

The clarity and vibrant colors of the water were mesmerizing, and the gentle waves lapped softly against the boat, creating a soothing rhythm. The beaches, with their inviting allure, were dotted with a mix of vacationers and local beachgoers, adding a lively and joyful ambiance to the scene.

Emma and Jasper took full advantage of the spectacular views, their spirits lifted by the sight of such natural beauty. All of a sudden, Emma let out a joyful, excited scream. "Look, Grandpa! Look!" she exclaimed, her voice brimming with delight. She pointed eagerly towards the side of the boat.

Jasper turned around and followed her gaze, his eyes widening in surprise and wonder. Just alongside Arabella, a small school of dolphins was leaping and playing in the water. Their sleek bodies glistened in the sunlight as they frolicked beside the boat, their playful antics creating a spectacle of graceful arcs and splashes.

Emma's laughter and cheers were filled with pure joy as she watched the dolphins, her enthusiasm infectious. Jasper grinned, captivated by the sight of the dolphins' acrobatic displays and the sheer beauty of the moment.

It was a magical encounter, definitely one of the highlights of their journey that perfectly complemented the stunning scenery.

To make the moment even more special, Scott and Samantha, who were now traveling just a day ahead of Emma and Jasper, called. They planned to meet up with Emma and Jasper in Apalachicola, perfectly timed before their crossing of the Gulf Coast.

That night, Emma and Jasper anchored Arabella next to a small island with a stunning white-sand beach. The island's pristine shoreline gleamed under the setting sun, casting a warm, golden glow across the tranquil waters. The peaceful surroundings offered a perfect retreat after a day of exploration. The beach, framed by lush vegetation and with no signs of human development, felt like a secluded paradise.

As the sun dipped below the horizon, Emma and Jasper took a moment to appreciate the beauty of their temporary anchorage. They enjoyed a quiet evening on deck, the sky above painted with hues of orange and pink as twilight settled in. The view was breathtaking, and the peaceful ambiance made it an ideal setting for a relaxing night.

Jasper awoke as usual for his morning routine, brewed a fresh cup of coffee, and settled into the cockpit with his book, waiting for Emma to stir.

After some time, he heard splashing noises and looked up to see Emma swimming back towards the boat. She had woken up early, swam to the nearby island, and was now returning with a bright, enthusiastic smile.

"Come on in, Grandpa! The water's a bit cool, but it's beautiful!" she called from the water. Jasper grinned back at her. "Give me a minute, I've got a better idea," he replied.

He quickly disappeared into his cabin and in a short time reappeared with a cooler bag and a case.

Lowering the dinghy into the water, Jasper started rowing towards Emma. "Grab onto the back Emma," he instructed. Emma held onto the dinghy as Jasper rowed them to the island.

Once they reached the island, Jasper pulled out the case inside was masks and fins and a yellow and red box with two long coiled hoses coming out of it. "What's that?" Emma asked, pointing to the equipment laid out on the deck.

"It's a Hookah diving system," he replied, grinning. "I bought it for cleaning and working on the bottom of the boat, but I hear there's some fantastic coral around here. I thought we'd check it out."

"Really? That sounds amazing!" Emma's eyes sparkled with excitement. Emma nodded, her curiosity growing. "How does it work?" "Simple the box floats and inside is a battery and compressor that pushes the air down the hose to us." he said, showing her the gear.

"We'll go over the signals to use underwater, and I'll make sure you're comfortable with everything. Once we're down, just relax and take it all in. The coral should be vibrant, and you might even see some cool fish."

After a quick briefing, they donned their masks and fins, then slipped into the water, the warm waves enveloping them. As they descended, sunlight filtered through the surface, casting shimmering patterns on the ocean floor.

Emma's breath caught in her throat when they reached the coral reef. It was a kaleidoscope of colors—blues, purples, and yellows danced together in a mesmerizing display. Fish darted among the corals, adding to the vibrant scene.

Emma signaled, pointing to a school of bright parrotfish grazing on the reef. He smiled, nodding, and together they floated above the coral, their worries forgotten in the wonder of the underwater world.

After their dive they made their way to a picturesque spot on the beach. Jasper spread out a blanket and unpacked containers of food he had brought. "I thought it would be nice to have breakfast on the beach before we set off again," Jasper said, his eyes twinkling with excitement.

Emma's face lit up with delight as they settled onto the blanket, enjoying the tranquil beach setting and the delicious breakfast Jasper had prepared. It was the perfect start to their day,

"This is such a perfect spot," Emma said, her eyes scanning the idyllic beach and sparkling water. "Couldn't we stay here for the whole day?" Jasper shook his head with a gentle smile. "I'm afraid not. We promised Scott and Samantha we'd meet them tomorrow. But don't worry—there will be plenty of other spots like this one, I promise."

Emma's smile faltered slightly, a touch of disappointment in her eyes. "Well, okay. It looks like it's going to cloud over soon anyway," she conceded, glancing up at the darkening sky.

After they enjoyed their leisurely breakfast on the beach, they packed up and returned to Arabella. As the clouds began to gather, Jasper and Emma set off, ready to continue their journey with the anticipation of reuniting with their friends and exploring more beautiful destinations ahead.

Later that evening, Jasper and Emma arrived at the marina in Apalachicola and carefully maneuvered Arabella into their assigned slip. The location was conveniently close to where Scott and Samantha's boat, Singing Swallows, was docked.

After securing the lines and ensuring everything was in place, Jasper and Emma made their way over to Singing Swallows. Jasper knocked on the cabin door and waited. After a short pause, Scott's head appeared from the hatch. "Hi, guys! How about grabbing some dinner?" Jasper asked.

Scott looked back into the cabin, where Samantha's giggling was clearly audible. "Give us ten... twenty minutes," Scott replied, his voice tinged with amusement. "We're just finishing up something." Realizing they had interrupted a private moment, Jasper and Emma quickly offered, "Take your time. We're just moored over here—when you're ready."

With that, they retreated back to Arabella, trying to hide their smiles. They then settled in for a bit.

After what turned out to be closer to an hour, Scott and Samantha finally arrived at Arabella. Scott greeted them with a warm smile, "Hi guys! Sorry about the delay. It's great to see you again."

Emma and Jasper, still feeling a bit embarrassed from their earlier interruption, returned the greeting with friendly smiles. "Great to see you too," Jasper responded, trying to hide his lingering discomfort. "Yes, wonderful to see you," Emma added with a nod.

Samantha quickly took charge of the next part of the evening. "So, where do you guys feel like eating?" she asked.

Jasper and Emma exchanged glances, noting the casual attire of their friends—Scott in cutoffs and a t-shirt, and Samantha in yoga shorts with a sports bra, casually draped with a shirt. The laid-back outfits suggested a preference for a relaxed dining experience.

"Somewhere casual?" Jasper said, catching on. "We're up for anything that's local and laid-back." Emma nodded in agreement. "Yes, a casual spot would be great. We're looking forward to a relaxed evening."

"How about just the restaurant here at the marina? It looks like it has a nice patio" Asked Emma. "That sounds great sweety" Samantha said emphasizing her S's. With that the four headed up the dock to the restaurant's patio. As they walked, the conversation flowed effortlessly, filled with stories and laughter, making it clear that the reunion was already off to a fantastic start.

After they were seated and had placed their orders, the conversation naturally shifted to discussing their journeys and experiences since they last met. Emma began sharing updates about her family with Samantha.

"I've been keeping in touch with Antoine and my dad regularly. We still video chat most nights," she said, her eyes lighting up as she spoke. "One night, I even managed to set up a three-way video call and introduced my dad to Antoine. It was a pretty special moment for all of us."

Samantha smiled warmly. "That sounds wonderful." Emma nodded. "It's always great to see their reactions and share some of this journey with them, even from afar. It made me feel a bit closer to home."

As the evening continued, Jasper and Scott joined in, recounting their own experiences and catching up on the latest developments. The camaraderie and shared excitement about their travels made for an engaging and enjoyable dinner, setting the stage for a memorable night of reconnecting and storytelling.

However after a few hours Jasper announced he had a long day and was ready to go back to bed. Scott then said "I'm actually tired myself so I'm going back as well. You girls coming?". Samantha quickly said "You're not tired are you Emma?"

Before Emma even got a chance to answer Samantha continued "We are going to stay and have a couple more drinks we will see you guys back onboard."

Jasper looked at Emma and she gave him a smile as she shrugged her shoulders "Ok we will see you later then" answered Jasper. Scott turned to Emma "Ok goodnight Emma" Then turned to Samantha, winked at her and said "I'll be waiting for you sexy" and gave her a kiss.

Once the guys were out of hearing range, Samantha turned to Emma with a curious expression. "So, things are getting really serious with Antoine? Does your dad like him?" she asked, her tone eager and inquisitive.

Emma smiled, enjoying the chance to share more about her personal life. She answered Samantha's questions to the best of her ability, discussing her relationship with Antoine and the positive feedback from her dad. Their conversation flowed easily, touching on various aspects of her life.

After a few hours, Samantha made a comment that made Emma's heart lift. "I can't wait to meet him," Samantha said, her enthusiasm clear.

Emma was heartened by Samantha's comment about looking forward to meeting Antoine. It made her feel that their friendship would continue even after this adventure. "Well, we could video call him now on my phone," Emma suggested, excited about the idea.

Samantha started shaking her head. "No, not tonight. I've been drinking and I want to make a good first impression," she explained, her tone firm but polite. Emma found this response a bit odd coming from Samantha but accepted it, thinking that perhaps Samantha simply wanted to be at her best when meeting Antoine.

"Well, it's getting late, and we have an early start tomorrow. This will be our first leg of the big bend.

Are you ready for some open ocean?" Emma asked, shifting the focus to their upcoming journey. Samantha nodded with confidence. "We've already tackled Lake Michigan, and the weather looks promising for tomorrow, so I'm sure I'll be fine. You're right, though—it is getting late."

With that, the two friends settled their bill and headed back to their respective boats for the night.

The next day proved to be a bit of a marathon of a journey. The group was up before dawn, their excitement tempered by the long day ahead. As they cruised along the sun slowly began to rise, casting a warm, golden glow that gradually transformed the dark, inky blue of the night into vibrant shades of amber and coral.

The water, calm and nearly mirror-like, began to catch the light, creating a dazzling display of ripples that sparkled as if adorned with thousands of tiny diamonds. As the sun rose higher, its light spread across the deck of *Arabella*, warming the cool morning air. The gentle breeze carried the fresh scent of saltwater, and the soft lapping of waves against the hull provided a soothing accompaniment to the sunrise.

They spent the next sixteen hours crossing the first leg of the Big Bend, navigating the open waters of the Gulf of Mexico.

As night began to fall, they neared Cedar Key. The sky had darkened significantly by the time they approached their anchorage. Navigating through the dark waters and finding their way required careful coordination and concentration. Finally, they managed to secure their boats in the anchorage.

With the anchor set, the group slipped into their evening routine. Exhaustion was evident, but there was also a deep sense of satisfaction from having successfully completed a challenging leg of their journey.

As the stars began to emerge in the clear night sky, they took a moment to enjoy the peaceful surroundings and reflect on the day's adventure. The quiet of the anchorage, provided a placid end of a demanding but rewarding day.

The next day followed a similar pattern, though it was a bit shorter in duration. Taking advantage of the more relaxed pace, Emma and Jasper decided to enjoy a later start. Their laid-back approach, however, meant they arrived at Crystal River after dark again.

This time, they were docking at a marina conveniently situated in town. As they eased into their slips and secured Arabella, Jasper turned to Emma and informed her that "because higher winds are forecasted, we'll be staying in Crystal River for a couple of days," he explained. "I've already spoken to Scott and Samantha. We're planning to have brunch together tomorrow. Is that ok?"

Emma's face lit up with anticipation. "That sounds fantastic! It'll be great to stay still for a couple days. Maybe get in a couple more writing lessons."

With the boats safely docked and plans in place for a leisurely brunch, Emma and Jasper settled in for the night. The marina, with its proximity to town, offered a different kind of charm, and they looked forward to exploring the area the following day.

The next morning arrived with a gentle, leisurely pace. After a while, Emma turned to Jasper and asked, "Should we start getting ready to head out for brunch?" Jasper glanced at the clock and replied, "Scott and Samantha are meeting us at the restaurant around eleven-thirty, so we still have some time."

As the morning progressed, they took their time preparing, enjoying the relaxed atmosphere that the marina and Crystal

River offered. Eventually, the clock edged closer to their planned meeting time, and Jasper and Emma made their way to the restaurant.

As Emma and Jasper arrived at the restaurant, they entered and began searching for the table where Scott and Samantha were supposed to be seated. Their eyes scanned the room until Emma's gaze landed on a familiar face at a table that included Scott, Samantha, and - unexpectedly - Antoine.

Emma's breath caught in her throat, and her eyes welled up with emotion. "Wha..." she began, her voice trembling. Without waiting for a response, she rushed over to the table and enveloped Antoine in a heartfelt hug. "What are you doing here?" she asked, her voice a mix of surprise and joy.

Antoine's smile was warm and reassuring. "It's my winter vacation. I'm joining you for the next two weeks, till just after Christmas" he said, his eyes twinkling with excitement.

Emma's heart raced, her emotions a whirlwind of happiness and disbelief. The unexpected reunion was more than she could have hoped for, and as she held Antoine close, the moment felt surreal and perfect.

Samantha beamed with excitement as she explained, "He flew into Tampa, and Scott and I rented a car early this morning to pick him up.

I didn't want to call him last night because I was afraid I'd spoil the surprise."

Jasper added with a grin, "Yes Antoine messaged me and we arranged most of this, then I enlisted the help of Scott and Samantha to pull it off.

That's also why I didn't want to stay an extra night on that island. I was already bending the cruiser's golden rule of 'Don't travel on a schedule,' but we needed to be here today. And yes, Antoine will be with us for two weeks. I'm not putting you guys up in a hotel this time, but I'll swap cabins so you can have the larger one during his visit."

Scott then chimed in, "We rented two double kayaks for this afternoon to explore the manatees and the crystal-clear waters. I was hoping Jasper would join us, but it seems he is set on staying behind." Jasper shrugged and replied, "I'll be tackling some maintenance while you're out. But enjoy kayaking! I'll make sure everything's in top shape for when you get back."

Emma finally released Antoine from her tight embrace, her eyes still glistening with joyful tears. "But you don't know how to kayak, and you're scared of the water?" Antoine smiled warmly and replied, "I know, but you love kayaking, and I figured it's time to face my fears.

I've been taking lessons back home." Emma's tears of happiness flowed freely as she pulled Antoine back into a heartfelt hug. The gesture meant more to her than words could express.

Samantha, with a playful tone, broke the emotional moment. "Okay, if you two are done, can we please order brunch? I'm starving!" With a collective chuckle, they agreed and settled into their seats.

After brunch, they wheeled Jasper back to Arabella and then made their way to the kayak rental place. The process was quick; they filled out the paperwork and paid the deposit.

As Emma took her seat in the kayak, she was immediately struck by the vibrant colors beneath the surface. The clarity of the water revealed a mesmerizing underwater landscape, with rocks and sand shimmering in hues of turquoise, pink and emerald.

Her awe quickly turned to delight when she spotted a group of manatees gently moving through the water. There was a whole congregation of these gentle giants, their movements and endearing faces captivating Emma.

She couldn't help but marvel at how adorable they looked as they floated and grazed, their grayish bodies contrasting beautifully against the clear water.

Emma was so excited as she whispered to Antoine, pointing out the manatees. "Look at them! They're even cuter than I imagined!" The experience was magical, a perfect blend of natural beauty and personal triumph as Antoine faced his fears and Emma reveled in the stunning surroundings.

As Emma paddled through the crystal-clear waters, surrounded by the gentle manatees, she couldn't help but reflect on how much her life had transformed since last spring. From never having ventured beyond her hometown in the Adirondacks to kayaking with manatees in Florida alongside a man who truly loves her, she felt a profound sense of gratitude and contentment.

But in the midst of her joy, a shadow of doubt crept in. She couldn't shake the worry that, once this trip was over, Antoine might discover her phobia and be disappointed.

The thought of their long-distance relationship ending loomed in the back of her mind, and she grappled with the fear that such relationships often didn't survive the distance.

Yet, as she looked around at the idyllic scene—the sunlit water, the playful manatees, and Antoine's supportive presence—she reminded herself that those concerns were for another day.

She was living in the present, savoring every moment of this extraordinary journey. With that realization, her smile returned, bright and untroubled. Emma resolved to focus on the happiness of today, letting go of worries about the future and fully embracing the magic of the moment.

The two pairs spent the day kayaking through the enchanting waters of Crystal River, exploring the clear blue depths and delighting in the playful manatees.

As the evening approached, they returned to their marina, their hearts full from the day's adventures.

After docking and switching cabins to accommodate Antoine, Emma settled into her new space with a sense of anticipation. Once everything was in order, she eagerly picked up her phone and called her dad to share the exciting news. "Dad, you won't believe the day we had!" Emma began, her voice brimming with enthusiasm. "We spent the whole day kayaking in Crystal River, and Antoine is here with us for the next two weeks!"

She went on to recount the beauty of the clear waters, the awe-inspiring manatees, and the surprise of having Antoine join them. She relished every moment of sharing these special details with her dad. As the conversation continued, Emma's joy was evident. She was grateful for the unexpected turn her journey had taken and couldn't wait for her dad to hear all about it.

For the next couple of days Jasper, Emma, Antoine, Scott, and Samantha enjoyed their time in Crystal River, savoring the relaxed pace and exploring the charming surroundings. The anticipation of their next leg of the journey lingered in the air as Jasper and Scott closely monitored the weather conditions, waiting for the ideal window to continue their trip across the Gulf.

Finally, after two days of patience, Jasper and Scott agreed that the conditions were right. They decided to depart that night around eleven, aiming to make the most of the favorable weather and reach Tarpon Springs before dusk the following day.

Emma was both excited and apprehensive about the night cruising ahead. She had never done much at night before, and the idea of navigating in the dark was new to her. Antoine, on the other hand, found a certain reassurance in the night's obscurity, figuring that the reduced visibility might actually help ease his anxiety about the open water.

As they set out under the cover of night, the water was calm, and the skies were clear, allowing them to make steady progress.

The tranquil darkness provided a serene journey, and the gentle rocking of the boat was soothing.

When dawn finally broke, the sunrise over the Gulf was nothing short of spectacular. The sky was painted in brilliant hues of orange, pink, and gold, reflecting off the calm waters. The sight was a perfect reward for their overnight journey, a breathtaking reminder of the beauty that awaited them as they continued.

Emma, Antoine, and the others watched in awe as the sun climbed higher, illuminating their path and signaling the approach of another exciting day.

As they continued across the Gulf, the day wore on. Antoine's initial fear had faded, but the journey was growing tedious. At last, he spotted land and shouted, "Land Ho!" His laughter brought a few smiles to the crew. As they approached, the channel became visible, and shortly after, they reached the anchorage.

After both boats had anchored securely, Scott called across the water to Arabella with a cheerful shout. "How about after we eat, you guys come over? Samantha will blend us some drinks, and we can celebrate crossing the Gulf!"

Jasper glanced over at Emma and Antoine, who were both nodding enthusiastically. "Sounds great. We'll let you know when we're done eating," Jasper responded. "Perfect! See you then," Scott replied.

Antoine turned to Jasper with a bright smile. "Oh, and just so you know, Jasper, Emma and I are making supper tonight. We're preparing a traditional French-Canadian meal called Guédille. We found all the ingredients at a market in Crystal River."

Jasper grinned and said, "As long as it's not Poutine—my stomach can't handle that super greasy stuff!" Scott chimed in, "Nope, no Poutine, just Guédille. It's not greasy at all." "Sounds great," Jasper said, pleased. He was always eager to try new foods and was relieved he didn't have to cook tonight.

In the galley of Arabella, Emma and Antoine worked seamlessly together. Antoine took charge of the cooking, while Emma kept him company and helped with preparations. They made three plates of Guédille, each featuring two freshly baked buns resembling hoagie rolls more than hotdog buns. These were generously filled with tender lobster pieces and a mix of complementary ingredients.

When they were ready, Emma and Antoine brought the plates out to the cockpit where Jasper was waiting. He took his first bite and exclaimed, "Mmm, this is delicious! It's a lot like a New England Lobster Roll, right?" Antoine laughed and replied, "I wouldn't know; I've never had a Lobster Roll before!"

They finished their meal with satisfaction, savoring the rich flavors and the company. Afterward, they radioed Scott and Samantha to let them know they were ready and then made their way over to Singing Swallows for drinks and a celebratory evening.

As they enjoyed their drinks, Scott stood up and clinked his glass to get everyone's attention. "I have a toast to make," he began, a broad smile on his face. "Here's to three great new friends. Even though it hasn't been that long, it feels like we've known each other much longer. And to continue our friendship even after we cross our wake in Jersey; To Emma, Jasper, and Antoine—may our shared experiences continue to create lasting memories and strengthen our bond. Cheers! "

Everyone raised their glasses and joined in the heartfelt toast. "Cheers!" they echoed, their glasses clinking in celebration. Then Emma quietly turned to Jasper "what does 'crossing our wake' mean?" Jasper whispered back "Finished the loop. Remember they started in New Jersey".

As the evening progressed, laughter and conversation flowed freely, the perfect end to a day full of new experiences.

Emma, feeling content and surrounded by friends, reflected on how much this journey had given her so far. From the stunning views of the Gulf to the camaraderie with Scott, Samantha, and of course Antoine, it was clear that this adventure was more than just a trip—it was an unforgettable chapter in her life.

Chapter 13

Umm, No, It's Just That...

After covering just fifteen miles the following day, Emma, Jasper, and Antoine anchored in a delightful spot right next to the Clearwater Marine Aquarium.

Jasper glanced at Emma with a grin and said, "You know, Emma, I've always had a soft spot for aquariums. I bet you'd love this one, especially since it doubles as a rehabilitation center. It's actually quite famous—there's a movie about a dolphin that lost its tail and got a prosthetic one from this place."

Emma's eyes lit up with excitement. "I know that movie! It was so touching. Oh please, can we go? It sounds amazing!" Antoine, who had been listening intently, chimed in, "I'm in too. I've always wanted to visit a place like this."

Jasper chuckled, "Great! I'll call Scott and Samantha to see if they want to join us. In the meantime, could you get my wheelchair into the dinghy?"

With Scott and Samantha opting for a relaxing day aboard their boat, Emma, Jasper, and Antoine set off to explore the aquarium.

Upon arrival, they were warmly greeted by the friendly staff and the vibrant atmosphere of the Clearwater Marine Aquarium.

The aquarium's dedication to marine animal rescue and rehabilitation was immediately apparent and deeply impressive.

Their first stop was the sea turtle rehabilitation area, where they watched several turtles recovering from injuries. Jasper was fascinated by the advanced techniques used in their care and admired the top-notch facilities designed to aid their recovery. Emma and Antoine were both moved by the touching stories of each turtle and their progress back to health.

They then visited the dolphin and manatee exhibits, marveling at these incredible creatures up close. Wandering through the touch tanks, Emma's face lit up with joy as she gently handled starfish and sea urchins, while Antoine enjoyed seeing her excitement and learning about marine life.

Before leaving, Emma, Jasper and Antoine stopped by the gift shop, where Emma picked out a small dolphin figurine as a memento of their visit. Returning to their boat late in the afternoon, Emma was eager to call her dad and share her experiences at the aquarium, along with the incredible stories she had learned about the marine animals. Ben was thrilled to hear all about her day.

After a few minutes of catching up, Ben finally managed to interject, "Emma, there's something I want to talk to you about." Emma's excitement faded as she asked, "What is it Dad? Are you okay?"

Ben's voice was calm and reassuring. "I'm fine, sweetheart. But I've been doing some thinking. I've always loved your mother dearly, and I always will. After the accident, it was just you and me, and you became my entire world. But now, I've come to realize that I need to start living for myself too. You won't be living at home forever."

He continued, "A coworker of mine set me up on a blind date recently, and it went really well. We've been seeing each other more often, and now I guess I have a girlfriend. To be honest, it was your courage and zest for life that inspired me to take this step."

Emma listened, her heart swelling with a mix of happiness and shock. After a long pause, she finally replied, "I'm sorry Dad, I'm just in shock. Please tell me more about her." Ben chuckled softly. "Her name is Audra. She has auburn hair and she's twenty-two years old."

Emma's eyes widened. There was another long pause before she finally managed to speak. "Twenty-two? Are you serious Dad? That's the same age as me!" Ben responded, "Do you think that's too young for me? Do you think I'm too old?"

Emma stammered, "Umm, no, it's just that..."

Ben cut her off with a laugh. "Relax, Emma! I'm just messing with you. Twenty-two is way too young for me. Audra is actually about the same age as I am, and I think you'd really like her. And don't worry, we're taking it slow."

Emma's initial shock began to dissolve into laughter. "Okay, you got me. I'm glad to hear that you're both happy and taking things at your own pace. I'm really happy for you, Dad."

Ben's voice was filled with relief and happiness. "Thank you, Emma. I was a bit nervous about telling you, but your support means the world to me. I just wanted to be open with you about what's going on in my life right now."

Emma's curiosity was piqued. "So, tell me more about her?" "Well, she's divorced, has green eyes, and owns a charming little antique shop down in Whitehall. What else do you want to know?" replied Ben.

Emma laughed softly. "Just everything, Dad. Absolutely everything."

Ben's voice softened with sincerity. "Audra is a truly wonderful person. She spends her days curating and restoring unique pieces, and she loves sharing the stories behind them. We've been having such a great time together—exploring local events, cooking new recipes, and just enjoying each other's company. It's been a long time since I've felt this content."

Emma's eyes softened with affection. "I can't wait to meet Audra when I get back." Ben's tone was full of anticipation. "I'm looking forward to that, too. It'll be great for you to meet her. Thanks for being so understanding and supportive. It means a lot to me."

Ben and Emma continued their conversation for hours. Unlike their usual calls where Emma did most of the talking, this time Ben took the lead, sharing stories and details about his new relationship. Emma found herself deeply moved by her father's happiness.

The next day, the two boats continued down the Gulf Intracoastal Waterway, navigating through a densely built-up area where houses and buildings lined the shoreline.

As the sun began to set, they approached their chosen anchorage with caution, noticing a group of people doing yoga on stand-up paddle boards nearby.

After finally settling the boats for the night, Jasper and Emma prepared to enjoy their meal. Just as they were about to start eating, Emma's phone rang. It was Samantha.

"Hi Emma! I've got some exciting news," Samantha's voice came through cheerfully. "I talked to the coach of that yoga class we saw, and they can fit us in for a session tomorrow morning. I know Scott isn't interested, and I doubt Antoine and Jasper will want to join us, but how about you and I give it a try? I think it could be a lot of fun!"

Emma hesitated. "I've never done yoga before, and doing it on a paddle board sounds really intimidating."

Samantha chuckled softly. "I understand, Emma. I've done yoga instructional videos, but I've never tried it on a paddle board either. I'm probably going to end up in the water more than you will. But come on, yoga isn't that difficult, and sometimes you've got to face your fears. Plus, you know Antoine says the same thing about facing your fears."

Emma thought about it for a moment. "It could be fun, and Antoine did give the same advice about facing your fears. "Okay, why not? I'm in!" Samantha's enthusiasm was evident. "Great! I'm excited. It'll be an amazing day, and we'll have a blast. See you in the morning!"

"Um, Emma, by any chance, do you have another swimsuit besides the... let's call it 'classic' black swimsuit you wore the other day?" Samantha asked hesitantly.

Emma was taken aback. "What's wrong with it?"

Samantha, sounding apologetic, replied, "I'm sorry, it's just a bit out of style. By which I mean, a nun would think it covers too much." Emma's eyes widened. "Well, I do have a bikini I've never worn before. It was a gift, and it doesn't cover much. To be honest, I'm embarrassed to wear it."

Samantha burst into laughter. "Emma, you need to relax! You have a great physique, and I'm sure you'll look fantastic in it. I can't wait to see you in it. The class is at eight, so I'll pick you up in the dinghy at about quarter to eight. Have a great night, and I'll see you in the morning!"

Emma ended the call, feeling a mix of anxiety and excitement. Despite her initial embarrassment, she decided to embrace the challenge and the fun of trying something new. She settled into their nightly routine, mentally preparing for the unique experience ahead.

The next morning arrived early. Emma had set an alarm to make sure she was up in time, and the sound of it roused both her and Antoine. As Emma prepared for the day, Antoine popped his head out of the cabin hatch and noticed Jasper already settled in his spot. "Coffee, Jasper?" Antoine called out. "Please," Jasper replied.

Antoine quickly made three coffees, handing one to Emma. "I know you don't function well before your morning coffee, so take a minute and enjoy."

He then went to the cockpit to give Jasper his coffee. A few minutes later, Emma emerged wearing the pink and white striped bikini she had. She felt self-conscious and tried to cover herself with her arms and hands. Antoine's eyes lit up as he exclaimed, "Wow, Emma, you look amazing!" Jasper, chuckling, added, "Antoine, close your mouth, you're drooling!"

The group shared a laugh, and Emma's embarrassment began to fade. They enjoyed a brief, relaxing moment with their coffees.

Soon, they heard the sound of Samantha rowing over. She appeared in a red satin bikini that left little to the imagination—much more revealing than Emma's. Everyone's eyes widened in surprise at how little it covered. As Samantha bent over to tie off her dinghy to Arabella, it became clear that the bottom was just a thong.

Emma shot a sharp glance at Antoine. "Eyes over here," she said with a smirk. Antoine didn't care; in his mind Emma was the most beautiful girl in the world and he thought Samantha was a bit too bold for his taste.

Samantha joined them with a cheerful wave. "Ready for some yoga?"

The two girls set off in the dinghy and met up with the group, which was already gathering. As the class began, there was a lot of splashing and laughter.

Emma and Samantha found themselves struggling to stay balanced on their paddleboards while trying to follow the yoga poses. Emma spent more time in the water than on the board, but she didn't mind at all. She was having an absolute blast, laughing along with Samantha and the others.

After an hour of fun-filled attempts and plenty of tumbles, the class concluded. Both Emma and Samantha returned to their boats thoroughly soaked but beaming with happiness. Once back aboard, Emma headed below deck to dry off and change, eager to shed her wet swimsuit and enjoy the rest of the day.

After Emma had finished changing, the group weighed anchor and set off again. It turned out to be a perfect day—neither too hot nor too cold, with a gentle breeze guiding them along the Gulf Intracoastal Waterway. They arrived at a large marina in Cape Coral by evening. Eager for a change of pace, the group decided to go out for food and drinks.

As they sat at the table, enjoying their meal, Jasper turned to Emma and said, "Scott and I were talking, and tomorrow we'll start on the Okeechobee Waterway. It cuts across Florida and exits at Stuart, which is about a hundred and twenty miles north of Miami.

I know I said we could see Miami when we left, but that would mean days there and days back. Scott and Samantha have been there many times, and I've never had much desire to go. But I don't want to let you down. If you want, we can go and meet up with Scott and Samantha somewhere further along the loop."

Emma glanced at Antoine, who suggested, "We could plan another trip to Miami at a later date, perhaps fly or drive down."

Emma noted the look of reluctance on Jasper's face and saw how much he preferred not to go to Miami. She also appreciated traveling with Scott and Samantha and knew if she didn't go now, she might never get another chance. She also knew there was no way she was getting into a car or airplane.

"No, it's not worth it," Emma decided. "Let's just head north from here." Jasper looked relieved. "Are you sure?" "Yes, I'm sure. There are still lots to see yet along the loop," Emma affirmed.

"Well, it's getting late. I think I'm going to head back to the boat," Jasper said. "Yep, I agree," Scott added. With that, they settled the bill and made their way back to their boats, content with the decision.

The next morning, as they began their journey through the Okeechobee Waterway, Jasper took a moment to remind Emma of a few important things. "Emma, just a heads-up. Parts of the waterway passes through the Everglades, which is home to some potentially dangerous wildlife. I know on occasion you enjoy going for a swim, but it's important to be cautious here. Alligators and other critters are known to roam these waters."

Emma was thrilled about exploring this new section, so different from the Adirondack Mountains where she was raised.

The prospect of experiencing the unique landscapes and wildlife of the Everglades intrigued her.

"I'm really excited about this," Jasper smiled, pleased with her enthusiasm and understanding. "That's the spirit. It's going to be an amazing experience, and you'll get to see a whole different side of Florida. Just stay aware, and you'll be fine."

As they continued their journey through the Okeechobee Waterway, Emma was captivated by the striking contrast from the bustling urban areas they had passed to the subtropical wetlands of the Everglades. The transition from cityscapes to the vast expanses of the Everglades was breathtaking, and Emma eagerly took in every detail.

It wasn't long however till everything started to look the same. It started to make for a very long day.

At least navigating through the locks added a welcome change of pace to their day.

The nice wind that accompanied them throughout the day was a blessing, keeping the heat at bay. However, because of that same wind, Jasper and Scott decided it would be wiser to take the protected route around the southern edge of Lake Okeechobee rather than risk crossing the open waters of Florida's largest lake.

After more than eight hours on the water, they finally reached their anchorage at the southern end of the lake. The spot was idyllic, nestled among lush vegetation and featuring a large tree adorned with dozens of cormorants perched on its branches.

The sight was both peaceful and picturesque, offering a great end to their long day of travel.

As evening settled in, Jasper called over to Emma with a hint of excitement in his voice. "Look, right there, going into the water!" Emma turned swiftly, her eyes widening as she caught a glimpse of an alligator sliding beneath the surface.

"That was incredible!" she exclaimed, her voice filled with delight. Jasper chuckled, "I know! It's hard to believe it took us this long to finally spot one." With that they retired for the night, Tomorrow was going to be another long one.

The following day, they completed the final stretch of the Okeechobee Waterway, navigating through lush, verdant landscapes and tranquil waters, offering a peaceful end to their crossing. By afternoon, they reached their anchorage, located at the Eastern terminus of the St. Lucie River.

This anchorage was perfectly situated near where the St. Lucie River converges with the Atlantic Intracoastal Waterway. The location provided a strategic vantage point, with views stretching out towards the broader, more open waters of the Intracoastal. It was a picturesque spot, offering a mix of calm waters and the occasional sight of boats making their way along the busy waterway.

The area around the anchorage began to come alive with the soft glow of the setting sun reflecting off the water. The quiet was punctuated by the occasional call of distant birds and the gentle lapping of water against the hulls of the boats. The two boats took advantage of the beautiful evening, enjoying a relaxed dinner on deck and discussing the day's travels.

The transition from the peacefulness of the Everglades to the bustling waterways that lay ahead marked an exciting new chapter in their voyage.

Chapter 14

Reverberate Through Their Very Bones

Ben and Audra were nestled into a cozy booth at Tico's Diner, The soft hum of conversation and the clinking of dishes created a comforting backdrop as they delved into their discussion about the upcoming Christmas holidays.

The diner, decked out in its festive decorations, added a touch of holiday cheer to their conversation. Twinkling lights adorned the windows, and a cheerful Christmas playlist softly played in the background, setting a nostalgic tone.

Audra, her green eyes sparkling with excitement, leaned forward slightly. "So, have you given any thought to how you want to spend Christmas this year?" she asked, her tone brimming with anticipation.

Ben, his expression thoughtful, stirred his coffee absentmindedly. "I've been thinking about it. This will be our first Christmas together, so I want it to be special. Maybe we could do something traditional, like decorating a tree and cooking a big holiday meal. But I'm also open to new ideas. What do you have in mind?"

Audra's smile softened, her auburn hair catching the light from the diner's vintage-style lamp. "I love the idea of decorating a tree. We could have a cozy night with holiday movies and some homemade cookies. However, I've been hearing you talk about your wonderful daughter and how much you miss her since I met you. Why don't we take a little trip together?"

Ben's expression grew somber as he stirred his coffee. "I'd love that, but... she's with my father right now, and I've mentioned how I feel about him."

Audra's gaze grew sympathetic. "Yes, but you haven't shared why. I understand it's a sensitive topic, but it seems to me that the trip you're describing sounds like something special for her. Perhaps the good he's doing now might outweigh the mistakes of the past?"

Ben's voice sharpened, his emotions evident. "No. I appreciate your concern, but I can't reconcile that part of my past with the present. I'm sorry, Audra. Is there any chance we can change the subject?"

Audra, sensing the weight of his feelings, nodded gently. "Of course, Ben. Let's talk about something else. I just want you to know that I care about you and understand that there are things we might need to work through."

Ben gave her a grateful smile, appreciating her willingness to shift the conversation. They both took a moment to breathe, and soon, their discussion turned to lighter, more pleasant topics, as they continued to enjoy their meal their conversation flowed easily, punctuated by laughter.

Meanwhile, Antoine, Emma and Jasper were eager to start their day. As they weighed anchor and set their course, a pod of dolphins emerged, playfully darting alongside the boat. Emma's squeals of delight filled the air; their appearance always brought her immense joy.

"This is such a special moment," Jasper said, glancing at Emma with a grin. "We're no longer heading away from home; we're actually on a direct path back. Though, it's still about four or five months until we get there."

Emma's eyes sparkled with excitement as she watched dolphins leaping and swirling in the water. "I can hardly believe it! Even though we're heading home, there's still so much ahead of us."

As the dolphins gradually faded into the distance, the boat continued its journey northward. After a pleasant day of travel, they anchored in a large and bustling anchorage.

Emma reflected on the contrast between this lively, urban environment and the isolated stretches of the Canadian and Midwest rivers they had previously explored. "It's amazing how each town or city seems to blend seamlessly into the next," she mused, appreciating the dynamic and ever-changing scenery around them.

The following morning, as Emma and Antoine emerged into the cockpit, they found Jasper looking unusually emotional, his eyes glistening with unshed tears. "Guys, I want to make some time today," Jasper said, his voice unsteady.

Emma, noticing Jasper's distress, asked gently, "Sure, but are you okay?" Jasper met her gaze, trying to steady himself. "Yes, I'm fine. I just received a long message. I'll explain more about that later. But it's not the reason I want us to make it to Titusville before tomorrow morning."

Emma, sensing his urgency but trying to lift the mood, asked, "I don't understand why the rush. I thought you said you should never try to keep a schedule on a boat?"

Jasper managed a small, reassuring smile. "Well, there's a big surprise waiting for us. You'll see tomorrow morning if we make it." Emma's curiosity was piqued. "Okay Grandpa. I have to admit, your surprises so far have been pretty spectacular." She glanced at Antoine with a grin. "Can't wait to see what this one will be."

"Oh, and I also wanted to ask," Emma continued, "when is the next major provisioning stop?" Jasper responded, "We can do that before we leave Titusville. We're in no rush after that. Why?" Emma's face brightened. "Actually, with Christmas coming up, I was thinking of making a special meal. I wanted to get the ingredients for it."

Jasper's eyes lit up. "Well, if you don't mind, I thought I'd put you up in a hotel over Christmas. It's my Christmas gift to you. I figured you might enjoy some time without me. And to be honest, I'd rather be alone for the holidays. It's just a personal preference. Maybe someday I'll explain it to you, but not today."

Emma's expression softened with gratitude. "If you're sure, then thank you so much." Antoine nodded in agreement. "Yes, thank you, Jasper. You've already done so much for us." Jasper gave them both a warm smile. "It's my pleasure. I'm glad to do it."

"Emma, could you call Scott or Samantha and let them know I want to make it to Titusville today?" Jasper asked, his tone serious yet excited. "Sure, right away," Emma responded, heading to the radio.

A few minutes later, she returned with an inquisitive look on her face. "Grandpa, Scott thinks it's a great idea and says he knows why, but he wouldn't spill the beans to me either."

Emma's confusion was evident, and Jasper chuckled. "Don't worry about it, Emma. It's not about the town itself, so don't waste too much time trying to guess." Emma turned to Antoine, hoping for some insight. "Do you know what's going on?" Antoine shook his head. "Nope, Jasper never mentioned anything to me. And I've never heard of Titusville before, so I'm just as much in the dark."

Jasper grinned, clearly enjoying the mystery. "It's a surprise. You'll just have to wait and see. Trust me, it's worth it."

The rest of the day passed quickly as they continued their journey. By the time they reached their next anchorage, night had already fallen, and the area was bustling with activity. As they finished anchoring, Jasper commented, "Well, dawn comes early."

Antoine, with a playful grin, chimed in, "Yeah! Happens every morning just about sun up." It was a line he'd picked up from a movie. Jasper couldn't help but smirk at the reference. "Yes, Antoine, ha ha. Anyway, we should get some rest tonight."

With that, they each retreated to their cabins, ready to recharge for the exciting day ahead.

At four thirty the next morning, Jasper began knocking on Emma and Antoine's cabin door with increasing urgency. "Wake up, wake up! Come on, guys, wake up!" Emma and Antoine jolted awake. "Is everything okay? What's going on?" Antoine called out, still groggy.

"Yes, just come out into the cockpit. It's time for your surprise!" Jasper's voice rang back, full of excitement. Emma glanced at the clock and then at Antoine.

"A surprise at four thirty in the morning? I think he's lost his marbles. Well, let's go."

The two of them stumbled into the cockpit, still half-asleep. To their surprise, most of the boats in the anchorage were also awake, and almost everyone was gathered in their cockpits, eagerly awaiting something.

Emma looked around in confusion. "What is going on?" Jasper's face lit up with a grin that could only be described as mischievous. "You'll find out in about four minutes."

The wait felt like an eternity, with the anticipation building by the second. Finally, the silence was shattered by an incredibly loud noise, much louder than thunder, that seemed to reverberate through their very bones. A bright light appeared behind the trees, and then, piercing the sky, a rocket shot into space.

Antoine's eyes widened in shock. "We're at Cape Canaveral!"

"Yep!" Jasper shouted back, his enthusiasm unmistakable.

For the next ten minutes, Emma, Antoine, and everyone else watched in awe as the rocket soared into the heavens, their eyes fixed on the brilliant spectacle. As the rocket became a mere dot in the sky, Jasper turned to Emma and Antoine. "Well, I'm heading back to bed. See you later!" With that, he disappeared back into his cabin.

Emma and Antoine exchanged incredulous glances, their hearts still racing from the thrill. "How can he just go back to bed?" Emma asked. "I'm wide awake. How about you?" "Yep, wide awake," Antoine agreed. "Can't imagine going back to sleep now. What should we do?"

Emma smiled and began unbuttoning her pajama top. "Oh, I have an idea. Follow me." With a playful glint in her eye,

Emma led Antoine back into their cabin, both excited for what the morning might still hold.

Later that day, Emma and Antoine emerged from their cabin. It was now almost noon, and Jasper was lounging in the cockpit, deeply engrossed in his book. Emma carried a coffee in her hand, while Antoine had two—one for himself and one for Jasper. "Hello, Grandpa! That was something last night," Emma said, her eyes sparkling with reminiscence.

Jasper chuckled. "You mean this morning." Antoine, eager to make plans, spoke up. "I was thinking the five of us should take a taxi and tour the space center this afternoon."

Emma glanced at Jasper and then back at Antoine. "To be honest, I'm not feeling that great today. I'd rather pass on the tour. Space isn't really my thing."

Jasper's expression softened. "Actually, I'm not feeling too hot either. I think it's the early wake-up call. But Antoine, why don't you take the dinghy over, grab Scott and Samantha, and go on the tour? I'm sure you'll have a fantastic time."

Antoine nodded, and soon he was heading over to Singing Swallows in the dinghy. Jasper turned to Emma with a thoughtful look. "Emma, I know you would have loved to go, right? Was it the taxi that put you off?"

Emma lowered her gaze, a bit embarrassed. "Yes. Is that why you didn't go? Because I couldn't?" Jasper smiled warmly. "In a way. I didn't come on this trip just to spend time with them. I came for you—and well, to get out of that nursing home also."

Emma chuckled softly. As they continued their conversation, they heard rhythmic splashing approaching. It was Samantha, making her way over in the dinghy.

As Samantha tied up the dinghy to Arabella, Emma asked, "You didn't go with the guys?"

"Nope," Samantha replied, her tone teasing. "And I'm guessing you're feeling better than you let on. So, two questions: First, are you really okay? I'm guessing you wanted to go, right? Second, how about we take my dinghy into town and check out the temporary farmer's market? It's better than just sitting here feeling sorry for yourself."

Jasper quickly chimed in before Emma had a chance to respond. "You're absolutely right. Let's go into town!" Emma nodded, her mood lifting. "Yes, you're both right. Let's go. And Samantha, this will be a great chance for you and me to shop for Christmas presents for our guys, it's only two days away. As for your first question, I'm fine."

The trio made their way to Samantha's dinghy, "Let's start at the market," Samantha suggested as they disembarked. "I've heard it's a great place to pick up some local treats and gifts."

The farmers market was alive with activity. Stalls were lined up with colorful fruits and vegetables, homemade jams, and artisan crafts. Emma's eyes sparkled with curiosity as she took in the vibrant scene. "This place is incredible," Emma said, her voice full of enthusiasm. "I love how local and authentic it feels."

Samantha grinned. "I thought you'd like it. Plus, it's a perfect spot for picking up some Christmas presents. Look at these handmade ornaments!" She pointed to a stall decorated with intricate, handcrafted decorations.

Jasper, who was enjoying the lively atmosphere, chimed in, "I'm just here to support your shopping spree." He laughed as he examined a display of locally made soaps.

As they wandered through the market, Emma picked up a jar of local honey, and a few jars of homemade preserves.

Samantha was on the hunt for some special holiday treats and found an array of delectable baked goods. "These cookies look perfect for Christmas," she said, adding a box of them to her basket. "We'll need something sweet for the holiday season."

Jasper took a keen interest in a stall selling nautical-themed artwork. "Look at this," he said, showing Emma and Samantha a beautiful painting of a sunset over the water. "This could be a great gift for Scott."

As they continued their shopping, they enjoyed the lively atmosphere and the friendly interactions with local vendors. Emma and Samantha's cheerful chatter filled the air as they compared their finds and discussed gift ideas.

After they finished at the farmers market, they strolled through some of Titusville's charming shops. They found a quaint boutique that sold vintage-style jewelry and a cozy bookstore with a selection of local authors. Emma picked up a book for herself and a couple of unique gifts for Antoine.

By early afternoon, their bags were filled with goodies and gifts. They headed back to the dinghy, each carrying their purchases with a satisfied smile. "I'm really glad we did this," Emma said as they made their way back to Arabella.It made for such a nice day".

Jasper, who had enjoyed his time at the market, added, "I agree. It was a nice day. Thanks for making this happen Samantha."

Back on Arabella, they started organizing their finds and preparing for their evening. The Christmas spirit was beginning to set in for Emma.

The next couple of days glided by smoothly as they navigated the Atlantic Intracoastal Waterway from Titusville to St. Augustine. The journey was marked by picturesque scenery, peaceful waters, and the occasional dolphin sighting.

Emma spent her time reading, taking photos, and enjoying the peaceful rhythm of the trip, while Jasper and Antoine took turns at the helm.

Upon reaching St. Augustine at dusk, they entered the bustling mooring field, an expansive area dotted with hundreds of white mooring balls, each spaced meticulously apart. The sight was a testament to the organized yet lively nature of the city's harbor.

Instead of dropping their own anchor, they opted for the convenience of the mooring balls, which allowed them to secure their boat without the hassle of anchoring.

Jasper expertly maneuvered Arabella into position and guided the boat towards one of the available mooring balls. With practiced precision, Emma and Antoine worked together to secure the lines, ensuring the boat was firmly in place.

As they settled into their new spot, Emma looked around with excitement. "I've heard so much about St. Augustine's history and architecture. I can't wait to explore tomorrow". "Don't forget tomorrow is Christmas eve and you two are going to be checking into the hotel" commented Jasper. Emma gave Jasper a warm smile "Thank you again for that" With that the three of them settled into their nightly routine.

Early the next morning, the two boat crews—Jasper, Scott, Samantha, Emma, and Antoine—took the two dinghies and prepared for a day of exploring St. Augustine. With the sun shining brightly and a gentle breeze in the air, everyone was eager to dive into the city's charm.

They set off together, walking through the quaint streets of St. Augustine. The group marveled at the classical architecture, with its mix of Spanish, colonial, and Victorian influences.

They paused to take in landmarks like the Castillo de San Marcos, the oldest masonry fort in the United States, and the picturesque Flagler College, a stunning example of Spanish Renaissance architecture.

Emma and Antoine, along with the rest of the crew, took a leisurely stroll through the historic district, enjoying the eclectic shops and boutiques that lined the streets. They admired the beautifully preserved buildings and the vibrant local art scene, soaking in the rich history and culture of the city.

Around midday, they decided to stop for lunch at a charming local café. This café was known for its Southern-inspired menu and cozy ambiance and offered a delightful variety of dishes. They enjoyed a leisurely meal, sharing plates of shrimp and grits, pulled pork sandwiches, and fresh salads.

After lunch, it was time to say their goodbyes. Jasper and the rest of the crew helped Emma and Antoine with their bags, ensuring they had everything they needed before heading to a beautiful classic resort. Jasper as usual found them one of the best hotels in town.

Emma and Antoine expressed their gratitude as they checked into the hotel. "Thanks so much for this Grandpa," Emma said with a smile. "We really appreciate it." Jasper, smiling warmly, replied, "No problem at all. Enjoy your time here, and Merry Christmas." With that everyone joined in and wished them a Merry Christmas. Jasper, Scott, and Samantha said their final farewells and headed back to the marina.

Emma and Antoine approached the resort with a sense of anticipation. The hotel's grandeur was evident even from the exterior, with its striking Spanish Revival architecture and elegant façade. The hotel was renowned for its historical charm and luxurious amenities, standing as a testament to the city's rich heritage.

As they entered the hotel lobby, they were greeted by a captivating blend of old-world opulence and modern comfort. The lobby was adorned with ornate chandeliers, intricate mosaic tile work, and lush, dark wood paneling that echoed the building's storied past.

Plush velvet chairs and sofas were arranged around a grand fireplace, adding to the warm and inviting atmosphere.

Emma and Antoine approached the check-in desk, where a friendly staff member awaited them with a welcoming smile.

The receptionist, dressed in a classic uniform, efficiently processed their reservation while engaging in light

conversation about their journey. "I hope you had a pleasant trip," the receptionist said, handing them their room keys. "I hope you'll enjoy your stay." Antoine nodded appreciatively, "We're excited to be here. This place is beautiful."

With their room keys in hand, Emma and Antoine made their way to the elevators.

The hotel's corridors were just as charming as the lobby, with their soft lighting and ornate artwork. The walls were adorned with vintage photographs and historical memorabilia, providing a glimpse into the hotel's illustrious past.

They arrived at their room and opened the door to find a luxurious suite awaiting them. The room was a perfect blend of elegance and modern comfort. Richly upholstered furniture, a sumptuous king-sized bed with plush linens, and large windows offering views of the city's historic district created a serene retreat.

The room was decorated in warm, earthy tones with intricate detailing that echoed the hotel's classic style. Emma and Antoine took a moment to explore their suite, appreciating the attention to detail and the blend of classic charm with contemporary amenities.

The spacious bathroom featured a deep soaking tub and a separate shower, providing a touch of luxury and relaxation. As they settled in, Emma couldn't help but admire the view from their window. "We have a great vantage point. The historic district looks stunning from here."

They took some time to refresh themselves before heading out to explore more of St. Augustine. The Hotels prime location allowed them easy access to the city's attractions, and they were eager to immerse themselves in the local culture and history.

After a day of sightseeing, they returned to the hotel, Jasper had made reservations at seven to dine at the hotel's renowned restaurant. Antoine and Emma thought that the restaurant, known for its exquisite cuisine and elegant ambiance, was the perfect end to their day.

Emma and Antoine approached the entrance of the elegant restaurant. Emma glanced at Antoine with a mix of excitement as they approached the Maitre d'. "Good evening,"

Emma said, her voice tinged with excitement. "We have a reservation under the name Nicholson."

The Maitre d' looked up from his podium and smiled warmly. "Ah, yes, Ms. Nicholson. Your table is ready. Right this way, please."

Emma and Antoine followed the Maitre d' through the restaurant, their footsteps echoing softly on the polished floors. As they walked, the restaurant's atmosphere enveloped them—soft lighting, elegant decor, and the murmur of other diners enjoying their meals.

When they reached their table. The Maitre d' gestured towards a table set for four, and to Emma's and Antoine's confusion, she saw two people already seated there. As they drew closer, Emma's eyes widened in disbelief.

There, sitting at the table, was none other than her father, Ben. The familiar face she had missed so much was smiling warmly, his eyes twinkling with a mix of joy and relief. Beside him sat a woman Emma assumed must be Audra.

Overwhelmed by the unexpected reunion, Emma's emotions surged. Tears welled up in her eyes, and she struggled to hold back the flood of emotions. She could hardly believe that her father was here, in St. Augustine.

Ben stood up quickly as he saw Emma approach, his own eyes glistening with emotion. "Emma!" he exclaimed, his voice choked with emotion. "I didn't know if we'd be able to pull this off. I wanted to surprise you." Emma, now fully overcome, rushed to her father and enveloped him in a tight embrace. "Dad!"

she sobbed, her voice muffled against his shoulder. "I can't believe you're here. This is... this is amazing!"

Antoine, witnessing the heartfelt reunion, stood back with a warm smile, giving Emma and Ben their moment. Audra looked on with a tender expression, happy to see the touching family reunion.

After a few moments, Emma and Ben pulled away, both with tears in their eyes. Emma took a deep breath, wiping away her tears, and turned to Audra. "I'm so happy to meet you, Audra," she said, her voice filled with gratitude. Audra smiled warmly, reaching out to hug Emma. "It's wonderful to finally meet you, Emma. I've heard so much about you."

As they all settled into their seats, the initial shock of the surprise began to give way to joy and laughter.

"How did you arrange this?" Emma asked, her eyes wide with astonishment. Ben looked at her with a hint of amusement. "I sent a letter to your grandfather a few days ago. I had planned to stay at a regular hotel, but he insisted on paying for this place and this restaurant."

Emma's face brightened with hope. "Does this mean you two are talking again?"

Ben's expression grew serious. "No. This was a one-time thing because I wanted to see you, and Audra practically twisted my arm about writing to him." Emma glanced at Audra and mouthed a heartfelt "Thank you," her eyes filled with gratitude.

The evening unfolded into a heartwarming celebration, filled with engaging stories, laughter, and the joy of reconnecting with family. As the night progressed, Ben excused himself from the table for a few minutes.

Antoine turned to Emma with a thoughtful expression. "Do you remember the morning we left for Titusville? Jasper came out of his cabin with tears in his eyes. I'm guessing that was the letter from your dad. It seemed like he didn't want to be alone for Christmas. He did all this for you."

Audra nodded in agreement. "Antoine's right. I'm not sure what was in the letter, but I have a feeling some of it wasn't very nice.

When I suggested this surprise, I just wanted your dad to have a happy Christmas. I didn't intend for anyone to get hurt."

Emma's eyes softened as she realized the depth of Jasper's gesture. Antoine, sensing her growing concern, suggested, "Once we've finished dinner and said goodnight to your dad and Audra, why don't we come back here, grab some desserts, and take them to Jasper, We could also give him the gifts we got him this afternoon?" Emma's face brightened at the idea. "That sounds perfect. Let's do it."

Soon Ben returned and he took his seat and smiled at Emma and Antoine, who exchanged knowing glances. The evening continued with lively conversation, delicious food, and an unmistakable sense of joy that filled the room.

As the dinner progressed, the conversation flowed naturally. Emma could feel a new, positive energy around her father, and the warmth of the evening made the surprise even more special.

After dinner, Emma turned to her father and Audra, her eyes brimming with gratitude. "Thank you both for this amazing evening. It's been the perfect surprise."

Ben looked at Emma with a warm, affectionate smile. "I'm really glad you enjoyed it. I wanted to make this Christmas special for you. And Audra and I were thinking, perhaps tomorrow morning after breakfast, we could go for a walk. Even though many places will be closed, I thought it might be nice to explore a bit."

Emma glanced at Antoine, who was nodding enthusiastically. "Yes, that sounds wonderful. I'd love to." With their plans set, they exchanged heartfelt goodbyes and Christmas wishes. "Good night, and Merry Christmas," Emma said, her voice filled with warmth and joy.

As Ben and Audra left to return to their hotel room, Emma and Antoine watched them go, then Antoine and Emma called over the waiter and ordered some desserts to go. Emma selected an assortment of pastries, chocolates, and a couple of rich, indulgent cakes.

The hotel lobby was beautifully decorated for the holidays, adding to the festive atmosphere. With the desserts in hand, Emma and Antoine made their way back to the marina to take the water taxi and head over to Arabella.

Emma's thoughts were focused on Jasper and how much he had done for her and Antoine. She wanted to make sure he knew how much he was appreciated, especially on Christmas eve.

When they arrived at Arabella, they quietly boarded the boat and made their way to Jasper's cabin. Emma gently knocked on the Hatch "Grandpa you awake". Jasper slid open the hatch. "Hey Grandpa," Emma said softly as she entered, holding out the box of desserts. "I thought you might like some company and treats. We wanted to thank you for everything you've done."

Jasper looked at Emma and Antoine, his face a mix of surprise and gratitude. "You didn't have to do that. But... Thank you. I really appreciate it."

"We also got you a couple of Christmas gifts," Emma said with a smile. Jasper looked surprised. "Oh, you didn't have to do that." "Yes, we did!" Antoine replied cheerfully as he handed Jasper a neatly wrapped little box. "Mine first."

Jasper unwrapped it to reveal a decorative wooden box. Inside was a brass compass engraved with the words, "Not all who wander are lost." Jasper's eyes lit up as he looked at Antoine. "Aw, thank you! I love it." "You're welcome," Antoine said, beaming.

Emma then handed over her gift. "Now, here's mine." Jasper took the elegantly wrapped package and opened it to find a framed photograph of himself and Emma aboard Arabella, taken inside a lock.

His eyes filled with emotion. "I remember this moment. It was at Jones Falls on the Rideau Canal. You were trying to take a selfie, and one of the lock staff offered to take the picture for us. Hard to believe that was over six months ago. Thank you so much." Jasper pulled Emma into a heartfelt hug. "This means a lot to me."

Afterwards Emma and Antoine set the desserts on the small table in the cabin, and they all sat down together. The mood was much lighter. After a while, Emma and Antoine bid Jasper goodnight, leaving him with a warm sense of being appreciated. As they took the water taxi back to the marina, Emma reflected on how this Christmas Eve was unforgettable.

"Thank you for the idea, Antoine," Emma said softly as they approached the hotel. "It meant a lot to me." Antoine smiled warmly. "It's been a memorable Christmas Eve. I hope we have a lot more like this."

Christmas morning Antoine and Emma slept in. They had been awake most of the night enjoying each other's company.

When Emma woke up, she saw Antoine already awake, his eyes meeting hers with a warm gaze. "Good morning my love," Antoine said softly. Emma smiled back. "Good morning."

Antoine reached behind him and pulled out a small, beautifully wrapped box, handing it to Emma. "Merry Christmas." Emma's eyes lit up as she quickly unwrapped the gift. Inside was a pair of stunning diamond earrings.

"Oh my God, they're absolutely beautiful! I love them. When did you buy them?" Antoine chuckled. "In Montreal, before I left." Emma smiled. "Ah, that would explain it." She got out of bed and went over to her bag, retrieving a neatly folded jacket with the NASA logo embroidered on it. "I got you something too, but I didn't have a chance to wrap it."

She handed the jacket to Antoine. "Oh wow, I love it! Let me guess where you bought it?" Emma laughed as Antoine tried on the jacket, which fit him perfectly. "Perfect fit, this is great. Thank you!" Antoine said, giving Emma a big hug and a kiss.

"What do you say we get ready and then call my dad and Audra to meet them downstairs for breakfast?" Emma suggested. "Sounds like a plan," Antoine agreed. They quickly got dressed and called Ben and Audra.

Ben answered, "Well, we were up early and already had breakfast, but since it's almost noon, how about we meet for lunch instead?" Emma laughed. "Okay, lunch it is. And after we eat, we can go for that walk around town we talked about last night." "Perfect," Ben replied.

With that settled, Emma and Antoine prepared to meet Ben and Audra, eager to enjoy the rest of their Christmas Day together.

After lunch, they left the hotel grounds and wandered along the river. As they strolled, Emma spotted a familiar figure approaching them. It was Samantha, walking alone.

Emma noted with a wry smile, 'At least she's wearing more clothes than usual today.' Samantha was dressed in white shorts over a one-piece swimsuit, with a sheer shirt draped casually over her shoulders.

When they were close enough to speak, Emma introduced her companions. "Hi Samantha, this is my father, Ben, and his girlfriend, Audra. Guys, this is Samantha, You know I mentioned her and her boyfriend Scott in our calls."

"Nice to meet you both," Samantha said warmly. "Nice to meet you too," Ben and Audra replied in unison. Emma then asked, "Samantha, why are you on your own?" Samantha hesitated before speaking.

"Scott and I had a major argument this morning. He's gone to spend time with Jasper, and I just needed some fresh air, so I decided to take a walk."

Emma offered, "Well, why don't you join us? We're out for a walk too. What happened, if you don't mind sharing?"

Samantha was candid. "We've been trying to conceive during this entire trip, and it's been really stressful. This morning, after exchanging gifts, we were having some fun. And in the middle, I suggested we see a doctor when we get home. Scott overreacted and got really angry. I think the constant togetherness might be wearing us both thin."

Audra, listening intently, asked, "Did you want a big family?" Samantha replied thoughtfully, "Not necessarily a big family, but yes, I always wanted a family." Ben looked at Audra, seeking her input before speaking. "Audra's previous marriage ended due to her struggles with her inability to have children."

Understanding the weight of the conversation, Audra gently took Samantha's hand and led her to a nearby bench. "You guys continue your walk. Samantha and I need to talk for a bit," Audra said, her tone firm yet kind.

Emma nodded, giving Audra and Samantha the space they needed. As she and Ben continued their walk with Antoine, she glanced back at Audra and Samantha, hoping the conversation would help mend things for her friend.

As Audra and Samantha sat on the bench, Audra prompted gently, "Okay, tell me exactly what happened." Samantha sighed and began, "This morning, Scott was on top of me, and my mind started to wander. You know how that happens sometimes, right? I began to think about how it's been almost eight months of trying, and maybe something's wrong.

We should probably see a doctor. It could be him or it could be me. So at that moment, I blurted out, 'When we get back, we should see a doctor together. Maybe your soldiers aren't ready to do battle.'

And before I could even say, 'Or it could be me,' he cut me off." Audra chuckled softly, "Yeah, that might be a bit tough on a guy's ego." Samantha nodded. "He was so mad he..."

Samantha shook her head, the humor of the situation softening the edges of her frustration. "

He was so mad he practically stormed out of the cabin. I tried to explain that I wasn't blaming him or anything, just that we needed to figure out what was going on, but he was already fuming. It's like I hit a nerve I didn't even know was there."

Audra listened intently, her expression sympathetic. "It sounds like it really shook him up. I can understand why—he might be feeling like his manhood is being questioned, even though that wasn't your intention."

Audra placed a reassuring hand on Samantha's arm. "It's a tough situation, and it's bound to stir up strong emotions. Maybe he needs a little time to cool down. Once things settle, you can both talk more calmly and figure out how to approach the situation together.

Besides it's your first baby it can take a lot more than eight months to get pregnant. I have a friend that took a year and a half. Plus in the worst case scenario there are other options that can help like In vitro or hormones, there are tons of options."

Samantha took a deep breath, feeling a bit more grounded. "Thanks, Audra. It really helps to talk this out. I just hope he can see that I'm coming from a place of concern and not criticism."

Audra squeezed Samantha's hand gently. "I think he will. And remember, you're not alone in this. Once he calms down I'm sure he will be there for you, and you've got the strength to get through this, no matter how tough it seems right now."

Meanwhile as Emma, Antoine and Ben walked along the riverbank, they chatted about the various sights and sounds of the town, though Emma's mind kept drifting back to Samantha and Audra.

She hoped that their conversation would bring some clarity or relief to Samantha. The afternoon sun cast a warm glow over the water and the surrounding trees. The serenity of the river and the distant hum of the town created a peaceful setting, contrasting sharply with the turmoil Samantha had described.

Eventually, Emma, Antoine and Ben turned back toward the bench where Audra and Samantha had settled. Samantha was now visibly more relaxed, her posture more at ease. Audra had her arm around Samantha's shoulders.

As Emma, Antoine and Ben approached, Audra gave a reassuring smile and said, "We've had a good talk. Samantha's feeling a bit better now." Samantha looked up, her eyes reflecting a mixture of gratitude and relief. "I really appreciate you both. I needed to talk it out, and Audra's been amazing." Ben looked at them and said "Yep I know she is, I'm a lucky man"

Emma laughed at her dad and then spoke "I'm glad you had that conversation. Sometimes, just talking things through can make a big difference."

As they continued their walk, the atmosphere lightened considerably. The conversation drifted to more neutral topics like local eateries and scenic spots.

Samantha seemed more engaged now, though Emma could tell she was still processing the morning's events. They all walked Samantha back to the water taxi. As they looked out at the boats, Emma noticed that Scott's dinghy was back at *Singing Swallows*. "Good luck, Samantha," Emma said warmly as she boarded the water taxi.

"It was nice to meet you," Ben said with a friendly smile.

"You take care of yourself," Audra added, her tone genuine.

Antoine simply gave a wave and said, "See you guys tomorrow."

With a final wave, Samantha's water taxi pulled away from the dock. The four of them continued their walk, their steps leisurely and relaxed. As they neared the hotel, the sky was awash in hues of pink and orange, signaling the approach of evening.

The peaceful end to their day was a welcome change from the earlier tension and they all took a moment to enjoy the tranquil beauty of the sunset.

Emma, Antoine, Ben and Audra returned to the hotel and enjoyed a quiet dinner together, reflecting on the day's events. The meal was filled with light conversation and laughter, providing a perfect end to an emotionally charged day.

Afterwards, they agreed that an early night was in order. As they wrapped up their evening, Ben suggested, "Let's all get together for breakfast tomorrow morning before Audra and I need to catch the airport shuttle at eleven." Everyone nodded in agreement, appreciating the chance to share one last meal together before their departure.

With plans set, the two couples headed to their separate rooms for the night. Emma and Antoine retired to their room, their conversation soft and intimate, while Ben and Audra prepared for their journey home.

In the morning, after a pleasant breakfast, the two couples checked out of the hotel and made their way to the shuttle departure point. The mood was a mix of warmth and bittersweet farewell.

Antoine, with a sincere smile, extended his hand to Ben. "It was great meeting the two of you," he said. Ben shook Antoine's hand firmly, a sign of genuine appreciation. "It's our pleasure," Ben replied, his eyes reflecting the sentiment.

Audra then stepped forward, her affection clear as she enveloped Antoine in a warm hug and placed a kiss on his cheek. "We'll see you in the future, right?" she asked, her voice full of hope. Antoine's smile was heartfelt. "Absolutely - nothing will stop me."

Turning to Emma, Audra said, "My dear, you are everything your father bragged about. Meeting you has been a true pleasure. I'm sure we'll stay in touch—maybe I can even join one of those famous video chats I've heard so much about."

Emma laughed softly, touched by Audra's words. "I would really like that. It's been wonderful getting to know you, and thank you for coming into my dad's life. You're perfect for him."

Emma then faced her father, her smile tinged with sadness. "Dad, it was so great to see you. I've missed you so much. I can't believe it's going to be so long until I see you again." Her eyes filled with tears as Ben reached out to her. "Sweetheart, it will pass before you know it. We'll stay in touch constantly and you'll enjoy the rest of your trip. You deserve this so much. I love you."

Ben pulled Emma into a tight hug, his embrace filled with fatherly affection. Emma whispered, "I love you too, Dad," into his ear. With their goodbyes said and promises made, Ben and Audra boarded the shuttle. Emma and Antoine watched as the vehicle pulled away.

Emma and Antoine made their way back to the water taxi, exchanging glances that reflected a mix of contentment and nostalgia. The ride was peaceful, the sun casting a gentle glow over the water as they neared Arabella.

Upon arrival, Jasper looked up from his book, a welcoming smile on his face. "Hello, guys," he greeted as they boarded the boat. Emma and Antoine returned the greeting, their smiles bright despite the lingering emotions from their goodbyes.

As they settled in, Jasper closed his book and joined them for a chat. The conversation naturally shifted to Scott and Samantha, and the recent visit with Ben and Audra. They reminisce about the highlights of their time together.

"I'm glad you had such a wonderful time," Jasper said thoughtfully. "It sounds like the visit was a real success." Emma nodded, her eyes still reflecting the joy of the past few days. "It really was. I didn't expect it to be so emotional, but it was perfect." As the day unfolded, they continued to talk and relax on the boat, savoring the calm after a whirlwind of events.

Chapter 15

Full of Drama

The next morning, as the first light of dawn filtered through the windows of Arabella, it was time to resume their journey. Emma, Antoine and Jasper prepared for another leg of their trip, their destination set for Jacksonville. They were eager to get underway, hoping to reach their destination before nightfall.

Jasper yelled over to Singing Swallows "You guys up" Scott quickly appeared "Yep, but you guys go ahead, I have some work to do, Ok if we will meet you in Savannah ?" Jasper nodded and yelled back "of course, we will see you there". The two friends waved goodbye.

The air was cool and fresh as they started the engines and set their course. The early morning tranquility gave way to the rhythmic hum of the boat cutting through the water. Jasper navigated and kept an eye on their progress as the boat glided through the water, the day's journey felt both familiar and exciting.

The scenery shifted with each passing mile, a constant reminder of the ever-changing landscape they were exploring. The anticipation of reaching Jacksonville was mixed with the bittersweet knowledge that another farewell loomed on the horizon.

Their destination was not just another stop on their journey; it was the place where they would part ways once more. The next morning, after arriving in Jacksonville, Emma and Jasper would say goodbye to Antoine, who would be heading home back to Canada.

By the time they reached Jacksonville, the sun was beginning its descent, casting a warm, golden glow over the cityscape. The marina, bustling with activity, greeted them with its lively ambiance and vibrant energy. They expertly maneuvered Arabella into their designated slip and the boat settled gently against the dock.

As evening embraced the city, Emma, Antoine, and Jasper took a moment to absorb the scene around them. The twinkling lights of the city reflected off the water, creating a mesmerizing dance of colors.

The air was filled with the sounds of the marina—laughter from nearby restaurants, the gentle clinking of glasses, and the distant hum of the city.

Jasper, looking forward to some much-needed downtime, chose to stay aboard Arabella and relax. Meanwhile, Emma and Antoine, intent on making the most of their last night together before parting ways, were determined to seize the evening. After freshening up, they set off to explore Jacksonville.

Their destination was a charming restaurant perched along the waterfront, offering a panoramic view of the river.

At the restaurant, they were greeted warmly and seated at a table with a perfect view. The menu boasted a variety of local seafood and other regional specialties, and Emma and Antoine took their time choosing dishes that would " complement their final night together. The evening unfolded with easy conversation, laughter, and a shared appreciation for the beautiful setting.

As they dined, they savored each course, from freshly caught shrimp to rich, decadent desserts. Emma and Antoine talked about their favorite memories from the last couple of weeks and speculated about future adventures, while Jasper, back on the boat, enjoyed his quiet time with a book and a cup of coffee.

After their meal, Emma and Antoine decided to take a leisurely walk along the waterfront. They strolled hand in hand, taking in the city lights and the tranquil water, reflecting on the trip's highlights and what the future might hold. It was a fitting way to end their time in Jacksonville.

As the evening wore on, they returned to the marina, feeling content and at peace. Jasper welcomed them back with a relaxed smile, and together they spent a quiet night on the boat.

The next morning dawned early, with a crisp chill in the air. The marina was just beginning to stir as Antoine prepared for his departure. Emma and Jasper were there to see him off, the atmosphere tinged with a bittersweet sense of finality.

Antoine and Jasper exchanged a heartfelt handshake, the gesture reflecting both their gratitude for the journey shared and the friendship they had developed. "Safe travels, Antoine. It was great having you on board," Jasper said, his voice sincere. Antoine nodded, a smile on his face despite the sadness of parting. "Thanks, Jasper. It's been an incredible experience."

Emma stood a short distance away, fighting to keep her tears in check. As she moved toward Antoine, her emotions overwhelmed her. She wrapped her arms around him, her voice quivering as she whispered, "I'm going to miss you so much. Thank you for everything. I love you."

Antoine embraced her warmly, tenderly stroking her back. "I'll miss you too, Emma. We'll stay in touch every night until we're together again. I love you too."

Emma's grip tightened as if she were trying to hold onto the moment forever. Antoine's embrace was warm and reassuring. As they pulled back slightly, their eyes met, a mix of sadness and hope reflected in their gazes. "Promise me you'll take care of yourself," Emma said softly, her eyes glistening.

Antoine nodded, brushing a stray tear from her cheek. "I promise. And you do the same. We're just a call away from each other, remember?"

Emma gave a shaky smile and nodded. The distance ahead seemed daunting, but in this moment of parting, their words and shared feelings built a bridge of reassurance. They lingered in their goodbye, each knowing that though the separation was difficult, their connection remained unbreakable.

The departure was a poignant moment, with Antoine finally stepping towards his waiting taxi. Emma watched him go, her eyes filled with tears. Jasper stood beside her, offering silent support as they both watched Antoine's figure recede into the distance.

As the early morning sun began to cast its light over the marina, Emma took a deep breath, trying to steady herself.

She turned to Jasper, who placed a reassuring hand on her shoulder. "It's always hard to say goodbye," he said quietly. Emma nodded, wiping away her tears."

With Antoine's departure, the marina slowly stirred to life, and the reality of moving on began to sink in. Jasper fired up the engine, the hum resonating softly through the boat.

Emma made her way to the front to weigh anchor, a task that usually filled her with excitement. Today, however, it filled her with sadness.

The sky above was overcast, casting a muted gray light over the water. Without the usual breeze, the waterway's surface was eerily still, like a mirror reflecting the somber clouds. The only movement was the gentle wake left behind by the Arabella as it glided through the glassy expanse.

After a long and exhausting day, Emma and Jasper finally reached their anchorage in front of Cumberland Island. The sky was dimming as they lowered the anchor, the boat settling into its temporary resting place. Emma and Jasper swapped back to their respective cabins, and Emma found herself once again in the small, familiar rear cabin.

The tiny space felt even more confining tonight, amplifying her sense of isolation. She lay down on the narrow bed, feeling the weight of the day press down on her. All she wanted was to reach out and hold Antoine, to find solace in his presence. But tonight, she couldn't even call him; he was still on his way home, miles away from where she needed him.

She was overwhelmed by a profound sense of loneliness and sadness, making her unwilling to engage in conversation with anyone else. She murmured a quiet goodnight to Jasper, who was understanding enough to leave her to her thoughts, and then she sent a brief message to her father, letting him know that she was too tired to talk and would catch up with him tomorrow night.

As the boat gently rocked with the subtle movement of the water, Emma stared up at the ceiling of her small cabin, the shadows cast by the dim light seeming to reflect her inner turmoil.

She felt a deep ache in her chest, the kind that only time and a familiar embrace could soothe. For now, she closed her eyes, trying to find some small measure of comfort in the rhythm of the boat and the quiet solitude, hoping that tomorrow would bring a glimmer of clarity and peace.

With a good night's sleep and the warmth of her morning coffee, Emma's spirits lifted. She felt a renewed sense of optimism as she sipped her coffee, letting the soothing ritual ease her into the day. Jasper too, seemed in high spirits, his usual cheerfulness evident in the way he moved about the boat.

"I was doing some research last night," Jasper said, his eyes sparkling with enthusiasm. "This island looks amazing. Would you mind if we went to check it out today?" Emma's curiosity was piqued.

"Sure, but did you find out if you can use your wheelchair there?" Jasper's smile widened. "Actually, no, I can't use my own wheelchair there." Emma's brow furrowed in confusion. "But if you can't use your wheelchair, how are we going to manage?"

Jasper's smile remained unwavering. "They have special all-terrain chairs available. They're designed to handle different surfaces, including the beach. It'll make it easy for me to get around and explore."

Emma's eyes brightened with relief and excitement. "That sounds incredible! Let's go." "Well can we eat breakfast first" remarked Jasper. Emma laughed "Yes and if you like I can pack a picnic." Jasper nodded his head in agreement.

Soon enough they were on the island and received the special wheelchair. It was like a regular wheelchair except it had really big balloon tires. Jasper laughed comparing it to being in a bouncy castle.

Their first stop was the main visitor center on the mainland, where they gathered essential information about accessible routes and highlights. Armed with maps and insights from the friendly staff, they set off with renewed excitement.

The island welcomed them with a diverse tapestry of landscapes—dense forests, sweeping dunes, and pristine white sand beaches. They were immediately captivated by the untouched expanses of sand stretching out before them.

Despite the challenges posed by the uneven terrain, Jasper's off-road wheelchair, built for rugged conditions, allowed him to navigate these diverse paths with impressive ease. Emma, ever supportive and attentive, helped guide Jasper through the island's varied environments, ensuring they could fully savor each moment.

Their exploration soon led them to the Plum Orchard Mansion, a grand estate renowned for its historical significance and striking architecture.

As they approached, Jasper admired the elegant design, while Emma reveled in the expansive, lush grounds. Emma and Jasper both agreed this would be the perfect spot to have their picnic lunch. There were plenty of picnic tables and shade was provided by these giant oak trees covered in Spanish moss.

The island's wild horses, roaming freely, added a touch of magic to their journey. They watched in awe as these majestic creatures trotted along the sandy shores and through the island's wooded trails. The remnants of old ruins they encountered along their path spoke of the island's rich history, adding layers of intrigue to their day.

With each turn and new vista, Jasper and Emma uncovered more of Cumberland Island's charm.

After spending most of the day there they decided it was time to go back to the boat. Jasper was tired and Emma couldn't wait to video call Antoine and her dad and tell them about her day.

The next morning, Emma could barely contain her excitement. She woke up early, brimming with energy, got ready for the day and then sat in the cockpit, eagerly waiting for Jasper to join her. After the delightful day they'd had yesterday, she was thrilled to see what the new day would bring.

When Jasper finally came up, coffee in hand, he had some news for Emma. "Well, Emma, I hate to break it to you, but I was thinking we might want to make some distance today and tomorrow. There's still plenty to see along the way. In fact, I know we'll pass a beautiful lighthouse today."

Emma was fine with that. "That's perfectly fine. I actually enjoy days that are more about the journey. It's shaping up to be a beautiful day." And it was. They made excellent time, taking in stunning landscapes as they traveled. By evening, they arrived at a perfect, secluded anchorage, a tranquil spot that promised a peaceful night under the stars.

The following day mirrored the previous one, with smooth sailing and pleasant weather. They reached Savannah and docked at a marina, settling into their assigned slip, which was on the opposite side of the marina from the Singing Swallows. By the time they were ready to call it a night, they decided to wait until morning to get in touch.

After settling into their cabins, Emma picked up her phone, eager to call her dad. To her surprise, it was Audra who answered."Hi Emma, it's me Audra," she said, her tone warm. Emma was taken aback. "Hi Audra, um why are you answering my dad's phone?" "Oh, he had to go into work and left his phone here," Audra explained."

Emma hesitated for a moment, processing the information. "Audra, can I ask you something?" "Of course," Audra replied.

"Are you living with my dad now?" Emma asked. Audra paused, choosing her words carefully. "You know Emma, it's something we haven't really discussed in depth. To be honest, other than a brief stop to pick up some clothes when we came to visit you, I haven't been back to my place in a while. But let's just say I'm not ready to give up my apartment just yet. We'll see how things evolve. Are you worried I'll still be around when you get back?"

Emma chuckled softly, feeling reassured. "No, not at all. I actually like you a lot and think you're great for my dad. It's been a long time since I've seen him this happy. I was more concerned about Antoine and me. The only way I see us being together after I return is if I move to Montreal or if he moves to Ticonderoga.

I don't know if I'm ready for that or if it's even feasible legally to work in each other's countries."

Audra's voice took on a thoughtful tone. "Yeah, I think that's something we have all been wondering about. It sounds like you two have a lot to figure out. I wouldn't rush into any major decisions until you're closer to the end of your trip. See how things stand then, but starting your research now is a good idea.

If you need any help or advice, your dad and I are here for you." Emma felt a wave of gratitude. "Thank you Audra. I really appreciate your support. I'll keep that in mind and let you know if I need anything."

"Absolutely," Audra said warmly. "Just focus on your journey right now. We'll take care of things here, and we'll talk soon." With a sense of reassurance, Emma was grateful for Audra's support and for the clarity it brought as she continued to navigate her own uncertainties.

Emma, feeling a bit more grounded, said "Thanks Audra. I'll keep that in mind." Audra happily replied "Anytime.... Oh I just heard your dad walk in, do you want to talk to him?" Emma quickly replied "He did? I thought you meant when you said 'went into work' you were being discrete for 'went drinking beers with his co-workers'?"

Audra paused then in a serious voice replied "um no I've never seen him go drinking with his co-workers. In fact, other than a glass of wine when we go out to eat, I've never seen him drink, I didn't even know he liked beer. Is there something I should know?"

Emma was grappling with mixed emotions. While she was relieved that her dad wasn't out drinking, she couldn't shake the concern that she might have unintentionally complicated things with Audra.

Trying to downplay the situation, she said, "No, not at all. It's just that occasionally he goes out with his co-workers. It's not a big deal."

Audra's voice was soothing as she responded, "Oh, okay. You kind of scared me with how you said that. Do you remember when your dad mentioned that my inability to have children was a factor in my divorce?

The real issue was that my ex wasn't open to discussing surrogacy or adoption. Instead, he turned to drinking - a lot - and he was abusive when he drank. I might be living in Whitehall now, but I'm originally from Tucson, where he still lives. A friend of mine took me in, which led to me getting my shop and a place of my own."

Emma's concern grew. "Oh my god, are you worried he might come after you?" Audra laughed lightly, trying to reassure her.

"No, it's not one of those situations. I did have a restraining order against him, but he's never violated it or tried to contact me.

If he wanted to find me, he could. I'm not exactly hiding; I'm active on social media. Besides, now he has the opportunity to find someone who can have children."

Emma felt a wave of relief wash over her. "I'm glad to hear that you're at least safe." Audra's tone brightened. "Your dad is right here now. Would you like to talk to him?"

Emma smiled. "Sure, It was really nice talking to you." Audra added quickly, "And Emma, if you ever want to talk, just give me a call. I'm hoping we can become good friends." Emma's smile widened. "I'd really like that, I'll get your contact info from my dad." "Great," Audra said. "Here's your dad."

Audra passed the phone to Ben, and Emma greeted him warmly. They enjoyed their usual nightly conversation, where she filled him in on the details of her day. Since she hadn't left the boat and had only seen the scenery from the water, the conversation was brief. As they spoke, Emma's anticipation for her nightly chat with Antoine grew stronger.

The next morning, Emma was roused from sleep by a knock on her cabin door. Still groggy, she slid open the hatch to find Samantha standing there with a cheerful grin.

"Good morning sleepyhead!" Samantha said with a lot of enthusiasm. Emma squinted in the early light, noting that Jasper and Scott were already in the cockpit with Samantha.

"Ugh, it's too early," Emma mumbled, trying to shake off her drowsiness.

"Actually, it's about ten thirty" Jasper chimed in, looking up from the cockpit. Emma blinked at him in surprise "Oh well, I was up late talking to Antoine. Give me a few minutes to get ready." "Sure thing sweetie. I'll get you some coffee" Jasper offered with a smile.

Emma nodded and disappeared back into her cabin. It didn't take her long to freshen up and she soon reappeared, looking more awake and ready to start the day. Samantha greeted her with a laugh. "Okay, let's try this again - 'good morning'!" Samantha said, her cheerfulness undiminished.

Emma smiled at the three of them. "Good morning everyone." She took a seat in the cockpit, her eyes brightening at the thought of what the day might hold.

Samantha's eyes sparkled with excitement. "You know, you really inspired Scott and me. Yesterday, we went out and bought ourselves some bicycles. It's a much better way of getting around while on the boat and will be great for exercise when we get back home.

I was hoping Scott and I could go for a ride this morning, but he needs to go to a chandlery to buy some parts for the boat. We thought it would be a good idea for Jasper to join Scott, and you and I could go for a bike ride instead. What do you think?"

Emma's face lit up with enthusiasm. "I would love that! But first, do you think I could have something to eat?" "Of course!" Samantha said. Emma was already heading towards the galley.

A little while later, after Emma had eaten and the two groups had set their plans in motion, Emma and Samantha set out on their bicycles to explore Savannah.

The city's charm unfolded before them as they pedaled through the historic district, taking in the stunning architecture and the picturesque squares that seemed to be frozen in time. The vibrant atmosphere of Savannah was alive with the hum of activity, and their bike ride gave them a unique vantage point to soak it all in.

They made stops along the way to visit famous landmarks, including the iconic bench from the movie Forrest Gump. They enjoyed leisurely breaks at local cafes, savoring the flavors and ambiance that the city had to offer. The bicycles allowed them to cover more ground and discover hidden gems that might have otherwise gone unnoticed.

While cruising down a bike path, Emma spotted a green and white sign. "Samantha, do you know what that is? I saw a similar sign in Titusville and St. Augustine."

Samantha glanced at the sign and smiled. "Oh, that indicates we're on the East Coast Greenway. When it's completed, it will be a trail stretching from the Canadian border all the way down to Key West, Florida. A lot of it is already finished, but some sections still require riding on roads. I've seen it in Philadelphia, Trenton, and even in Manhattan on our little road trips."

"That's very cool," Emma replied, her mind racing with possibilities. She thought to herself, *I wonder if Antoine would ever be interested in a trip like that in the future. It sounds amazing.*

The two friends continued their exploration of Savannah, enjoying the freedom and adventure that the bike ride brought.

Eventually, hunger began to set in, and they decided it was time to head back.

They made their way to the marina, where they met up with Jasper and Scott.

As the evening approached, the four of them gathered on the patio of the marina's restaurant. They shared stories from their day, laughed over delicious food, and enjoyed the peaceful ambiance of the setting sun over the water. It was a fantastic end to a day of discovery and camaraderie, blending the charm of Savannah with the joy of good company.

The next day, after a leisurely start, the two boats set out to continue their journey north up the Intracoastal Waterway. As they approached the expansive Port Royal Sound, the wind picked up from the southeast, coming directly off the ocean. This made the crossing particularly choppy and challenging.

A particularly massive wave slammed against the side of Arabella, drenching both Jasper and Emma. Despite the rough conditions, they persevered and eventually made their way back into the calmer waters of the Beaufort River.

After about an hour of navigating through the river's sheltered waters, they finally reached their anchorage off the town of Beaufort. Relieved to have completed such a demanding day, they were ready to relax and enjoy the peace of their new setting.

The subsequent morning they were eager to explore this charming town known for its classic beauty and Southern hospitality. Emma made sure Jasper's wheelchair was ready for the day's venture.

The weather was perfect—clear skies and a gentle breeze made for an ideal day of exploration.

The group started their visit with a leisurely stroll along the scenic waterfront park. The park offered stunning views of the harbor and was adorned with lush greenery and colorful flowers, making it a picturesque setting for their outing.

Scott, who had been researching local attractions, suggested they visit the historic district, which was renowned for its antebellum architecture and quaint streets. Emma and Samantha agreed, and the group headed toward the heart of Beaufort's historic area.

As they explored, they stopped by some of the town's notable landmarks, including the Beaufort History Museum and the stunning John Mark Verdier House.

During their tour, they also made sure to visit some local shops and cafes. Beaufort's downtown area was filled with unique boutiques and cozy eateries. Emma and Samantha picked out a few souvenirs including a little wooden dolphin, while Scott and Jasper relaxed at a nearby café, enjoying some refreshing beverages and local treats.

For lunch, they chose a charming restaurant with a patio that overlooked the harbor. The restaurant was known for its delicious seafood and Southern fare and the group indulged in a leisurely meal while taking in the beautiful views.

After lunch, they decided to explore the nearby Spanish Moss Trail, a scenic route that offered a unique view of the surrounding landscape. Emma pushed Jasper's wheelchair along the well-maintained trail, which was shaded by ancient oaks draped in Spanish moss. The tranquility of the trail provided a peaceful respite from the busier parts of the town.

As the afternoon drew to a close, the group made their way back to the anchorage. The town's charm had left a lasting impression on everyone.

In the evening, they gathered on the deck of Singing Swallows for a casual dinner and conversation before calling it a night.

Dawn broke early, and Jasper was eager to get underway. He was determined to reach Charleston Harbor before nightfall.

The weather was perfect, with clear skies and a gentle breeze—ideal conditions for their journey however as Jasper explained it to Emma "The area we are traveling though today is called the lowlands and this is going to be a very stressful day. We are going to be dealing with some very strong currents and we have to be extra vigilant watching the tides as this area is famous for shoaling; shoaling is the accumulation of sediment in shallow areas, which can greatly reduce the depth of the water. So basically we can hit the bottom and get stuck.

The good news is unless you're at absolute high tide. When the water rises it usually frees you".

With that, they weighed anchor and set off, navigating through the intricate waterways. As they cruised, Emma was captivated by the natural beauty surrounding them. The landscape was teeming with life; birds soared overhead and in one particular spot, she spotted a Great Blue Heron, a cluster of Cormorants, and just a few feet away, a pair of dolphins frolicking in the water.

Emma thought to herself 'This is truly beautiful, this is one of those moments in life where you just look in awe'

As it turned out, the day was flawless, and none of Jasper's concerns materialized into actual problems. However, by the time the two boats finally arrived at the Marina in Charleston, it was quite late. Given the hour, they decided to call it a night.

The following morning the four of them were off to see Charleston. Emma, Jasper, Scott, and Samantha were excited to explore the city, and they had planned a day filled with sights and experiences that everyone could enjoy.

The group headed towards the historic district. They navigate the charming, tree-lined avenues and past beautifully preserved antebellum homes. The city's rich history was evident in every corner, from the ornate ironwork on the historic mansions to the well-maintained public squares.

Their first stop was the historic Charleston City Market, a bustling area full of local vendors and artisans. The market offered a delightful array of crafts, food, and souvenirs.

Emma and Samantha took turns pushing Jasper's wheelchair through the market, allowing him to take in the lively atmosphere and browse the unique stalls. Jasper was particularly intrigued by the local handmade crafts and enjoyed engaging with the vendors.

From the market, the group made their way to the waterfront area, where they explored the scenic Battery promenade. The promenade provided stunning views of the harbor and was lined with classic mansions, each with its own story. They stopped frequently to admire the views and take photographs.

For lunch, they chose a renowned local restaurant known for its Southern cuisine. The restaurant's outdoor patio was accessible, and the group enjoyed a delicious meal featuring Charleston specialties like shrimp and grits, she-crab soup, and fresh seafood.

Jasper appreciated the opportunity to savor the local flavors while enjoying the pleasant weather and views of the surrounding cityscape.

After lunch, they visited the Nathaniel Russell House, an elegant 19th-century mansion that offered a glimpse into Charleston's past. The house was well equipped with ramps and accessible routes, allowing Jasper to explore the beautifully restored rooms and learn about the history of the house and its former inhabitants.

As the day drew to a close, the group took a leisurely stroll through the nearby Waterfront Park. The park's iconic Pineapple Fountain and pretty surroundings provided a relaxing end to their day of exploration.

When they returned to their marina in the evening, everyone was content and fulfilled. The group settled back for a second night on the deck of Singing Swallows for a relaxed dinner, sharing their favorite moments from the day and reflecting on the beauty and charm of the city.

The next few days were spent cruising up the sheltered Intracoastal Waterway. They made a stop in McClellanville to collect their forwarded mail and visited the stunning Hopsewee Plantation.

Their journey continued until they reached Georgetown, where they found a well-protected, though somewhat busy, anchorage. The town offered all the amenities needed to restock the boats and a charming harbourfront boardwalk for leisurely strolls.

While walking along the boardwalk, Jasper paused and addressed the group. "Do you all like this city?" he asked.

Everyone either nodded or replied affirmatively. Jasper's smile faded slightly as he delivered some unexpected news.

"The forecast has changed. A major storm is approaching late tonight, and we're expecting heavy rain afterward. It looks like we might need to stay here for about a week."

The group's smiles quickly disappeared. Scott was the first to voice his thoughts. "I do like this town, but not that much. At least it's a practical stop. We're not paying for a marina, and it's easy to get into town, even if it's going to be rainy."

Samantha chimed in with a suggestion. "Since this might be the last sunshine we see for a while, how about we head out to find a patio for dinner? It would be nice to enjoy the weather while we still can."

Everyone agreed, and they quickly found a restaurant with a patio offering panoramic views of the harbor. They spent a few pleasant hours enjoying their food and drinks, but as expected, the wind began to pick up, and dark clouds loomed on the horizon.

As the weather took a turn, Jasper said, "Well folks, I guess that's our cue. Let's settle up and head back to the boat before the storm hits."

Later that night, as Emma was speaking with Antoine, the storm arrived with a vengeance. The roar of thunder and the pounding rain were so overwhelming loud that Emma had to cut their conversation short.

Despite Jasper's reassurances that she was relatively safe from lightning, the storm still terrified her. She attempted to comfort herself by reminding herself that there were numerous sailboats nearby with their masts raised, so if lightning were to strike, it would likely hit them first.

The storm made for a long, restless night, but eventually, the intensity subsided, leaving only the steady patter of rain.

Over the next week, the rain came down relentlessly, so much so that Jasper couldn't resist joking about Noah's Ark. The persistent downpours kept them mostly confined to the boat, with only a few excursions into town during brief breaks in the weather.

Emma took advantage of the downtime to have a few writing lessons and call Ben and Antoine frequently.

She spoke with them so often that she eventually ran out of new things to talk about.

After days of waiting and enduring the dreary weather, the skies finally cleared, and they were ready to continue their journey. Emma was relieved; she felt like she was on the verge of losing her sanity from the prolonged confinement.

On the final day in Georgetown, Emma ventured into town alone to buy groceries and pick up a few other necessities. Jasper was impressed by her newfound independence. She had once been apprehensive about exploring new places by herself, but now she navigated strange towns with increasing confidence.

The following morning, Emma experienced an immense sense of relief as they readied to weigh anchor.

The weather was absolutely perfect for travel—clear skies and a brilliant sun overhead. Emma and Jasper were invigorated by the splendid conditions, savoring the peaceful sensation of the boat smoothly slicing through the water under the sunny sky.

They arrived at an anchorage in Wrightsville Beach, a charming little tourist town. Although the day's journey had been pleasant, Emma found herself unusually eager to call Antoine. Typically, she would start with a call to her dad before reaching out to Antoine, as their conversations often stretched late into the night. But tonight, she decided to call Antoine first.

After chatting with Antoine for a while, they decided to set up a three-way call with Ben. As luck would have it, Audra was also present and joined the conversation. The group enjoyed a lively discussion for several hours. Eventually, the call returned to just Antoine and Emma, who continued their conversation for the rest of the evening.

The next morning, as usual, Emma woke up a bit late. "Sorry, Grandpa. I was up late again talking to Antoine," she said, rubbing her eyes. Jasper chuckled, "I'm used to it by now."

Emma looked around, taking in the stunning scenery. "Wow, this really is a beautiful part of the country," she remarked.

Jasper grinned and said, "You know those Nicholas Sparks movies full of drama? Well, a lot are set and filmed right around here." Emma laughed, "Well, if there's ever a place for a little more drama, this is it. Antoine and I were actually talking about how it might be easier to work in each other's countries if we got married."

Jasper's eyes widened in surprise. "NO. It's way too soon for that. You should try living together first or something similar." Emma continued to laugh, "Well, we thought we would like to get married before we have a kid."

Jasper shook his head. "Let's hope that's still a ways off." Emma grinned, "Well, we know it'll be less than nine months from now."

Jasper was momentarily speechless. "Wha...?" was all he could manage. Emma's expression turned serious. "I'm pregnant. I bought a couple tests back in Georgetown, but I only did them yesterday."

Jasper took a deep breath, trying to process the news. For a moment, he was silent, the weight of the revelation settling in. Then, a broad smile spread across his face. "Emma, that's amazing!" he exclaimed, his voice filled with genuine joy.

Emma's eyes filled with tears of relief and happiness. "You really think so? I was so nervous about how you'd react."

Jasper moved closer and pulled her into a warm hug. "Of course, I think so! This is incredible news. I'm so happy for you. And for Antoine, too. You're going to be an amazing mom. I'm guessing you told Antoine and your Dad last night?" Jasper asked.

 Emma sat with Jasper, feeling the weight of the conversation settle between them. She took a deep breath and continued, "Yes, and they were both extremely happy when I told them. Antoine was eager for me to come straight home, but I was so anxious about revealing my phobia to him at that moment. So, I suggested we do a three-way call with my dad. I thought having him on the call might help."

Jasper nodded, encouraging her to go on. Emma sighed and added, "Antoine thought my dad would be on his side and insist I come home immediately, but both Dad and Audra told him that it's crucial for me to finish this trip,

especially since nothing major typically happens in the early stages of pregnancy. Dad even offered to pay for a private ultrasound when it's time, which is really comforting."

Jasper looked relieved. "That's great to hear". Emma smiled faintly. "Yes, and I'm planning to call my family doctor today. Audra has a friend who's a gynecologist, and she's going to check if she can arrange a video consultation for me until I can get home."

Jasper gave her a reassuring look. "You're handling everything so well. It's good that you're getting all the support you need. Just remember, we're all here for you, and you don't have to go through this alone."

Emma felt a surge of gratitude for Jasper's understanding and support. "Thank you, Grandpa. It means a lot to me to know that I'm not alone in this."

Jasper smiled "Sounds like you have it figured out". Emma chuckled softly. "Yep, it was a long call, but I'm feeling more settled now."

She paused before continuing, "Grandpa, I want this baby to have a full family. I need to understand what happened between you and my dad. I want to know why he's not here with us." Jasper's expression grew somber as he sighed. "Emma, that's not something I can fully explain.

If it were up to me, your dad would be right here with us. You'll need to talk to him directly to get the answers you're looking for."

Emma reluctantly accepted this and then brightened. "Do you think Samantha and Scott would want to go for breakfast?

I can't wait to tell them." Jasper smiled. "Sure, why don't you call and ask them?"

Chapter 16

Scarlett O'Hara

Scott and Samantha were still lying in bed when Samantha's phone rang. The phone was charging in the galley, so Samantha got up to answer it. After a brief conversation, she returned to their stateroom.

Scott, propped up in bed, greeted her with a warm smile. "Hold on a second," Scott said, his gaze fixed on her. Samantha, completely naked with the morning sun casting a soft glow around her, paused in the doorway, looking at him with curiosity.

Scott's smile widened. "I'm sorry, I just couldn't help but admire you. You know, you get more beautiful and sexy every day. And I'm really sorry for the way I acted before when you mentioned going to see a doctor."

Samantha walked over and lay down beside him, resting her head on his shoulder. "Well, I guess my timing could have been better," she replied softly. Scott chuckled. "If we're not pregnant by the time we get back, we'll both go see a doctor ok. So, who was on the phone?"

Samantha looked up at him with a mischievous glint in her eye. "That was Emma. They want us to meet them for breakfast in about an hour. She mentioned they have something to tell us. But that leaves us with a whole hour to ourselves."

With a playful grin, Samantha climbed on top of Scott, her intention clear. The two of them enjoyed their private moment together, making the most of their time before heading out for breakfast.

Well over an hour later, the two couples gathered at the marina restaurant, taking their seats at a sunny table with a view of the water. After placing their orders, Emma surveyed the group and remarked, "Wow, everyone seems so happy today."

Samantha flashed a bright smile and shared, "Scott and I have decided that if we're not pregnant by the time we get home, we'll go see a doctor.

Emma and Jasper exchanged glances, and Emma reflected, 'I hadn't considered how Samantha might react to this news. It might be difficult for her to hear. I can't bring it up now.' Turning back to Scott and Samantha, Emma said, "Antoine and I have decided to get married."

Both Samantha and Scott looked at her in shock. Scott spoke up, "But you've only been dating for less than a year, and you've spent even less time together in person."

Jasper then interjected, suddenly grasping what Emma was doing. "Yes, but it's mainly to facilitate working across the border. And let's be honest, in today's world, it's just a piece of paper, right?"

Jasper couldn't believe the words coming out of his mouth. This was far from his true feelings, but he recognized that Emma needed a lifeline in this conversation.

Samantha and Scott, now smiling, turned their attention to Emma. "Congratulations!" Scott said warmly. Samantha, beaming with excitement, enveloped Emma in a big hug. "Yes, congratulations! So, are you planning to get married as soon as you return, or will Antoine be joining you along the way again? Either way, I hope I'm invited!"

Before Emma could respond, Scott added, "It's less than a day's drive from our place to yours. We definitely want to be there."

Jasper quickly shifted the focus of the conversation. "So, what's the plan for today?" Scott replied, "I thought we'd cover a few miles and then stop at the next anchorage by dusk." Jasper's face lit up with a smile. "That sounds like a great idea. Let's wrap this up and get moving."

Later, as they traveled along, Emma turned to Jasper. "Grandpa, I wanted to thank you for what you said back there. I know it wasn't exactly your true opinion. I just realized I picked the worst moment to drop the news about the pregnancy and I panicked."

Jasper smiled warmly. "No problem at all. But just a heads-up—at some point, Samantha might notice there's something a bit different about you," he said, gently pointing at her belly. Emma chuckled, "Yeah, I know. I'm hoping Samantha and Scott might have their own news by then, and it won't be such a big deal."

Jasper raised an eyebrow. "That's one way to look at it. But honestly, if Samantha doesn't get pregnant and you wait, it might end up making things more awkward." Emma sighed thoughtfully. "I'll think about it. Thanks for the advice."

As the day wore on they were heading up the Intracoastal Jasper started looking at Charts etc looking at Anchorages. He was starting to get tired and figured they would be stopping for the night soon.

When a Coast Guard boat cut them off and pulled up fairly close alongside them, one of the crew members yelled across "This section of the Intracoastal goes through a secure area and will be closed for the next two hours while they are doing firing range practice.

As dusk began to settle in, the Coast Guard crew member added, "You can either anchor here and wait for the passage to reopen, or head back to the last proper anchorage for the night. It's your call."

Jasper quickly glanced at his charts and then radioed Scott. "We have two options: either go back an hour to the last decent anchorage or wait here for a couple of hours and continue to the next anchorage, but it'll be pitch black by the time we get there."

Scott's voice crackled over the radio, "I really don't like the idea of going backward. I've got a huge spotlight on board. Let's push forward." Jasper agreed. "All right, we'll continue forward."

Samantha then suggested cooking dinner for everyone and eating aboard the Singing Swallows while they waited. Jasper and Scott maneuvered their boats alongside each other, rafting them together, and Scott lowered his anchor. Emma decided to lend a hand in the galley. "Samantha, I need to ask you something," Emma said as she helped with the preparations.

Samantha looked up from where she was chopping vegetables. "Sure, what's on your mind?" Emma hesitated for a moment before speaking. "Do you think getting married just for a piece of paper is a bad idea? Honestly."

Samantha set down the knife and looked thoughtful. "You know, I tend to be pretty open-minded about most things, but the idea of marriage just for paperwork doesn't sit well with me. That said, I understand the need to make it easier for you two to be together."

Emma offered a slight smile. "What if I told you there was another reason behind it?"

Scott and Jasper were lounging on the deck, enjoying a cold beer as the sun began to set. The peaceful evening was suddenly interrupted by a loud, astonished "WHAT" coming from inside the cabin.

Jasper, with a knowing smile, took a sip of his beer. Scott, however, jumped up in alarm and rushed inside.

Inside the cabin, Scott found Samantha and Emma in a heartfelt embrace, both women visibly emotional with tears streaming down their faces. The scene was one of intense, raw emotion, and Scott's heart raced as he asked, "What's going on? What happened?"

Emma and Samantha pulled apart slightly, their faces still wet with tears. Emma looked at Scott, her eyes brimming with a mix of happiness and nervousness.

"I'm pregnant," she said softly, her voice trembling with the weight of the news.

Scott's eyes widened, but then a broad smile spread across his face. "So those are happy tears!" he exclaimed, clearly overjoyed. He stepped forward and gave Emma a warm, congratulatory hug. "Congratulations! That's wonderful news." Emma returned the smile. "Thank you, Scott."

Sensing the need for some privacy, Scott nodded. "I'll leave you two to talk." He gave them one last encouraging glance before heading back out to the deck, leaving Samantha and Emma to share their moment of joy and support.

Scott returned to the deck to rejoin Jasper, his mind clearly preoccupied. "Wow, that's some news," he said soberly, settling into his seat. Jasper, noticing Scott's serious tone, asked, "Yes, are you alright? You seem a bit unsettled."

Scott nodded, though his expression remained troubled. "Yes, I'm okay. It's just... this news might put even more pressure on Samantha. It's already a sore spot for us."

Jasper, understanding the delicate situation, responded thoughtfully. "Scott, Emma and I had already discussed this. She even considered not telling Samantha to avoid adding to the stress. But I convinced her that hiding it wouldn't work in the long run—Samantha would notice eventually. I'm truly sorry if this adds more pressure, but we couldn't see another way. You know Emma is going to need her friends right now."

Scott's face softened as he considered Jasper's words. "You're absolutely right," he said with a genuine smile. "I'm sorry for my reaction. You're right, Emma does need support and we'll be here for her."

After a couple of hours, the Coast Guard signaled that the restriction was lifted. The two boats untied and prepared to resume their journey. Singing Swallows took the lead as darkness fully enveloped the waterway.

Emma and Samantha settled at the bows of their boats, eyes straining in the night to spot any potential hazards. The calm, gentle sound of the boat cutting through the water mixed with the night's chorus of crickets and frogs, creating a peaceful atmosphere that Emma found extremely blissful.

As they continued on, the hours slipped by until they finally arrived at their chosen anchorage. Singing Swallows had already found a spot, and now it was up to them to locate theirs.

Emma switched on their spotlight, illuminating the water, while Jasper navigated the boat at a crawl, keeping a close watch on the depth finder. When they found a suitable spot, Jasper shifted the engine into neutral and told Emma to drop the anchor.

Once the anchor was secured and Emma returned to the cockpit, Jasper turned to her with a serious look "Emma, there's something we need to talk about," he began. Emma, concerned asked "What's up?" Jasper sighed "With your pregnancy, I don't think it'll be feasible for you to handle anchoring duties as you get further along. We'll need to stick to marinas for the latter part of our trip."

Emma's face fell. She loved the peaceful nights at anchor, and she knew Jasper did too. "I'm really sorry, Grandpa," she said, feeling guilty. Jasper shook his head reassuringly. "Don't worry about it. Your health and the baby's safety are what matter most. We'll adjust our plans and make it work. The marinas will be fine, and we'll still enjoy our journey."

The next day, after a short but delightful cruise, the two boats anchored near a beautiful barrier island with a pristine beach. They spent the day swimming in the clear waters and sunbathing on the soft sand. Jasper, looking around at the idyllic scene, reminded Emma, "This is our last opportunity for these beachside pleasures until we reach New Jersey."

To fully enjoy the moment, they set up a picnic on the beach, making the most of their time in this secluded spot before their journey continued.

As the day started to draw to a close they weighed anchor just to move to an anchorage closer to the town of Beaufort for the night. Emma couldn't help but notice that they already went through Beaufort South Carolina and now there in Beaufort North Carolina.

Jasper laughed "Yep but there is a way to tell them apart. It's in the pronunciation, The last Beaufort is pronounced Bew-Fort and this one is pronounced Bo-Fort" Emma still chuckled, finding it still a little amusing. With that they settled into their evening routine Jasper relaxing with his book and Emma on the phone.

The next day, after a brief stroll around Beaufort, they continued north. The route began to veer inland from the ocean, transitioning from a river-like passage to a large bay and then back to a narrow canal.

This pattern persisted for the following days, alternating between expansive bays and narrow rivers. They anchored each night until they reached Belhaven, where they docked at a marina that resembled more of a resort. The main building had once been a plantation.

It was already getting late, so they decided to call it a night.

The following day, the group set out to explore the marina before taking one of the complimentary electric golf carts into town for provisioning. Scott and Samantha had left early to get a head start and planned to meet up with Emma and Jasper later in the evening.

Emma took the wheel of the golf cart, eager to control the pace. She started off slowly, but as the day went on, she found herself driving faster than Jasper had anticipated. The convenience of the cart made their errands a breeze, allowing them to easily pick up everything they needed for the trip.

Jasper, mindful of the journey ahead, was determined to make the most of this opportunity. He knew they needed to stock up on supplies thoroughly, as he wanted to cover some significant distance without making another stop until they reached Norfolk. The day's successful provisioning meant they were well-prepared for the leg of their journey that lay ahead.

When they returned to the marina, Jasper and Emma noticed a couple in their late thirties posing for wedding photos next to Arabella. The bride was resplendent in a stunning white wedding dress and the groom was dressed in elegant formal wear. Jasper and Emma hesitated, not wanting to intrude on their special moment.

Jasper finally approached them with a friendly smile. "Excuse me, but that's my boat you're taking pictures with." The groom turned, a bit flustered, and quickly apologized. "Oh, I'm so sorry! I've always had a passion for antique boats, and she is truly a masterpiece."

Jasper's expression softened as he saw the genuine admiration in the groom's eyes. "Well, if you'd like, you're welcome to come aboard and take some more pictures there.

I'd be happy to show you around." The groom's face lit up with excitement. "Seriously? That would be amazing!" He glanced at his bride and the photographer, who both nodded in agreement.

The photographer seemed momentarily lost in thought before finally addressing Jasper. "We still have a couple of hours before the dinner. Do you think it's possible for us to take a short cruise for some additional photos? I'd be happy to pay for the favor."

Jasper chuckled "Absolutely, I think that's a wonderful idea. But I couldn't possibly take your money." The bride and groom exchanged delighted looks, their smiles widening as they processed the offer. Vivian, the bride, gave a grateful nod, while Rhett, the groom, seemed thrilled. Emma, with a smile stepped in and said, "Alright, everyone on board!"

Once they were all aboard Arabella, Jasper and Emma introduced themselves. "I'm Jasper, and this is my granddaughter, Emma. And you are?" Rhett extended his hand with a friendly grin. "I'm Rhett and this beautiful bride is Vivian." Vivian waved and said, "It's such a pleasure to meet you both. We're so grateful for this opportunity."

Jasper let out a chuckle. "I haven't heard the name Rhett since the movie 'Gone with the Wind.'" Rhett grinned. "Yeah, my mom was a huge fan of the film."

Vivian added, "And I get—" Emma interrupted with a playful smile, "Pretty Woman, right?"

Everyone turned to Emma with curiosity. Jasper looked at her and explained, "In 'Gone with the Wind,' the main couple are Rhett Butler and Scarlett O'Hara. Scarlett was played by Vivien Leigh. So, I'm guessing Vivian gets that reference more often." Vivian burst into laughter. "Yes, that's true. I have to say, this is the first time someone's referenced 'Pretty Woman.'"

Emma blushed slightly. "I have to admit, I've never seen 'Gone with the Wind,' but I definitely will now. And by the way, what's your name?" She turned to the photographer. "I'm Lisa," she replied with a smile. "Thank you so much for doing this." Jasper nodded, "It's our pleasure."

With that, Jasper started the engine, and Arabella gracefully slid away from the dock, setting out on a scenic cruise. The photographer busily snapped photos of the couple, the gentle ripples of the water, and the elegant lines of the boat.

The air was filled with laughter and the soft hum of the engine, capturing the perfect moments for Rhett and Vivian's special day, while Emma and Jasper enjoyed the unexpected joy of sharing their boat with such a charming couple.

Once they were out of the harbor, Jasper suggested they stop the boat for a moment. "What about if Emma took the photographer in the dinghy for some shots of the couple from farther back? It'll give you a better perspective."

Vivian and Rhett eagerly agreed and Lisa prepared her gear for the dinghy shoot. Emma helped her into the smaller boat, and Lisa set up her camera to capture the couple from various angles.

As the dinghy maneuvered around the larger vessel, Lisa snapped photos of Rhett and Vivian striking different poses. They even did the classic 'I'm flying' pose off the bow, with Rhett holding Vivian as she stretched her arms out, laughing joyfully.

Lisa also took some professional shots of Jasper and Emma, capturing their genuine smiles and the tranquil beauty of the setting sun reflecting off the water.

When the photo session was over, everyone returned to the main boat, where Rhett and Vivian expressed their heartfelt thanks. Vivian hugged Emma and Jasper, "This has been incredible. Thank you so much for making our day so special."

Jasper smiled, "We're glad we could be a part of it. It's not every day we get to share Arabella with such a lovely couple."

Once back at the marina, Rhett and Vivian expressed their gratitude once more. Vivian, with a warm smile, said, "Since you've given us such a wonderful wedding gift, it seems you have no choice but to come to our reception!" Rhett chimed in enthusiastically, "Yes, please join us. It would mean a lot to have you there."

Jasper and Emma exchanged a glance and then turned to the couple. Emma spoke up, "We'd love to come, but we're actually traveling with another couple." She gestured toward Swinging Swallows. Before Emma could continue, Rhett interrupted, "Bring them along! We'd love to have everyone join us."

Emma and Jasper smiled, feeling genuinely touched by the invitation. Emma said. "Thank you so much for including us." With the plans set, the two couples parted ways, looking forward to the evening's festivities and the chance to celebrate the newlyweds.

Later that evening, Emma made her way over to Swinging Swallows to share the exciting news about the day's events and to extend the wedding reception invitation to Scott and Samantha. As she explained the afternoon's adventure and the kind invitation from Rhett and Vivian, she saw their initial excitement turn into hesitation.

Samantha was the first to speak, "Oh that sounds amazing, but we really don't have anything appropriate to wear. I'd feel so out of place." Scott nodded in agreement. "Yeah, we don't have anything that nice. I think we'd just feel uncomfortable."

Emma tried to reassure them, "Grandpa is just planning to wear a dress shirt and slacks, and I'm going with a simple sundress. It's a casual wedding reception. You guys would be perfectly fine!" Despite Emma's efforts to convince them, Scott and Samantha remained firm in their decision. Samantha sighed, "We really appreciate the invitation, but we just don't feel right about it."

Emma, though disappointed, understood their hesitation. "Okay, I get it. If you change your minds, just let us know. It'll be a fun evening!" With a friendly wave and a promise to fill them in on the details later, Emma left Swinging Swallows, her mind already thinking about how to make the most of the upcoming celebration.

When it was time to head out, Jasper was already waiting in the cockpit, looking sharp in his dark slacks, gray pinstripe shirt, and matching tie. Emma emerged from her cabin, and with a playful smile, she said, "Wow, you clean up nice!" Jasper grinned and replied, "You look fantastic yourself."

Emma was wearing a light blue sundress adorned with a delicate seashell print, which fluttered slightly in the evening breeze. Together, they made their way to the old plantation where the reception was being held.

As soon as they entered, Rhett and Vivian spotted them immediately. The newlyweds enthusiastically greeted them, their faces lighting up with smiles. "I'm so glad you could make it!" Vivian said, guiding them through the elegant venue.

Rhett took over, introducing Emma and Jasper to various guests. "These are the wonderful people who helped us with our wedding photos this afternoon," he explained. "They took us out on their beautiful boat and gave us some truly memorable shots."

Throughout the evening, Emma and Jasper mingled with the other guests, enjoying the warm ambiance and celebrating the newlyweds. The reception was filled with laughter, heartfelt toasts, and the clinking of glasses, making for a delightful night in honor of Rhett and Vivian.

Jasper and Emma had a great night that ran quite late, but before they left Vivian gave them her contact information so she could make sure to get them the pictures from today.

The next morning they were both woken up by knocking on the cabin. Jasper and Emma slid open their respective hatches and Scott was outside. "Sorry, were you guys still sleeping? I was just wondering when we are going to get going."

Jasper answered "Sorry it was a late night. We are up, just give us a few minutes and we will be on our way ok?" Scott smiled "sounds good, we will be waiting". Before long they were back to traveling.

Chapter 17

The Expansive Command Bridge

After a late start to the day, the crew of both boats finally resumed their journey, slipping back into their routine of navigating the waterways.

The hours passed with the steady hum of engines and the gentle sway of the boats as they cut through the Alligator River. The sun began its slow descent, casting a warm, amber glow over the water.

As evening approached, Emma and Jasper, along with Scott and Samantha, decided it was time to find a suitable spot to anchor for the night. They navigated their way towards a small, secluded bay off of Albemarle Sound, a promising location they had identified earlier in the day.

The bay was nestled in a quiet corner, shielded from the more open waters of the sound. It offered a tranquil haven, perfect for a restful night after a day of steady travel. As the boats glided into the bay, Jasper maneuvered their boat with a practiced hand, finding a spot where the water was calm and the depth suitable for anchoring.

Scott followed suit, positioning Singing Swallows nearby. Once both boats were securely anchored, the crew set about their evening routines.

As they settled into their evening, the day's fatigue seemed to melt away, replaced by a sense of contentment. The bay's ambiance provided a great end to a productive day of travel.

The morning sun broke over the horizon, casting a golden glow on the anchorage where Jasper and Scott's boats had spent the night. The peaceful waters and quiet surroundings of the anchorage had provided a restful respite, but the day ahead promised new decisions.

As the boats prepared for departure, Jasper and Scott talked on the phone. The conversation turned to the choice they faced; the Virginia Cut route or the Dismal Swamp Canal route.

Jasper explains the two options. "We've got two main routes to consider. The Virginia Cut is shorter and more direct, but it's often busier, less scenic and can be quite rough. The Dismal Swamp Canal, on the other hand, is a bit longer and slower, but it's known for its beauty and tranquil scenery."

Scott looked thoughtful, considering the choices. "We've had a lot of open water recently. A change of pace could be nice. The Dismal Swamp Canal sounds like it could be an interesting experience." Samantha nodded in agreement. Emma, listening in on the conversation, glanced at Jasper "I'm leaning towards the Dismal Swamp Canal too".

Jasper looked up, his eyes reflecting the same enthusiasm. "I agree. The Dismal Swamp Canal it is then. It may take a bit longer, but I think it will be worth it. Plus, it'll be interesting to explore a route that has so much historical significance."

With their decision made, the group set about preparing for the day's journey. The engines roared to life, and the boats began their slow exit from the anchorage.

As the boats re-emerged into Albemarle Sound, the tranquility of the previous anchorage was quickly replaced by the tumultuous conditions of the open water. The waves crashed and churned, sending sheets of spray over the deck. The once-gentle breeze now roared with a fierce intensity, and the water seemed to writhe in agitation.

Inside the cabin, Emma braced herself against the lurching of the boat, her heart racing with the uncertainty of the rough waters. She glanced through the porthole, watching the chaotic scene outside, and felt a rising sense of unease. The boat rocked and pitched with each wave, making it difficult to stay steady.

Jasper, with his eyes firmly on the horizon and his hands deftly maneuvering the tiller, was focused on guiding Arabella through the challenging conditions. He knew that this stretch of water could be particularly volatile, but he had faith in his vessel's capabilities.

As the boat pitched and swayed, Jasper made a point to reassure Emma. "Don't worry Emma," he called over the noise of the stormy sea. "We're heading for the sheltered waters of the Pasquotank River soon. Arabella is designed to handle much worse than this. She's built for the roughest seas."

Emma nodded, trying to calm her racing thoughts. She knew Jasper had extensive experience and a deep trust in Arabella's seaworthiness, but the violent waves and the relentless spray made it hard for her to relax. Still, Jasper's steady voice and confident demeanor were comforting.

The rough passage seemed endless, each wave battering the boat with renewed vigor. But Jasper's skill and experience kept them on course. He maintained a steady pace, carefully navigating the tumultuous waters with precision. Emma clung to the reassurance that they were making progress toward the calmer waters of the river.

Finally, after what felt like an eternity, they started transitioning from the open sound to the sheltered river which brought a welcome reprieve. The water began to smooth out, and the violent spray lessened, allowing Emma to venture back above deck.

Emma felt a sense of relief as the boat eased into the calmer, more sheltered waters of the river. The river's gentle current and the protective embrace of its banks offered a stark contrast to the previous chaos. Emma took a deep breath, her tension easing as she looked around at the serene surroundings.

Jasper's reassuring words and steady handling of the boat had proven true. They were safely on their way to a more tranquil part of their journey.

The Pasquotank River seemed to gradually close in on them, the riverbanks creeping closer together as if drawing the boat into a more intimate embrace.

Tall trees and lush vegetation lined the banks, their reflections shimmering in the slowly calming water.

The landscape offered a stark contrast to the chaos they had just left behind. The sky above was a clear, tranquil blue, and the gentle lapping of the water against the hull was a soothing sound after the tumultuous conditions of the sound.

Emma felt her tension ebb away as they glided along, surrounded by the beauty of the untouched wilderness.

As they moved forward, the river's width continued to decrease, and the surroundings grew even more serene. The once spacious waterway now seemed to funnel them towards a new destination. Jasper's focus was unwavering, his eyes scanning the charts and the narrowing channel ahead.

"Looks like we're getting close," Jasper remarked, glancing over at Emma with a reassuring smile. "We'll be entering the Great Dismal Swamp Canal soon."

Emma looked around, observing the narrowing passage with a sense of anticipation. The trees on either side seemed to stretch their limbs towards each other, creating a lush, green tunnel that beckoned them forward. The gentle curve of the river guided them along, hinting at the intriguing journey ahead.

Finally, as they rounded a bend, the Pasquotank River seamlessly transitioned into the Great Dismal Swamp Canal. The change was subtle but unmistakable. The river's width had constricted to a narrow channel, and the dense vegetation along the banks seemed to envelop them in a lush, green world.

The Great Dismal Swamp Canal stretched out before them, a testament to nature's unspoiled beauty and man's ability to harness it. The water was calm and reflective, and the air was filled with the earthy scent of the swamp. The towering trees and tangled vines created a sense of seclusion and mystery.

Arabella's bow cut through the calm waters with a steady rhythm. Emma felt a renewed sense of wonder as they entered this new phase of their journey. As they continued along the canal, the sense of being surrounded by nature's untouched splendor deepened. The Great Dismal Swamp Canal offered a unique and picturesque setting.

Emma was pleasantly surprised when she saw the locks appearing once again along their route.

There was something oddly satisfying about the process, a blend of anticipation and precision that she found oddly comforting.

As they approached the first lock, Emma watched with keen interest. The old, sturdy gates loomed ahead with their weathered wood and ironwork. As they began to open, Jasper maneuvered Arabella into position, skillfully guiding the boat into the lock chamber. Emma readied herself on the deck, prepared to handle the lines as they entered.

Once inside, Emma took a moment to appreciate the quiet. The surrounding walls of the lock created a cocoon of calm, muffling the sounds of the outside world. She looked at Jasper, who was focused but seemed relaxed.

The lock gates closed behind them, the water slowly rose till the chamber was full. Then the lock gates opened again, revealing the next stretch of the canal, Emma's face lit up with a smile. She enjoyed the brief pause it provided and the sense of achievement that came with successfully navigating through the lock.

After navigating through the narrow confines of the canal, the boats emerged back into the open rivers. The familiar sensation of wider waters greeted them as they continued their journey.

As the sun began to set they headed to a marina that was part of the Nauticus Maritime Center and Naval Museum, a place he thought would offer both a convenient docking spot and an interesting visit for the next day. As they approached the marina, the lights of the Nauticus complex twinkled invitingly in the distance, their reflections dancing on the water's surface.

Both boats, Singing Swallows and Arabella, maneuvered into their assigned slips with practiced ease.

The slips were conveniently located right across from each other, providing a perfect arrangement for easy access between the two boats.

With the boats securely docked and the day's journey coming to an end, the group took a moment to unwind. The night was growing late, and the excitement of the day had left them ready for a good night's rest. Jasper and Emma, along with Scott and Samantha, exchanged brief goodnights before heading to their respective boats.

The next morning dawned clear and crisp, with the promise of a day full of exploration and discovery. Jasper, Emma, Scott, and Samantha awoke to the gentle sounds of the marina—seagulls calling and the soft lapping of water against the hulls of their two boats.

After a hearty breakfast aboard their respective vessels, they made their way to meet on the docks, eager to start their day.

The Nauticus Maritime Center and Naval Museum stood just across from their slips, its modern architecture a stark yet welcoming contrast to the classic lines of the boats they had been traveling on. The group strolled across the dock.

Entering the museum, they were greeted by an impressive array of exhibits showcasing maritime history. The center's galleries were filled with artifacts, interactive displays, and informative panels that offered insights into the evolution of naval technology and the significance of maritime exploration.

Emma's eyes sparkled with interest as she moved from one exhibit to the next, taking in the rich history and diverse collections.

Scott and Samantha, equally captivated, marveled at the various models of antique ships and the detailed accounts of naval battles. Jasper, with his extensive knowledge of maritime history, shared fascinating anecdotes and insights, adding depth to their experience.

After spending a few hours immersed in the exhibits, the group made their way to the adjacent Battleship Wisconsin, a massive and formidable vessel that had been transformed into a museum. The battleship's sheer size and significance were awe-inspiring.

Boarding the Wisconsin, they quickly realized there were sections that Jasper would not be able to go through. He was however able to go onto the main deck and into a room called the Ship Experience Access Room. This specially designed room was developed for visitors that want to experience the Battleship, but are unable to physically take the tour.

The room has been designed to mimic a control center. Visitors are able to sit at a station and create their own tour of the Wisconsin as they navigate the software. While Jasper spent his time there, the rest of the group toured the ship.

They explored the vast deck, peered into the intricate machinery of the engine room, and marveled at the expansive command bridge. Each area offered a glimpse into the daily life of the sailors and the operational complexity of such a powerful warship. After the tour they met up with Jasper on the main deck "I'm sorry you couldn't come with us" Emma said thoughtfully. "Yeah buddy it was a lot of stairs and ladders. Truthfully at one point I was jealous of you" Scott said with a slight chuckle.

Jasper said "Thanks guys but it was fine that S.E.A.R room they set up was truly a great experience".

As the afternoon wore on, the group gathered on the deck of the Wisconsin, overlooking the tranquil waters of the harbor. They reflected on their day, sharing their favorite parts of the museum and battleship tour.

With the sun beginning to dip toward the horizon, they returned to the marina. They decided to enjoy a relaxed dinner together at a nearby waterfront restaurant.

Jasper checked the weather forecast one last time. The prediction was favorable—clear skies and calm winds for the next few days. Seizing the opportunity to make the most of the good weather, Jasper realized that an early start the following morning would be ideal for covering more distance and enjoying smoother traveling.

Gathering the group, Jasper shared his plan. "With the forecast looking so promising, I think it's best if we get an early start tomorrow. We can take advantage of the calm conditions to cover some good mileage and make the most of the pleasant weather."

Emma, Scott, and Samantha nodded in agreement, all appreciating the thought of making significant progress on their journey. Recognizing the importance of a good night's rest to ensure they were all well-prepared for an early departure, they agreed to call it a night earlier than usual.

The two boats, Arabella and Singing Swallows, slipped away from the docks at Nauticus just as the sun began to break over the horizon, creating a beautiful sunrise. As they navigated up the Elizabeth River, the bustle of the major port came into view.

Large cargo ships, their hulls gleaming in the morning light, loomed overhead like giants. Cranes swung back and forth, busy with the rhythm of loading and unloading. Emma stood at the bow of Arabella, her heart racing at the sight of the massive vessels.

The sounds of the port - the honking of horns, the calls of seagulls, the distant hum of machinery—filled her with both excitement and apprehension.

As Arabella and Singing Swallows glided past the naval base, the sheer scale of the vessels docked there took Emma's breath away. Massive destroyers, with their sleek lines and powerful silhouettes, towered above them, their intimidating presence a reminder of the might of the navy.

Nearby, aircraft carriers loomed like floating cities, their flight decks wide and flat, ready for planes to take off at a moment's notice.

The hulls of the ships were painted in shades of gray, blending seamlessly with the water beneath them. She could see sailors moving about on the decks, small figures against the vast machinery of war and she felt a swell of admiration for their service.

"Look at that one!" Scott called from Singing Swallows, pointing excitedly at a destroyer that seemed to slice through the water with effortless grace. "I read that they can go over 30 knots!"

As they continued along the waterway, the naval base slowly receded behind them, the impressive ships becoming mere silhouettes against the horizon. Emma felt a sense of accomplishment that they had navigated past such formidable vessels.

The Chesapeake Bay opened up before them, vast and inviting. Emma turned to Jasper, her fears now overshadowed by excitement. "What's next?" she asked, her eyes sparkling with anticipation.

"We're heading toward Gwynn Island," Jasper replied, a smile spreading across his face. "It's a beautiful anchorage. You'll love it."

As Arabella and Singing Swallows navigated toward Gwynn Island, the scenery transformed into a tranquil paradise. The water shimmered under the afternoon sun.

They rounded a sandy peninsula, revealing a sheltered cove that felt like a hidden gem. Jasper expertly maneuvered Arabella into position, and Scott followed suit with Singing Swallows. The two boats lowered their anchors, their lines stretching taut as they settled into the calm embrace of the water.

Emma looked around from the deck. Soft sand kissed the shoreline, and the gentle rustle of trees added to the idyllic atmosphere. It felt like stepping into a postcard. Looks like we've found a little piece of heaven," Emma remarked, glancing over at Jasper.

Samantha leaned over and called out from Singing Swallows, her eyes wide with excitement. "How about a swim? I could use a refreshing dip after that ride." "Count me in!" Emma agreed.

The allure of the sandy shore and clear water beckoned them like a siren's song. Once they were all ready, they made their way to the beach, the warm sun warming their skin as they stepped onto the soft sand. The shoreline was dotted with shells and bits of driftwood".

As the sun began its descent, they all felt a sense of peace, anchored behind the sandy peninsula of Gwynn Island.

The next couple of days were nothing short of spectacular. With clear skies and gentle breezes, Emma, Jasper, Scott and Samantha relished every moment on the water. The next night they anchored in the Solomons, where they explored quaint shops and enjoyed fresh seafood.

The next morning they were off for Annapolis, the sailing capital of the USA.

As they approached the vibrant city, the iconic skyline of Annapolis came into view. The spires of the Maryland State House and the charming historic buildings painted a picturesque scenery against the deep blue of the Chesapeake Bay.

They navigated through the busy harbor, where sailboats glided gracefully and the air was filled with the sound of seagulls.

"Let's keep it simple tonight," Jasper suggested. "How about we have a quiet evening aboard our boats and meet in the morning to explore the town together?" Samantha nodded enthusiastically. "I love that idea! A little downtime will be nice."

In the morning they all gathered on the dock. Jasper pointed toward the bustling waterfront. "Welcome to Annapolis! There's so much to see here." Emma's eyes sparkled. "I can't wait! What should we do first?"

Samantha chimed in, "Let's start with a stroll along the waterfront. I've heard the shops and cafes are fantastic." As they disembarked and made their way to the shore, the charm of Annapolis enveloped them. They wandered along the streets, admiring the colonial architecture and vibrant flowers adorning the homes.

The air was rich with the scent of blooming magnolias and freshly brewed coffee. Their first stop was a charming café where they enjoyed pastries and steaming cups of coffee. As they sat outside, the lively atmosphere of the harbor buzzed around them—people chatting, laughter echoing, and the distant sound of music drifting through the air.

Afterward, they explored the U.S. Naval Academy, marveling at the impressive buildings and learning about the history of this prestigious institution. Emma felt a swell of pride as they walked through the grounds, appreciating the dedication and sacrifice of those who served.

Later, they strolled back toward the docks, where the sight of sailboats bobbing gently in the water was mesmerizing. Jasper pointed out various vessels, sharing stories of famous races and sailing techniques.

As the sun began to set, casting a warm golden glow across the harbor, they found a cozy spot to watch the sunset. The sky transformed into a canvas of oranges, pinks, and purples, reflecting beautifully in the water. "Today was perfect," Emma said, leaning back against Jasper. "I can't believe how much we've done in just one day."

The next day they decided they were only going as far as Baltimore harbor. It was another perfect day as they left Anapolis and crossed the Chesapeake Bay. As usual Arabelle led the way. They did this because Singing Swallow was a trawler and could go faster. Having Arabella in front meant it was easier to keep pace.

They had been cruising on the bay for just a couple of hours when Emma emerged from the forward cabin, a tray of snacks in her hands. As she looked around at the sparkling water, a puzzled expression crossed her face. "Um, where did Singing Swallows go?"

Jasper turned back, scanning the horizon for any sign of their friends' boat. "That's a very good question. They were right there the last time I looked," he replied, frowning slightly. Jasper stopped Arabella quickly and called Singing Swallows. Scott

came on the radio "Sorry our engine died, I'm trying to restart it now."

Jasper's heart sank as he heard Scott's voice crackle over the radio again. "We're officially dead in the water," Scott said, his tone edged with frustration. "The engine won't restart."

"Okay, we're on our way back," Jasper replied, his mind already racing through possible solutions. He quickly started the engine on Arabella and maneuvered the boat around, setting a course back toward Singing Swallows.

As soon as they arrived, Jasper expertly maneuvered Arabella alongside Singing Swallows and tied the two boats together. He grabbed his toolbox and crossed over, determination etched on his face. "I'll take a look. I'm not a mechanic, but I've got plenty of experience with these diesels," he assured Scott as he climbed into the engine room.

After a few tense moments of silence, Jasper finally reappeared, wiping his hands on a rag. He looked at Scott, his brow furrowed. "Um, Scott, let me ask you something—did you not notice how hot your engine was running or smell anything unusual?" Scott looked oblivious, his brow furrowed in confusion.

Jasper looked at Scott, disappointment etched across his face. "Well, it looks like your belt wore out, which would have been a simple fix. But because you weren't monitoring your engine temperature, it seriously overheated and did some major damage. I'm sorry buddy, but this is really going to cost you. I can tow you to Baltimore Harbor, but that's the best I can do."

Scott's expression shifted from relief to worry. "Do you think they can fix it?" he asked, his voice tinged with anxiety.

Jasper hesitated, the weight of the situation hanging heavily between them. "It depends on how badly it's damaged. You could be looking at warped cylinder heads, leaking head gaskets, and scored cylinder walls—all of which are very expensive to repair. Worst case, you might need to replace the entire engine." Jasper continued.

"But first, we get you to a marina where they can take a look at it," Jasper replied, his tone firm but reassuring. "Once they assess the damage, you'll have a better idea of your options."

Scott looked over at Samantha, his expression shifting from guilt to resolve. "I'm really sorry. I didn't know it was getting that bad. But whatever happens, I won't let this ruin our trip. We'll just be stuck in Baltimore for a bit."

Samantha smiled gently, wrapping her arms around him in a comforting hug. "Accidents happen, Scott. We'll get it fixed, no matter the cost. Just promise me that now that you know, you'll keep a closer eye on things. We can't afford to let this happen again."

He nodded, her words sinking in. "I promise. I've learned my lesson the hard way." Emma nodded in agreement, trying to provide a sense of hope. "And who knows? Maybe it won't be as bad as it sounds."

Jasper grabbed a tow line and prepared to connect it to Singing Swallows. "Let's get you moving," he said, his focus shifting to the task at hand. "The sooner we get you to a proper dock, the sooner we can start figuring this out."

As Jasper secured the tow line, Scott took a deep breath, bracing himself for the challenges ahead. "Thanks man, I really appreciate it," he said, his voice full of gratitude mixed with apprehension.

We could be in Baltimore for quite a while, and I don't want you two to be stuck there the whole time. So tell you what, you guys continue your trip. We should catch up to you before we cross our wake in Tom's River."

Jasper looked at him sympathetically. "Well, we did want to visit Baltimore anyway, so we'll stay until we at least know how long you'll be. Then we'll decide. How does that sound?"

Scott nodded, relief washing over him. "That sounds fair. We'll keep you updated on the repairs. I'll make sure to push them to get it fixed as quickly as possible."

Samantha chimed in, "And in the meantime, we can explore the city together. There's so much to see and do. We can't let this setback keep us from enjoying the journey."

Emma smiled, feeling a wave of optimism. "Exactly! We can turn this into a little adventure. Who knows what we might discover?"

"But for now, let's get you into a marina," Jasper said, with determination in his voice. They quickly finished setting up a tow line between the two boats, ensuring everything was secure.

Once ready, Jasper throttled up his engine, and the line went taut. They slowly started moving, the gentle hum of the engine blending with the sounds of the water.

Jasper glanced at Emma, a playful smile crossing his face. "Pulling a boat larger than ours is going to make for a slow day. I'll have to keep a close eye on our engine temperature so we don't end up like them. I'm just glad it's a calm day. I'd hate to do this in waves."

Emma chuckled, appreciating Jasper's lightheartedness in the situation. "Yeah, I can't imagine trying to tow them through choppy waters. We'd probably be stuck for hours!"

As they made their way toward the marina. Jasper kept a steady pace, his focus shifting between what's ahead and the temperature gauge. "We'll get them there safely," he assured Emma.

After many hours of steady towing, Jasper finally radioed into the marina, explaining their situation. "We're bringing in a disabled boat," he said, "and we need a clear end dock for easy access."

The marina staff quickly confirmed they would have a space ready, emphasizing that they had full boat repair facilities available. Jasper relayed the information to Scott, reassuring him that help was on the way.

With precision, Jasper guided the boats as they passed slowly by the end of the dock. Scott prepared himself, ready to jump onto the dock as soon as they were close enough. When the moment came, he sprang onto the solid surface, quickly making his way a few feet down the dock before stopping Swinging Swallows.

Scott then skillfully walked the boat up to the end, ensuring there was enough space for Jasper to turn around and moor behind him.

Once they were all secured, Jasper let out a sigh of relief. "We made it," he said, glancing at Scott, who was tying off the lines. "Thanks for the smooth ride," Scott replied, his expression a mix of gratitude and determination. "Now, let's see what kind of repairs we're facing."

Scott and Jasper made their way to the main office, eager to settle the docking fee before heading over to the workshop to speak with the mechanic. After a brief conversation about the issues with Swinging Swallows, they learned the mechanic would be down shortly to assess the situation. Feeling a sense of urgency, they hurried back to their boats.

As they approached Arabella, they noticed Samantha already on board, chatting with Emma in the cockpit. Scott smiled, relieved to see them both in good spirits despite the circumstances. "The mechanic will be down shortly to have a look," he announced.

"Wow, that was fast," Samantha replied, glancing back at Scott with a look of optimism.

Scott then continued, "Why don't you three go into town while I deal with this? It's my fault anyway, and I'm sure I'll have plenty of time to explore it for myself."

Emma, Samantha, and Jasper exchanged glances, realizing this was a perfect opportunity. "Are you sure?" Emma asked, wanting to make sure Scott was okay with the plan.

"Absolutely," Scott reassured them, waving his hand dismissively. "I'll be fine here."

Samantha, Jasper and Emma decided to explore Baltimore. They start their day at the Inner Harbor, admiring the classic ships and enjoying a walk along the waterfront and grabbing some crab cakes from a local vendor. Later, they stroll through the historic Fells Point area, browsing quirky shops and stopping for coffee at a cozy café.

Samantha's phone buzzed, it was Scott, letting her know he was finished at the mechanic and wanted to join them for dinner. Happy, she relayed the message to Jasper and Emma.

They quickly decided to head to a nearby restaurant known for its lively atmosphere and delicious seafood. As they arrived, the smell of grilled fish and spices filled the air, teasing their appetites. They found a table on the patio, where they could enjoy the warm breeze and watch the sun dip toward the horizon, casting a golden hue over the marina.

Once seated, Scott looked sheepishly at Samantha. "Well, I have good news and bad news," he began, the playful tone in his voice contrasting with the serious content. "Bad news first. The engine is not worth repairing."

Samantha's expression dropped, but Scott continued, "The good news is we're getting a new engine! The only thing is... I had to promise them our firstborn to pay for it."

Samantha shook her head, a slight smile breaking through her concern. "Well, I guess we don't have a choice. How long is it going to take?" Scott's tone shifted to serious. "About a week." Samantha stared at him, processing the news.

The weight of the situation hung in the air, but then she took a deep breath. "Well, I don't want to think about it right now. Let's just enjoy this beautiful night."

Emma and Jasper nodded in agreement, and the atmosphere lightened. They ordered a variety of seafood dishes to share, drinking glasses of white wine.

As the sun set, the patio filled with laughter and chatter from other diners, the sounds of clinking glasses and sizzling dishes creating a lively backdrop. Emma felt a warm sense of camaraderie, the worries of the day slipping away as they shared stories and made plans for the future.

"Let's not let this hiccup ruin our trip," Samantha suggested, her eyes sparkling with enthusiasm. "We'll make the most of our time in Baltimore." "Absolutely," Scott chimed in. "And we can plan a few fun outings while we wait for Swinging Swallows to be ready." Later that night, as the stars twinkled above and the gentle sound of water lapping against the hull of Arabella created a soothing ambiance, Jasper and Emma sat in the cockpit, deep in discussion.

"What do you think our next move should be?" Jasper asked, his brow slightly furrowed. After a moment of contemplation, Emma replied, "I think we should stay in Baltimore for about half a week. It gives Scott and Samantha time to sort out their engine issues."

"Good point," Jasper agreed, nodding. "And since it's mostly open water between here and New Jersey, Singing Swallows should be able to travel faster. They'll likely catch up to us in no time."

Emma smiled, her heart lightening at the thought. "And as long as we're together to celebrate them crossing their wake, I think that's what really matters."

"Absolutely," Jasper said, his face breaking into a grin. "It'll be nice to have this time to explore Baltimore. There's so much history and culture here. We can make the most of it while we wait." They spent the next few moments brainstorming places to visit, from the vibrant Inner Harbor to local seafood joints.

During the next few days in Baltimore, the group immersed themselves in the city. They visited the National Aquarium, where colorful fish and playful sea otters captivated their attention. Emma squealed with delight as she watched the dolphins perform their tricks, while Jasper admired the intricate ecosystems on display.

They also spent time at Patterson Park Observatory, marveling at the sweeping views of the city and the lush greenery surrounding them. The highlight of their trip came when they explored Fort McHenry, where they walked the grounds that inspired "The Star-Spangled Banner." Emma felt a deep connection to history.

Samantha and Emma made the most of their time together, often grabbing bikes to ride through the city's numerous trails. They laughed and chatted as they pedaled along the scenic routes, the warm sun shining down on them. The city felt alive.

When the day finally arrived for them to leave, there was a bittersweet feeling in the air. They gathered at the harbor, the boats bobbing gently in the water. Scott and Samantha came over to say their goodbyes, a mix of gratitude and hope in their eyes.

"Take care of yourselves out there!" Scott said, clapping Jasper on the back. "We'll catch up soon." With promises to reunite soon, Jasper and Emma waved farewell as they cast off from the dock.

As they navigated away from the harbor, the skyline of Baltimore faded into the distance, but the memories they created would remain etched in their hearts. They were ready for the next chapter of their journey, the open waters of the Chesapeake Bay stretching before them, full of possibility.

The weather was not as nice as it had been but at least the wind was blowing from the South-East meaning it was coming from shore and the waves were not too bad.

After a long day Emma was happy when they entered the Chesapeake and Delaware Canal. Even though this canal gave shelter from the open waters of the Chesapeake it was a major connection between the two bays and it was frequented by very large commercial ships which always put Emma on edge.

The canal is about fourteen miles long and about one third of the way in, Jasper and Emma anchored for the night in Chesapeake City, a quaint town. As the sun set, they enjoyed the views of the waterway while they ate in the cockpit.

The next morning, the mood shifted as Jasper gathered Emma on the deck to share some unsettling news. "I'm sure you noticed the treetops swaying. The wind is still blowing hard, and while that's manageable up north in the Chesapeake, it's a different story on the Delaware. It'll be coming straight up the bay, creating some very rough water."

Emma's expression faltered for a moment, her excitement dimming as she processed the implications. But just as quickly, she pushed through the gloom, finding a silver lining. "Well, so be it. That's part of the adventure, right?" She flashed Jasper a big smile, determination shining in her eyes.

Jasper couldn't help but soften at her optimism, though he remained serious. "The forecast suggests it'll last a few days, though." Emma maintained her upbeat demeanor.

"Well, I guess Scott and Samantha will have a chance to catch up during that time."

Her spirit was contagious, and Jasper found himself warming to the idea. "Yeah, you're right," he replied, finally allowing a smile to creep onto his face. "They can use the extra time to get repaired in Baltimore. And we can take a breather, maybe explore some local spots ourselves."

The quaint little town had an undeniable charm, with colorful storefronts and inviting sounds drifting through the air. Emma pointed out, "Look over there! I can see an ice cream shop and a museum!" Her eyes sparkled with excitement.

"I've been craving ice cream," she said, beaming. "Why don't we grab a couple of cones and take a stroll through town?" "That sounds like a great idea," Jasper replied, smiling back at her enthusiasm. Emma quickly got to work, maneuvering Jasper's wheelchair into the dinghy with practiced ease.

Once they were both settled, she expertly navigated the small boat to the dinghy dock. They made their way to the ice cream hut, where the colorful menu tempted them with an array of flavors.

Indulging in their favorites—Emma with her beloved mint chocolate chip and Jasper opting for a classic vanilla. After they finished savoring the delicious treat, they wandered through the town, taking in the charming scenery.

Their next stop was the C&D Canal Museum. As luck would have it, admission was free. Eager to learn about the canal's history and its significance to the region, they ventured inside. The museum was filled with intriguing exhibits, and they marveled at the old photographs that depicted the canal in its heyday.

Jasper's attention was captured by a massive old steam engine on display, its intricate mechanisms a testament to engineering ingenuity. "Can you imagine the power this must have had?" he mused, running his fingers over the cold metal.

They spent time reading about the various boats that once navigated the waterway and even struck up a conversation with a friendly museum guide, who shared captivating stories of the canal's construction and the community that thrived around it. Emma found herself lost in tales of adventure, her imagination ignited by the history surrounding them.

After finishing their tour, they headed back to Arabella, where Jasper started to prepare dinner. The aroma of his cooking smelled so good. Emma smiled, feeling grateful for the day and the cozy evening ahead.

They settled in for a delightful meal, discussing everything they had learned and experienced, content in the knowledge that sometimes the unexpected detours were the most rewarding parts of their journey.

Early the next morning, Jasper stepped into the cockpit with his coffee and a book in hand. As he settled into his favorite spot, he took a moment to appreciate the view.

A layer of fog hung over the water, no more than a foot high, creating a quiet and ethereal atmosphere. There was something about these foggy mornings that always put Jasper at ease, inviting him to linger a little longer in the tranquility of the moment.

He set his book down, savoring the quiet. However, his peaceful morning was abruptly interrupted by a series of unmistakable sounds coming from Emma's cabin.

The unpleasant noise repeated, confirming what he already feared: morning sickness had struck. With a sigh, Jasper returned to his cabin for a moment, gathering a few thoughtful items before re-emerging. He made his way to

Emma's cabin and gently knocked on the door. "Emma, sweetheart, I'm coming in."

"Okay," came her weak voice from inside. Jasper slid the hatch open, and the sight that greeted him tugged at his heart. Emma was hunched over the toilet, looking pale and uncomfortable. He quickly approached, concern etched on his face. "Sweety, I brought you a couple of things," he said softly. "A glass of water to rinse your mouth, a wet cloth to wipe up, and a cup of ginger tea to help settle your belly."

Emma turned her head slightly, managing a weak smile. "Thank you," she murmured, her voice barely above a whisper. Jasper carefully placed the items on the counter beside her, then knelt down to be closer to her. "Just take your time, okay? I'm right here." As she sipped the water and ginger tea, Jasper's heart ached for her discomfort. "I know," she replied, her voice steadier now. "I just didn't think it would hit me this hard."

"It's all part of the adventure," Jasper said . "You always know how to make me feel better." replied Emma.

"Just doing my job," Jasper replied with a wink. "Now, let's take it easy today. How about a cozy morning aboard before we figure out our next steps?" Emma nodded, feeling a sense of calm wash over her. "That sounds perfect." With that, they settled into the day, surrounded by the soft sounds of the morning, the fog slowly dissipating as the sun began to rise.

By lunchtime, Emma was starting to feel a little better, though the thought of food still made her stomach churn.

Jasper, ever attentive, approached her with a plate of plain crackers. "Here, eat these. It might help settle your stomach."

Emma accepted the crackers with a grateful nod. "Thank you," she replied softly, nibbling on one cautiously. Jasper watched her with a sympathetic expression. "I think we should just spend the rest of the day onboard. No rush to go anywhere until you're feeling up to it."

Emma managed a weak smile, grateful for his understanding. "That sounds nice. I'm really sorry I'm not having more fun right now."

"Hey," Jasper said gently, "you don't have to apologize. Just focus on resting. I'll take care of everything else." Feeling reassured, Emma sank back against the cushions of the cockpit, the gentle sway of the boat lulling her into a sense of calm.

"It's so peaceful here," Emma remarked, leaning against the railing, feeling the gentle breeze against her skin. "Yeah, it really is," Jasper agreed, looking out over the water. "And it'll be even better when you're feeling 100% again." Emma smiled, appreciating his optimism. "I can't wait for that."

The next morning, Emma stepped into the cockpit to find Jasper beaming at her. "How are you feeling this morning?" he asked, a hint of hope in his voice. Emma grinned back, her spirits lifted. "I feel great! I guess it was just a one-day thing."

Jasper chuckled lightly, relieved but cautious. "I hope you're right." However, fate had other plans. By noon, Emma was back in her cabin, doubled over and groaning. "I thought this was called morning sickness!" she exclaimed, frustration coloring her tone.

Jasper, trying to keep the mood light, replied, "Well, I think it's just a name. In my experience, it can hit any time of day." Emma let out an exasperated "Ugh, that sucks!" as she clutched her stomach, the irony of it all hitting her hard.

Jasper, being supportive, asked her. "Want me to bring you some ginger tea or crackers?" he offered gently. "Yes, please," Emma sighed, grateful for his help. "I'll take anything that might make this a little more bearable."

As Jasper prepared the tea, he couldn't help but feel sympathy for her. He returned to her cabin with the warm mug and a few crackers, setting them down on the small table. "Here you go. Hopefully, this will help a bit."

Emma took a sip of the tea and nodded appreciatively. "Thanks, Grandpa. I really hope this doesn't last long." Jasper settled beside her, his expression softening. "Just remember, I'm here for you. We'll get through this together." She smiled weakly, comforted by his presence. "You make it easier," she admitted, taking another sip.

"Good. That's the plan," he replied. "In the meantime, let's just take it easy today. We don't have to go anywhere until you're feeling better."

The next few days unfolded much the same way, with Emma struggling through the afternoons while Jasper remained a steadfast support. Each day, she felt fine in the morning, only to be sidelined by nausea as the sun climbed higher. They spent their time on the boat.

On the fourth evening, a familiar sight broke the monotony as Singing Swallows glided into the anchorage. Excitement bubbled in Jasper as he waved, and it wasn't long before Scott and Samantha paddled over in their dinghy.

"Hi, guys! How are you doing?" Samantha called out, tying up alongside Arabella. "I'm fine, but Emma is a little under the weather," Jasper replied, glancing toward the cabin.Scott climbed aboard, concern evident on his face. "Is it a cold?"

Jasper chuckled lightly. "Yeah, one that lasts about nine months!" "Oh, morning sickness!" Samantha laughed, her voice ringing with understanding. She turned to the cabin. "Do you think she'd mind if I went in to see her?" Emma's voice drifted from inside, a mix of weariness and warmth. "Tell her to get in here!"

Samantha grinned and exchanged a knowing look with Scott and Jasper before heading inside to check on her friend. Once the two women were settled in, Jasper turned his attention back to Scott. "Listen, I was looking at the weather, and it seems like the wind is going to die down this evening and stay calm through tomorrow."

Scott raised an eyebrow. "That's good news, but what about the day after?" Jasper nodded, steadying himself for the next part. "I was thinking we might be able to cross the entire Delaware Bay in a single day." Scott pondered this for a moment, scratching his chin. "But that means navigating into the Cape May Canal at night."

"Not if we leave really early in the morning," Jasper replied, his eyes gleaming with determination. Scott's expression shifted as he considered it. "How early?" With a satisfied smile, Jasper laid out his plan.

"I did the math, and if we leave around three in the morning, we should be fine." Scott looked taken aback, a mix of surprise and intrigue crossing his features. "Okay, so be it. Let's do it. But what about Emma's morning sickness?"

Jasper paused, his brow furrowing slightly. "Well, as long as tomorrow is like the last few days—she wakes up fine, then gets sick in the afternoon, and is okay in the evening—she should be fine for both the departure and arrival. I just hope the forecast holds and it's not a bumpy ride."

Scott nodded, still considering. "Alright, then. Let's get this plan into action. We'll all need a good night's rest."

As they wrapped up their discussion, laughter echoed from inside the cabin, drawing Jasper's attention. He peeked in to find Emma and Samantha deep in conversation. Samantha, with her warm and encouraging demeanor, was trying to lift Emma's spirits.

"It won't last forever, and it's worth it in the end," Samantha assured her, her tone hopeful. Then, with a playful glint in her eye, Samantha shifted her approach. "Emma, it's not for sure, but I think soon I'll know exactly how you're feeling right now."

Emma looked at her, puzzled. "What do you mean?" Samantha smiled brightly, a hint of excitement creeping into her voice. "I haven't taken a test yet, but I'm late."

Emma's eyes widened, and a huge smile broke across her face. Gathering her strength, she wrapped Samantha in a tight hug. "Oh, that's wonderful! We need to get you a test, but I'm sure it'll be positive!" Samantha squeezed her back, still grinning. "I really hope you're right. But, sweetie, can you not talk anymore until you rinse your mouth?"

Emma instantly broke the embrace, turning away in embarrassment. "Oh, I'm so sorry!" Samantha just laughed, her eyes twinkling. "Don't worry about it." With a newfound energy, Emma replied, "I guess it's all part of being pregnant, right?"

"Exactly!" Samantha said, still smiling. "But I wasn't kidding—please rinse!" Emma chuckled and took a swig of water, rinsing her mouth. "Okay, now we can talk," she said, her laughter mingling with Samantha's.

Arabella and Singing Swallows set out at three in the morning, determined to finish their journey along the C&D Canal and cross the Delaware Bay. The early morning was tranquil, with a gentle breeze and the stars fading as dawn approached.

As they navigated the calm waters, the sunrise painted the sky in soft pastels, mirroring the surface of the wide open bay. By evening they had finished crossing the bay and entered the Cape May Canal, where they enjoyed the lush scenery and the sounds of nature surrounding them.

Finally arriving at the marina in Cape May, the two boats tied off and Samantha walked over immediately and asked Emma "You ok sweetie? Did you get sick" Emma smiled nope not at all today. Maybe I just need to keep moving" she said laughing.

Emma continued "That was a long one today. I know Jasper is planning on taking a nap right away so I think tonight we'll just relax and go into town tomorrow if I still feel good. Is that ok?"

"Absolutely, I think a nap is all Scott wants as well. And maybe tomorrow we can find a drug store to buy a pregnancy test" Samantha said smiling. Emma smiled back "For sure. Well I'm going to say goodnight and I'll see you in the morning " "Sounds good" Samantha replied".

With that Samantha went back to Singing Swallows and Emma went to see Jasper. "Grandpa, why don't you take a nap in the cockpit and I will cook for us. You have been taking such good care of me the last few days, it's my turn" Jasper grinned "I'm not going to argue with that, Jasper grabbed a cushion and lied down in the cockpit while Emma went below and prepared dinner for them.

After she finished she went out in the cockpit to wake Jasper. He had fallen asleep with his phone in his hand. Emma didn't want him to drop it as he woke so she gently removed it from his hand. As she did the screen lit up and she could see what looked like the end of a letter and at the bottom was written "Thank you – Ben."

Emma's heart raced could this be the letter her dad sent to Jasper. She knew she shouldn't read it. If she did it would be a major violation of Jasper's trust. On the other hand it could explain what the fight was about between them. Maybe she could fix it if she knew what the fight was about. She finally decided in the long run it would be better if she knew but didn't tell anyone.

So she quietly took the phone back into the cabin. Her heart racing as she read it. She was so scared of getting caught or finding out why her dad hated Jasper, maybe she would hate him too after reading it.

As soon as she finished reading it she put it next to Jasper . "Grandpa wake up, Grandpa wake up, it's time to eat". Jasper slowly woke "Mmmm thank you, that smells good". As they ate Emma's mind was elsewhere "Emma are you ok?" Jasper asked. "Yes, just tired. It was a long day. I think I'm going to lie down as soon as I'm done eating" replied Emma.

Sure enough as soon as she finished eating she retired into her cabin. And the first thing she did when she got there was grab her phone and call her Dad. After some small talk Emma's voice took a more serious tone "Dad I have something to confess to you".

"What's that?" Ben's voice also became serious. Emma went on to explain what happened this evening and that she read the letter "I'm so sorry dad" Emma said apologizing. She could barely speak as she was holding back the tears.

"It's ok Emma. But tell me, do you now understand better?" Emma took a deep breath "a little but there is still one big question I have." Ben sounded sincere "what's that?". "I get that you blame him for Mom and Grandma but wasn't it just an accident?" Emma asked.

After a long silence Ben started talking solemnly " When I was a child, my dad took my mom and me on grand adventures around the world. We visited bustling cities and pretty landscapes, but as I grew older and started school, our travels became limited to summer vacations.

It was during those years that I began to sense his restlessness. Although he never explicitly voiced it, I could see the way he looked at the walls of our home—like he was trapped. Occasionally, he would escape on solo trips, leaving my mom and me behind, as if to reclaim a piece of his freedom.

Once I became an adult and moved out, he resumed his explorations with my mom. She thrived in those adventures, always eager to embrace new cultures and experiences. But then came my wedding day—a significant moment in my life that he couldn't be bothered to attend.

A week later, he showed up unexpectedly and gifted us a honeymoon trip to Costa Rica. It was classic Dad—timing dictated by his schedule, a grand gesture to compensate for his absence, and then he was off again, leaving us to navigate our new life without him.

When you were born, he missed that too. I still remember the conversation; he called to say he wouldn't be able to make it, and in the background, I heard my mother's quiet sobs. It hurt her to be absent yet again.

Then came that terrible year when you were eight. We had asked him every single year to visit with us at Christmas. We wanted to have a family Christmas including my parents. But every year they were off in some far away location.

Finally he said they were coming for Christmas. He arrived on Christmas Eve. and had plans to fly out on Christmas Day, so he was only there for one night.

He made plans for all of us to drive from Ticonderoga to New York City to see the Radio City Rockettes. The show started at eight o'clock, and afterward, we could drive back home.

After the show everyone could see the fatigue in his eyes, yet he insisted he was fine. We pleaded to stop for the night, but he brushed off our concerns, saying he was fine. We all knew the real reason was if we stopped for the night he would miss his flight the next day.

It was a reckless decision. He fell asleep at the wheel. The car veered off the road, crashing into a pillar on an overpass. In an instant, he shattered our family. My mom, my wife—gone. And you? You were left with a phobia that still haunts you. The weight of that night, the loss, and the regret are burdens I carry every day."

Emma was at loss for words. She never saw this side of Jasper but she was out with him on an adventure so wouldn't see that side of him.

This is where Jasper was his happiest but at what cost. Emma couldn't imagine choosing travel and adventure over her family. She had a lot to think about tonight.

Chapter 18

Just a Little More Time

The next morning, Scott and Samantha strolled over to Arabella. Jasper was already perched in the cockpit, sipping his coffee as the sun glinted off the water. "Are you guys ready to go explore?" Scott called out, his enthusiasm contagious.

Jasper smiled faintly but shook his head. "I'm afraid Emma isn't feeling well this morning."

Samantha's brow furrowed with concern. "Oh no, morning sickness again?" "To be honest, I'm not sure," Jasper replied, glancing toward the cabin. "I'm assuming so."

Scott exchanged a look with Samantha, his face softening. "Well, what about you? Do you want to come and explore?" If you don't mind pushing me," Jasper said with a hint of playful reluctance. Scott let out a hearty laugh. "Of course! Just go tell Emma you're going and let's get your wheelchair."

After a quick visit to Emma, who was nestled in the cabin, they made sure she was comfortable before embarking on their day. The trio set off into town, the sun shining warmly above them.

They navigated through the streets lined with charming Victorian homes, their colorful facades adorned with blooming flower boxes.

The scent of salt air mingled with the sweet aroma of breakfast being served in nearby cafes.

As they rolled along the picturesque pathways, the inviting beaches came into view, beckoning them with their golden sands and gentle waves. Laughter filled the air as Scott and Samantha pointed out whimsical shops and quaint eateries, but despite the vibrant atmosphere, Jasper felt a lingering emptiness.

"Hey, can we head back?" he admitted after a while, his voice tinged with wistfulness. "It just isn't the same without Emma."

Samantha nodded, her expression understanding. "I get it. Let's go check on her."

The trio turned around, the lively sights of the town fading behind them as they made their way back to Arabella.When they reached the boat, Emma was sitting up in the cockpit, a weak smile on her face. "How was it?" she asked, her eyes lighting up at the sight of them. "Not the same without you," Jasper replied, his voice softening. "We missed you."

Samantha smiled, brushing a stray hair behind her ear. "I'm sorry I wasn't feeling well earlier. Maybe I'm just hormonal," she laughed lightly. "I'll try not to ruin any future plans." "It's okay sweetie, we understand" Samantha reassured her. "Right now, you need to take care of yourself."

Emma's eyes brightened as she suggested, "How does this sound: tonight we grab some drinks, and tomorrow we head down to the Seawall Promenade and check out the lighthouse, plus everything in between?"

"That sounds great!" Scott said excitedly, his enthusiasm infectious. "I can't wait to explore more!"

Samantha grinned "Perfect! A little fun tonight and a big sight seeing tomorrow. Just what we all need."

The following day, after a hearty breakfast, and taking care of some boat chores, the four travelers set out to explore the charming town. They started their day with a leisurely stroll down to the waterfront, where the fresh sea breeze invigorated their spirits. There, they found a cozy café with a stunning view of the harbor and stopped for a delicious lunch. The seafood was fresh, and the conversation flowed easily, filled with excitement for the day ahead.

Once they finished eating, they continued along the scenic seawall promenade, taking in the breathtaking views of the ocean on one side and the large Victorian mansions on the other. The sun shone brightly, casting a warm glow on their faces as they chatted and laughed, enjoying each other's company.

As they walked along Sunset Boulevard, Scott spotted a well-trodden trail leading into the woods. "Let's check out the observation tower!" he suggested, his eyes sparkling with enthusiasm. The group agreed, and they ventured down the trail, surrounded by the sounds of chirping birds and rustling leaves.

After a short hike, they reached the observation tower, with Scott and Emma helping Jasper up the one stairwell. They were rewarded with a stunning panoramic view of the Cape May Wetlands. They stood in awe, taking in the expansive landscape dotted with rich greens and shimmering blues, snapping photos to capture the moment.

After soaking in the beauty, they made their way back to the main road, and continued on their way till they reached the tall cylindrical lighthouse whose white base and red top stood proudly against the sky.

Jasper and Scott decided to wait at the bottom while Emma and Samantha climbed to the top. Once they reached the lantern room They looked out at the breathtaking view. It was a perfect spot to appreciate the coastal scenery and the endless horizon.

Afterwards, the four headed back into town, ready for dinner. They found a restaurant directly on the seawall promenade, its outdoor seating perfect for enjoying the evening breeze. As they settled in, the sounds of the waves crashing nearby created a soothing setting to their meal.

They shared plates of local specialties and clinked glasses in a toast to a day well spent. After dinner, feeling content and a little more connected to one another, they returned to their boats for the night. The stars began to twinkle overhead, and as they settled in, the gentle rocking of the water lulled them into a peaceful state, ready to dream about their next day.

Late the next morning, after a leisurely breakfast, the group decided it was time to get going again. They set their sights on Wildwood, about an hour north, where another marina awaited them.

Both Scott and Jasper had been there before numerous times, but this trip held special significance for Samantha. She was excited to show Emma the town where she had grown up, sharing stories and memories that shaped her childhood.

As they navigated their way out of the harbor. The journey was smooth, but short. Once they arrived in Wildwood, the sights and sounds welcomed them.

After docking at the marina, Scott and Jasper decided to stay behind on the boats to tackle some much-needed maintenance. They had a few repairs and checks to handle before setting off again.

Meanwhile, Samantha told Emma to wear her swimsuit under her clothes in case they go to the beach or something. Then Samantha took Emma to explore the town. The vibrant energy of Wildwood was contagious, with its bustling boardwalk. and the enticing aroma of funnel cakes wafting through the air.

Samantha guided Emma through the streets, sharing anecdotes that brought the town to life. Samantha eagerly pointed out familiar landmarks, reminiscing about her favorite ice cream shop and the boardwalk where she spent countless summers. Emma listened intently, fascinated by the stories of sandcastles and beach bonfires.

After a delightful lunch at a local eatery, where they savored fresh seafood and classic boardwalk fare, Samantha suggested they go to the beach. Maybe even for a swim.

Laughter filled the air as they raced each other down the beach. Samantha reveled in the joy of sharing this experience with Emma, creating new memories while reliving the thrill of her own childhood.

As evening approached, after stopping at a drugstore to get a test for Samantha, they made their way back to the marina, filled with laughter and excitement. They arrived at Singing

Swallows first and Scott was wrapping up his maintenance tasks.

"How was the water?" Scott asked, raising an eyebrow. "It was amazing! You missed out!" Emma chimed in, grinning from ear to ear. Emma gave Samantha a hug goodbye as she headed back to Arabella.

When Emma returned to the Arabella, she felt a mix of excitement and exhaustion from their day in Wildwood. As she stepped onto the boat, she didn't immediately see Jasper, so she made her way to his cabin. Curiosity piqued, she gently opened the hatch, calling out, "Grandpa?"

What she saw inside froze her in place. Jasper was lying on the floor, his body contorted in an unnatural pose. Panic surged through her, and she yelled out in fear, "Grandpa!" Her heart raced as she jumped down into the cabin, rushing to his side.

"Grandpa, are you okay?" she exclaimed, her voice trembling. She knelt beside him, her mind racing with worry. She reached out to check for signs of life, desperate to know he was alright.

When Emma saw that Jasper was unresponsive, a wave of panic washed over her. She quickly stuck her

head out of the hatch and screamed at the top of her lungs, "Scott! Samantha! Somebody help me!"

Her voice echoed across the marina, filled with urgency and fear. She turned back to Jasper, her heart pounding as she knelt beside him, shaking his shoulder gently. "Grandpa! Please, wake up!"

Moments later, she heard hurried footsteps approaching. Scott and Samantha appeared at the hatch, concern etched on their faces. "What's going on?" Scott asked, his expression shifting from confusion to alarm as he saw Jasper on the floor.

"Help him! I don't know what's wrong!" Emma cried, her voice trembling. She stepped aside, letting them rush in.

Samantha quickly knelt next to Jasper, checking for any signs of life. "Jasper, can you hear me?" she asked, her tone steady but urgent.

Scott moved in closer, assessing the situation with a steady demeanor. "Call 911," he said, his voice calm yet urgent. Emma grabbed her phone, dialing immediately as she felt the weight of the moment pressing down on her. Within minutes, a small crowd of other boaters began to gather on the dock outside the Arabella, their curious faces reflecting concern.

An older woman stepped forward, her presence commanding. "I'm a retired doctor, I'm coming in!" she called out, making her way onto the boat. As she entered, Emma quickly informed her, "I'm on the phone with 911."

The woman nodded, her focus shifting to Jasper. "Okay, who knows him best?" she asked, scanning the cabin.

Emma stepped forward, her voice shaky but determined. "I'm his granddaughter."

"Alright, we need to make some room," the doctor said, glancing at the cramped cabin. The doctor looked at Samantha and Scott " could you please step outside?"

They complied, giving the doctor space. Once they were outside, she turned back to Emma. "What's your names?"

"I'm Emma, and this is Jasper," she replied, her worry evident. The doctor began to examine Jasper, checking his pulse and listening to his breathing. As she worked, she asked Emma a series of questions to gather important information.

"What's his medical history?" Emma took a deep breath, trying to stay composed. "He had a stroke about a year ago, but he's been doing okay since then."

The doctor nodded, as she continued her examination. "What about medications? Does he take anything regularly?" "Yes, he takes blood thinners and medication for his blood pressure," Emma responded quickly, recalling the details she had learned along the trip.

The doctor gave the information to the operator on the phone. "He has a history of a stroke, he is non-responsive, but he still has a pulse and is breathing lightly. We need an ambulance here immediately." Emma watched anxiously, her heart racing as the doctor continued to assess Jasper.

"He's going to be okay, right?" she asked, her voice barely above a whisper. The doctor glanced at her, her expression firm yet reassuring. "We're going to do everything we can. Just stay close."

As the sound of sirens approached in the distance, Emma felt a tumult of emotions—fear mingled with a flicker of hope. She knew Jasper was in good hands with the retired doctor, and she couldn't help but pray that he would pull through this.

The doctor suddenly yelled out from the cabin, "Sir, can you come back in here?" She was referring to Scott. As he stuck his head in the hatch, the doctor explained, "The paramedics won't be able to get a stretcher in here. Time is of the essence; we need to get him out onto the dock."

Scott nodded, his face set with determination. He turned to the gathering crowd of concerned boaters and focused on the strongest-looking gentleman. "Sir, could you help us, please? We need to get him out of the cabin." "Sure thing," the gentleman replied, stepping forward with a sense of urgency. He followed Scott into the cabin, where the doctor was still checking on Jasper.

"On the count of three, we're going to lift him," the doctor instructed, her voice firm and steady. "Emma, make sure he's stable as we move him." Emma nodded, her heart racing as she positioned herself beside Jasper. "Ready," she said, squeezing his hand reassuringly.

"One... two... three!" Scott and the gentleman lifted Jasper carefully, their arms supporting him as they maneuvered him toward the hatch. Emma felt a surge of adrenaline, willing Jasper to hold on.

With great care, they managed to get him through the narrow space and onto the deck. The doctor quickly assessed him again, keeping a watchful eye as they laid him down gently on the dock.

Within moments, the paramedics arrived, their sirens fading as they jumped into action. "What do we have?" one of them asked, swiftly approaching the scene. The doctor spoke up, her voice clear and authoritative. "He has a history of a stroke, is non-responsive but has a pulse and is breathing lightly. We need to monitor him closely."

The paramedics nodded, quickly setting up their equipment. Emma watched with bated breath as they worked, grateful for the expertise surrounding her. She felt Scott and Samantha's reassuring presence beside her, and together they hoped for the best as the medical team continued their efforts to stabilize Jasper.

As the paramedics finished loading Jasper into the ambulance, they turned to Emma. "Are you coming?" one of them asked, their tone urgent but compassionate.

Emma's eyes widened at the question. She knew she needed to go, but the thought of climbing into that ambulance paralyzed her. She just stood there, rooted to the spot, her heart racing as she battled the fear rising within her.

"Ma'am, are you coming?" the paramedic asked again, concern creeping into his voice. "Ma'am, we need to go!" he urged, glancing at the clock.

Emma reminded herself of what Antoine had said about facing her fears. She took a deep breath, pushing aside the panic that threatened to overwhelm her. Without saying a word, she climbed into the back of the ambulance, determination overcoming her hesitation. She thought to herself 'no windows, just like the elevator. Come on, face your fears.'

As the doors closed behind her, the sterile smell of antiseptic filled the space. She quickly positioned herself near Jasper, who lay on the stretcher, his face pale but still breathing. The paramedics worked efficiently, checking his vitals and preparing to transport him.

"Stay with him, okay?" one of them instructed Emma as they began to drive. "Talk to him. Let him know you're here."

Emma nodded, her voice trembling slightly as she leaned closer to Jasper. "I'm here, Grandpa. I'm right here," she said softly, holding his hand tightly. "You're going to be okay. We're getting you the help you need."

As the ambulance sped through the streets, the lights flashing outside, Emma felt a mix of fear and resolve. She was facing her fears head-on, Emma thought to herself 'just concentrate on Grandpa, you can do this, face your fears.'

At that moment she decided no matter what Jasper had done in the past she forgave him. For Jasper, she would do anything.

Once they arrived at the hospital, the ambulance doors swung open, and the paramedics quickly unloaded Jasper on the stretcher. Emma hurried to his side, her heart pounding as they wheeled him into the emergency room.

Bright lights and the bustling atmosphere surrounded them as medical staff moved with purpose. Emma felt a rush of anxiety but clung to Jasper's hand, determined to stay with him. "You're going to be okay," she whispered again, squeezing his fingers gently.

The paramedics relayed vital information to the waiting team of doctors and nurses, who immediately began their assessments. looking at Jasper's vitals on the monitor. "Let's get an IV started and run some tests."

Emma stepped back slightly, allowing the medical team to work but never letting go of Jasper's hand. She felt a mix of helplessness and determination, hoping that her presence would offer him some comfort.

As the doctors began their examinations, Emma caught snippets of their conversation. "History of stroke, non-responsive, but stable..." Their professional tone both reassured and terrified her.

After what felt like an eternity, one of the nurses turned to Emma. "You can wait in the family area. We'll keep you updated on his condition." Emma hesitated, glancing back at Jasper. "I want to stay with him," she said, her voice steady despite the chaos around her.

The nurse smiled gently. "We understand, but we need to focus on him right now. He'll be in good hands. You can wait just outside, and we'll come to you as soon as we have more information."

With a heavy heart, Emma nodded. She reluctantly released Jasper's hand, reassuring herself she wouldn't be far. She stepped into the waiting area, surrounded by the sterile scent of disinfectant and the low hum of anxious conversations.

Sitting down, she pulled out her phone, fingers trembling as she typed a quick message to Scott and Samantha to let them know where they were. She felt alone but tried to focus on the hope that Jasper would pull through.

As she waited, Emma took deep breaths, reminding herself of Antoine's words about facing fears. She was determined to be strong for Jasper and to support him in any way she could.

About half an hour later, the familiar faces of Samantha and Scott appeared in the waiting area, their expressions a mix of concern and relief. They rushed over and enveloped Emma in a big hug, their warmth offering her a sense of comfort amidst the uncertainty.

"How are you holding up?" Samantha asked, stepping back to look Emma in the eyes. "Do you have any news?" Emma shook her head, feeling a wave of frustration wash over her. "No, nothing yet. They took him in for tests, but it feels like forever."

Scott placed a reassuring hand on her shoulder. "You're doing great, Emma. Just being here for him is so important." Samantha nodded in agreement. "Have you been able to talk to anyone?" "Not really," Emma admitted. "Just the nurse told me they'd keep me updated. I wish I could be with him."

"Let's find out more together," Samantha suggested. "We'll wait with you until we hear something." Emma felt a surge of gratitude for their support. "Thank you. I really appreciate it."

Minutes ticked by slowly, each second feeling like an eternity. Emma found herself constantly glancing at the entrance, hoping for a glimpse of a doctor or nurse with news. But the waiting was agonizing, and she fought to stay hopeful, comforted by the presence of her friends.

Feeling the weight of the moment, Emma took a deep breath and decided to call her dad. She stepped away from Samantha and Scott, needing a little privacy as she called. "Hey Dad, it's me" she said, trying to keep her tone steady despite the turmoil inside her. "Emma! What's going on? You sound upset."

Tears pricked at her eyes as she explained, "We are in Wildwood, New Jersey. It's Grandpa. He collapsed on the boat, and we rushed him to the hospital. They're running tests, but I haven't heard anything yet."

"Oh no, Emma! I'm so sorry. Is he... is he okay?" "I don't know yet. They said he's stable, but he's non-responsive right now. I just feel so helpless."

"I'm on my way," her dad said immediately, his voice firm. "I'll be there as soon as I can. Just hang in there, okay? You're doing the right thing by being there for him." "Thanks Dad, I just wish I could be with him. It's hard waiting."

"I know, sweetheart. Just stay strong. I'll be there soon." Emma nodded, even though he couldn't see her. "Okay, I'll keep you updated. Love you. " "Love you too, Emma. I'll see you soon."

After hanging up, Emma returned to her friends, feeling a mix of relief and anxiety. "My dad's on his way," she said, trying to keep her voice steady. Samantha reached out, squeezing her hand. "You're doing everything you can, Emma. We're here for him and for you." Scott nodded in agreement. "And we'll keep you company until he arrives. You're not in this alone."

Feeling the warmth of their support, Emma settled back into the waiting area, bracing herself for whatever news would come next.

A few minutes later, Emma's phone buzzed, and she quickly answered. "Dad?"

"Hey, Emma! I just wanted to let you know I'll be flying into Philadelphia," Ben said, his voice steady. "I'm renting a car and will be there as soon as I can." "Okay, that sounds good," Emma replied, feeling a mix of relief and apprehension. "Do you have any idea how long it'll take?"

"Traffic can be tricky, but I'll do my best to get there quickly. I'm just so sorry I can't be there right now," he said, his tone full of concern. "It's okay Dad, I understand. Just drive safely, okay? I'll keep you updated if anything changes."

"I will, and remember, you're doing great. Just focus on being there for Jasper," he reminded her. "I'll see you soon."

"Thanks Dad, Love you."

"Love you too." As she hung up, Emma felt a little lighter knowing her dad was on his way. She returned to Samantha and Scott, who had been waiting expectantly.

"He's flying into Philadelphia and renting a car," Emma explained. "He'll be here as soon as he can." "That's good to hear," Samantha said, offering a reassuring smile. "You'll have your dad here with you soon." Scott nodded. "And we'll be right here too. You've got a solid support team."

Feeling a bit more grounded, Emma settled back into her chair, trying to distract herself by engaging in conversation with her friends while they waited for news. The minutes stretched on, but she held onto the hope that soon, they would have some answers about Jasper's condition.

After several hours of anxious waiting, Emma felt her heart leap when a doctor finally emerged from the double doors of the emergency room. Calling out her name. She stood up, her breath catching in her throat. "How is he?" she asked, hope and fear intertwining in her voice.

The doctor took a deep breath, his expression serious. "Your grandfather has suffered a massive hemorrhagic stroke. We performed emergency surgery to repair the broken blood vessel and to remove excess blood that was putting pressure on the brain."

Emma felt her knees weaken, but she took Samantha's arm, determined to stay strong. "Is he... is he going to be okay?"

"He's in recovery now, but he's still sleeping. We'll be monitoring him closely as we're not out of the woods yet," the doctor explained. "It's crucial that we keep a watch on his vital signs and brain activity."

Samantha and Scott stood by her side, their expressions grave yet supportive. "Can we see him?" Emma asked, her voice barely above a whisper.

Yes, you can go in for a brief visit. Just keep in mind that he may be disoriented when he wakes up," the doctor replied. "But your presence can be comforting for him."

"Thank you," Emma said, her voice steadying as she followed the doctor's lead. He guided them down a hallway to a recovery room, where Jasper lay peacefully, surrounded by medical equipment. The rhythmic beeping of monitors filled the air.

Emma's heart ached at the sight of him, vulnerable but alive. She approached the bed, taking a deep breath as she reached for his hand. "Grandpa," she said softly, her voice trembling. "I'm here. We're all here for you."

Samantha and Scott quietly stepped back, giving Emma a moment alone with Jasper. She leaned closer, her heart racing as she spoke to him, hoping that somehow he could hear her.

As the night wore on, Emma remained by Jasper's side, talking softly to him and holding his hand. The comforting beeps of the monitors became a steady rhythm, anchoring her in the moment.

Eventually, a nurse entered the room, her expression warm but professional. "I'm sorry, but we need to ask Scott and Samantha to leave for the night," she said gently. "Only one visitor can stay with him after visiting hours end."

Emma looked up, her heart sinking slightly at the thought of being alone, but she knew it was important for her to stay. "I can stay?" she asked, glancing between the nurse and her friends. "Yes, you can," the nurse confirmed with a nod. "He'll be in good hands with you here."

Scott and Samantha exchanged glances, and Scott placed a reassuring hand on Emma's shoulder. "You're doing the right thing, Emma. We'll check in first thing in the morning," he said. Samantha added, "Just call us if you need anything. We're just a phone call away and we will check on Arabella for you."

"Thank you," Emma replied, feeling a mix of gratitude and determination. She hugged them both tightly, holding onto their support before they reluctantly made their way out of the room.

Once they were gone, the nurse adjusted the monitors and checked Jasper's IV. "He's stable, and we'll be monitoring him closely throughout the night," she reassured Emma. "Just talk to him; it helps to hear familiar voices."

Emma nodded, settling back into her chair. As the nurse stepped out, she turned her attention back to Jasper, her heart full of love and hope. "I'm not going anywhere, Grandpa," she whispered. "I'll be right here with you."

Late in the night, Emma had picked up her phone and dialed Antoine's number. As the phone rang, her heart raced, both from the weight of the moment and the comfort she hoped he could provide. "Emma?" he answered, his voice warm and soothing. "What's going on?"

With trembling lips, she managed to share the devastating news. "It's Grandpa," Emma explained what had happened. "I'm here with him, but I don't know what to do." "Oh Emma, I'm so sorry," Antoine replied, his voice filled with compassion. "I wish I could be there with you right now. You're not alone in this."

Tears streamed down her cheeks as she felt the warmth of his words wrap around her like a comforting blanket. "It hurts so much. I can't imagine losing him." "I know," Antoine said gently. " It's okay to feel everything you're feeling. I'll take the bus down as soon as I can, but it'll probably take a day to get there."

"Thank you," Emma said, her voice barely above a whisper. "Just knowing you're coming helps. I feel so lost right now."

"I'll be there for you, I promise," he reassured her. "In the meantime, just stay with him. Talk to him. I know how much he means to you, and I'm sure he can feel your love." "I will. I just want him to know he's not alone." Emma replied.

Exactly, just keep holding his hand and sharing those memories. I'll get there as fast as I can." After hanging up, Emma felt a small flicker of hope amidst the despair.

Really early the next morning, Emma was jolted awake by the soft sound of the door opening. She blinked through her sleep, expecting to see the nurse come in for a routine check. Instead, a doctor entered, his expression grave.

"Ma'am, I'm sorry," he began, his voice steady but filled with sorrow. "We've done everything we could, but we don't think he will make it." Emma's heart shattered at his words. The reality of the situation crashed down on her like a tidal wave, and she felt tears streaming down her cheeks uncontrollably. "No... no,

please," she gasped, her voice breaking. "He can't... he can't."

The doctor's eyes softened with compassion as he approached the bed. "I know this is incredibly difficult. Your grandfather fought hard, but his condition is critical. We want to ensure he's as comfortable as possible. If he wakes up, you should say your goodbyes."

Emma felt a whirlwind of emotions—fear, anger, and overwhelming sadness. She grasped Jasper's hand tighter, as if willing him to respond, to prove the doctor wrong. "Grandpa, please," she whispered through her tears. "You have to fight. I'm right here."

The doctor stepped back, giving her a moment of privacy while still watching from a distance. Emma's sobs filled the room, a raw expression of her grief. She felt so helpless, so small in the face of such immense loss. "I don't want to lose you," she cried, her voice trembling. "I need you to wake up. Please."

The room felt heavy with silence, and Emma knew time was slipping away. She wanted nothing more than for Jasper to know how much he meant to her, how much he was loved.

"I love you, Grandpa," she whispered, her heart aching. "I always will."

A short while later, the door opened, and Emma's heart lifted slightly as she saw Samantha enter, followed closely by Scott. But her breath caught in her throat when she spotted her dad behind them.

"Emma!" Ben exclaimed, rushing to her. Her eyes welled up as she ran into his arms, the weight of the world pressing down on her. "The doctor said he won't make it," she choked out, her voice trembling.

Ben held her tightly, his own heart breaking for her. "Oh, sweetheart," he murmured, stroking her hair. "I'm so sorry. I wish I could take this pain away."

Samantha and Scott stood nearby, their expressions full of concern and sorrow. Samantha stepped forward, wrapping her arms around Emma as well, offering her support. "We're all here for you, Emma. You're not alone in this."

Emma clung to her dad and her friends, feeling the warmth of their presence as a small comfort in her grief. "I don't want to lose him," she said, tears streaming down her face.

Ben pulled back slightly to look into her eyes. "We'll face this together, one step at a time. Just be with him. Talk to him. He needs to know you're there."

"Ben, Ben, is that you?" a very weak voice came from the bed. Emma's heart raced as she yelled out, "Grandpa!" Everyone rushed to the bedside, their worries momentarily replaced by a glimmer of hope.

"You're awake, Grandpa!" Emma exclaimed, tears of relief streaming down her face.

Jasper turned his head slowly, trying to open his eyes. "Ben, you're here," he whispered, his voice fragile but filled with emotion. "Yes Dad, I'm right here," Ben replied, stepping closer, his heart swelling at the sight of his father's struggle to connect. Jasper managed a faint smile. "I want you to know I'm so sorry."

"Dad, no. Now is not the time for that," Ben said gently, feeling a rush of emotions he hadn't expected.

"Then when is it time?" Jasper asked, his voice barely above a whisper. "Dad, I forgive you," Ben replied, his voice steady. "I think I forgave you a long time ago, but I was too stubborn to admit it, even to myself."

Emma watched the exchange, feeling the weight of their shared history and the power of reconciliation. She could see the relief in Jasper's eyes, a flicker of peace in the midst of uncertainty.

"Thank you, son," Jasper whispered, tears glistening in his eyes. "That means more to me than you will ever know."

Emma squeezed her grandfather's hand, overwhelmed with emotion. "We're all here for you, Grandpa. You're not alone."

"Emma," Jasper said, barely above a whisper, his voice fragile yet filled with warmth. "Do you remember when we met in the nursing home and I told you there were two things I needed before I died?" Emma looked at him, her heart swelling "Yes, Grandpa, I remember."

Jasper managed to smile, his eyes twinkling with a mix of love and mischief. He pointed at Ben. "Number one," he said, then turned to Emma. "Number two." Finally, he pointed at Emma's belly, a gentle smile spreading across his face. "And a half. I got them thanks to you. You have made my life complete."

Emma felt a wave of warmth and joy wash over her. She smiled through her tears and leaned in, wrapping her arms around him in the best hug she could muster, wanting him to feel every ounce of her love. "Thank you, Grandpa," she whispered.

Jasper then turned his gaze to Ben, beckoning him closer. "Come here, son," he whispered, and Ben leaned in, curiosity etched on his face. Jasper leaned in and whispered something in Ben's ear, his expression serious yet filled with affection.

Emma watched, holding her breath, knowing that whatever Jasper had to say was important. She could see the emotion flicker across Ben's face, a mixture of surprise and understanding. Whatever words passed between them felt monumental, a legacy of love and connection being shared in those final moments.

As the warmth of the moment lingered in the air, Jasper's eyes fluttered, and he slowly drifted back into a peaceful sleep. Emma, still holding his hand, felt a mix of gratitude and heartache wash over her. They had shared so much in those brief moments—love, forgiveness, and connection.

Time seemed to stretch as she sat there, watching over him, wishing for just a little more time. Ben and Samantha stood close, their hearts heavy with unspoken words.

Eventually, the soft sounds of the monitors became a background hum, and Jasper's breaths grew shallower. Emma sensed the shift in the room, a quiet stillness settling over them. "Grandpa?" she whispered, her voice trembling. "We're still here with you."

But Jasper's breathing slowed, the gentle rise and fall of his chest becoming more sporadic. Emma felt a cold wave of fear wash over her, but she held tight to his hand, willing him to feel her presence.

"Please, don't leave us," she urged softly, tears streaming down her cheeks. "You've fought so hard."

With a final, gentle sigh, Jasper's body relaxed completely, and the monitors began to beep in a steady, somber rhythm. Emma's heart sank as she realized what had happened. She looked at her dad, whose expression mirrored her own heartbreak, and then at Samantha and Scott, who stood by her side, ready to offer support.

In that moment, Emma felt a profound sense of loss, but also a deep gratitude for the love they had shared. She leaned closer to Jasper, whispering through her tears, "I love you, Grandpa. Thank you for everything."

As they stood together, surrounded by the memories and the love that would always connect them, Emma knew that while Jasper's presence would be missed, his spirit would forever remain a part of her life.

The next morning, the four of them sat in a cozy restaurant, the sun streaming through the windows. The air was filled with the smell of fresh coffee and pastries, but the weight of their loss hung heavily over their conversation.

Ben took a deep breath, looking around at Emma, Samantha, and Scott. "Well, the first thing Emma and I need to figure out is what to do with Jasper. Other than us, he doesn't have any other family." He paused, his voice steady but tinged with sadness. "I think we should have him cremated."

Emma nodded, feeling a mix of emotions. "I think that makes sense. It's what he would have wanted, right? To be free and... to not have to worry about anything."

Samantha reached out and squeezed Emma's hand. "Whatever you decide, we're here to support you both. Maybe we can hold a small memorial service, just for us and anyone who knew him. A way to celebrate his life."

Scott chimed in, "That sounds like a good idea. We could share stories, remember all the good times. It might help with the healing process."

Ben looked thoughtful. "Yeah, I like that. Jasper loved being around people, and I know he cherished his time with all of you. It would mean a lot to honor him that way."

Emma smiled through her tears. "I want to make sure we do it right. He deserves that." Ben said I'll find out what is involved in having that done.

Samantha then turned to Emma, her expression gentle. "What about you, sweetie? Does this mean you don't get to finish the loop?" Before Emma could respond, Ben interjected.

"My father whispered his wish to me last night before he passed. Do you want to know his thoughts?"

The group leaned in, curiosity piqued. Emma nodded eagerly. "Yes, please." Ben cleared his throat, the weight of his father's words hanging in the air. "He told me to be there for Emma and to take Arabella and finish the loop for him and for her."

Emma's heart swelled at the thought of continuing their adventure together. "And?" she prompted, eager for more.

Ben looked at Emma very seriously. "Well, I thought about it, and the truth is, my dad didn't just leave me Arabella. He also left me a great deal of money, so I'm thinking finishing the loop with you is the perfect way for me to start my retirement."

Emma's eyes widened in disbelief. "Are you serious?" Ben smiled softly. "Absolutely. I want to honor his memory by doing something he loved. And I know how much it means to you too. It would be a way to keep him close, even if he's not physically here."

Samantha and Scott exchanged glances, their expressions a mix of surprise and joy. "That sounds like an incredible plan," Samantha said. "It would be a beautiful way to celebrate his life."

Emma felt a rush of gratitude and hope. "I'd love that, Dad. I want to finish the loop with you—together," Emma said, her eyes bright with excitement. "But I have to ask, when did the three of you meet?" Ben laughed. "Actually, we really haven't! We just arrived at the same time."

Emma smiled softly. "Well, Dad, this is my friend Scott and Samantha. I've talked about them endlessly on our phone calls." "Nice to meet you both! I've heard a lot about you."

Ben said, extending his hand. Scott shook it eagerly while Samantha smiled warmly. "It's great to finally meet you," Samantha said "And Emma has told us so much about you!"

Emma blushed slightly. "Only the good stuff, I promise." Ben chuckled, his eyes twinkling. "I hope so! It sounds like you all have had quite the time together."

"We have!" Scott replied. "From wild storms to beautiful sunsets, it's been unforgettable." "Yeah, and we're really glad Emma's been with us," Samantha added. "She's made everything more fun." Emma grinned, feeling a swell of pride. "I couldn't have asked for better friends to share it with."

Chapter 19

Treasures That Awaited Them

As they sat there discussing their next steps, Emma felt a renewed sense of purpose. While the pain of losing Jasper would linger, the promise of continuing together gave her something to look forward to. With her dad and friends by her side, she felt ready to embrace whatever came next.

That afternoon, Emma waited anxiously at the bus station, her heart racing with excitement. The sun shone brightly overhead, but all she could think about was Antoine and the comfort he would bring.

As the bus pulled in, her stomach fluttered. When the doors swung open, a rush of passengers spilled out, and there he was—Antoine, with his warm smile and open arms.

"Emma!" he called, spotting her instantly.

Without hesitation, she rushed toward him, wrapping her arms around him tightly. The warmth of his embrace felt like a lifeline amidst the whirlwind of emotions she had been navigating. "I'm so glad you're here," she whispered, pulling back to look into his eyes. "I missed you so much," he replied, brushing a stray tear from her cheek. "How are you holding up?"

Emma took a deep breath, grateful for his presence. "He passed away this morning. It's been really hard, but I'm trying to focus on what we can do to honor Grandpa." Antoine nodded, understanding the weight of her words. "I'm here for whatever you need. Just let me know how I can help."

Together, they walked toward the marina, where the others were waiting for them. Emma felt a sense of relief and comfort wash over her. With Antoine by her side, she knew she could face the challenges ahead.

As they approached, she could see her dad, Samantha, and Scott gathered. As they approached the group, Emma turned to her friends and spoke up. "Hey guys, you all remember Antoine?"

Everyone started nodding, smiles spreading across their faces. "Good to see you!" Ben said, extending his hand to Antoine. "How long do we have you for?" Antoine returned the handshake, his expression warm. "For about a week, then unfortunately I have to get back." Emma was a bit disappointed but quickly masked it with gratitude. "I'm just glad you're here now".

Samantha chimed in, "Absolutely! We're all in this together, and it means a lot to have you here, Antoine." As they stood by the water, a gentle breeze rustled the leaves around them, creating a sense of calm. Ben cleared his throat, gathering everyone's attention.

"Well, let's make the most of the time we have together. Jasper wouldn't want us to dwell on sadness. He'd want us to celebrate life." Emma smiled at her dad's words.

In the days that followed, Ben and Emma made the arrangements for Jasper's cremation. On the day of the cremation, they gathered at a chapel surrounded by greenery, with Antoine, Samantha, and Scott by their side for support. The atmosphere was quiet, a comforting stillness that allowed them to reflect on Jasper's life.

After the service, they made their way to the crematorium, where a small ceremony was held. Emma held onto the urn that contained Jasper's ashes, feeling a mix of sorrow and peace.

"You'll always be with us, Grandpa," she whispered, imagining him smiling down on them.

"Thank you for everything," Emma said, her voice trembling. "We love you, Grandpa."

The next morning, There was a sense of renewal in the air, and Emma felt a mixture of excitement and nervousness as she took a deep breath. Ben, standing at the edge of the dock, scratched his head. "I have to admit, I'm a bit rusty after all this time. It's been a while since I've handled a boat."

Emma smiled reassuringly. "No worries, Dad. I'll take the lead. Just follow my instructions, and we'll be fine."

With a nod, Ben and Antoine moved to untie the boat, their movements steadying as they got into the rhythm of their tasks. Emma climbed into the cockpit, her heart racing a little as she turned the key to start the engine. The familiar roar of the motor filled the air. "Ready when you are!" Emma called out, her voice buoyant with confidence.

Antoine untied the last line, stepping back to take a look at Emma. "You've got this". Emma glanced back at him and gave a thumbs-up.

Once everything was in order, she navigated the boat out of the slip with precision, feeling a rush of freedom as they glided onto the open water. "Feels good to be back out here!"

Ben said, his eyes sparkling as he took in the expansive view. With Antoine by her side and her dad's encouragement, Emma felt ready to embrace whatever lay ahead, eager to complete the loop.

After a full day on the water, Ben began to regain his confidence, the rhythm of boating coming back to him with every passing hour.

As the sun dipped lower in the sky, they finally approached the marina in Atlantic City. Once the boats were safely moored the group stood together on the dock. Ben, Scott and Samantha couldn't help but exchange skeptical glances.

"Not exactly our favorite place," Scott muttered, shaking his head. Emma, however, was practically buzzing with excitement. "Come on! The lights, the energy—it's so vibrant! I really want to see it!" Antoine stood beside her, equally eager, his eyes sparkling with anticipation.

Ben chuckled, " You two go enjoy the boardwalk; we'll hold down the fort." Emma grinned, grateful for their understanding. "Thank you! We'll bring back some photos to show you!"

As they stepped onto the boardwalk, the atmosphere shifted dramatically. The sound of laughter and music filled the air, and the scent of popcorn and saltwater taffy wafted toward them. Emma and Antoine walked hand in hand, soaking in the sights and sounds.

"Look at those lights!" Emma exclaimed, pointing toward the towering casinos that illuminated the night sky like beacons.

They strolled along the long boardwalk, taking in the various attractions. Emma snapped photos, capturing the colorful neon signs and the joyful faces of passersby. "Let's stop here!"

Antoine said, motioning toward a small stand selling funnel cakes. They indulged in the sweet treat, sharing bites and laughing as powdered sugar dusted their fingers.

As they continued down the boardwalk, Emma felt a sense of freedom and joy. For the first time since Jasper's passing, she allowed herself to truly enjoy the moment. The lights, the sounds, and the company of Antoine filled her heart with warmth. "Thanks for coming with me," she said, glancing up at him, her eyes sparkling with gratitude.

"Always," Antoine replied, smiling down at her. " I'm happy to be by your side."

As they walked, hand in hand, Emma couldn't help but feel that even amidst the uncertainties, moments like this reminded her that life continued to offer beauty and joy. And for tonight, that was more than enough.

The following day, the sun rose bright and clear as the group got ready to set out for Toms River. For Scott and Samantha, this leg of the journey held special significance—it was where they would finally cross their wake and complete their loop.

"I can't believe we're finally doing this," Scott said, glancing back at Samantha, who wore a radiant smile.

"I know! It feels surreal," she replied to the group. "All those times we talked about this moment... it's finally here! Plus, I have more great news! I did the tests last night. Scott and I are going to be parents!"

The group erupted into cheers, their voices mingling in joyous celebration. "Are you serious? That's incredible!" Ben exclaimed, his voice filled with emotion. Emma jumped up and down, clapping her hands. "Oh my gosh! This is amazing news!"

Antoine grinned, joining the celebration. "You two are going to be fantastic parents. I can't wait to meet the little one!" Samantha laughed, a few happy tears spilling down her cheeks. "Thank you! We're a bit overwhelmed, but so excited."

The group continued to celebrate, sharing hugs and laughter as the reality of the news sank in.

Ben, Emma and Antoine shared in their enthusiasm, the camaraderie making the journey all the more special. Emma could feel the weight of the past few days lifting slightly, replaced by a sense of accomplishment and joy for her friends.

They eventually un-tied Arabella and Singing Swallows, ready to set their course for Toms River. The morning sun glinted off the water, creating a shimmering path ahead. As they pushed away from the dock, excitement buzzed among the crew.

"Let's go!" Emma exclaimed, her eyes sparkling with anticipation. Ben took the helm of Arabella, while Scott steered Singing Swallows alongside them. Antoine and Emma settled comfortably on deck, enjoying the refreshing sea breeze.

The boats moved in harmony, as they made their way up the coast. Ben navigated, feeling more at ease with each passing wave. "We're almost there, just a bit further!" he shouted.

As they approached Toms River. "Look, there's the entrance!" Samantha yelled out across the water.

Scott guided Singing Swallows carefully into the river, while Ben followed closely with Arabella. The scenery shifted to lush greenery lining the banks and charming houses dotting the shore.

Finally, they spotted the marina, and the moment of crossing their wake drew near. "This is it!" Samantha yelled, her voice trembling with excitement.

As they docked and secured the boats, a cheer erupted from both crews. "We did it!" Samantha shouted, beaming at Scott.

With hugs and high-fives all around, they celebrated not just the completion of their journey, but the friendships and memories they had built along the way. It was an achievement that would forever be etched in their hearts.

As Scott and Samantha walked up the dock toward the office, the familiar sights of the marina wrapped around them like a comforting embrace. Suddenly, a voice rang out from the crowd, cutting through the air with unmistakable excitement.

"Scott, you're back!"

Scott turned to see a few fellow boaters approaching, their faces lit up with joy. It was their friends welcoming them home.

"Hey, everyone!" he called out, his spirits lifting as he quickened his pace. He extended his arms for hugs and handshakes, grinning from ear to ear. "Congratulations on finishing the loop!" one of them exclaimed, clapping Scott on the back. "We've been waiting to hear all about your adventures!"

"Thanks! It was incredible, with a lot of surprises along the way," Scott replied. Samantha beamed beside him, clearly proud of their journey. "These are our friends Ben, his daughter Emma and her boyfriend Antoine."

"Nice to meet you" One boater said as the others nodded and shook hands. "Did you bring back any good stories?" another boater asked Scott, leaning in closer. "Plenty!" Scott laughed.

After a few moments of catching up, Scott glanced back toward the office. "We should check in and get settled. I'm sure there's a lot to organize after our trip." With that, the group made their way toward the office, laughter and chatter filling the air. The feeling of homecoming was electric, and Scott couldn't help but feel grateful for the friendships that made this journey worthwhile.

Once in the office, the friendly receptionist greeted them with a warm smile. "Welcome back, guys! I have some exciting news for you. "The yacht club is holding an impromptu reception tonight in honor of you!" Samantha's eyes widened in surprise. "Really? That's amazing! But when did you arrange this?"

"Well when you called a couple days ago to arrange a couple of slips we went to work contacting everyone. It's a celebration for you both completing the loop" replied the receptionist. Scott and Samantha gave her a big smile "Thank you so much. We didn't expect this at all!"

The receptionist continued, "The reception starts at seven. There will be food, drinks, and a chance for you guys to share stories from your adventure." As they left the office, the buzz of excitement filled the air. The thought of a gathering with friends and sharing their news made the day even more special.

As evening fell, Ben, Emma and Antoine made their way to the yacht club for the reception celebrating Scott and Samantha. The atmosphere buzzed with excitement, the scent of fresh food and sweet pastries wafting through the air as they approached the entrance.

"Are you ready for this?" Ben asked, glancing at Emma and Antoine, who both nodded eagerly.

Inside, the room was beautifully decorated, with twinkling lights strung overhead and tables adorned with flowers. Friends and fellow boaters mingled, laughter filling the air as people exchanged stories and raised glasses in celebration.

"Look, there they are!" Antoine pointed toward Scott and Samantha, who were surrounded by well-wishers. They looked radiant, clearly overwhelmed with happiness.

Ben, Emma, and Antoine made their way through the crowd, smiles on their faces. As they approached, Scott caught sight of them and broke into a wide grin. "You made it!" he exclaimed, pulling them into a group hug. "Thank you for being here!"

Samantha beamed, her eyes sparkling. "We're so glad you came! This is incredible!" The trio spent the evening celebrating alongside the couple, sharing stories and laughter. They raised their glasses in a toast, honoring not just Scott and Samantha's journey but the bonds they had all formed along the way.

As the night wore on, Emma found herself reflecting on how much had changed since they first set out on their trip. The thought of new life, the promise of friendship, and the beauty of shared experiences filled her with warmth. "Here's to new beginnings!" she raised her glass, and the crowd echoed the sentiment.

The next morning, as the sun began to rise over the marina, Scott and Samantha made their way down to Arabella. Their hearts, still full from the night's celebrations.

"Hey, you two!" Emma called out from the deck, a smile spreading across her face. "Thanks for coming down."

"We just wanted to say goodbye before you head out," Scott replied, his voice warm. Samantha nodded, her eyes sparkling with excitement. "Plus, we wanted to thank you for being such amazing friends," Samantha added, her smile bright.

Ben stepped out from below deck, rubbing the sleep from his eyes. "You guys deserve every bit of the celebration. We're so happy for you!"

Scott and Samantha exchanged glances, a mixture of gratitude and happiness in their expressions. "We're going to miss you all," Scott said, pulling Emma and Ben into a heartfelt hug. "But we can't wait to hear about the rest of your loop." "Thank you," Emma replied, a touch of sadness creeping in. "Just remember, you have a whole crew ready to support you whenever you need us."

As they shared warm farewells, Antoine stepped forward, a playful grin on his face. "And don't forget to send updates! I expect plenty of pictures of the little one!" "Same to you" Samantha replied. Laughter filled the air, lightening the moment as they all envisioned the future.

"We'll be in touch," Samantha promised, wiping a tear of happiness from her cheek. "This isn't goodbye forever; it's just the start of a new chapter." With one last wave, Scott and Samantha turned to head back up the dock. Emma, Ben, and Antoine stood in the cockpit, watching them go, their hearts full of hope for their friends.

Eventually Ben fired up the engine and Antoine untied them, and Arabella was off on her own again. Today was going to be a really long one and one Emma had been dreading for months.

After another two hours of protected waters they exited the Point Pleasant inlet and now they're out on the open ocean for the next eight hours. Luckily the tide was with them as they exited and the wind had been calm for days.

Finally, after navigating the open ocean, Arabella approached the Verrazano-Narrows Bridge, One of the longest suspension bridges in the Americas. The sight of its imposing towers rising majestically into the sky brought a wave of relief and excitement.

Emma stood at the bow, her heart racing. "We made it across!" she shouted, her voice nearly lost in the breeze. The bridge stretched across the harbor like a colossal guardian. Ben looked out from the cockpit, squinting against the sun. "This is an incredible moment," he said, awe evident in his voice. "It feels like we've crossed into a new territory."

Antoine leaned against the railing, taking it all in. Look at how beautiful it is!" A testament to engineering marvel and resilience. As they got closer, the scale of the structure became even more apparent.

The roar of traffic overhead was a stark reminder of the bustling city life above, contrasting with their tranquil journey below. Emma snapped photos, capturing the grandeur of the bridge against the deep blue ocean.

As they passed beneath the bridge, a sense of accomplishment washed over them. The scary ocean had tested their resolve, but now, the Verrazano-Narrows Bridge was behind them and the sun dipped lower on the horizon.

They soon arrived at their anchorage behind Lady Liberty, the iconic statue standing proudly against the scenery of the Manhattan skyline. Emma let out a gasp of delight. "Look at that view!" she exclaimed, her eyes sparkling as they dropped anchor. The twinkling lights of the city began to flicker on, creating a stunning contrast with the deepening twilight.

Initially, the anchorage felt a bit rolly due to the wakes from passing boats, making the vessel sway gently.

Emma clutched the railing for balance, but it was all part of the adventure. Soon enough, however, as night fell and the boat settled into the water, the rocking calmed, and a peaceful serenity enveloped them.

Antoine stepped to the bow, gazing at the view. "This is incredible. We're anchored right behind Lady Liberty! I can't believe it," he said, his voice filled with wonder. Ben joined him, leaning against the railing as the lights of Manhattan began to reflect off the water.

"It's surreal, isn't it? This is one of those moments you dream about," he replied, taking a deep breath of the salty air.

As the stars began to twinkle above, Emma pulled out her camera again, wanting to capture the moment. "Let's take some photos! This is too beautiful not to remember," she said, excitement bubbling in her voice.

They gathered together, posing with Lady Liberty in the background, the Manhattan skyline glowing behind them. Laughter and joy filled the air as they snapped pictures, making memories that would last a lifetime.

Once they settled in for the night, Emma couldn't help but reflect on their journey. The challenges they had faced only made this moment sweeter. Surrounded by friends, with the world's most recognizable symbol of freedom nearby, she felt a profound sense of gratitude for all they had experienced and all that was yet to come.

The following morning, the three travelers sat in the cockpit, sipping coffee as the sun rose over the harbor. The conversation turned to their plans for exploring the city. "I think we should stay at the marina on 79th Street," Emma suggested, her eyes sparkling with excitement. "That way we can walk or use the city's Citibike system. It's perfect for getting around!"

Antoine furrowed his brow, shaking his head. "I prefer the marina in New Jersey. We could take the Path train, and it would be faster, easier, and much cheaper!" His passion for the idea was clear as he leaned forward, making his case. Emma countered, and soon the two were engaged in a spirited debate. Ben watched, chuckling quietly at the familiar back-and-forth.

"What's so funny?" Emma finally asked, narrowing her eyes at her dad. "Oh, nothing," Ben replied with a grin. "It just reminds me of your mother and me back in the day. But seriously Emma, if you don't tell him right now, I'm going to."

Emma shot him a glare, a mix of irritation and apprehension. "Dad, please don't..."

But Ben raised an eyebrow, unwavering. "Tell him."

With a reluctant sigh, "Okay... fine" Emma turned to Antoine. "I have something called Tachophobia." Antoine looked puzzled. "Tachophobia? What's that?" Emma took a deep breath, her heart pounding. "It means I'm afraid of speed. Other than the ambulance ride the other day, I haven't really been in a car, train, or plane since I was a kid. That's why I never left Ticonderoga."

Emma felt a knot tighten in her stomach. "So all those times I suggested doing something that required a car or a bus, you came up with something better just to avoid telling me the truth?" She searched his eyes, hoping for understanding, but instead found a mix of hurt and frustration.

"I wasn't trying to deceive you," she said, her voice trembling slightly. "I was scared—scared I'd lose you if you knew the truth." Antoine's expression began to soften. "I get that, but you should have given me the benefit of the doubt. You should have trusted me enough to share this with me. And you should have told me when you found out you were pregnant. I'm not going anywhere."

A smile crept across Emma's face, warmth flooding her chest. "Really? You mean it?" "Of course I do," Antoine replied, his tone gentle. "We're in this together, no matter what." In that moment, the weight of her fears began to lift, and she felt a surge of relief.

"Oh, thank you so much!" Emma exclaimed, her voice filled with joy as she jumped into his arms. "I love you," she added, her heart racing with relief and affection. Antoine wrapped his arms around her, holding her close, feeling the warmth of their connection. "I love you too," he said softly, a smile spreading across his face.

In that moment, all the fears and uncertainties faded. Antoine looked at Ben "Thank you" Ben smiled "So 79th street it is. Are you guys ready?"

With a huge smile, Emma exclaimed, "Absolutely! Let's weigh anchor and get going!" Her excitement was infectious as she quickly moved to prepare the boat for departure. Antoine chuckled, his spirits lifted by her enthusiasm. "All right, captain! Let's make the rest of this trip unforgettable."

Before long, they were on their way again, and soon they found themselves tying off in the boat basin, ready to explore the vibrant city. Excitement bubbled between them as they discussed their first destination, Central Park. Fortunately, the boat basin was just a few blocks away, making it the perfect starting point.

As they entered the park, the grandeur of Belvedere Castle caught their eyes. Emma couldn't resist snapping a few photos, the castle framed by lush greenery. After soaking in the view, they continued their journey through the Ramble, where the winding paths and hidden nooks felt like an enchanting escape from the city's hustle.

They stopped to rest at Bethesda Terrace, the sound of the fountain providing a serene backdrop.

Emma sitting on the edge, taking in the beauty of the angel statue and the vibrant mosaic tiles beneath their feet. "This place is magical," she remarked, her eyes shining with delight.

Refreshed, they continued down the Mall, where the majestic trees created a beautiful canopy overhead. The atmosphere was alive with laughter and chatter as people strolled by. Eventually, they crossed the Central Park Zoo. With a shared look of excitement, they decided to grab some bicycles at Pulitzer Plaza.

The bicycles proved to be a fantastic way to explore the city. With stations scattered throughout Manhattan, they could easily pick one up at a nearby location, ride to their next destination, and drop it off at another station.

Pedaling through the bustling streets filled with life and energy. Emma and Antoine took turns leading the way, navigating the vibrant neighborhoods while soaking in the sights and sounds around them. Each stop was a new opportunity to experience something different.

They managed to take in most of the sights of Midtown and Lower Manhattan before nightfall. The energy of the city was infectious, and they reveled in the stunning views as they navigated their way through iconic spots.

As darkness fell, the city transformed into a dazzling display of lights. They wandered through Times Square, where the neon signs flickered vibrantly, and the buzz of excitement surrounded them.

The Empire State Building loomed majestically above, its lights twinkling against the night sky, and they paused to capture the moment in photos.

After a long day of exploration, they finally returned to the boat, fatigue settling in. Emma stretched her arms and let out a contented sigh. "What a day! I can't believe how much we saw." Antoine chuckled, rubbing his tired eyes. "It was incredible, but I'm exhausted. And I have to catch that early train back home in the morning."

Emma's heart sank a little at the thought of him leaving so soon. "I wish you could stay longer," she said softly. "Me too," Antoine replied, pulling her into a gentle embrace.

At six-thirty the next morning, the alarm rang, pulling Emma and Antoine from their sleep. Emma had decided she was ready to navigate her way from the train station back to the boat basin on her own, so they moved quietly to avoid waking Ben, slipping out of the boat together.

Once back on land, they grabbed a couple of bicycles and pedaled toward Penn Station, the early morning air was refreshing. As they rode, they shared stories and laughter, trying to savor every moment before Antoine's departure.

When they finally arrived at the station, a sense of reality began to settle in. Emma's heart sank as she realized their time together was coming to an end. They shared a long, heartfelt embrace, her eyes welling up with tears. "I'll be home tonight. Call me, okay? We have a lot to figure out."

Antoine nodded, his expression softening. "I will. You're stronger than you know, Emma. We'll tackle everything together." As the announcement for his train echoed through the station, they both knew the moment had come.

Antoine took a step back, and with one last lingering look, he turned and headed toward the platform. Emma watched him go, her heart heavy but filled with hope for the future.

As Emma rode the bicycle back to the boat basin, she couldn't resist stopping at a diner to pick up breakfast for herself and her dad. The aroma of freshly brewed coffee and pancakes filled the air, and she smiled at the thought of surprising him.

When she arrived back at the boat, a little chuckle escaped her lips. There, sitting in the cockpit in the exact same spot as Jasper, was her dad, reading a book and sipping coffee, looking like a younger version of her grandpa. "Hi, Dad! I brought breakfast!" she called cheerfully.

Ben looked up, a smile spreading across his face. "Oh, thank you! Is it okay if we eat while we get going? I'd like to cover some distance today." "Sure, sounds like a great idea!" Emma replied, setting the breakfast down in the cockpit.

With the smell of pancakes wafting through the air, Ben started the engine while Emma untied the boat. The familiar rhythm of their morning routine set a comforting tone for the day ahead.

Before long, they found themselves passing under the iconic George Washington Bridge, which marked their departure from the bustling city. The overcast sky lent a soft, muted beauty to the landscape, and Emma felt a sense of peace wash over her as they drifted past the Palisades and the Hudson Highlands. She particularly loved the lighthouses, standing as steadfast beacons.

They finally arrived at their anchorage for the night, nestled behind an island that boasted the ruins of a castle. The sight was enchanting, the crumbling stone walls silhouetted against the evening sky, creating an amazing view for the night.

The next day, the rain fell lightly, a soft rhythm of droplets that came and went. Undeterred by the weather, Emma and Ben decided to set off anyway, keeping the cockpit enclosure up to stay dry. The cozy interior felt like a refuge as they navigated the river, the gentle sound of rain creating a simple calmness.

As the river straightened out, their progress picked up, and the scenery passed by in a blur of greens and grays. They enjoyed the quiet beauty of the landscape, the mist rising from the water adding a magical touch to the morning.

By late afternoon, they arrived in Kingston, New York, eager to explore the town. Ben had mentioned a marine museum that he was excited to show Emma, hoping to share its rich maritime history with her. However, as they approached, they discovered it was closed for the evening.

"Looks like we'll have to save that for tomorrow," Ben said with a hint of disappointment, glancing at the locked doors. Emma smiled reassuringly. "That's okay! We can still check out the town a bit. Who knows what other surprises it holds?"

With that, they strolled through the charming streets of Kingston, taking in the quaint shops and cozy cafes. The warm glow from the windows and the inviting aroma of food wafting through the air made for a comforting atmosphere, despite the drizzle.

They stopped at a small bakery to grab a treat. As the day turned to evening, they made their way back to the boat, excited for what the next day would bring, rain or shine.

The next morning, Emma and Ben were jolted awake by a loud crack of thunder that echoed through the marina. The storm had arrived with a fury, and it was quickly decided that they would stay in Kingston for at least that day. Both of them agreed it was better to wait it out than venture out in dangerous conditions.

By the afternoon, the storm had mostly passed, but the rain continued to fall steadily. Rather than let the weather dampen their spirits, they resolved to make the best of it. They grabbed a couple of umbrellas and donned their rain jackets before heading out to the marine museum.

The streets were slick and glistening, but Emma found beauty in the rain-soaked town. As they approached the impressive brick building, they were filled with excitement. The museum, with its tall ship models and vibrant maritime art, promised a journey into the past. Inside, they were greeted by the warm, inviting smell of aged wood.

Their first stop was the gallery showcasing the history of the Hudson River. Ben marveled at the intricate ship models, each one telling a story of adventure and trade. "Look at this one!" he exclaimed, pointing to a model of a majestic sloop. "I can imagine sailing on it."

Ben, always the history buff, shared fascinating facts about the river's role in commerce. "Did you know that during the 19th century, this was a major route for transporting goods?" he asked, eyes gleaming with enthusiasm.

Next, they wandered into an interactive exhibit where visitors could learn about navigation. Ben eagerly tried his hand at using a sextant, while Emma laughed, playfully pretending to be lost at sea. They both enjoyed a virtual reality experience that let them steer a historic vessel through stormy waters, their hearts racing with the thrill of adventure.

As they moved through the museum, they stumbled upon an exhibit dedicated to shipwrecks. A short film played, showing dramatic reenactments of famous disasters. Emma watched, captivated "This is incredible," she said.

After a couple of hours of exploration, they decided to go to a local restaurant for dinner. They sat and ate and discussed their favorite parts of the day. Emma loved the ship models, while Ben couldn't stop thinking about the shipwreck stories.

The next day, they set off again, the rain finally subsiding but the sky remaining overcast and gray. Emma couldn't shake the feeling of wondering if the sun would ever break through the clouds again. Despite the gloom, the air felt fresh, and the calm water made for a smooth journey.

As they navigated the river, the scenery continued to unfold, with charming towns and lush landscapes flanking either side. They made good time and, by evening, arrived at a city dock in Albany.

The bustling atmosphere of the capital city was a change from the quiet town of Kingston. After securing the boat, Emma felt a rush of excitement. "I can't wait to call Antoine!" she exclaimed, her mind racing with thoughts of sharing their adventures with him.

Once they settled in, Emma found a quiet spot in the park adjacent to the dock and pulled out her phone. She dialed Antoine's number, anticipation bubbling within her. When he picked up, his warm voice instantly brightened her mood.

"Hey, it's me!" she said, grinning from ear to ear. "Emma! How's the trip going?" Antoine replied, his tone full of genuine interest. "It's been amazing! We went and saw the

Maritime museum in Kingston and now we are stopped in Albany".

As she talked, Emma felt a sense of happiness wash over her. Sharing these experiences with Antoine made everything feel even more special, and she cherished the connection they maintained despite the distance. After they finished talking, Emma hung up with a smile, looking forward to the next part of their journey.

The next morning, Emma and Ben were eager to dive into their exploration of Albany. They set out and walked across a long pedestrian bridge that spanned the massive highway dividing the city from the waterfront.

Their first stop was the impressive State Capitol building, a stunning example of Classical and Romanesque architecture. Its intricate stonework and grand arches stood in stark contrast to the sleek, modern lines of the Empire State Plaza across the street. They wandered around the grounds, admiring the statues and manicured gardens, before crossing the street to the plaza itself.

Once there, Emma marveled at the large reflecting pool that sat in the middle, flanked by fountains that danced gently in the cool breeze.

On one side stood four medium-height skyscrapers, while a single tall skyscraper towered on the other, creating a striking skyline. Emma was particularly drawn to the performing arts center, which resembled a giant suspended egg, a modern architectural marvel that piqued her curiosity.

At the far end of the plaza loomed the New York State Museum, Emma thought its unique design resembled an upside-down pyramid. A grand staircase led up to the entrance, and Emma felt a thrill of excitement at the thought of exploring its exhibits.

"Let's check it out!" she urged, but Ben suggested they grab some lunch first. They headed below the plaza into the mall, navigating through shops and food stalls until they found the bustling food court. The aroma of various cuisines wafted through the air, making their mouths water.

After enjoying lunch, they were fueled and ready to tackle the large museum. Emma's anticipation grew as they approached the entrance, eager to uncover the stories and treasures that awaited them inside.

As Emma and Ben entered, they were greeted by a spacious atrium filled with natural light filtering through large windows. The atmosphere was lively, filled with the sounds of excited children and adults alike exploring the exhibits.

"Wow, this place is huge!" Emma exclaimed, taking in the grand space. The museum was known for its extensive collection, showcasing the history, culture, and natural wonders of New York State.

As they continued through the museum, they stumbled upon a special exhibit featuring the Hudson River School of art. The vibrant landscapes painted by 19th-century artists captured the beauty of the New York countryside, and Emma felt a deep connection to the scenes depicted. "These remind me of our travels along the river," she said, her heart swelling with pride for her home state.

After spending hours wandering through the various exhibits, ranging from colonial history to modern art, they left the museum and went across the way to the Corning Building, which is the tallest building in Albany.

They went inside and entered the elevator, finally arriving at the observation deck. From there, they could see a breathtaking panoramic view of Albany and the Hudson River below. Emma took a deep breath, soaking in the moment.

"This has been amazing," she said, turning to Ben. "I'm so glad we came here." Ben smiled, clearly pleased. "Me too. It's nice to learn more about our state and its history together."

With their spirits high, Emma and Ben made their way back to Arabella, the excitement of the day still buzzing between them. "I'm ready for the next stop already," Emma remarked, her eyes sparkling with enthusiasm.

Ben smiled at her eagerness. "Well, we still have some daylight left, so we could make it to Waterford for the night." "Let's get going then!" Emma replied, her energy infectious.

They quickly prepared the boat for departure, Emma deftly untying the lines while Ben started the engine.

As Arabella pulled away from the dock, the familiar hum of the engine filled the air and the scenery of Albany began to recede behind them. The Hudson River stretched ahead, and the gentle breeze carried the fresh scent of the water.

Emma took the helm, guiding the boat with confidence as they navigated the river. The overcast sky from earlier had begun to clear, allowing the sun to peek through, casting a warm glow over the landscape.

As they cruised along, Emma pointed out various sights along the riverbanks—the lush greenery, the quaint houses dotting the shore, and the occasional bridge arching gracefully overhead. "This is so beautiful," she said, her voice filled with wonder.

"Just wait until we get to Waterford," Ben replied. "It has its own charm with the locks and the historic architecture." The journey was smooth, and they soon found themselves approaching Waterford. As they neared the docks, Emma's anticipation grew. "I can't wait to explore!"

Ben nodded. "Let's get settled, then we can go for a stroll. I know a great place for dinner."

After securing Arabella at the dock, they stepped onto solid ground, taking a moment to soak in the quaint, small-town atmosphere. The restaurant Ben had in mind was a charming diner right on Broad Street, the main thoroughfare of Waterford. It wasn't fancy, but it had a welcoming vibe, with good food at good prices served by a friendly staff.

Ben loved eating there whenever he passed through town, and Emma could see why. After their satisfying meal, they decided to explore, even though the night had settled in around them. They headed toward the large first lock of the Erie Canal, the area well-lit and bustling with activity. Emma marveled at the massive structure. As they approached, its presence was awe-inspiring.

"Can you believe how much traffic must have passed through here in its heyday?" Ben mused, his eyes scanning the lock's mechanisms. Ben continued "this lock and those that came before it were a vital part of the canal system, changing the way goods were transported across New York."

After enjoying the sights, they strolled along the canal, the gentle sounds of water lapping against the sides providing a soothing background to their walk. The moon cast a silvery glow over the water, enhancing the atmosphere.

Eventually, they reached the visitors center, where Arabella was tied up. In front of the building, was a map of the Erie Canal laid out on the ground, created with different colors of paving stones. Nearby, a statue of a horse stood proudly, its side painted with a tourist map, serving as a whimsical welcome to visitors.

Emma laughed softly. "This place has a lot of character. I love it!" Ben smiled, taking in the scene. "It really does. It's these little moments that make the journey worthwhile." They stood together for a moment, soaking in the sights and sounds of Waterford, grateful for the day's trip.

Chapter 20

Crossing Her Wake

The next day was a straightforward one. Ben and Emma got an early start, greeted by a bright sun that promised a pleasant day ahead. They navigated through a couple of locks, feeling the familiar thrill as Arabella rose with the water.

As they made their way along the scenic route, the landscape shifted, revealing lush greenery and charming waterways. After a day of leisurely cruising, they arrived at the first lock of the Champlain Canal. After passing through, they found the Fort Edward Town Dock, where they decided to spend the night.

Ben prepared a simple dinner, and they settled in the cockpit, enjoying the soft evening breeze and the peaceful sounds of the water. It was a perfect end to a simple yet fulfilling day.

The next day was dedicated to navigating the Champlain Canal, a stretch of water that promised both ease and beauty. Emma and Ben set off early, the sun rising steadily, illuminating the calm waters ahead.

As they cruised along, Emma marveled at how straight and well-maintained the canal was, making for a smooth ride.

The lush greenery lining the banks swayed gently in the morning breeze, creating a beautiful setting.

They tackled nine locks throughout the day, each one a small experience in itself. With each lock they completed, Ben's excitement bubbled over, especially as they approached Whitehall—his long-awaited destination.

As they neared the town, Emma could sense Ben's anticipation. "Audra is going to be waiting for us," he said, his eyes shining. "I can't wait to see her!"

Finally, they pulled into the town dock, just before the last lock of the canal. Emma tied off Arabella, her heart racing with excitement to see her dad so happy. They stepped onto the dock and walked toward a small park that overlooked the water.

And there she was - Audra, standing under a blooming tree, her smile radiant as she spotted Ben. "Ben!" she called, her voice filled with warmth.

He rushed forward, enveloping her in a tight embrace. Emma stood back for a moment, watching their reunion unfold. It was clear how much Audra meant to her dad. His face lit up with joy, the stresses of the journey melting away.

The three of them settled on a nearby bench, taking in the lovely surroundings. The park was alive with the sounds of birds chirping and laughter from families enjoying the day.

Ben couldn't contain his enthusiasm. "You're going to love Whitehall, Emma. Audra knows all the best spots. We should grab lunch at that little café she loves." Audra nodded, a smile on her face. "Oh, it's a hidden gem. You'll definitely want to try their famous sandwiches."

They all stood up and began walking toward the café, with Ben animatedly sharing stories about the journey so far. Emma felt a warmth in her heart to see Ben so happy and relaxed.

The café turned out to be a cozy spot, with charming decor and the tantalizing aroma of freshly baked bread wafting through the air. They found a table by the window, and as they sat down, Emma felt a wave of contentment wash over her.

Lunch was filled with laughter, shared stories, and delicious food. Audra regaled them with tales of life in Whitehall, and Emma chimed in with anecdotes from their travels.

Ben beamed, clearly enjoying the company of two important women in his life. After they finished eating, Audra suggested taking a stroll through the town to see some local sights.

"There's a little museum dedicated to the history of Whitehall that I think you'd both love, and in the park is the hull of the original USS Ticonderoga. Oh and up there on the hill that's Skene manor overlooking the town." she said, her enthusiasm infectious.

Ben looked at Emma "There is something I want to ask you. Is it ok with you if Audra joins us tomorrow as we go home and you cross your wake?" Emma's eyes lit up "of course. I would absolutely love that."

"Well, Arabella is yours tonight," Ben said, looking at Emma with a grin. "I'm spending the night at Audra's, but we'll be back early in the morning to finish crossing the wake with you."

The next morning, Emma was awake bright and early, the soft glow of dawn illuminating the cockpit. She felt a wave of excitement wash over her as she anticipated the day ahead. As she waited for Ben and Audra, her mind raced with thoughts of the journey's culmination.

When she finally spotted them walking down the dock, Audra carried a cooler bag under her arm, a wide smile lighting up her face.

"Hi, Emma! You ready?" Ben called out, his eyes sparkling with enthusiasm. "Absolutely! I can't wait to get going!" Emma replied, her heart racing at the thought of finishing her journey.

Audra set the cooler down on the deck and grinned. "I brought some breakfast for us to enjoy on the way. Thought it might be nice to start the day right!"

Ben chuckled, "Well, you may not be getting a party when you cross your wake, but we brought champagne to celebrate!" Emma's face lit up at the mention of champagne. "You guys are the best!" she exclaimed.

As they pulled away from the dock and headed toward the very last lock, Ben commented, "The weather is perfect for your last day. Clear skies and calm waters—it doesn't get better than this!"

Emma nodded, taking in the beautiful scenery. The canal sparkled under the sun, and a light breeze rustled the leaves on the trees lining the shore. "I can't believe this is the last day," she said, her voice filled with a mix of nostalgia and anticipation. "It feels like just yesterday I started this adventure."

"Here we go!" Ben announced as they entered the lock, the anticipation building. Emma held her breath, ready to mark this moment forever. The doors of the lock closed behind them, and the water level began to rise. Excitement coursed through her veins, and before she knew it, they were through, emerging into the shimmering waters of Lake Champlain.

"Time flies when you're having fun," Audra said, handing Emma a breakfast wrap from the cooler. "Let's make the most of it!"

As they enjoyed their breakfast, the gentle sway of Arabella felt comforting. Emma took a moment to soak in the view—the vast lake stretched before them, framed by the distant mountains and the sky painted in shades of blue.

She felt a wave of gratitude for the journey and the people who had shared it with her. Each wave that kissed the hull of the boat felt like a reminder of her grandfather's words, encouraging her to embrace this milestone.

"I can't believe I'm finally crossing my wake," Emma said, her voice almost a whisper. "It feels surreal." Ben grinned, "You've earned this moment, Emma. Every lock, every wave, every challenge—it's all brought you here." "Absolutely!" Audra added, her eyes shining with excitement. "And we're here to celebrate it with you!"

As they glided across the lake, Emma felt a swell of emotion. She thought of all the moments that had led her here; the laughter, the challenges, the friendships. "I wish Grandpa could see this," she murmured, her heart a mix of joy and longing.

"He's with you in spirit," Ben said softly, his voice warm and reassuring. "And I know he's proud." With the sun shining down they made their way across the lake, Emma's heart swelling with a sense of accomplishment.

During the crossing, Audra turned to Emma with a curious expression. "So, now that you're finishing this journey and with the baby on the way, what are your plans?" Emma beamed. "I think I'll write a book about all of this—my adventures, the people I've met, and everything I've learned along the way.

During the day, as they cruised across the sparkling waters of Lake Champlain, Ben turned to Emma with a gentle expression. "I'm sorry the end of your trip won't be like Scott and Samantha's," he said. "But when we get to the dock, we'll crack open the champagne and celebrate. Then you'll ride your bicycle back home, while Audra and I take the boat across the lake to the marina. We'll grab a taxi back."

Emma nodded, trying to contain her excitement. The thought of finishing her journey was exhilarating, even if the end wasn't as grand as she had imagined. As they continued their ride, the familiar scenery began to emerge on the horizon.

Not much later the boat ramp where she had started came into view, her heart raced with anticipation. She was just moments away from crossing her wake. "I can't believe this is happening!" she exclaimed, her eyes wide with joy.

As they approached the dock, she noticed someone leaning against their bicycle, watching them intently. Emma squinted, her heart fluttering. "Is that...?" she began, a smile breaking across her face.

Ben glanced over, a knowing grin on his lips. "Looks like someone wanted to be here for the moment." As they drew closer, Emma recognized the figure—it was Antoine, looking as eager as she felt. His presence filled her with warmth and excitement, and she could hardly wait to share this achievement with him.

"Hey, Emma!" he called out, his face lighting up. "I wouldn't miss this for the world!" With the boat finally docked, Emma felt a rush of emotions. This was it—she was about to cross her wake, a full circle in her journey. She hopped off Arabella, her feet touching the familiar ground, and turned to face the water.

"This is it!" she announced, her voice trembling with joy. "I'm finally here!"

Ben and Audra stepped off behind her, carrying the cooler with the champagne. "Let's do this right," Ben said, his eyes twinkling as he uncorked the bottle. Emma took a deep breath, ready to embrace the moment.

Antoine wrapped his arms around her "You did it baby". Emma let out a final cheer. "I did it". Ben laughed "I know I said you had to bike back home but I didn't say you had to do it alone". Emma turned to Ben "Thank you so much for your help in finishing this."

Ben, still laughing "I'm not done. We did some research and it turns out getting married and having a baby together isn't the only way to allow Antoine to work here. It turns out owning a company also helps.

That's why Audra sold Antoine her shop for one dollar. She won't be needing it anymore as thanks to my Dad we will both be retiring together. In fact, you and Antoine can have the house and the car. Antoine will need the car to go to work and we don't need the house anymore because we plan on taking

Arabella and doing the loop as the first of many adventures for us.

Emma's eyes widened in surprise. "Really? That's incredible!" " But we are not leaving the area till late fall, I want to meet my grandchild first. Plus we will be back most summers and every Christmas".

Emma felt a mix of emotions—joy, disbelief, and gratitude. This wasn't just the end of one chapter; it was the beginning of so many new adventures. She looked at Antoine, whose eyes mirrored her excitement, and she knew they were ready to face whatever came next together.